After a bloody *coup de' état*, the nation of Asante lies peaceful and prosperous on Africa's rich western shore...like a drowsy lioness dining on the evening's kill.

Over the feast presides the enigmatic "Little Captain," *Anokye*—the President who engineered the coup. Is Anokye another petty tyrant...or is he an African Napoleon, capable of uniting the continent under his rule?

It takes a ruthless cynic like Peter Tangent, undercover man for American oil interests, to see the horror that lurks behind the festive mask of Anokye's regime.

And to propose an even greater horror, all his own...

THE TANGENT FACTOR

LAWRENCE SANDERS

Berkley Books by Lawrence Sanders

THE FIRST DEADLY SIN
THE PLEASURES OF HELEN
THE SECOND DEADLY SIN
THE TANGENT FACTOR
THE TANGENT OBJECTIVE
THE TOMORROW FILE

Lawrence Sanders
The Tangent Factor

A TOTEM BOOK
TORONTO

This edition published 1979 by Totem Books
A Division of Collins Publishers
100 Lesmill Road
Don Mills, Ontario M3B 2T5

Published by arrangement with
Berkley Publishing Corporation and
G. P. Putnam's Sons

Totem Books
A Division of Collins Publishers
100 Lesmill Road
Don Mills, Ontario M3B 2T5

Printed in the United States of America

Author's Note

The names of existing nations, organizations, and institutions have been used, but this is a novel, and individuals and events described are fictitious. Where actual official titles are used, no reference is implied to persons presently holding those positions, nor should such reference be inferred. Names and characters are wholly imaginary.

1.

THE NIGHTCLUB HAD originally been a barn. Stalls had been converted to booths. The loft had been ripped away to expose splintery beams, now festooned with ropes of onions and red peppers. Feeding troughs were planted with plastic orchids in bark chips. An unpainted plywood bar ran the length of the back wall, facing the dance floor and tables. The acrid odor of manure lingered, mixing with the edgy scents of hashish, the sweat of dancers, fruity perfume.

Yakubu was the only customer at the bar. He wore a red bandanna knotted about his head. A small gold loop hung from the lobe of his left ear. His blue workshirt was open to the navel. A necklace of yellowed shark teeth gleamed on smooth black skin.

1

He lifted his eyes to glance at the other customers in the club: two black men sitting at a far table. They wore white shirts, flowered ties, sedate suits of European cut. They sat quietly, finishing a carafe of Algerian red.

Yakubu motioned to the bartender. The man came over slowly, polishing a glass with a towel made from an opened flour sack. He had a walleye that stared at the rafters. Yakubu found it difficult not to look up there, to see what was happening.

"Would you care for an additional beer, sir?" the bartender asked.

He spoke Twi. Yakubu replied in that language.

"Thank you, no," he said. "That man at the table. . . . The large one with his back against the wall. . . . I have seen him before. Is it possible you know the name?"

"Ah, that one," the bartender said. "You are not of Togo, sir?"

"I do not have that good fortune. But the man seems familiar."

"Perhaps you have seen his image in the Lomé newspaper," the bartender said. "He is Nwabala. A politico."

"Oh yes," Yakubu nodded. "The very man. I have read of him. He wishes to join the land of Benin to Togo. He leads a band of followers."

"So it is said. The man with him is his bodyguard. Very ill-tempered, that one."

Yakubu smiled. He finished his beer, left the bartender a small dash, sauntered out of the cabaret. The two men at the back table watched him go, but he didn't glance in their direction.

Ten minutes later, a white woman walked into the club. She paused, looked about curiously, then moved to the bar. Her long blonde hair was braided into a single plait, coiled, pinned atop her head. She wore a tie-dyed brown Apollo, the loose shift ending just above her knees. Her legs were bare, hairless, pale.

"Scotch whisky and Perrier, if you please," she said to the bartender, speaking French.

"At once, madam. Does the lady desire ice? It is available."

"Thank you, no. No ice."

At the far table, the two men straightened slowly in their chairs. Nwabala lifted the glass of wine to his lips, staring over the rim at the blonde.

"A sympathetic woman," he said to his companion. "She is a tourist?" He spoke Hausa.

The bodyguard shrugged. He was younger, thinner, harder.

"Undoubtedly a tourist," he said. "She wonders, Is it true what they say about black men? So she comes to West Africa to find out."

The big man laughed. "Perhaps I can help her. Go to the bar. Ask her if she wishes to join us for a drink. Speak to her politely in French."

The younger man glared angrily, then pushed back his chair with a clatter. He strode to the bar, spoke to the woman a moment, then returned to the table.

"She does not wish to join us," he said.

Nwabala stared at him a moment.

"Fool," he said. "You do not know how to speak to a white woman. You spoke to her in an uncultured manner."

Nwabala rose to his feet. He was tall, heavy, with long, dangling arms, big hands.

"Could she have a weapon?" he asked.

The bodyguard looked at him, then turned away without speaking.

Nwabala went to the bar, bowed to the woman. In a moment, they were smiling, shaking hands. They chatted easily, laughing occasionally. The walleyed bartender had retreated to the end of the bar, leaving them alone.

After a few minutes, Nwabala smiled, lifted the woman's hand, kissed the knuckles. Then he returned to the table. He sat down, picked up his wine.

"She is French," he said in a low voice. "Parisienne. Her name is Yvonne. Staying for two weeks in a bungalow she has rented. I will join her there in thirty minutes. See how easy it is if you speak in a cultured manner?"

They sipped their wine slowly. They watched as the white woman paid for her drink, left a dash, and departed.

Soon after, they finished their wine and moved to the bar to settle their bill.

Nwabala paused at the doorway. "Take a look," he said. "A good look."

The younger man went outside alone. He looked up and down the deserted street. It was almost 0200. Thin clouds slid oilily across a watery moon. The bodyguard strolled to the corner, staring about. He checked the alley alongside the cabaret. He peered into shadows. Then he returned to the club.

"All clear," he reported.

They drove in a black Peugeot, doors locked and windows up, although the night was muffled with heat. Beads of moisture gathered on the hood.

The bungalow sat alone, deserted, on a small plot of land halfway to Porto-Seguro. The earth around it was packed hard, treeless. Bare dirt gleamed whitely.

The bodyguard drove the Peugeot off the road, stopped next to the little porch. Lights were on in the bungalow, coming through narrow chinks in the closed venetian blinds.

"Take a look around," Nwabala ordered.

The bodyguard got out of the car. He slid a hand into the right pocket of his suit jacket. He made a complete circuit of the house, then returned to the car.

"All clear," he said.

"Inside too, you fool," Nwabala said.

The younger man went up the porch steps, knocked on the screened door. In a moment, the inner door was opened. The white woman stood there. She was wearing a blue peignoir over a lighter blue nightgown. Her feet were bare.

"I must search your house," the bodyguard said stolidly. He spoke a harsh French.

She looked beyond him to the parked Peugeot. Behind the closed glass, Nwabala waved to her and smiled. She waved back and unlatched the screened door, letting the bodyguard inside. Then she went to sit on a couch. She crossed her legs, adjusted the peignoir carefully to cover her knees.

The bodyguard didn't look at her. He marched slowly through the living room, kitchen, bathroom. He pulled drapes aside and opened closet doors. Then he went into the bedroom. There was a chest of drawers, chair, small dressing table and bench, and the bed. There was one closet door, louvered, with a loop of soiled string hanging from the hole where the knob should have been.

The bodyguard pulled the loop of string slowly. The door opened. Yakubu stood inside, arms folded. The two men stared at each other a moment. Then Yakubu handed over an unsealed envelope. The bodyguard took it, opened the flap, counted the CFA francs slowly with blunt fingers. He nodded, tucked the envelope into an inside pocket, swung the closet door shut on Yakubu. Then he went back outside.

"All clear," he said.

Nwabala climbed out of the car.

"Wait here for me," he said. "An hour. Perhaps two or three. It depends..."

He went into the bungalow. The woman locked the door behind him. She had a bottle of Italian brandy uncorked, two little paper cups beside it.

"Yvonne!" Nwabala said. "But how nice!"

Twenty minutes later they were naked in bed. She had unpinned her hair. It hung about her shoulders. He was enchanted to see that her pubic hair was also flaxen.

He lay atop her.

"Am I too heavy?" he inquired solicitously.

"No, no," she breathed. "Oh no."

He spread her smooth thighs, pulled up her knees.

"Oh, you're so big," she recited. "Oh, what a man you are. Oh, I've never had a lover like you before."

And so on. He grinned with pleasure.

She put her arms about his broad, buttery back. She hooked ankles and feet behind his knees.

"Hold me," she whispered fiercely. "Hold me tight!"

Obediently he slid his arms beneath her. Her weight locked them there. Her arms and knees held him imprisoned.

"Oh!" she cried. "Now!"

The closet door opened silently. Yakubu crossed to the bed in one smooth step, flowing, the knife held knuckles down. It was not a heavy blow, but a graceful thrust, the blade going in alongside the spine, angled upward. In, in, until forefinger and thumb pressed soft flesh. Yvonne watched Nwabala's eyes as he realized he was dead.

Yakubu helped her roll the body away. It thumped to the floor. Then Yakubu went outside and got into the front seat of the Peugeot, next to the driver.

"It went well?" the bodyguard asked.

Yakubu nodded and offered a Gitane. Both men lighted up and smoked slowly, not speaking. The car windows were open now. The night air seemed to be clearing, a fresh wind blowing from the west.

Twenty minutes later Yvonne came out of the house. She was wearing the brown Apollo and carrying a small overnight case. She turned off the final light, locked the door, left the key on a ledge over the porch window. Then she came down to the car. She sat alone in the back seat. No one spoke. They drove directly to the airport. The bodyguard let them out and drove away.

An hour later the Piper Aztec landed at the new Mokodi International Airport in Asante. They taxied to a remote section of the field used by the Asante National Air Force. Yvonne was met by Sgt. Sene Yeboa, who took her bag and led her to a waiting Land-Rover. Yakubu alighted and looked around. A bright red Volkswagen was parked in the dim light coming from the corrugated iron hangar. A bare arm extended through the opened sunroof and beckoned. He walked over and got in alongside Sam Leiberman.

The mercenary had a pint bottle of American whisky. He handed it to Yakubu, waited patiently while the black took three slow swallows. Then Leiberman took one deep gulp and belched.

"How'd it go?" he asked.

"As you planned," Yakubu said.

"He died happy," Leiberman said. "Now what? You going back to pimping in Abidjan?"

"Ah . . . well, no," Yakubu said. "Not Abidjan. I have a little trouble there."

"*Little* trouble?" Leiberman scoffed. "And death is an inconvenience. What in Christ's name made you take on a Muslim girl?"

"I didn't go to her. She came to me."

"Her brothers catch you, they'll pound a tent peg up your ass."

"I know," Yakubu said mournfully.

"Want to stay in Mokodi?" Leiberman asked.

"Can I?"

"I can arrange it," Leiberman nodded. "But we'll have to get you a respectable job. How would you like to manage a whorehouse?"

2.

THE ASANTE NATIONAL ARMY was passing in review on the parade ground of the Mokodi barracks. Newly armed with American-made M16A1 automatic rifles, three brigades of black soldiers stepped smartly past the reviewing stand, weapons carried at port arms. Flags and guidons snapped on the fiery morning wind. Toward the rear, growl of engines increasing to a roar as they approached the stand, came the Asante National Tank Corps. Ten new AMX-30 tanks, hatches open, tankers at the salute.

On the reviewing stand was the guest of honor, Gen. Kumayo Songo of the Togolese army. Standing at his left was his son and aide, Capt. Jere Songo. On his right was the President of Asante, Obiri Anokye, wearing an army uniform without decorations or indication of rank.

As the tanks clanked past, Anokye told General Songo that the commander, the tall, bearded man in the lead tank, was Col. Jim Nkomo. "Very capable," Anokye said.

The President spoke French, as did his guests.

"A formidable man," the general smiled. "A veteran of your coup?"

"Yes. He was with me."

A company of machine gunners came last, trundling their heavy .50 Browning M2 guns on two-wheeled carts, and then the parade was at an end.

"Very impressive, Mr. President," General Songo said. "You have accomplished wonders in a short time. I congratulate you."

"Thank you. But there is still much to be done. Particularly in weapons training."

"Morale?"

"Excellent," President Anokye said. "To be an Asante soldier is a thing of pride. Our people are grateful to the army for ending the tyranny of King Prempeh."

"Of course," Songo nodded. "And no doubt the new rifles also help morale?"

"That is true," Anokye said. "You still have the MAS?"

"Still," Songo said disgustedly. "And old Garands and Mannlichers, even a few Lebels. My country has money for everything but new guns."

"I know," the President said sympathetically. "It is a problem. Shall we seek the shade?"

He led the two officers down the wooden stairway. The stand was surrounded by a cordon of the President's personal guard, commanded by Sgt. Sene Yeboa. The guardsmen wore khaki with white spatterdashes and white silk ascots. They carried Thompson submachine guns and Colt .45 sidearms in white leather holsters.

"Captain," Anokye said, "would you please ask the sergeant to call the cars?"

"Of course, sir. At once, sir."

The young Songo moved away briskly. The President led the general into the shade beneath the reviewing stand. Anokye, still called "the Little Captain" by Asantis, was only five feet four. He easily stood erect beneath the planked platform. Songo, a brooding, slumpish man with his brown leather belt cinched under a heavy paunch, had to duck his head. He appeared to be in obeisance to the Little Captain.

"General, I deeply regret you must cut short your visit."

"I also, sir. This Nwabala business. . . . My government is much concerned."

"I understand," Anokye said gravely. "But surely it was a personal matter? It is said the man was a womanizer."

"He may have been," Songo said angrily. "But it was no jealous husband or lover who killed him. This was a political assassination."

"Political?" the President said. "Can you be certain?"

"The bodyguard has fled to Benin," Songo said grimly. "We have demanded his return, but they refuse. The border has been closed. On both sides."

Anokye shook his head sorrowfully. "I do not like to see neighbors in angry confrontation. We are all brothers, all Africans."

"Sir, it is not the first time they have tried our patience," Songo said. "They have much to answer for. There is only one way to answer a bully, and that is to stand up to him. We must bring an end to these insults and provocations against the people and government of Togo."

"And you believe the killing of Nwabala was a Benin plot?"

"I know it was," the general said furiously. "He spoke for peace between Togo and Benin, a closer relationship, perhaps even a merger of the two countries. His death was their answer. Very well. If they don't desire peace, they must suffer the consequences."

"Please be assured of my understanding," President Anokye said gently. "I am ready to help in any way I can. Will you convey my sympathy to your government?"

"I shall be happy to, Mr. President," General Songo said. "Ah, here are the cars..."

"One moment more, if you please, general. I was happy to hear of your son's promotion. A fine boy."

"Thank you, sir."

"You are aware of his interest in my younger sister Sara?"

"Aware of it and welcome it, sir," Songo said. "A charming girl."

"Thank you. I hope our families may become better acquainted. Who knows..."

They moved out from under the platform into bright sunlight and crossed to the waiting cars. Guardsmen stood at attention by opened doors.

"With God's smile, go in good health and return in good health," President Anokye said, speaking Akan.

"May Allah bless your days and your family," General Songo replied, in Twi. Then he switched again to French. "Thank you, Mr. President, for your generous hospitality. I was much impressed by the discipline and training of your fine army."

"We progress," Anokye said gravely. "I hope to have four fully armed brigades within six months. One difficulty..."

"Oh?" Songo said. "What is that?"

"A critical shortage of dependable field and general officers. I myself, of course, am Commander in Chief of the Armed Forces. I have personally planned and directed the reorganization of the army following the end of the Prempeh regime. But I find my time increasingly spent on affairs of state. Domestic politics, foreign relations, matters of finance, and so forth. Yet I have no generals of education, training, and experience to whom I can safely entrust this new army. You are a graduate of St.-Cyr, are you not, general?"

"Yes," Songo said, straightening his shoulders, pulling in his paunch, "that is true, Mr. President."

"Ah," Obiri Anokye said softly, "if only Asante had a commander like you."

The Songos' limousine left for the airport a few moments later, but not before a blushing, stammering Captain Songo had asked the President of Asante to give a folded note to his sister Sara.

"But I am too old to be playing Cupid," Anokye said solemnly. "But perhaps plump enough." Then, when the young captain blushed even more, Anokye laughed and said, "I shall deliver it with pleasure, captain. I know I speak for Sara—and all my family, of course—when I express the hope you may return soon for a longer visit."

After the Togolese departed, President Anokye entered his black Mercedes-Benz limousine. He was driven across the parade ground to the barracks gate, chauffeured by Sgt. Sene Yeboa. Preceding them was a military Land-Rover with four guardsmen. Both vehicles flew small Asante flags from their front fenders.

The cars moved slowly south on Asante National Highway No. 1, the country's only paved road, then swung west on a laterite road, avoiding the built-up section of Mokodi. They made a wide circle, and approached the city again, through a section of large estates bordered with bougainvillea hedges. At a deserted place on the road, the cars stopped and were exchanged. The four guardsmen drove the limousine back to the Asante National Palace, flags whipping. President Anokye and Sergeant Yeboa got into the Land-Rover, after removing the fender flags.

They went on for a few kilometers, then pulled into the pebbled driveway of a handsome private home. It was stucco painted a light pink, on a single level, gracefully rambling, with several small wings. Yeboa drove the Land-Rover around to the back, through the open door of a galvanized iron garage. Both men got out and walked the few steps to the back door of the house. They entered without knocking. The sergeant remained in the kitchen. President Anokye went down a hallway to the living room. Yvonne Mayer was waiting for him, wearing a blue peignoir over a lighter blue nightgown. Her feet were bare. Her hair was down.

"Bibi!" she said, holding wide her arms.

Later, sated and sweated, they lay in bed on their backs and watched the mad motes dance. Once, lying thus, Anokye had stared down at their naked bodies and said, "We are night and day." It was true; the abstract patterns formed when black and white entwined never failed to bemuse them.

His skin was dark as cordovan, with a ruddy burnish. He was stoutly made, already inclining to corpulence: thick waist, a layer of softness over the muscles of chest, shoulders, thighs. The young power was still there, but with the yield of padded suede. Black hair at armpits, chest, groin, was hard, with the spring of wire.

The woman, taller than he, was whalebone, as resilient. Blonde hair, pale skin. Arms and legs slender and sinuous. Strong hands and long, prehensile feet. A curious face: cameo features with a tough, distrustful cast. Her breasts were small shields with stiff pink bosses. All of her as sinewy as a vine.

"Bibi," she said lazily, "how did it go—the Nwabala business?"

"As I hoped," he said. "General Songo is furious. Togo has demanded the return of the bodyguard. Benin refuses. The borders have been closed."

"The bodyguard may speak."

"And reveal his own complicity? I do not believe so. Yvonne, there is a long history of enmity between these two countries. Borders have been closed a dozen times. I remember when it was necessary to go to Lagos in Nigeria in order to get into Benin. No visas were issued for travel from Togo. No, the bodyguard will remain in Benin. They will reject Togo's demands."

"I am glad—that what I did helps you."

"Yes, it helps. Did it bother you?"

"Nwabala? No. I have done worse things."

He turned his head slowly on the pillow to stare at her.

"Did you enjoy it?" he asked softly.

"Enjoy?" She shrugged. "A job of work. Yakubu was very good: fast and without useless talk afterward."

"He has moved into the Golden Calf?"

"Yes, into my old apartment. I think he will work out well. The girls like him. He is hard with them but does not demand special favors. You understand? He brings me the books every week. I believe he is stealing about five percent. I don't think that's too much, do you, Bibi?"

"No, let him have it. But no more than five."

"He wishes to raise rates. With all the Texas oilmen in town, he says we can charge more."

"How do you feel about it? The Golden Calf belongs to you."

"Yes, I think we can increase prices. Business has been very good."

"Do as you think best. Men came from London to speak with Willi Abraham. They wish to build a gambling casino on the beach, west of the Mokodi Hilton, near the Zabarian Restaurant. Sam Leiberman says these men are connected with a crime syndicate. But he says they are honest in money matters. What do you think?"

She considered a few moments. "Asante will share?" she asked.

"Yes. A percentage of the net to be negotiated."

"No," she said, "don't do that. They will hide all kinds of expenses and big salaries and skimming in figuring their net. Ask for a percentage of the gross."

"Then you think we should grant a license?"

"Yes, if Asante gets a percentage of the gross. And the tables must be completely straight. The house percentage is enough with honest games and wheels. And all employees, including croupiers, are to be Asantis. Insist on that."

"Yes," he nodded. "Good. I can always depend on you for excellent advice. Yvonne, I have to leave soon; I have a staff meeting at the palace. But first I wish to speak about us, about you."

Now she turned her head to look at him. Their eyes locked.

"What do you wish to say, Bibi?"

"You are happy with this house?"

"Oh yes, it is very fine. I have hired a housekeeper and cook, a maid, and a man to see to the grounds."

"Good. And as I promised, the Golden Calf is completely yours. Just be certain to pay your taxes!"

"I shall," she smiled.

"Now . . . oil from the Zabarian wells will begin to flow a week from next Friday. Actually, it has already begun to flow, but on that day we will have an official ceremony and celebration. The public relations man from Monrovia is arranging it. I will push a button, and everyone will see oil flow through a clear plastic pipe. Starrett executives are coming from America. Peter Tangent has arranged that. It will give me the chance to meet them and speak with them about my plans. Also, I am inviting Premier Da Silva of Benin."

"Ah," she said, still staring into his eyes. "And his daughter Beatrice?"

"Yes. His daughter Beatrice. I will ask to marry her while they are here. Ask him and ask her."

She shivered. Her eyes slid away. She stared at nothing over his shoulder.

"So soon, Bibi?" she murmured.

"It must be done," he said. "You know my plans. You agreed."

"To the marriage," she said reluctantly. "But I told you what I would do if you left me—I will destroy myself and put a curse on you and your plans."

It was his turn to shiver.

"I do not like to hear you speak of such things," he said. "I will not leave you; that I have sworn. But Da Silva knows of you, of us, and the only way I may win his friendship, and his daughter, is to make it appear to him that I have given you up. That is why I have taken you from the Golden Calf and given you this home. But it is not enough. You know there is little I do in Mokodi, in Asante, that can be hidden for long. Da Silva will learn that I am visiting you here. I cannot let that happen. So…"

"So?" she asked.

"I wish to make a suggestion. Just a suggestion. I want you to consider it carefully. I wish you to marry Sene Yeboa. Then this will become his home. And I will be able to visit without gossip. He is the commander of my guard and my oldest personal friend. He is my brother. It would be perfectly natural if I was seen—"

Her eyes flicked back to his, and widened.

"No," she said. "No, no, and no. Find another way. I don't want to marry Sene Yeboa, or any other man. I want only you. I want to love only you."

"Please listen to what I speak," he said patiently. "Sene is a good man. I have not suggested it to him until I spoke to you, but I am certain he will do as I wish. He follows me in everything. Since we were boys together. He will agree to marry you. He will—"

"No," she said fiercely. "No no no."

"He will not wish to make love to you," Anokye said quietly. "He has many other women. He is a bull. He will understand it is a marriage of—of convenience."

"Your convenience!"

"Yes," he agreed. "But what is good for me is also good for you, for all of you. You have sworn allegiance to me, to my destiny."

"I will not do it," she cried. "Not not *not!*"

"Then the love you speak of means nothing," he said, beginning to anger. "'Bibi, whatever you ask. Bibi, I will do anything for you. Bibi, I will die for you.' And so forth. But now I ask, and you say, 'No no no.' That is what your love means."

She struck his chest with her fist.

"And you?" she shouted. "What does your love mean? That I should marry another man?"

It went on and on, rising in intensity. Her blows against his chest and shoulders became harder, more frantic. He attempted to pin her arms. She squirmed to escape. He rolled his weight atop her. She wept with anger, head whipping from side to side, hair flinging. He caught her flailing legs between his. He crushed her torso within his arms.

And slowly, slowly, their disordered fury turned to a different frenzy. He smacked her jaw with the heel of his hand, ravaged her flesh with his teeth, fell violently upon her and forced penetration as her blows turned to a nailed grasp and her whippy body lurched up to meet his rage, and once more she called him, "My captain!" "My king!" "My master!" and what began as rape ended as . . . if not love, then need.

When, finally, they were finished and lay slackly, bruised and swollen, they stared at each other with dulled eyes. Both, not wishing to part in anger, moved about fretfully on the bed, each hoping the other might speak first. Or make a signal. She did, taking his fingers in hers, shifting to be close to him, head on his shoulder, her fine flaxen hair entangled in his black wire. He took a deep breath, held her body tightly, their slicked skin damply pressed.

"Bibi . . ." she murmured, stopped what she was about to say and instead said, "Bibi, this General Songo—you trust him?"

"He is a simple man," the Little Captain said. "A good soldier but a simple man. He can be valuable."

"And Sene Yeboa—is he a simple man?"

He looked at her a long moment.

"Many believe so. That is the impression he gives. But Sene Yeboa is not a simple man. Sene is deep, and he yearns."

"Yearns? For what?"

"Ask him after you are married."

"I will think about it," she said, and they left it at that.

The Land-Rover, flags replaced in fender sockets, headed back toward the Asante National Palace. President Obiri Anokye sat sprawled in the front seat, alongside Sgt. Sene Yeboa. The Little Captain's left arm was extended across the back of the driver's seat, touching the sergeant's thick shoulders.

"Sene," he asked, "it goes well with the mercenary? There are no problems?" As usual when they were alone, they spoke Akan.

"No problems, Bibi," the sergeant replied. "Leiberman makes many jokes. I must laugh at him. But he is a wise man. And brave. He plans well."

"He plans very well," Anokye agreed. "But he is white. Sene, as my plans grow, we must select special men."

"Special?"

"Prempeh had his secret police. We killed them all, but now I see why such men are necessary."

"You desire to have secret police, Bibi?"

"We would not call them that, of course. But I need men I can trust. These men would provide me with information of what happens in Asante, things I might not otherwise know. You understand? Who says what. Who plots against me. Who assembles guns. And so forth. But also, I need men in other countries, my men who could learn and tell me what I need to know. These men must be black. White men could not talk and listen and make friends and go to certain places in Africa. Leiberman could not."

"You speak the truth, Little Captain."

"Sene, I want you to find men who can do these things and who will be willing to serve me. We will pay them generously, for their tasks will not be easy. Perhaps dangerous."

"Yakubu is such a man."

"That is true. He kills well and has no fear. Can you find other such men?"

"I will find them, Little Captain. There are a few who serve in the guard. Quick men who do not fear death."

"Good. And then you must go to Lomé, to Cotonou, and find such men there. And perhaps other places."

Yeboa considered carefully a long moment. Finally he said, "I believe it would be better to select Asantis for the task and send them to other places rather than to select men of those countries. Then the men who serve can be trusted. They will be of our blood."

"Brother," Anokye said, and squeezed the sergeant's heavy shoulder. "You speak wisely."

They drove a few moments in silence. Then Yeboa spoke again.

"You asked the woman, Bibi?"

"I did," Anokye said. "I told her I had not yet spoken to you about it."

"What was her answer?"

"She will think on it. Sene, you are certain you are willing to do this thing for me?"

"I will do it, Little Captain."

They turned into the Boulevard Voltaire, passed the American embassy, circled the palace plaza, and pulled into the rear driveway. President Anokye glanced sideways at the sergeant. The husky soldier, with a machine gunner's massive neck and shoulder muscles, was hunched over the wheel, his thick, sensuous features intent and solemn.

"You are troubled, Sene?" Anokye asked gently.

"Little Captain," Yeboa said earnestly, "she is your woman. If I should marry with her, I would not go to her. You know that?"

"I know."

"But if she comes to me?"

"She will," Anokye said. "In time."

"Then what am I to do?"

President Obiri Anokye slapped a hand down on the man's broad knee.

"Are we not brothers?" he said.

"Yes *sah!*" said Sergeant Yeboa.

The palace and the grounds had been repaired and restored following the violent coup d'etat of August 5th. Armed guardsmen still stood at the entrances and patrolled the plaza, but the ground floor of the palace and certain chambers in the upper floors were open from 1000 to 1500 to all Asantis and tourists. An exhibition of Asanti art was currently on display in the main ballroom, and once a week the Asante National Dance Company presented a free performance of their most famous dances.

President Obiri Anokye had moved his aged mother and father, and his younger brother Adebayo and sister Sara, into chambers on the third floor. His older brother Zuni and his wife had elected to remain, with their children, in the original Anokye home on the island of Zabar, off the Asante shore, connected to Mokodi by a thrice-a-day ferry.

On this morning, the palace was already open to the public; the main floor corridors were crowded with Asantis and tourists. President Anokye was recognized and greeted with a spattering of applause. He smiled and stopped frequently to speak a few words with visitors, to exchange handshakes, salaams, bows. Anokye spoke French and Akan fluently, English carefully, some German and Italian, several African languages.

He welcomed a tour group of tall Swedes, speaking to them in English. He stood in his familiar stance: feet apart and firmly rooted, short torso bent slightly backward, erect, chest inflated, chin elevated and thrust forward, hands on hips.

He told them of his pleasure in seeing them in Asante. He said he hoped they would visit all of his nation, including the cooler hill country, and urged them particularly to seek the opportunity to meet with and come to know the friendly Asanti people. He said that with the revenue from the new oil wells beneath the sea off Zabar, plans were being made to provide more attractions for tourists. He said he hoped to make Asante a showcase for all of Africa, where citizens would enjoy the blessings of liberty and prosperity, and be free to work out their own destinies, whatever they might desire. The tourists were impressed.

"Mr. President," one of the Swedes asked, "do you believe there will be war between Togo and Benin?"

Anokye turned grave. "I pray to God it may not be so," he said. "We are all Africans, all brothers, and we must learn to live in peace with each other. Thank you again for visiting us, and I hope you may return home with many fond memories of our beautiful country."

Then he left them and marched up the wide mahogany staircase to his second floor conference room. He was closely followed by Sgt. Sene Yeboa, who never ceased glancing about, a hand hovering near his holstered pistol.

They were all waiting for him: his inner circle, the men who had been with him through the bloody events of August 5th and had proved their loyalty. The blacks were Premier Willi Abraham, Minister of State Professor Jean-Louis Duclos, Attorney General Mai Fante, and Col. Jim Nkomo. These men were Asantis except for Duclos, a fawn-skinned Martinicain. The two whites in the room were Sam Leiberman and Peter A. Tangent. Leiberman was a mercenary, currently under contract to Asante as a "military advisor." Tangent was still on salary with the Starrett Petroleum Corp., headquartered in Tulsa, Oklahoma, and New York. He was their Chief of African Operations, working out of Starrett's London office.

The Little Captain greeted his friends and insisted on

shaking hands all around. He apologized for having kept them waiting, then settled into the high-backed chair behind his wide desk. The legs of the chair had been lengthened so that he would be on eye level with visitors. All drew up chairs except for Sergeant Yeboa, who stood with his back against the single door.

Heavy drapes had been drawn across the tall windows, blocking out the fierce Asante sun. The air conditioning was going full-blast, a chilled breeze circulated by a four-bladed fan suspended from the ceiling. The fans had been installed by the French governor who built the palace. After Asante achieved independence in 1958, King Prempeh IV had the palace air-conditioned, but in one of his many extravagances had kept the old-fashioned fans. Obiri Anokye had retained them.

He picked up a desk ornament, a lead model of a black officer in the dress uniform of an Asanti captain. This, with nine models of Asanti enlisted men, had been Peter Tangent's personal gift to President Obiri Anokye to commemorate his inauguration. The gift had pleased the former army captain enormously. He fondled the little soldier as he spoke.

"About the casino project," he began abruptly, speaking French. "Willi, we will take our percentage from the gross rather than the net. Do you approve?"

Premier Abraham, a small, fine-boned, grey-haired man wearing a suit of dark tropical worsted beautifully tailored in a European cut, nodded at once.

"Good, Bibi. They will object, but they will finally agree."

"More profits for the whites," the Minister of State said angrily.

The Little Captain had a habit of turning his entire head in a magisterial way instead of shifting his eyes. Now he turned to stare at Duclos.

"We know how you feel, Jean," he said softly. "But there is an English saying about learning to walk before you can run. Is that not so, Peter?"

"Something like that," Tangent said.

"Besides," Anokye went on, "we will insist that all

employees of the casino, including croupiers, be Asantis. It will aid employment here and give us knowledge of their gross revenues."

"I'm not certain they'll agree to that, Bibi," Willi Abraham said dubiously. "They are hard men."

"Leiberman?" Anokye asked.

"They'll probably agree to Asantis for waiters, porters, bartenders, bouncers, cooks, and so on," Sam Leiberman said. "And I'd guess they'll be willing to train Asantis as croupiers. But they'll want their own guys at the top: pit bosses, the spooks behind the walls with glasses, cashiers, accountants, managers, and so on."

"All right," Anokye said. "We will settle for that. I am anxious this casino should be built. I believe it will help tourism and our balance of payments. Anything else before we hear Peter's report?"

"The personnel carriers?" Col. Jim Nkomo offered.

"I will discuss that with you personally," the President said. "It is a military matter. Anything else?"

"This Togo-Benin matter," said Mai Fante slowly.

"Yes?"

"There is talk of their submitting their differences to the Organization of African Unity for arbitration."

"Talk?" Anokye said sharply. "From where? Who talks?"

"I received a call from Benin," Mai Fante said. "A friend. He says it is under discussion. He asks our reaction. The call was to sound us out."

"We welcome any move that will insure peace," President Anokye said. "Any move that will help remove causes of dispute between Togo and Benin. That is our official reaction. Our public position. Is that clear to everyone? Good. Anything else? No? All right, Peter; take the floor. Tell us the bad news."

"Not entirely bad," Peter Tangent said. He rose to his skinny six feet five, seeming to unkink as he straightened up. He lounged about the paneled study as he spoke. Once he paused to pull a packet of Players from his inside pocket, lighted up, then passed the cigarettes about. Fante, Nkomo, Leiberman, and Sergeant Yeboa accept-

ed. President Anokye shook his head, but took a package
of Gauloise Blue from his top desk drawer and sat
listening with an unlighted cigarette between his lips.

Tangent was wearing a suit of navy blue silk, a white
cotton shirt with button-down collar, a maroon Countess
Mara tie. He had a gold Omega chronometer loosely
chained about his left wrist. His tasseled black loafers
gleamed with a dull gloss. Tangent's skin was pale,
cheekbones lightly freckled. Across his high forehead was
a discernible red mark; the panama he habitually wore
pressed too tightly.

"The meeting was held in Tulsa," he began, speaking
rapidly. "Present were five men besides myself. The vice
president and the general manager of the Tulsa office.
They handle domestic operations. And the vice president
and general manager of the New York office, responsible
for overseas operations. The fifth man was old Ross
Starrett himself, chairman of the board. He's the son of
the original owner of the company, Sherm Starrett, who
died about twenty years ago. Ross himself is no spring
chicken. Pushing eighty, I'd guess. I hadn't seen him for
several years, and he looked like death warmed over.
Suffers terribly from rheumatoid arthritis. But the brain
is still keen. Surprisingly, I found him the most
sympathetic. Just a feeling I had. He let the others carry
the ball and went along with their judgment. But I got a
definite feeling of interest from him. I'm very perceptive
to vibrations in the executive suite, and I got the
impression that Ross Starrett was curious and interested.
Perhaps even intrigued.

"In any event, I made my presentation, using a big map
of Africa. I had the research department of our London
office look up some numbers for me, and I threw them
fast: population of Africa, land area, present and
projected GNP, existing and estimated mineral deposits,
petroleum fields discovered and suspected, cereal grains,
everything. Then we got down to the nitty-gritty: what,
exactly, you wanted.

"Here I was hampered by your instructions, Mr.
President. I was to mention Togo and Benin, and nothing
else. They are not stupid men, and the general manager of

the New York office had done his homework and had all
the answers. The tribal volatility of the two countries,
their frequent changes of government, their lack of a solid
economic base: no oil, no gold, no diamonds, no
phosphates to speak of. Just palm oil and cassava. As he
pointed out, both countries would have been down the
drain years ago if it wasn't for the subsidies from France.
No argument there.

"To make this as brief as possible, they have no interest
in Togo or Benin. As the veep of Tulsa pointed out, Shell
had great hopes for offshore Benin wells but has nothing
to show for it but a string of dry holes and a gusher of red
ink. So it's no-go for any investment on Starrett's part.
But as expected, they're perfectly willing to advance
limited sums against anticipated revenue from Asante's
Zabarian wells."

"The same bargain they made on the coup," Professor
Jean-Louis Duclos cried bitterly. "They are kind enough
to lend us our own money!"

"We are not that badly off," Willi Abraham said. "We
don't need Starrett for loans. With oil production about
to begin, many sources of ready cash are open to us."

"I know all that," Tangent said patiently, "and I
explained it to them. I said what you sought was a kind of
partnership: an outright grant against future licenses to
explore for oil and prospect for minerals in lands that
came under Asante's hegemony. But since all I could offer
was Togo and Benin, they said no way. Too poor. Not
enough evidence of a potential return to justify the gamble. Then old Ross Starrett said something that made
me realize he was interested, and way ahead of the others.
He said their answer might be different if you had other
countries in mind."

President Anokye looked up quickly.

"Did he mention any specific countries, Peter?"

"Yes, he did. Nigeria and Zaire."

The men in the room looked at each other, smiling.
The Little Captain leaned back in his chair. He finally
lighted his cigarette and smoked slowly, blowing plumes
at the ceiling.

"Sene," he said dreamily, "how do you feel about all

this?" He straightened, leaned forward over the desk, spoke to the others. "I trust Sene's judgment. He is bush-wise. Perhaps he does not know economics, but he knows men and why they act as they do. Sene, what do you say?"

"Do not borrow their money," Yeboa said immediately. "If it is needed, get it elsewhere. If we crawl, pan in hand, they will think themselves our masters. If they are not willing to take the risk, they should not share the profit."

"Very good, Sene," Anokye said approvingly. "Ex-actly how I feel. The rest of you?"

They all nodded in agreement.

"And how did you leave it?" the President asked Tangent.

"I told them their decision would anger you, and might cause complications. That is the word I used: 'complica-tions.' I implied that after hearing their decision, you might have second thoughts about the lease arrangements on the Zabarian wells."

"Good," Willi Abraham said. "And their reaction?"

"Concern," Tangent said. "They were definitely concerned. That was when I suggested a man from Tulsa and a man from New York come over for the ceremony when the oil flow officially starts. I suggested they speak to you in person. They readily agreed. Ross Starrett was most anxious for them to come. He said, 'Maybe something can be worked out.' I quote his exact words."

"Sounds like my kind of guy," Leiberman said.

"He's almost twice as old as the others," Tangent said, "and has twice their nerve. He's an old man now, but still a wildcatter at heart."

"What do you suggest we do now?" the Little Captain asked. "What would be our wisest course of action?"

"I see several options," Tangent said, lighting another cigarette. "One: we can go elsewhere for the funds needed for the Togo-Benin campaign. Willi says they would be easily available."

"They would be," Abraham nodded. "Not for the purpose intended, of course, but we could say the money was needed for schools or hospitals or whatever."

"Two:" Tangent went on, "when the Starrett men come over for the oil ceremony, you could tell them in confidence, Mr. President, that our objective is actually Nigeria. If you decide to do that, I can state confidently that funds will be made available on a no-strings basis."

"Why shouldn't they?" Duclos burst out. "Nigeria—the richest nation in Africa!"

"No," Anokye said, "I do not believe it would be wise to reveal our plans to others at this time. It is enough that we alone know of it."

"There is one other option available," Tangent said. "I cannot say how viable it is, since I will not be consulted in the decision, but here it is.... While I was in the Tulsa office, I stopped by to say hello to old friends in production and development. We talked shop, of course, and I learned that Starrett's overseas operations are becoming increasingly strained by a shortage of refining capacity. To put it in a simplified way, the oil taken from Asante's waters will be shipped by tanker to Starrett's Ireland refinery. There the petroleum is broken down into gasoline, naphtha, kerosene, petrochemicals, whatever, and then must be shipped again by tanker to the end markets. In other words, if Africa wishes to buy Starrett gasoline or diesel oil, then Asante crude must be shipped thousands of miles and then shipped back again as finished products. Very uneconomical. So Starrett is investigating several areas where a refinery might be built to service all of Africa, a profitable market and a growing one. Asante is one of the areas under consideration as a possible refinery site. There is no way I can influence the decision. All the pertinent data is fed into a computer to find the location that maximizes profits. But since Starrett's leases with Asante and other oil producing African nations deal only with the drilling and pumping of petroleum, not refining, it occurs to me that the offer of generous terms to Starrett in granting a refinery license might result in a no-strings grant to Asante for the Togo-Benin campaign."

"Who do you work for?" Minister of State Duclos cried out. "Asante or Starrett?"

Tangent turned to look at him coldly. The young professor had jerked to his feet. His slight figure was quivering with fury. He shook a finger at the oilman.

"How do we know—" He tried to speak, choked on his rage, started again. "How do we know this is not a plot by your employer? Something they suggested you offer? In order to get favorable terms for their refinery? That will pollute our air and water? How do we know that? Eh? Eh?"

"My loyalty is with Asante and Obiri Anokye," Tangent said tightly. He turned to the desk. "Mr. President, if you do not believe that, then my value to you is at an end. I swear that no one at Starrett Petroleum brought up the subject of the refinery in connection with your request for funds. It was entirely my own idea. If you feel I am playing a double game, then I will withdraw at once."

"Peter, Peter," Obiri Anokye said soothingly, "I do not believe that for an instant. I have no doubts of your loyalty. To me and to my dream of a united Africa. Jean!" he spoke sharply to his Minister of State. "Sit down and do not speak. You shame me and my home by these false accusations. Peter has said the decision as to where the refinery will be located has not been made, and he cannot influence that decision. Perhaps it will be built in Guinea or Liberia or Ghana or Gabon. Is that not true, Peter?"

"That is correct, Mr. President. The matter has not yet been determined by the computer. But I felt you should be made aware of the possibility that Asante may be selected so that if it is, you may take full advantage of it."

"A refinery in Asante," Willi Abraham said, eyes gleaming. "It would help employment immeasurably."

"Only during construction," Tangent warned. "After it's in operation, it's almost fully automated, requiring only a minimal staff."

"Still," Mai Fante said enthusiastically, "it would be a boon to our balance of trade. Perhaps the harbor will be dredged and enlarged."

"Undoubtedly," Tangent said. "But it is too early to speak of such things. At the moment, our only two viable options are to take a loan from Starrett or seek it elsewhere, or to reveal the plan to conquer Nigeria and request a cash grant."

"Thank you, Peter," President Anokye said. "You have done well, performed a valuable service to Asante and to me personally. I will give the matter much thought. I will probably not reach a decision until after the visit of the Starrett people during the oil ceremony. If they bring up the matter of the refinery, then we will meet again and discuss it further. I thank you all. This meeting is at an end. Peter, will you remain a moment, please."

They filed from the room, excited and voluble. Duclos was still flushed with anger. When the room had emptied, Anokye made a motion of his head, and Sgt. Sene Yeboa also withdrew, to take up his station outside. He closed the door behind him.

"Peter, sit down and relax," the Little Captain said. "Here, next to the desk. Give me one of your cigarettes, please. How is it an American smokes English cigarettes?"

"Acquired taste," Tangent shrugged, still tense. He leaned forward to hold a flame for Anokye. "This lighter is French. My shoes are made in Spain. The suit is Italian."

"But your heart belongs to Africa?" Anokye said wryly.

"Yes," Tangent laughed, relaxing, "my heart belongs to Africa. As a matter of fact, that is the truth. I first saw Africa more than ten years ago, and I fell in love with it then. I have not changed."

"What do you love?"

"First it was the physical things. Incredible space. Unbelievable sky. The land itself. Then the people. Their humanness. More recently it's been the African way of life that attracts me. The soul of Africa. The spoken, visual, instinctive, *feeling* culture. A welcome alternative to my dull, unfeeling, mechanical world. Warm emotion as against chilly reason. Do I make sense?"

"Oh yes," Anokye nodded. "A great deal. Peter, I wish to apologize for Jean-Louis' outburst. It was not you, personally, he assaulted. In his eyes, no white man is capable of loyalty, sacrifice or, in fact, any unselfish motive."

"I understand the way he feels."

"Do you? I doubt it. Understand in your mind perhaps, but not in your heart. I assure you that *I* do not understand Jean's feelings. I have never hated the whites. Never. Perhaps because I never met a white I could not outwit."

"I'll remember that," Tangent laughed.

"Yes," Anokye said, showing his teeth, "do that." He sat back a moment, pondering. "Poor Jean. He does not realize how his hatred of the whites limits him. But he can be of value to me. In certain places. There are nations in Africa where the black leaders feel as he does, with better reason. In Rhodesia, for example. In South Africa. Zaire perhaps. Kenya. He will be a good representative for me in those places. Tell me, Peter—something that puzzles me—when you pleaded my cause before your employers in Tulsa, did they not suspect that your loyalty was now with me, and no longer with them?"

"It would never occur to them."

"Oh? Why not?"

"Because they could never believe that a white man would link his future to that of a black, would work for a black man."

"Ahh," Anokye said. He shook his head more in incredulity than disgust. "The reason I ask is that I wish to be certain that you know that should your employment with Starrett be terminated, I would want you to serve Asante full time. You will be an 'advisor' of one kind or another. At a very generous salary, I assure you. Admittedly, at this moment you are more valuable to me as the representative of Starrett Petroleum in Asante. But your value will not cease when your Starrett connection ends, if it should. You understand that?"

"I do, Mr. President, and I thank you."

"You think there is a chance of the refinery coming to Asante?"

"I think there is a very good chance. Asante is approximately halfway down the west coast of Africa. Starrett sells petroleum products from Morocco to Botswana. If that computer has any sense at all, it will select Asante for the refinery site."

"Yes, geography is everything, is it not? Look at this..."

He stood and led Tangent to the facing wall where, on a section of smooth hardwood paneling, a map had been taped. It was the *Michelin* No. 153, Afrique Nord et Ouest. The borders of Togo and Benin had been heavied with a red grease pencil. Anokye pointed at them.

"Why do you think I selected these two countries as the first targets of my drive southward?"

Tangent shrugged. "Because they are the closest to Asante? Because they are small and relatively weak?"

"Only partly that. If I had the military strength, I would strike directly at Nigeria or Zaire. Where wealth exists. Those are prizes worth the gamble. But to conquer those countries would require massive invasions. I may soon have sufficient soldiers, well armed and trained, but I do not have the means of invasion. It would require troop-carrying ships and amphibious craft to invade Nigeria from Asante, and probably a large air force to take Zaire. As conquests, Togo and Benin mean nothing economically. They are poor nations. Your men in Tulsa were quite right. But if I take Togo and Benin, then what do I have? Here... see? A border with Nigeria. There are roads across that border. I can go overland, on foot or in trucks. I can use tanks. No need for ships or aircraft. Togo leads to Benin, which leads to Nigeria. Once that is ours, all the southern half of Africa opens up. Perhaps, with Nigeria's wealth, I can leap-frog to Zaire or Angola."

"But Mr. President," Tangent protested, "Angola is in a state of rebellion."

"Peter," Obiri Anokye said gently, "all of Africa is in a state of rebellion."

3.

THE MOKODI HILTON, located on the beach west of the port area, was the highest building in Asante. Starrett Petroleum had leased the entire penthouse floor. It had been converted to offices and living quarters for J. Tom Petty, general manager of Starrett's Zabarian operation, and his staff. In addition, several suites were available for visiting VIPs. It was here Peter Tangent stayed during his frequent visits to Mokodi.

He had returned to the Starrett office following the palace conference, and had plunged immediately into a series of meetings with Petty and the chief engineers of the two offshore drilling rigs that straddled the ocean southwest of Zabar like steel spiders. Sitting in on the confabs were the technicians responsible for the tempo-

rary pipeline leading to a jerry-built floating dock in
Mokodi harbor. For the time being, it would serve as a
delivery site for the Starrett tankers that already floated
high in the water a few miles offshore, waiting for the
official ceremony before loading began.

Tangent listened to the progress reports, most of them
delivered in the harsh twang of West Texas or the softer
drawl of Oklahoma. Then he listened to the indignant
complaints: the unreliability of Asante contractors,
laziness of the niggers, high cost of American bourbon,
shortage of matériel, thievery of cab drivers, African heat,
the impossibility of getting a good bowl of chili. . . .

"WAWA," Tangent said finally, and when they looked
at him in puzzlement, he explained, "West Africa Wins
Again. Don't fight it; go along with it. These are good
people. Their way of life is not ours, but we'll get further
faster if we respect their method of doing things. You're a
long way from Tulsa and Houston. Relax. You'll get
better results if you treat them as equals. They've got a
great sense of humor. A good joke will get you more than
blowing your stack. Remember, it's their country. We're
here on sufferance. You're all making big money. Starrett
expects you to do your job, grin and bear it, then go home.
Everyone get the message?"

After they left, grumbling, Tangent spent the remainder of the afternoon on paperwork. He had a plate of
chicken sandwiches sent up from room service, and
munched on those as he worked, washing them down with
two bottles of Evian mineral water. Finally, about 2030,
he stuffed documents into an attaché case to take back to
London, and went into his suite to pack.

He was suddenly faced with empty hours, a realization
so abrupt and so painful he felt like weeping. He did not
know the cause. He was deeply involved with the plans of
Obiri Anokye, and this had meaning for him. But his
strength came from the passion of others. His hours alone
seemed to have no more significance than ticking, the
slow passage of time.

At the big picture window, drapes pulled back, he

looked out and down onto the lighted terrace. There
tourists dined, and he could imagine warm talk, cunning
lies, loud laughter. Life. And beyond was the black sea,
shirred with whitecaps. And farther beyond were the
twinkling lights of the oil rigs and the island of Zabar. All,
all, cheerful enough. Then why depression?

When the phone rang he moved slowly, still pondering
his gloom. Almost savoring it. A bittersweet hurt he could
not define.

"Tangent," he said.

"Leiberman here. Come have a drink with us. Dele and
me. We're going to the Zabarian. They've got a new
singer. A cunt from Accra."

"Thanks, but I can't," Tangent said. "I'm taking a
morning flight out, and I've got a lot of work to do."

"Cut the shit," Leiberman said. "There's more to life
than a barrel of oil and Sulka pajamas. Meet you at the
Zabarian in an hour."

"All right," Tangent said.

Dele was Leiberman's Ivory Coast girl, a little bundle
of giggling wickedness. She sat between Tangent and the
mercenary at the bar at the Zabarian and rubbed knees
with both of them. She and Leiberman and Felah, the
bartender, carried on an uproarious conversation in
Boulé, laughing continually. Tangent couldn't understand a word of it, but he felt better.

After a while the lights dimmed, the crowd quieted, a
spotlight came on, and the singer walked out. She was
carrying a mandolin. There was some polite applause.

She seemed enormously tall—Tangent guessed almost
six feet—and was stalk-thin. No breasts. No ass. She was
wearing a silver-grey silk gown, hung from her bony
shoulders with rhinestone straps. The shimmering stuff
was loose, but touched hard nipples, narrow hips. Her
naked arms were eels.

Her color was brown-black, deep, with no undertint.
Just matte. Black curls fitted her long skull like a tight
toque. A big, splayed nose, thick lips turned outward.
Heavy cheekbones, a chin like an elbow. Wide eyes

somewhat slanted. The entire face an African mask. Tangent looked for tribal tattoos, but there were none. Big gold hoops hung from pierced ears.

Leiberman leaned across to Tangent. "The queen of spades," he whispered, in English.

She strummed a few chords, then began to sing. Tangent listened a moment, then leaned across to Leiberman. "What is it?"

"Yoruba. About her guy who went to war and got greased. Very sad. Jesus, what a lousy voice. Great bod, lousy voice."

He was right, Tangent decided; the voice was bad: reedy, as mechanical as an old Victrola. But she could move. The sinuous body swayed. Arms lifted. The long throat was muscled ebony. Taut. There was something there, something. . . . But not the voice.

After a while, people began talking again and ordering drinks. She kept singing, and Tangent felt sorry for her.

"What is her name?" he asked Felah, in French.

"Amina Dunama, Mr. Tangent, sir."

"Where from?"

Felah rolled his eyes in his Rastus act.

"Here, there, everywhere. Mr. Tangent, sir. She up in Ghana before she come here. I think she Lagos-born."

"Let's have her over for a drink," Leiberman said.

"No," Tangent said.

Leiberman said, "Felah, though I've belted you and flayed you . . ."

"By the living God that made you . . ." Felah said.

"Get her skinny ass over here," Leiberman said.

"A duty and a pleasure, bwana," Felah said solemnly.

"Up yours," Leiberman said, "and have one on me."

"Oh, I had that a long time ago, Mr. Leiberman, sir," Felah said, and when the singer finished, to polite applause, he went to fetch her.

Leiberman and Tangent stood when she joined them. Felah made the introductions. Dele moved over so the singer could sit next to Tangent. But for a moment, he and Amina Dunama stood side by side.

"Look at you," Sam Leiberman said, "I could thread

both of you through one needle. What're you drinking, toots—hot goat's blood?"

She laughed and ordered a dry Beefeater Gibson, up. Her speaking voice was better than her singing voice: smooth, casual, mellifluous. Her French was fluent. A lot of Parisian argot.

"I enjoyed your songs, Miss Dunama," Tangent said politely.

"Thank you," she said.

"You got a terrible voice," Leiberman said. "You were lousy."

Tangent was embarrassed, but Amina Dunama looked at Leiberman with interest. "You're right," she said. "If it wasn't for the tourists, I'd starve."

"It's the carcass that gets them, honey," the mercenary nodded.

She looked down at her bodice.

"You think I should get silicone?" she asked.

"Nah," Leiberman said. "That stuff shifts. You're liable to end up a Babinga."

She threw back her head and laughed, long and hard. Her throat was thick, much bigger than her upper arm. A thigh of a throat.

Tangent looked from her to Leiberman and back, not understanding the exchange that made her laugh.

"Babinga?" he asked.

"Pygmies," Leiberman explained. "Some of them have steatopygia. Enormous great asses. You wouldn't believe."

"Oh," Tangent said.

Dele discovered that Amina spoke Boulé. The two women began to chatter. Leiberman got off his bar stool and came over to stand behind Tangent. He put a meaty arm across Tangent's shoulders.

"You drunk?" Tangent said, shrugging off the arm.

"Sure I am," Leiberman said cheerfully. "And loving every minute of it. I happen to be a very sweet drunk." Then he switched to English. "You fancy the beautiful cunt?" he asked.

Amina Dunama turned slowly and looked at the

mercenary. "I also speak English," she said in that language.

"So?" Leiberman said. "I just asked him an innocent question."

The singer shifted her stare to Tangent.

"Why don't you give him an innocent answer?" she said.

"Yes," Tangent said, "I fancy the beautiful lady."

Amina leaned forward and thrust a wet tongue into his left ear.

"Mazel tov!" Leiberman shouted. "May all your troubles be little ones. Felah!"

"Sir?" the bartender cried.

"But when it comes to slaughter..." Leiberman recited.

"You will do your work on water..." Felah answered.

"And you'll lick the bloomin' boots of 'im that's got it," they finished in unison, and Leiberman said, "The hell you will. Another round, chappie, and let joy be unrefined."

"I'm afraid he's drunk, Miss Dunama." Tangent said.

She looked into his eyes.

"Why are you afraid?" she asked softly.

They left Leiberman and his Ivory Coast girl at the bar. The loud, red-faced mercenary had attracted a circle of admiring tourists who were buying him drinks. Sam was regaling them with old *colon* jokes. ("When you first come to Africa, you pick a fly out of your beer. After six months in Africa, you swill the beer down, fly and all. After a year in Africa, you put a fly *in* your beer, for the protein!")

Amina was staying at the Moķodi Hilton. They strolled slowly back along the boardwalk. A three-quarter moon had come over. It laid a silver swath across the gently rolling sea. She had a fishnet scarf across her bare shoulders, but the mild night wind was warm and scented.

He wanted to ask her about her life, singing, home, childhood, likes, dislikes, everything.... But he was too content to speak, and she was silent.

They came into the lighted lobby, stopped, faced each other. He did not have to stoop to look into her eyes.

"I would ask you for lunch or dinner, Miss Dunama," he said, "but I must return to London tomorrow morning."

"Oh," she said.

"But I'll be back in a week," he said hastily. "Perhaps less than that. Will you be here?"

"For two weeks," she said. "Then on to Lomé."

"We'll have dinner when I return?"

"Of course."

"Can I bring you anything from London? I have no problems with customs."

"Just yourself," she said. They had been speaking French. Now she switched to Akan: "Go in good health and return in good health."

"The memory of your beauty shall keep me young and happy," he replied, and they both smiled. Then he said in French, "May I escort you to your door?"

"Please," she said. "Fourth floor."

At her door, he held out his hand.

"Thank you for a very pleasant evening, Miss Dunama."

She looked at the proffered hand in surprise, then looked up into his eyes.

"You're not coming in?" she said.

"Well... ah," he said. Then: "I haven't been invited," he giggled.

"Would you care to come in, Mr. Tangent?"

"Well... yes. For a moment."

Her hotel room was a shambles. Clothing tossed everywhere. Cosmetics. Perfumes. Cigarette butts. Used tissues. Half-empty glasses. A sandwich with one bite taken out, red lip rouge around the crescent. The bed mussed. She made no apologies.

"Let me see..." she said. "I think I have some banana liqueur. Or we can call room service."

"No, no," he said hurriedly. "Nothing, thank you."

"I have some cigars."

"Cigars?"

"Yes. I smoke cigars. Are you shocked?"

"Of course not," he said.

"Would you like a cigar?"

"All right," he said bravely. "I'll have a cigar."

They were really Spanish cigarillos, long, thin, black. They lighted up solemnly. Not bad. She threw clothes off chairs, and they sat close, puffing importantly. After a moment she reached up and switched off the lamp. But her balcony was over the lighted terrace; they could see each other dimly, in outline. Highlights: her bare shoulders, his tilted head.

"What Leiberman said . . ." he began. "You're really a good singer, Miss Dunama."

"I am not," she said without rancor. "He spoke the truth. I like him. He's alive."

"Then why . . ."

"Why do I continue? Because it allows me independence."

"But what is . . ."

"What is to become of me? What is to happen? I never fear of that. Do you know any African who plans the future, Mr. Tangent?"

"Yes," he said.

"Well, I do not."

"I would like to call you Amina, if I may."

"Of course."

"And my name is Peter."

"I know. But may I call you Mr. Tangent?"

"You may, of course. But why so formal?"

"I prefer Mr. Tangent."

"All right," he said equably. "If you prefer."

"In English, 'tangent' means going away from a straight line, does it not?"

"That's one meaning," he said shortly.

She got up, cigar clamped between her teeth, hiked up her silver-grey skirt, sat down in his lap. He squirmed about to accommodate her weight.

"Do you have a woman, Mr. Tangent?" she asked. "In London?"

"No."

"In Africa?"

"No."

"Anywhere?"

"No. No woman anywhere."

"That is sad."

"Yes," he said. "Sad."

"Would you like me to be your woman?"

His reply surprised him. Not what he said so much as how quickly he said it.

"Yes," he said. "I would like you to be my woman."

"All right, Mr. Tangent," she said.

She stunned him.

"Look here..." he said.

"Look where?" she asked innocently.

"I don't understand," he said.

"Don't understand what?"

"You. What you said. I don't understand why you would wish to be my woman."

"Will you pay?" she asked.

He drew a deep breath, pondered a long moment.

"Yes," he said.

She laughed.

"I don't wish payment," she said.

"You're mischievous," he said.

"Yes," she said, "I am. But I can save you."

"Save me?" he said indignantly. He shook his head. "Are you playing with me? Save me how? From what? What makes you think I need saving?"

"Don't you?"

"Of course not. From anything."

"Good," she said.

She stood and turned her back to him.

"The zipper," she said.

Obediently he pulled it down. It whispered derisively.

"Should we put out our cigars?" he asked nervously.

"What for?" she said.

He undressed shyly. He would not look at the naked wave on the rumpled sheet. He hung his jacket and shirt over chair backs. He shook out his trousers and draped them over a table edge.

"The socks," she said. "Rolled and tucked into the shoes."

He turned to her angrily.

"You think me a fool," he cried.

"Yes," she said. "A sweet fool. Now come to me."

He did, gingerly, rolling close to her.

"Oh my," she said. "So pale."

"Yes," he said.

"Freckled."

"Some," he said. "I can't go out in the sun. My skin can't take it. I used to go out in the sun all the time, but I reacted. Doctors told me that if I insisted on going out in—"

"Shut up," she said.

"All right," he said meekly.

After a while, he said, "I'm not going to make it."

"Is it so important?" she said.

"No," he said. "It's not," he said. With wonderment.

4.

TANGENT FLEW Air Afrique to Paris, planning to switch to Air France for the hop to London. There was food and drink all the way on the Mokodi-Paris flight, but he wasn't interested. Strapped into his seat in a half-empty cabin, he took a blank pad from his attaché case and stared at it.

He reviewed what he had said and done in Mokodi. The palace conference. He had made a mistake in admitting he was powerless to influence Starrett's decision on the refinery site. One did not publicly confess weakness. At worst, he should have said, "I'll see what I can do." He had not thought it through. Now, pondering, he saw that perhaps he might shape events. He grunted with pleasure, made a few cryptic notes.

Then, his writing hand reminding him of a white squid, something dead and apart from him, he put the ballpoint pen aside. He closed his eyes. He thought of Amina Dunama. Black wave on rumpled sheet. There again he had confessed weakness. Displayed it. But that was something entirely different. No power play there. Or if it was, of a different kind. And Amina had not cared. Said she did not care. Appeared not to care. It was difficult. He sighed, and dozed off.

The company limousine met him at Heathrow. He went immediately to Starrett's headquarters in an Edwardian townhouse in Mayfair. Only a minimal night shift was on duty, mostly in the communications center. But there was coffee steaming in a big perc and a tin of stale biscuits. Tangent helped himself to both, then placed a person-to-person call to Ed Gianelli in Tulsa. The time was right: about 2100 in London, 1500 in Oklahoma. The call went through without delay.

"Ed? Peter Tangent in London."

"Hey, Peter! And happy fish-and-chips to you."

"How're you, Ed? And the wife and bambinos?"

"Couldn't be better. You?"

"Fine, thanks. Ed, small problem. . . . You remember that thing we talked about when I was over—the refinery?"

"Yes?"

"It's out of the bag. A reporter from the London *Times* has been on my neck. He says he hears, quote, from an unimpeachable source, unquote, that it's going to Liberia. Anything to it?"

"No way. The choice right now is either Gabon or Asante. But not decided yet. At least that's what I hear."

"Good. I'll deny the report. Better yet, I'll just say, 'No comment.'"

"Right you are. When in doubt, keep your mouth shut."

"Thanks, Ed. Love to all."

Tangent rang off, grinning. Gabon or Asante. Interesting. He called Schwarzkopf's Adventure Tours, the travel agency that served as Tony Malcolm's cover.

The phone was answered on the first ring; a canned voice began: "Hello. This is a recorded message. There is no one in the office at present. But if you—"

Tangent hung up and called Malcolm's unlisted home phone. No answer. Then he tried Brindleys. Mr. Malcolm had signed in; "Just a moment, sir, and we will try to locate him." Finally, he was switched to the bar, and Malcolm came on.

"Who?" he said.

"Tangent. Hi, Tony."

"Peter! You're back. Or are you calling from darkest Africa?"

"I'm back. What're you drinking?"

"A bottle of Chateau Tannic Acid, vintage of yesterday."

"If I stand you a bottle of Latour fifty-three, will you meet me in the library in an hour?"

"Latour fifty-three? I'll meet you on the roof!"

Brindleys was a private club for gentlemen, in a refurbished townhouse on Park Lane. It was small, and expensive, although most members' bills were picked up by their corporations, embassies, trade organizations, etc., as a legitimate business expense. It was true that the world's business was frequently discussed and sometimes concluded at Brindleys. But it also offered an excellent kitchen and what was said to be the third largest wine cellar in London. Prices were not reasonable.

There were four men at the coppered bar when Peter Tangent strode in: Tony Malcolm down at the far end; the Stavros brothers in the middle, nursing little glasses of ouzo; and near the entrance, Julien Ricard hunched and glowering over a small balloon of brandy. Tangent hoped to slip by the Frenchman unobserved, but Ricard's hand shot out, he clutched Tangent's arm.

"Buy you drink," he said thickly.

"Raincheck," Tangent said, trying to smile pleasantly. "Got some business with Tony Malcolm."

Ordinarily at Brindleys, mention of "business" was sufficient excuse. For anything. But Ricard would not be put off; he did not release Tangent's arm. The American

thought, not for the first time, what an unattractive fellow
his captor was: dark, peevish, with a great livid birthmark
that ran down his right cheek on to his neck.

"You're in plastics, aren't you, Tangent?" Ricard said,
though he knew better.

"In a manner of speaking," Tangent said. "Oil,
actually. You're in snails, aren't you, Ricard?"

"Import-export," Ricard said angrily.

"Ah yes," Tangent said. "Snails *and* ticklers."

He jerked his arm away, and stalked down to Tony
Malcolm. He nodded to the Stavros brothers as he
passed. God only knew what *they* were in. Everything,
probably.

"Tony," he said. "Let's go into the library. Can't stand
that man!"

"He's a bit much," Malcolm said sympathetically. "I
expect it's the birthmark that makes him so nasty."

"No excuse," Tangent said, regaining his good humor.
"I've got the world's shortest cock, but I'm as nice a fellow
as you'd want to meet."

Malcolm laughed, and led the way.

There was only one other member in Brindleys library:
a gaffer deep in a leather club chair pulled up before the
fireplace. He was staring into the flames and giggling.
Tangent and Tony Malcolm sat far back in a secluded
corner. They watched Harold reverently uncork the
Latour.

"Should let it catch its breath, gentlemen," the old
waiter said. He poured a bit into a glass, paused
expectantly as Tangent sniffed and sipped.

"Loverly," Tangent said.

"It has a nice nose," Harold said, filling their glasses
halfway. "Please give it some time, gentlemen. We're on
the last case of this lot."

Malcolm savored.

"Velvet," he said. "Moonlight. Rembrandt. Mozart."

"How about Donald Duck?" Tangent asked.

"Philistine. When did you get back?"

"A few hours ago."

"See the papers?"

"Not yet."

"Starrett is up another three," Malcolm said. "Think I should hang on?"

"Definitely," Tangent said. "I am. It'll bounce even higher in a week or so. We're planning a refinery in Africa."

"Oh? Where?"

"Ah," Tangent said. "That's the reason for the wine."

"Didn't think it was my damp, white body," Malcolm said. "What's up?"

There was little point in trying to deceive; Virginia had good men in Togo and Benin, and Malcolm would guess what was going on. He looked like a plump, affable shoe salesman. But his brain, as Tangent once remarked, was "pure Borgia."

He told Malcolm of President Obiri Anokye's planned takeover of Togo and Benin. He mentioned nothing of Nigeria. He described Starrett's projected African refinery, and how it might affect Anokye's shortage of funds.

"I think they'll come through with the money he wants," Tangent said, "if he agrees to good terms on the refinery license."

"How do you know they'll build in Asante?"

"I checked with a friend in Tulsa. Just an hour ago. The choice has narrowed down to Asante or Gabon. That's where you come in."

"Is it?" Malcolm said lazily. He held his glass up to the dim light, peered through it, twirled it slowly. "You're really gung-ho for the Little Captain, aren't you?"

"Oh yes," Tangent admitted. "Burned my bridges. Metaphorically speaking. Look, Tony, this man has a great dream. A vision. He wants to unite all of Africa. All those sixty or so poor, suffering, undeveloped countries into one great nation, from the Mediterranean to the Cape, from the Atlantic to the Indian Ocean. That's something, isn't it?"

"You think he can do it?"

"I think he can do it," Tangent nodded. "You were impressed, weren't you, when you met him at the inaugural?"

"Yes," Malcolm admitted, "but I'm easily impressed."

"And shrimp can fly," Tangent scoffed. "You're the most realistic man I know. And you think he has a chance—don't you?"

"A lot of ifs, Peter," Malcolm sighed. "If he gets the money. If he gets backing from a powerful friend. If he keeps winning. If he isn't blown away himself. It's far from a sure thing."

"Didn't say it was. But the possibility is there, and the game is worth the candle. I'm not going to rend your heart with a recital of all the good things the Little Captain can do for the African people. Decent food, housing, health, education. All that. Just look at it from a balance sheet point of view. Minerals and oil discovered or not yet found. Millions of acres of underdeveloped or misused land. Great forests. Rivers and falls for hydroelectric plants. What a source of raw materials and cheap labor! What a potential market! Right now Africa is about where the U.S. was in eighteen-fifty. Just opening up . . ."

"I'm not certain Virginia should get involved," Malcolm said slowly.

"You'll be involved sooner or later, whether you want to be or not. I see the U.S. as that powerful friend you mentioned who's going to lead Africa into the Twenty-first Century. When the time is right, I'm going to start beating the drums in D.C. You know Starrett has some valuable contacts there. I think that if the Little Captain keeps winning, we can get State to pay more attention to Africa, to back Anokye politically and economically. We can become a world power!"

"'We'?"

"I mean Africa and President Anokye and the men backing him. Including me. The immediate problem is money. For arms, bribes, and so forth. That's why this Starrett refinery is important."

"And what do you want Virginia to do?"

"The choice is between Asante and Gabon—right? Well, Gabon is as French as the Champs-Elysées. I mean, they *own* the country. Oh, I know Gabon is supposed to be an independent republic, but the French run everything. Their advisors are everywhere, and I assure you that nothing big gets built in Gabon, no large investment is made, without a nod of approval from the Quai d'Orsay."

"Oh-ho," Malcolm said. "I begin to see your fine Italianate hand."

"Tony, you know how to do it. Just have Virginia leak to the—"

"All right, Peter, all right. You don't have to spell it out."

"It's worth a try, isn't it?"

"I'll think about it."

"Do that," Tangent said. "And always remember, the wine was a fifty-three."

"You conniving bastard!" Malcolm laughed.

Tangent pleaded weariness—"Only four hours' sleep in the last thirty-six"—and left Malcolm in the library. There was still a third of the precious bottle remaining. When the gaffer dragged himself out, still giggling, Malcolm took his place in the warmed club chair before the open fire. He sipped the wine slowly, staring into the flames.

Anthony Malcolm was a fleshy, pinkish chap who cultivated a manner of great good-humor. Candid, open, a genial fellow who was always delighted to stand a drink, tell a joke, offer a loan. Few of his pals at Brindleys would believe he had once killed a man with an umbrella. A very special umbrella.

Finally, sighing, he rose and took his final glass into the bar. The Stavros brothers had departed, but Julien Ricard still sat at one end, slumped over his brandy. He looked up as Malcolm entered from the library corridor. Malcolm looked at him and, no one else being present, the bartender busy with his accounts, jerked his head slightly. He drained his wine, left the glass on the bar, walked through the swinging door into the men's lavatory.

While he waited, Malcolm looked under the doors of the three toilet compartments. Then, just to make certain, he opened the three doors and glanced within. It was an old-fashioned loo with walls of white ceramic tiles and fixtures of cracked enamel: urinals as big as altars, sinks like baptismal fonts. Malcolm stood at one of the urinals, fly unzipped, and lighted a cigarette.

After a few moments, Julien Ricard came sauntering in. He glanced about, went to one of the huge sinks, began to soap his hands slowly.

"Poor Tangent," he said. "I give him a hard time."

"Keep it up," Malcolm said. "You're doing fine. You have anything for me?"

"Nothing since my last letter," Ricard said. "You received it? The new actuator?"

"Yes, I received it. We already had the actuator, but it's always comforting to get confirmation. Nothing else?"

"No. Nothing."

"Devaluation?"

"No, nothing on that as yet. Pending."

"Everything in France is pending," Malcolm said equably.

"True, my friend, true," Ricard chuckled. "We make haste slowly." He dried his hands on the roller towel. He looked into the mirror and began to comb his long, black hair, carefully, palm following the comb. Malcolm zipped up his fly, came over to a sink, began to rinse his hands.

"I have something for *you*," he said.

"Oh?" Ricard said.

"Starrett Petroleum is planning to build a refinery. In Gabon."

"Ah?" Ricard said. Then, "Tangent told you this?"

"In confidence. Apparently preliminary approaches have already been made in Libreville. In secret."

"Interesting," Ricard said.

"I thought you'd find it so," Malcolm said. "Your people should find it interesting, too. Help you score Brownie points."

"Brownie points?"

"American expression. Means getting credit for achievement."

"Brownie points," Ricard repeated. "Incredible."

5.

In Paris, on the avenue Montaigne, stands l'Escargot d'Or, a restaurant mentioned both in history books ("Bears on its facade the scars of musket balls fired during the French Revolution") and in the *Guide Michelin* (two stars).

L'Escargot d'Or serves the public on the ground floor. The smaller dining room on the second floor is available only for private parties, conferences, discreet meetings of publicly antagonistic politicos, industrialists, labor leaders, bankers, church dignitaries, etc. The second floor dining room is also the scene of the monthly banquet of Le Club des Gourmets, a prestigious association of food and wine connoisseurs.

Two nights following the meeting of Tony Malcolm

and Julien Ricard amidst the urinals of Brindleys, a not very successful dinner of Le Club des Gourmets was held at l'Escargot d'Or. The Beluga caviar was not properly chilled, the soufflé de homard à l'américaine was definitely chewy, and bits of shell were found in the Mont Blanc aux marrons. As for the wines—whispers of *"Merde!"* were heard. The hapless bishop who had provided the dinner (the twenty-four members of Le Club des Gourmets each planned and paid for the monthly banquet, in turn) was all apologies as Club members departed. They tried to be polite to the monseigneur, but there was little doubt that they would not soon forget this affront to their palates.

Left behind in the dimmed dining salon were Julien Ricard, the Man from the Palace, and the Man from the Bourse. The last two were portly men, wearing heavy, dark suits with high vests draped with golden chains. The Man from the Bourse wore the ribbon of the Legion of Honor. The Man from the Palace had been a hero of the Resistance. He had a black patch over one eye, a steel machine for a hand. Thin white hair did not conceal a metal plate set into his skull.

The three dawdled over minuscule glasses of kirschwasser and cups of espresso. They sat placidly until the table had been cleared and the waiters gone. Then Ricard rose and began to speak. He paced about the dim hall, occasionally pausing to look up at one of the scruffy chamois heads decorating the walls, or to touch his birthmark as a man might stroke a growing mustache.

"The original intelligence came from a friend in London," he told the others. "He has a valuable contact within Starrett itself. I am inclined to credit the report on those grounds. But to confirm, I sent Anatole Garde to Gabon. He speaks Fang and a few Bantu dialects. So far, he is unable either to confirm or deny. Those in government he has spoken to swear they have not been approached, in secret or openly, by Starrett representatives. Which means, of course, absolutely nothing."

"What do you recommend, Julien?" the Man from the Palace rumbled, hand and hook clasped comfortably across his paunch.

"I believe we should treat it as a matter of some consequence," Ricard said. "After what happened in Asante, we can no longer tolerate intrusions by the Americans into our sphere."

"What happened in Asante?" the Man from the Bourse asked blandly. "Merely a change of government. Hardly a world-shaking event. It was a change, incidentally, which has resulted in no loss to us."

Ricard was indignant.

"You think President Anokye will honor Prempeh's pledge to expropriate the oil wells?"

"He may or he may not," the Man from the Palace shrugged. "Meanwhile, Asante is becoming prosperous, which benefits us, of course. Subsidies will no longer be needed."

"But we're losing clout," Ricard cried angrily.

"'Clout,'" the Man from the Bourse smiled. "For a man who dislikes the Americans as much as you profess, dear Julien, you adopt Americanisms quickly. But no matter... let us get back to Gabon. Assuming the worst, that Starrett is attempting to maneuver secretly, what do you propose?"

"First, that we make the strongest representations possible to Libreville that we would view very dimly indeed any unilateral action on their part in negotiating this Starrett refinery. Second, that we make the strongest representations possible to the Americans that we would view very dimly indeed any attempts by one of their grotesque corporations to interfere without consultation in what is universally recognized as our sphere."

The Man from the Bourse sighed. "Julien, that is a formidable amount of 'strongest representations possible.'"

"Also," the Man from the Palace added, "a formidable amount of 'viewing very dimly indeed.' Still..."

The two looked at each other.

"I see no harm..." the Man from the Bourse began cautiously.

"Even if the report is without substance..." the Man from the Palace offered.

"True. The Americans want very much that nothing

should delay the Geneva conference."

"At the moment, they desire to be pleasant and cooperative on all matters."

"What better time to express our wish, delicately of course, that Starrett Petroleum should not take precipitous action within our legitimate sphere?"

"... That might, possibly, affect our interests and compromise the current spirit of cooperation and friendship that exists between France and the United States."

Ricard stroked his birthmark frantically.

"Well?" he asked. "Well?"

"Yes," the Man from the Palace said judiciously. "I think certain discreet representations may be made."

"Yes," the Man from the Bourse said thoughtfully. "We must treat the whole matter in an offhand manner, casually. But leaving no doubt of our concern and of our intentions."

Ricard sighed. "Thank you, gentlemen," he said, and wondered if he had scored Brownie points.

6.

PETER TANGENT CHECKED in at the Mokodi Hilton at about 1600 and went immediately to the Starrett offices on the penthouse floor. There he was handed a note that Jonathon Wilson had called, at 1330 that day, and requested that Tangent call back. Wilson was Cultural Attaché of the U.S. Embassy, having replaced the ineffectual Bob Curtin. He was Virginia's man in Asante.

Tangent called immediately.

"Wilson? Peter Tangent here."

"Hi. Good flight?"

"Good enough. An hour's delay in Conakry, for no apparent reason."

"Buy you a drink?"

Tangent paused a second. Then: "Sure. Where and when?"

"Cleopatra. Outside. In an hour?"

"Fine. See you then."

The Cleopatra, across from the palace on the Boulevard Voltaire, was a reasonably priced restaurant. "You will be amused," said the guidebooks, "by its Egyptian decor." Plaster sphinxes or not, its sidewalk café offered a most pleasant panorama of Mokodi. Handsome men and beautiful women of a dozen tribes, in costumes ranging from funereal European, to jeans and T-shirts, to brilliant native dress: bright gbariyes, flowing saparas, encrusted guriles. Head coverings from berets to fezzes, turbans to labarikas. Skin colors from fish-belly white to tunnel black. Flashing teeth. Cutting eyes. People moving to an inner rhythm. Scents that assaulted the nose, beguiled, sickened, wooed. Warm voices, warm laughter.

"Wilson," Tangent smiled, proffering a hand, taking a chair at the attaché's outdoor table. "Watching the passing parade?"

"Can't get enough of it," Wilson said, awed.

"I know exactly how you feel," Tangent said. "What're you drinking?"

"Gin sling."

"Very good," Tangent approved. "Won't cure the screaming trots, but makes 'em endurable. So it's said." He signaled the hovering waiter, pointed at Wilson's glass, held up two fingers. Then he stared at the Cultural Attaché. "The last time I saw you, you were peeling."

"Yes," Wilson laughed. "A mess. Tanning now. Finally."

"You are indeed. Are you enjoying Asante?"

"Very much," Wilson said, cutting short the "sir."

Tangent sympathized. This slight, eager young man wasn't sure of Tangent's status. Was he just another Yankee businessman? Or an undercover Virginia agent? Or an American executive offering close cooperation? A sleeper? A mule? A courier? A spook? What, exactly, was he? And not knowing, Wilson couldn't be certain what he might say—or even ask.

"Had a bullet," he said finally. "From Malcolm. For you."

"Oh?" Tangent said. "When?"

"Noon. Today."

They were silent while their drinks were served. They raised glasses in an unspoken toast, sipped gently.

"I'm glad you suggested this," Tangent said genially. "It tastes fine."

"Malcolm says to tell you the wine is working," Wilson said. "Mean anything?"

"'The wine is working'?" Tangent repeated. "Yes. Thank you."

"Good news? I hope."

Tangent flipped a hand back and forth, but didn't answer.

"That's all he sent," Wilson said. "For you." He looked out onto the street where as many strolled along the Boulevard, in traffic, as crowded the paved sidewalk. "What a country!" he said. "Marvelous!"

"Isn't it?" Tangent said. "I'm glad you like it. Getting on, are you?"

"Think so," Wilson said. "But slowly."

"Ah, yes," Tangent said. "A different rhythm here. Where were you before?"

"Copenhagen."

"My God!" Tangent laughed. "*Totally* different. Is there any way I can help?"

"Oh..." Wilson said, troubled. Not knowing how far to go. "President Anokye. Know him, don't you?"

"Oh yes. I have an appointment in the morning."

"Met him once or twice," Wilson said. "Official things. Embassy receptions. So forth." He leaned across the table, earnest, ingenuous. "What can you tell me about him?"

"Very ambitious," Tangent said promptly. "Very talented. An incredible orator. Sweep you off your feet. He's brave, as he proved during the coup. The people love him. The Little Captain. Very broad-based support. He's learning government as he goes along."

"He's also learning Portuguese."

"Is he?"

"I don't know where that fits in," Wilson said lamely. "Do you?"

"No, I don't."

"Marxist?"

"Anokye? No way. Starrett wouldn't be here if he was. No, we can work with him. A pragmatic man."

"Know anything about his personal life?"

"Very little. He smokes occasionally. He has a drink now and then. Never to excess, to my knowledge."

"Women?"

"I wouldn't know about that," Tangent said.

"Hear he was sleeping with a white woman," Wilson said, blushing faintly beneath his tan. "Ran a local cathouse. The Golden Calf. But now she's out. A black man is running the place."

"Ever been there?"

"What? Where?"

"The Golden Calf."

"Oh," Wilson said, blushing even deeper. "Ah ... no. Not yet."

"What happened to her?" Tangent asked. "The woman?"

"Living in a big, expensive house out in the Evogu district. Talk is she's going to marry a soldier. Sergeant. Commander of the President's personal guard."

"You do get around," Tangent said slowly. "Ready for another?"

"All right. One more. You know anything of this?"

"No," Tangent said. "Nothing."

"Story is that Anokye dumped the white woman— Yvonne Mayer, her name is—so he can marry the daughter of the premier of Benin."

"Interesting," Tangent said.

"Fascinating!" Wilson said enthusiastically. "Larger than life. Italian opera."

Tangent laughed and paid for the drinks.

"What else have you heard?" he asked the keen young man.

"Well..." Jonathon Wilson said, leaning forward again, carried away by his own prescience. "Some evidence that Anokye is organizing a kind of secret police."

"Oh?"

"Not secret police exactly. Domestic spies. To keep a tab on things. No one's been arrested or tortured. Nothing like that. Yet. Just a few men. No uniforms. They go around and, you know, ask questions. At the moment, it's all very vague."

Tangent nodded. "You're filing all this with Virginia, aren't you?" he asked casually.

"Of course."

"Good," Tangent said, reflecting ruefully that Tony Malcolm knew more of what was going on in Asante than he did.

He spent the early evening with J. Tom Petty, reviewing plans for the oil ceremony. There would be a luncheon at noon—Starrett had reserved the entire Zabarian—with President Anokye and other honored guests attending. Then, after the ceremony and speeches in the afternoon, guests would be welcomed to an open house at the palace, culminating in an evening gala with music, dancing, fireworks.

"It's shaping up to be a real brawl," Petty said enthusiastically. "My boys can hardly wait."

"Try to keep them under control," Tangent said, somewhat nervously.

"Oh hell, Pete, you know what oilmen are like. If they get too rough, we'll kick their asses back to the rigs. I'll have the small boats standing by. That sergeant—what's his name? The light-colored nig in the palace?"

"Yeboa?"

"Yeah, Yeboa. He promised his guards would take it easy. No one gets locked up unless they start tearing the place apart."

"Good," Tangent said. "It's important that everything goes well. What about the booze?"

"It won't run out," Petty assured him. "And if it does, the hotel manager said we can draw on him. Jesus, this is going to be a blast!"

He was a hulking man with a bourbon complexion.

Muscles running to flab. Clothing perpetually rumpled and sweat-stained. On the rigs, or on the *Starrett Explorer* anchored offshore, he was a tiger, and needed. In an executive suite, he was too big, too raucous, too everything, including chewed cigars.

"Listen, Peter," he said, frowning importantly, "these hotshots coming in from Tulsa and New York..."

"Yes?"

"You reckon they'll want tail?"

Tangent paused. "I hadn't thought of it. I suppose they will."

"They go for caramel ass, y'suppose?"

Tangent reflected a long moment.

"I'd guess so," he said finally, with some distaste. "Exotic Africa. Something to tell the boys about back home. Can you line it up?"

"Sure I can."

"Not too black," Tangent said hastily. "High yaller. Clean, for God's sake. The last thing in the world we want..." He left the sentence unfinished.

"Gotcha," Petty said. "I'll have something sweet up here waiting for them when they come back from the palace. That way they won't have to be seen in public with the cunts."

"That's good," Tangent said faintly. "You take care of it."

But was it, he thought mournfully, any worse than what he had done when the Man from Tulsa and the Man from New York had visited London? He remembered his mother saying, "Everyone has to eat a peck of dirt before they die." Sometimes his peck seemed bottomless.

He finally got back to his own suite, took off jacket, loosened tie, kicked off tasseled moccasins. He mixed a gin sling at the little bar, and carried it over to the bed. He called her room number.

"Amina? Peter Tangent."

"Mr. Tangent! You're back! How nice."

"Are you working tonight?"

"Yes, I am."

"Time for some food? Before or after?"

"After would be just right," she said. "But I have a late show. I'll be through about one o'clock. Too late for you?"

"Oh no. Suppose I meet you at the Zabarian?"

"We'll eat there?"

"If you like," he said. "Or we could come back here. The terrace serves until four. Or any place you prefer."

"Why, Mr. Tangent," she said, mocking, "you mean you don't mind being seen with me in public?"

"No," he said happily, "I don't mind."

He took a nap, awoke, showered, dressed carefully and, about midnight, strolled along the boardwalk toward the Zabarian. He could have gone earlier and caught her act. He felt guilty about that—but not very; she really had no singing voice at all.

Amina was just finishing her last set when he entered. He sat at the bar, exchanged greetings with Felah, ordered another gin sling. He took a handful of salted ground nuts, swiveled to look at her.

Tonight she was wearing an off-the-shoulder gown of bottle green. A lot of flounces. It was too much for her stick body. Still, those marvelous arms were bare. And when she turned slowly, in time to strummed chords, her bare back was revealed. To below the waist. A hard, sinuous back. Polished. Rippled with muscle.

"Much woman," Felah whispered.

"Yes," Peter Tangent said.

She finished to apathetic applause. She saw Tangent at the bar, came over, handed her mandolin to Felah.

"I wowed them tonight," she said, picking up Tangent's drink and taking a deep swallow. "How are you, Mr. Tangent, sir?"

"Very well, thank you. And you, Amina?"

"Jack-dandy," she said.

"Jim-dandy," he said.

"What's jack-dandy?"

"There isn't any. There's Jack Daniels. That's an American whisky."

"Gee, Mr. Tangent," she said, "you know everything. Going to feed me?"

"I am," he said. "Where?"

"You say," she said. "I'm too tired to care. Can I have a drink here?"

"Of course."

"What you're having. I liked that."

Tangent ordered, and asked Felah if Sam Leiberman had been around. Felah said no, Mr. Leiberman had been scarce lately. Probably busy moving. Moving where? Tangent wanted to know. Felah said Mr. Leiberman felt his quarters over Les Trois Chats were not suitable for an advisor to the Asante national government, so he had rented a larger apartment over Le Café du Place, a slightly more reputable cabaret located behind the French embassy, near the palace.

"He's living over *another* nightclub?" Tangent marveled.

"That's what he say," Felah chuckled. "He say, 'If I have my life to live over again, I want to live it over a bar.'"

"That's Leiberman," Tangent smiled.

"Can we have a party?" Amina Dunama asked. Her hand was on Tangent's arm. "With him and Dele? I liked them."

"Sure," he said. "I'll look him up tomorrow. Will you be here for the oil ceremony?"

"No," she said. "I'm moving on to Lomé."

"Sadness," he said. "But you'll come back?"

"Maybe," she said. She looked into his eyes. "Or maybe you come to Lomé, Mr. Tangent?"

"Maybe," he said, feeling a shiver.

He felt very happy with her, very relaxed. A few tourists were staring at them, whispering. But there was no hassle. They talked about...later, he couldn't remember. He did remember that she wanted him to put two cigarettes in his mouth, light both from one match, then give her one. Just like an American movie star she had seen. He couldn't do it, he told her, he just couldn't; it was too silly. But he mollified her by lighting one cigarette between his lips and placing it between hers.

They sauntered slowly back to the Mokodi Hilton, and

he learned a little about her. She was a Nigerian Hausa,
but from a rural animist family, not Muslim. She spoke
Hausa, of course, and Yoruba, some Akan and Ewe, and
less of Fond, Dende, Mina, Edo, and others. Also, French
and English.

"Also love, Mr. Tangent, sir," she said. "I also speak
the language of love."

"Do you now?" he said.

They dined on the tiled terrace of the Mokodi Hilton
and watched a gecko lizard dart between the empty tables.
An old morose waiter, whose bare feet obviously pained
him, listened to their order in silence, then brought them
what was available at that late hour: a pot of pepper
chicken, a salad of oiled greens, a bottle of Asti
Spumante. A few others were dining, but the terrace was
uncrowded, so hushed they could hear the gush of sea on
the strand beneath the terrace wall.

"Why isn't there a moon?" he said crossly.

Still, the breeze was warm and scented, the ocean
heaved gently, palm fronds rattled a bit. It was, he
judged, oh, about 80°F., a smell of rain in the air. The
lights of the oil rigs and the island of Zabar twinkled
offshore. A fishing boat went bobbing past. What more
do I want? he asked himself. What *more*?

She tucked in to the food. As she nibbled, he watched
her, fascinated. Her strong white teeth stripped the meat
away and, once, cracked the bones. Then she sucked the
juice.

"I'm glad you're not hungry," he said. She giggled, but
didn't pause. He could not understand where it all went;
she was as skinny as he, and harder. She finished
everything, sopping up the remainder of the chicken sauce
with cold fufu. Then she sighed, patted her napkin to her
lips, took a swallow of wine, and belched.

"Take me," she said. "I'm yours."

"Not if you eat that way all the time," he said. "I
couldn't afford you."

"Being with you makes me ravenous," she said.

He was about to ask her what she meant, but thought
better of it.

He learned a few other things. She came from a large family: three sisters and four brothers. Many, many aunts, uncles, cousins. All living in Nigeria. In the west. She had the Nigerian equivalent of a grade school education, then had gone to work in the kitchen of a village bar-cabaret-restaurant.

"And then it was onward and upward?" he asked.

"Mostly outward," she laughed. "I wanted to see the world. The whole wide world."

"And have you?"

"I've seen West Africa. Have you been to Paris, Mr. Tangent?"

"Yes. Many times."

"Tell me about it."

He did, telling the things he thought she wanted to hear. Her eyes glistened as he spoke; her thick lips parted.

"Oh," she said. "Oh. Some day..."

"Yes," he said.

They had a liqueur, some peppermint atrocity, then rose to leave. She chatted a moment with the old waiter.

"What were you speaking?" Tangent asked, as they strolled into the hotel.

"Twi," she said. "His feet hurt. He's tired."

"I guessed that," he said.

"I'm tired, too," she said. "My feet hurt."

"Then I'll say good-night, Amina," he said holding out his hand.

She looked at him.

"Mr. Tangent, sir," she said, "I just mentioned I was weary. I did not mean you should depart from me."

"Oh," he said, feeling foolish, "I thought..."

"Leave the thinking to me," she said. "And the singing to you."

He thought that the funniest thing he had heard in a long time, was still laughing when they entered her room and she locked the door behind them. She kicked off her shoes, went padding through the mess.

"I'm going to turn off the air conditioner and open the balcony door," she said. "Okey-dokey?"

"Okey-dokey," he said.

"What's wrong?" she said.

"Nothing's wrong."

"Your voice sounded strange."

"You're very quick, Amina," he said. "It's just that—uh—well, 'okey-dokey'—it's—it's dated."

"I like it," she said.

"Oh, I do, too," he said hastily. "Nothing wrong with it."

"Okey-dokey," she said. "Say it."

"Okey-dokey," he said obediently.

She undressed in the dimness, pulling a zipper somewhere in those ridiculous flounces.

"Lousy dress," she said. "Is 'lousy' okey-dokey?"

"Applied to that dress, 'lousy' is definitely okey-dokey."

She was naked then, and unconcerned. A glinting shadow moving gracefully. She went out onto the little balcony, and he followed. Nervous. Hesitant. She slumped into a chair with plastic webbing.

"You'll get a waffle pattern on your ass," he giggled.

She didn't answer, but closed her eyes. He stood a moment, then knelt before her, fully clothed, and began gently to massage her long, bony feet.

"I like that, Mr. Tangent," she murmured.

"Must you call me 'Mr. Tangent'?"

"Yes."

The balcony hung over the terrace, blocked from view from above and the sides. They were floating in space. Alone in the night. After a while, he put her feet softly aside and sat down next to her. He rested his cheek against the warm velvet of her knee and thigh. Her fingers absently tangled in his hair.

"I thought of you," he said. "Amina."

"Did you?"

"Are you falling asleep?"

"No."

"I thought of you."

"Did you?"

"Raise your knees."

"All right."

She raised her knees, spread them slowly, hooked heels onto the edge of the chair. She let her long, slender arms rest along the chair back. Her forearms drooped limply. She looked like some great black bat, hovering. She looked down at him gravely.

"Oh, Mr. Tangent," she said.

"Shut up," he said.

"Yes, sir."

She had a smoky flavor, dark and savory. Like nothing he had ever tasted before. Neither wine nor food nor anything. Almost metallic, he thought. Almost corky. Almost the taste of loam. Almost a lot of things. But not quite. Different.

Her spine stiffened with delight, head bent back, heavy throat hard. She stared dreamily at wavery reflections of the sea on the balcony above. Her body began to move, to twist, to squirm. His tongue pursued, and he knew her flow, the pour within her, an easy rhythm ending in a deep, deep paroxysm, then onward, upward, outward to the whole wide world. He looked up and she looked down to see hard nipples and flat breasts tight and sheened.

"Mr. Tangent," she breathed. "Sir."

"Yes," he said. "Oh yes."

The reception desk was in the entrance lobby, flanked by two stolid palace guardsmen. The receptionist was a plump, middle-aged Asanti lady wearing a neat black dress with white collar and cuffs. Her hair was precisely corn-rowed.

"Good morning, Mr. Tangent," she said. Her smile revealed three gold teeth and a gap, waiting.

"Food morning, Mrs. Odunsi," he said. In Akan, he asked, "Do you have health?"

"I have health," she replied, and asked, "Do you have sadness?"

"I have no sadness," he said, completing the ritual, then switching back to French: "And how is your father feeling?"

"He recovers, thanks to Allah."

"I am happy to hear it. Is there anything I may do to help? Perhaps medicine from London?"

"I thank you, Mr. Tangent, but he has what is needed. Now it is just a matter of waiting."

"The hardest part," he said. "And speaking of waiting, may I see the President? I have an appointment."

"Just a moment, please, sir." She called on her desk phone and spoke softly, then replaced the receiver. "You may go right up, Mr. Tangent. Second floor conference room."

Sgt. Sene Yeboa opened the door at his knock, grinning, and shook hands formally. He motioned Tangent to a chair near the door. President Anokye and Sam Leiberman were standing behind the big mahogany desk. They raised their hands in greeting.

"In a moment," Anokye called.

"No hurry," Tangent said.

Yeboa went back to the desk. The three men bent intently over what appeared to Tangent to be a pile of maps. They conversed in low voices. At one point, they appeared to be arguing. Finally, the Little Captain began to speak in a somewhat louder tone, his forefinger tracing a route on the top map. The other two listened carefully. When the President stopped speaking and looked at them in turn, Yeboa to Leiberman, they nodded. More than consent, Tangent thought; they nodded approval.

Anokye straightened up, and now he spoke in normal tones; Tangent could hear. "The timing is most important," Anokye said. Then he folded the maps, slipped them into his top desk drawer. He shook hands with Sam Leiberman. The mercenary picked up a floppy linen hat, started for the door, paused at Tangent's chair.

"Balles de golf!" he said. "You look like the cat that ate the canary."

"Something like that," Tangent said. "Going to be around for a while, Sam?"

"Why?"

"Thought we might get together for a party."

"Not before the ceremony," Leiberman said. "Maybe after."

"Too late," Tangent said. Then, in a lower voice,

"She'll be gone by then."

Leiberman stared at him.

"The singer?" he said finally.

Tangent nodded, feeling ridiculously proud.

Leiberman laughed and slapped a meaty hand on his shoulder.

"You sly goyische devil," he said. "Now you know what they mean by 'the white man's burden.'"

He went out laughing, shaking his head. Tangent rose and, when Anokye motioned, took the lounge chair in front of the desk. The President murmured something to Yeboa, and the sergeant departed—to take up his station, Tangent was certain, outside the door. Anokye sat down in his long-legged chair and took a deep breath.

"Perhaps I was happier as an army captain," he said.

"I cannot believe that, Mr. President," Tangent smiled.

"No, of course it is not true," Anokye said. "It is simply that I do not have enough hours in the day to do what must be done."

"Perhaps you need more people," Tangent suggested. "A larger staff."

"That, certainly. But people I can trust."

"I understand the difficulty," Tangent said. "But surely it can be done. In addition, perhaps your administration should be reorganized. I am not speaking of the government now; I mean only your own activities. Perhaps they require restructuring, better organization."

Anokye was interested.

"I had not thought of that. How would I go about it?"

"Call in professionals," Tangent said promptly. "There are good management consultants in London and New York. They have experience in such work. They will come in, study your setup, make recommendations for changes they feel will result in increased efficiency."

"I like that," President Anokye nodded. "Yes, very much. They charge a fee, of course?"

"Of course. But I don't believe your operation here is so extensive, as yet, to require a lot of time and a big fee. Perhaps this is the right moment to have it done. So you may expand your activities in an orderly manner. Shall I put someone in touch with you?"

"Please do. What is the word I want? Modernize? Yes, I will modernize my administration."

"According to proved managerial concepts," Tangent said.

"Yes. Excellent idea. I thank you. Now... what did you wish to discuss?"

"I hope this may prove to be good news, Mr. President," Tangent said. "It concerns the refinery Starrett plans to build in Africa."

He told the Little Captain of how he had learned that Starrett's choices had narrowed to Asante and Gabon. He said he had spoken to a friend about the matter, a friend in a position to alert the French to fictitious secret negotiations between Starrett and the Gabonese.

"You can imagine the reaction of the French to such a report," Tangent said. "I felt they would take steps immediately to make their displeasure known both to Libreville and to Starrett, through diplomatic channels. I received a message yesterday from London saying that is indeed what the French are doing. I cannot guarantee it, Mr. President, but I think it likely that when the Starrett executives come here for the oil ceremony, they will wish to sound you out on the possibility of building the refinery in Asante. Should that happen, you will be in a stronger position knowing they have already been warned away from Gabon. Under those circumstances, your chances of getting a no-strings grant for the Togo-Benin operation are considerably enhanced."

Obiri Anokye listened to this recital without change of expression. But when Tangent had finished, he rose to his feet, grinning. Tangent also stood up. The two men shook hands warmly, then sat down again.

"I recognize and declare my debt to you," Anokye said. "But who assisted?"

"A certain friend," Tangent said.

The Little Captain thought a moment.

"The gentleman from London who attended my inauguration?" he asked.

"I didn't think you'd remember," Tangent said.

"I remember," Anokye said. "I thought then he was not what he appeared to be, but more. I would like to reward him."

"He won't take money," Tangent said.

"What, then?"

"Well... he collects African art."

"Ah," President Anokye said. "I will select something fine. You will deliver it?"

"Of course."

"Tell him it is only a small token of friendship. I still consider myself in his debt. He may call on me."

"He will understand."

"And my congratulations to you on a very elegant plan."

"Thank you, Mr. President. And speaking of congratulations—are mine in order?"

Anokye stared at him.

"On what?" he asked.

"Perhaps I am being premature, Mr. President. But I have heard rumors of your impending marriage to the daughter of the Benin premier."

A different look came into Obiri Anokye's eyes. A deepening. Darkening. Then his glance cleared, he smiled coldly. He rose slowly, sauntered to the long window overlooking the palace plaza. He put his hands on his hips, stared down. His back was to Tangent.

"Congratulations?" he said. "Well... possibly. Premier Da Silva comes for the oil ceremony. Then we shall see."

"May your every wish be granted," Tangent said, in Akan.

"And may your smallest dream come true," Anokye replied solemnly in the same language. Then he returned to English: "It is very difficult to keep a personal secret in Asante."

"That is true, Mr. President," Tangent said.

"For instance," Anokye said, almost lazily. "This singer... Amina Dunama? You enjoy her company, Peter?"

Tangent gulped. "Yes, sir," he said.

"Nigerian?"

"Yes, sir. Hausa. But not a Muslim."

Anokye nodded, still staring down from the window.

"I am looking now at the exact spot where we came running across the plaza," he said dreamily. "Screaming and firing our weapons. I remember how surprised I was when I glanced around and you were right behind me. I had ordered you to remain in the telephone exchange."

"I apologize for disobeying your orders, Mr. President."

"I am thankful you did," Anokye said. He laughed softly. "I would never have gained the terrace if you had not offered your back. Why did you charge with us? It was not your war."

"I've asked myself that question several times," Tangent said. "I just don't know."

"To prove something?"

"Partly that perhaps. Partly the noise and excitement and madness of the moment."

"Maybe you wished to determine what kind of a man you are?" Anokye said thoughtfully.

"There may have been that also, Mr. President."

Anokye turned slowly, came back to the desk, sat down again. He leaned forward, elbow on the desk, heavy chin cupped in his palm. He looked at Tangent, into his eyes, through and beyond.

He sat in silence, and the American marveled that this young man (Anokye was now twenty-seven; Tangent, ten years older) should possess such gravity, such deep weightiness. His seriousness, somehow, invested life with significance. It was not to be flung to wine and roses, but measured out gravely with an acknowledgment of the consequences of one's acts.

"Physical courage is a curious thing," Obiri Anokye mused. "Those whose physical courage has never been tried believe it is not so important. I have read the words of men—wise, honored men—who have said that moral courage is the equal or superior of physical courage. That is not the truth, Peter. Physical courage is the root of all else. It is certainly the root of my success. Everything I have done, and shall do, grows from physical courage. That is why I must lead my men. Always. In person. On the field. I cannot rule from behind a desk. Then my power would surely fall away, and they would turn to a braver leader. And all my political and economic dreams for Africa would come to nothing. Men respect physical courage, and I must exhibit it."

He paused, but Tangent was silent.

"I believe you are a brave man, Peter," Anokye said suddenly.

"Thank you, Mr. President. Coming from you, that is praise indeed."

"But courage and foolhardiness are different," the Little Captain said gently. His thousand-yard stare shortened until his eyes were locked with Tangent's. "You must not be foolhardy."

"I don't intend to be," Tangent said stoutly.

"Good," the President of Asante said, still in that quiet, silky voice. "I am happy to hear that."

The meeting was concluded, and Tangent departed with an indefinable impression that he had been warned. But of what, he could not have said.

7.

THE BORDER BETWEEN Togo and Benin remained closed.
Though he now had a diplomatic passport identifying
him as an official advisor to the Republic of Asante, Sam
Leiberman thought it best to enter Benin from Nigeria. So
he flew from Mokodi to Lagos on the twin-engined Piper
Aztec, pride of the Asante National Air Force. Their
other two planes were aged Broussards. Airworthy, but
just.

In Lagos, he rented a Citroën 2-CV. Not very elegant
transportation, but sturdy. He figured the dusty car
would blend perfectly with Cotonou's taxi fleet. He drove
up through the Nigerian rain forest on an improved road
and crossed the Benin border without incident. He was
carrying no weapon, nor anything else that might

endanger his assignment. He came down to the coast road at Porto-Novo. He drove through the sleepy capital without stopping and arrived in Cotonou before noon. The siesta had just started; Benin's largest city appeared as somnolent as the capital.

Leiberman had a vague plan in mind, not detailed but sufficient to get him started. He drove directly to Akpapa, across the Nokoue lagoon. He registered at a crummy hotel he had stayed at once before when he had no choice. He rented a single room and wasn't surprised to find he was sharing it with flies, mosquitos, roaches, bedbugs, lizards, spiders, and a goodly selection of other African fauna. The stained toilet was down the hall, and you provided your own paper. Leiberman had come prepared. The hotel had one advantage: the other residents were thieves, pimps, whores, and drunks. Questions would not be asked.

He changed to a short-sleeved shirt in a wild batik pattern. It hung loosely outside maroon slacks. He suspended a cheap Japanese camera from a leather thong about his neck. He put on a pair of big green sunglasses with white plastic frames. He replaced his shoes with strap sandals over white cotton socks.

He took all his valuables and identification with him. He left only a cheap cardboard suitcase, a few items of clothing, and toilet articles in the room. The door had a lock, but he knew a determined push would spring it.

He drove back to Cotonou, down to the waterfront. After a few false turns, he found what he was looking for. He parked a few squares away and walked back. The siesta was ending; yawning dogs were getting up from the middle of the street.

It had once been a ships' chandler. The original sign, faded, chipped, still swung over the doorway on rusted iron chains. It read ARMAND DUBOIS ET CIE. But up and down the coast of West Africa, from Dakar to Douala, the place was now known as Harry Chime's.

The owner's name was nowhere displayed, but the dust-encrusted, bug-spattered windows bore many hand-lettered cardboard signs: U NAME IT, OUI HAVE IT; WE BUY JUNK AND SELL ANTIQUES; IF YOU DON'T FIND IT HERE, YOU WON'T FIND IT ANYWHERE.

The last was not an empty boast; Harry Chine's was a cluttered warehouse of clothing and hardware, kitchen utensils and camping gear, boat fittings and plumbing supplies, cordage and wire, tools and cutlery... and everything else. All piled higgledy-piggledy in a confusion that only the proprietor could solve. Nothing was new; everything had passed through one, three, a dozen owners, and was now torn, rotted, broken, dented, rusted, or bent. No matter. Some of the things could be found nowhere else in West Africa. Harry bought from anyone and sold to anyone. He did very well indeed.

When Sam Leiberman entered, the door struck a bell that jangled loudly in the cluttered shed. But the owner, sitting behind a scarred counter, didn't look up. He was busy prizing blue stones from a tarnished copper bracelet with the point of an awl.

"Hello, you stinking Limey shit," Leiberman called.

Startled, the man looked up, the awl clattered to the counter, he stared at the mercenary.

"Hello, you lousy Jew bastard," he said finally. "Where's my hundred francs?"

"Right here," Leiberman said. He walked to the counter. He took a roll of bills from his trouser pocket and counted off 100 CFAs. Harry Chime grabbed the notes, but couldn't take his tiny, tiny eyes off the roll. He was saddened when it disappeared back into Leiberman's pocket.

"Prosperous?" he asked.

"Sure. I'm being kept by a wealthy Montenegrin countess."

"And I shall be Queen of the May," Harry Chime said. "What's with the clown suit?"

"You mean *Tailor & Cutter* wouldn't approve? I'm Terre Haute, for God's sake. Can't you tell? Close up shop and let's go in the back room and talk business."

"Sure," Chime said. He locked the street door and put

up a sign: CLOSED BECAUSE OF DEATH IN THE FAMILY. Then he led the way toward the rear, threading a path through the piles of jumbled merchandise.

He was as tall as Leiberman, but about a hundred pounds heavier. He wore soiled khaki jeans, the fly straining at its buttons. The seat had been let out and patched with a wedge-shaped section of stained blue denim. On his bare feet were ripped U.S. Army combat boots of World War II. The top straps were unbuckled and flapped about as Chime walked, showing punky ankles. He also wore a sweated dark blue undershirt, revealing a billowing belly and bulbous breasts.

He led Leiberman into a small back room used for sleeping and cooking. It smelled like it. Leiberman sat down at a rickety wooden table and waited while Harry Chime dug out two jelly glasses and a demijohn of wine in a wicker basket. The outside bore the label of a good Italian volpolicella, but inside was Benin palm wine. Leiberman wasn't surprised. Chime sat down heavily, filled the two jars, and they drank.

"Losing a little weight, aren't you?" Leiberman said.

"Maybe a few pounds," Chime said.

Leiberman leaned across the table and dug a cruel thumb into Chime's belly.

"When was the last time you saw your cock, Harry?" he said.

"June 21, 1958," Chime said. "You come in here to feel me up or to talk business?"

They spoke a crude argot all their own, a mixture of several languages. "Donne-moi the fuckin' botella of vino, mein imbecile." They gossiped about old mercs. Who had died, and how. Who was down with bilharzia. Who had disappeared. Who was fighting where for how much. Most of their comrades from the disastrous Biafran campaign were now shooting at each other in Angola.

"You got anything besides this piss?" Leiberman asked, draining his jelly jar.

"Maybe some rum," Chime said reluctantly.

"Ho-ho-ho," Leiberman said. "Bring it out, Harry, or I'll take my business to Monoprix."

"Take it to Harrod's for all I care," Chime said, but he dug a half-full quart of Meyers's dark from under his littered sink and put it on the table. Leiberman filled his jelly jar. Chime poured some into what was left of his palm wine.

"What's going on around here?" Leiberman wanted to know.

"Aagh, they got this thing with Togo," Chime said disgustedly. "Ever since that wog got knifed in Lomé. The border's closed. How the hell did you get in?"

"I waltzed," Leiberman said. "What else?"

"Aagh, the fuckin' Reds are all over the place."

"No kidding?" Leiberman said. "I thought the French had the first mortgage."

"Still do," Chime said, "but the place is crawling with Russians and Chinks."

"Interesting, but not very," Leiberman said. "Enough of this bullshit. Harry, I need some stuff. A few little items."

"Like what?"

"Odds and ends."

"Pick out anything you want," Chime said, the rum getting to him. "No cost. Absolutely no cost to you, Sam."

"Thanks, Harry."

Leiberman sucked in his gut, opened the top of his trousers, unzipped a silk money belt. He carefully extracted a small square of onion-skin paper. He slid it across the table to Chime.

"Here's my list."

Chime rooted around in the table drawer and found a pair of glasses with bent wire frames. He put them on and scanned Leiberman's list. Then he looked up, blinking through thick magnifying glass.

"*This* will cost you," he said, and when Leiberman laughed, Chime said, "What the hell." He read the list again. "What's the thermite for?"

"I'm blowing the bank," Leiberman said.

"The hell you are," Chime said. "The government's taken it over. The place is full of barefoot soldiers."

"Goodbye bank," Leiberman said. "They'll suck it dry in a month. You got this stuff?"

"Most of it."

"The thermite, too?"

"Well... it's not new."

"How old?"

"Thirty, maybe forty years."

"Jesus Christ, Harry!"

"Best I can do."

"What is it?" Leiberman asked.

"Incendiary grenades. Wehrmacht potato mashers. Some of the stuff abandoned when Montgomery and Rommel were chasing each other across the desert."

"It's not leaking, is it?" Leiberman asked.

"Maybe a little corroded. Just a little. I'll throw in a pair of gloves."

"That's sweet," Leiberman said. "Thanks, but no thanks."

They sat staring at each other. Chime looked down at the list again, looked up and said, "Fuse?"

"Just what I was thinking," Leiberman said. "You got it?"

"Miles of it," Chime assured him.

"Fast or slow?"

Chime shrugged. "Who the hell knows? Cut off a piece and time it."

"Okay," Leiberman said. "Now something that's not on the list—I need a piece."

"Aagh, that's hard," Harry Chime said. "This ain't New York, you know. You want to rent it or buy it?"

Leiberman considered a moment.

"Buy, I guess," he said finally. "What can you get?"

"A 'thirty-four Beretta."

"Lousy vintage. How about a 'fifty-one?"

"Haven't got."

"This 'thirty-four Beretta—it works?"

"Sam, would I sell you defective merchandise?"

"Sure you would," Leiberman said cheerfully.

"Well... maybe it jams a bit."

"Beautiful."

"But all you do is smack the butt on the heel of your hand, and it unjams."

"And blows my balls off," Leiberman said. "All right. And two loaded magazines."

"When?"

Leiberman told him he'd pick up everything that evening at 2100. At that time he would inspect what he was buying, and they'd arrive at a price.

"Cash," Harry Chime said. "No tickee, no shirtee."

Sam Leiberman drove north on the improved road that ran up the length of Benin like a spine. It was tarred as far as Bohicon, about 150 kilometers north of Cotonou. But before Bohicon, and the turnoff for Abomey, was the village of Ighobo. And the Musée Ethnographique. Perhaps not as large as the one in Porto-Novo. But Ighobo's museum had an older and more valuable collection. And, as the Little Captain had pointed out, it was in a small village and probably lightly guarded.

The museum was housed in a whitewashed mud-brick, one-story building said to have been a collection center for slaves, before they were marched south to be sold to European traders at Porto-Novo. Rusted chains and manacles still hung from the rough-hewn posts supporting the thatched roof. A wooden floor had been added in modern times.

A tour bus had arrived just before Leiberman pulled into the dirt parking area. There were at least thirty tourists, mostly Canadians, and the mercenary was happy to note that many of the men were dressed in costumes not unlike his own: demented shirts, maroon slacks, strap sandals, necklaces of cameras. He casually fell in at the rear of the group as they followed their French-speaking Benin guide into the museum.

The L-shaped building had been divided by plywood partitions into a dozen small galleries, each devoted to the ancient arts and crafts of one of Benin's many tribes: Fulani, Bariba, Fon, Yoruba, Adj, etc. Objects were hung from walls and partitions, stood upright on the wooden floor, or were displayed in open cases.

Following the gawking tour group, listening to the enthusiastic spiel of the Benin guide, Sam Leiberman understood why Obiri Anokye had sent him on this mission, and not a black man. The Musée Ethnographique was an awesome treasurehouse of African culture. Marvelously carved Gelede masks. Wood and bronze sculpture. Ceremonial robes of shell and feathers. Intricate ironwork. Brilliant Glélé tapestries. Arms for court rituals and arms for battle. Thrones carved from a single block of mahogany. Kings' stools. Bracelets and necklaces of ivory, copper, gold. Grave ornaments. Phallic staves. Monoliths and deities.

But it was the juju charms and the grisgris that would keep this sacred place safe from despoilment by most black Africans. The spirits of ancestors dwelt here. Their clothing was here, their jewelry, arms, grave markers, images of the gods they worshiped. To defy the amulets, to scorn the fetishes, was to court doom in this world, the next, and all worlds to come. So Sam Leiberman, white mercenary, unbeliever, had been sent. He appreciated the Little Captain's reasoning.

But he was not totally immune to the shivery appeal of this art. It stirred the same fear and devotion he had felt as a boy watching the solemn ceremony in his father's temple, seeing the sacred objects and hearing the chants of exaltation. But that had been in another time, in another world, and now his faith was dead and gone. Not even a corpse left behind.

He came out into the bright sunlight and wandered around to the rear of the museum. He held his camera near his chin, as if seeking a suitable scene to photograph. There was an outdoor toilet, remarkably like a Chic Sale. And there was a kind of open shed, no more than a tilted thatched roof supported by four rough-hewn posts. In the shade squatted a single Benin soldier, barefoot, tending a charcoal fire within a clay pot. He hunkered comfortably on his hams, blowing into the embers of his fire pot. On the bare ground alongside him were three small yams and

a chicken leg, most of the feathers still attached. Leaning
against one of the posts was the soldier's rifle. It appeared
to Leiberman to be a MAS 49. He strolled closer, and the
soldier looked up.

Leiberman smiled, lifted his camera, pointed at the
soldier and nodded hopefully. The soldier scowled and
shook his head no. He did not want his soul captured on
film and taken from him. He was a young man, no more
than twenty. His khaki shorts and short-sleeved shirt were
clean. He wore a shoulder patch Leiberman could not
identify. He carried no sidearms. Just the rifle.

Leiberman made a circle of the museum. As far as he
could see, there was no alarm system. Several of the glass
windows were broken. There was a side door, but it had
been padlocked from the outside. Hasp and lock were
rusty. Leiberman completed his circuit and returned to
the parking area. The tourists were piling back into their
bus. He waited a few moments, then drove slowly back to
Cotonou behind the bus. He thought the young soldier, or
another, would probably be on guard all night. He tried to
figure a way to avoid killing him, but could not.

He followed the bus into Cotonou. When he saw where
the tourists were staying, he parked the Citroën and
walked back to the hotel dining room. He was greeted in
English by a maître d' who knew Terre Haute when he saw
it. Leiberman stayed in character by ordering *bifteck aux
pomme frites*, with a bottle of Löwenbräu dark. He
dawdled over a second beer, but it was only 1800 when he
finished; he had three hours to fill.

He strolled along the dirt sidewalks, watching the
laughing Cotonais hurry home to their town *quartiers*. He
stopped at the poolside bar of the Hôtel du Port and had a
double arak. It didn't help. He kept thinking about the
African art now standing in lonely splendor in the locked
museum. Brilliant enough to light up the night. He
thought of that, and of the young soldier on guard.

He went back to the Citroën and drove to his sleazy
hotel in Akpapa to change and pack. There was a small
restaurant and smaller bar attached. The place was
almost empty: a few villains drinking millet beer, a

handsome black fegela eating a cold rice salad, a white
woman sitting at the bar. She must have been pushing
fifty, Leiberman guessed. A French tart from the looks of
her. He sat at the other end of the counter and avoided
glancing in her direction. He didn't need her. It would
make him like men he knew who couldn't go into action
unless they were half smashed.

A half-hour later he and the French tart were naked
under the mosquito net in his cruel room. She had shaved
her pubic hair, and across her bristly groin was tattooed,
in French, ALL HOPE ABANDON YE WHO ENTER HERE. He
laughed to think that Harry Chime was putting his crazy
signs everywhere.

He was at Chime's at 2100, changed back into his
khakis. He had given the tart ten dollars Yank, and she
had been grateful. He never had learned her name,
thought no more of her, and would not—unless in a few
days he found himself wearing his pickle in a brown paper
bag.

Bamboo shades were down across the windows.
Leiberman knocked and waited. Eventually, the fat man
unlocked, let him in, relocked the door, and led the way to
the back room. He had everything ready in there.
Leiberman sat down at the table to inspect what he was
buying.

He stripped the Beretta. "Just to make sure there are
no old cigarette butts in here." The parts of the gun
appeared worn but serviceable. The barrel was clear.
Leiberman had lived with guns most of his adult life and
had respect for them, figuring that anything enabling an
ounce of lead to waste 200 pounds of flesh deserved
respect.

He reassembled the pistol. He unloaded the two
magazines and tested the springs. They weren't as strong
as he would have liked, but he thought they'd do. He
reloaded the magazines, slammed one into the butt of the
gun, jacked a round into the chamber, put loaded gun and
extra magazine into the pockets of his bush jacket.

"Piece of shit," he growled.

"Beggars can't be choosers," Chime said smugly.

"And a fuck in a bed is worth two in the bush," Leiberman said.

He took up the coil of fuse and measured a length from his wrist to his elbow, and cut it off. He put the piece on the floor, lighted one end, glanced at his watch. He and Chime watched the fuse sputter to the end. It took fifty seconds to burn. It also left a scar across the kitchen-bedroom floor. Chime made no objection.

"Fifty seconds," Leiberman said. "That's slow."

"Is it?" Chime said.

"Slow enough," Leiberman said. "I'll need, oh, say twenty-five feet."

Then he inspected the three battered gasoline cans. A gallon in each. He sloshed the contents, unscrewed the caps, sniffed cautiously.

"Not that you'd sell me sea water," Leiberman said.

"Aagh," Chime said.

Leiberman examined the metal Togolese army badge. It seemed to be authentic; he'd have to gamble on that. The sap was a good one: a canvas tube about a foot long, filled with sand and stitched with heavy, waxed twine. The canvas was sweat-stained. One end looked like it had been dipped in brown paint. But it wasn't paint.

Leiberman swung it experimentally a few times.

"Very nice," he said. "Reminds me of my days as a Boy Scout. Okay, Harry, now much for the lot?"

"Well now—" Chime started.

"Forget it," Leiberman said. "I'll give you half that."

After ten minutes of peppery argument, they agreed on 875 French francs, and Leiberman paid. Chime helped him carry the stuff out to the car, after carefully scouting the street.

"Thanks, Harry," Leiberman said. "You've been a great help."

"Tell your friends," Chime said.

"Not likely," Leiberman said. "That's another thing: you haven't seen me for years, have you?"

Chime looked at him.

"I don't see you now," he said.

"Very good," Leiberman approved. "Keep it that way."

To get into the car, he had to brush close to Chime.

"Tell me something, Harry," he said. "You ever take a bath?"

"What the hell for?" Chime said. "I sleep alone."

He drove north slowly toward Ighobo. Dark, dark. A quarter moon dimmed by thick overcast. Moisture on the tarred road. Rains coming; maybe soon. Not too soon, he hoped. Turned off for the Musée Ethnographique. Headlights out. A dim glow behind the building: the guard's fire.

Turned, drove back again. Nothing to be seen. All quiet. Parked a hundred meters down the road to Cotonou. Backed off the verge, partly into the bush. Got out. Locked the car. Everything inside. Took only the Beretta, extra magazine.

Walked on the road. Then cut into the bush. Moved slowly. Circled wide. Came up from the rear. Crouched. Saw the outhouse silhouetted in the small fire they had going. *They.* Two of them. Two guards, two rifles. Should have known: African soldiers don't like the night. Fight badly at night. So two guards, for company when the shadows close in.

Retreated. Went back to the car. Got the canvas sap. Went back to the museum again. Sap in hip pocket, gun in hand. Again, silent approach, circling, crawling the last few meters. Stopped short of the cleared area of packed dirt.

What were the children doing? Kneeled, lifted his head to see. Cavorting in firelight. Striking poses. Shouting things. What? Then rushing to flip pages of a tattered magazine near the fire pot. Looked at pictures. Then took a stance. "Eeeyah!" Answered by "Heeyuh!" Then hands chopping at each other. Feet kicking. Laughing and giggling. The one he had seen during the day and another just like him. Two young boys.

"Eeeyah!"

"HEEYUH!"

Then a spatter of howled Fon.

Got it. Practicing karate or judo. Martial arts magazine. Screaming with laughter as they assumed the rigid poses, made the formal moves. Fun.

Studied the scene. Two rifles leaning against posts of the shed. Fire in clay pot. Bottle of water or palm wine. No handguns or machetes. He moved cautiously. Coming closer to thatched-roof shed. But too far to use the Beretta. Get them apart. Take them one at a time. How?

Hunkered down on his heels. Watched. Waited, waited. No more karate now. No dancing about. Quiet. Both near the cook pot. Lying on packed earth. Talking softly. Grinning. Good palaver. Thirty minutes. Hour. No action. No inspection tour of museum. Sleep? Go to sleep, for Christ's sake. For your sake.

Then, finally, one gets up. Stretches. Says something. Other laughs. Standing soldier ambles toward privy. Built for tourists. Luxury for soldiers. Leiberman is on his feet, crouching, hot. Moves to edge of cleared area. Soldier goes into outhouse. Door closes.

Chance now. Good chance. Moves fast. Lightly. Runs across clearing. Gun out. Kicks rifles away. Spins to face astonished soldier rising to his feet.

Soldier rushes him. Eyes swollen. Teeth wet. Hand held high like a cleaver.

"EEEYAH!"

"Sonny, sonny," Leiberman groans sadly. He shoots. Three in the face. Fast. Slams boy backward. Crashing onto cook pot. Leiberman runs to privy. Waits at side. Crouching. Sweat dripping. Door smashes open. Soldier stumbles out. Pulling up shorts. Eyes glaring. Mouth open. Doesn't see Leiberman. Swish of sap. Down hard across back of skull. Soldier crumples. Doesn't move. Alive, but out.

Then Leiberman worked fast, whistling a merry tune. Left the soldiers where they lay. Ran along the road to car. Backed up to museum area. Parked on road in front. Quickly now. Found the front door locked. Good lock.

New. Back to the car for a tire iron. Ripped away old padlock and hasp on side door. When he yanked, the entire door came off rusted hinges.

Inside with first can of gasoline. Dribbled a path in and out of galleries. Gas soaking into dried flooring. Never raised his eyes to icons on the walls. Second can completed the soaked trail around interior walls. Third can pouring a dark trace out the side door.

Heeled depression in packed earth. Filled with last of gas. Propped end of fuse between two stones. Suspended in fumes over gas pool. Carefully uncoiled fuse toward road. Three gasoline cans inside museum. Placed Togolese army insignia near outflung hand of dead soldier. Live one still out. Not stirring.

Check his pockets. Gun, extra magazine, sap. Final look around. Lighted end of fuse with wooden kitchen match flicked on thumbnail. Fuse caught. Started to sputter. Flame began to crawl. Glanced at watch.

He drove slowly toward Cotonou for five minutes. Stopped on the verge. Got out of the car. Lighted a cigarette. Gauloise. Looked back. Waiting. Very patient. No panic. Waiting. Then, heard a distant *"whump!"* Saw a crimson ball of flame float up into the night sky.

He got back into the Citroën and drove steadily, at a legal speed, through Cotonou and Porto-Novo. Just before he came to the Nigerian border, he stopped on a deserted section of road in the rain forest and threw Beretta, extra magazine, and sap far out into the bush. Then he drove on and crossed the Nigerian border without incident. As he came into Lagos, it began to rain, heavily. But it was too late.

8.

THE LATE KING PREMPEH IV had been a Muslim, with
four wives, a plenitude of children, a superfluity of poor
relations. To accommodate this mob in the living quarters
on the third and fourth floors of the palace at Mokodi,
jerry-built interior walls and partitions had been erected.
They destroyed the fine proportions of the original
sleeping chambers and family rooms designed by a
French architect for the first governor of Asante.

When Obiri Anokye deposed the King and became
President of the Republic, one of his first acts was to order
the removal of Prempeh's alterations; the spacious old
rooms were restored, as closely as possible, to their
original splendor. Only one of King Prempeh's additions
was retained: an enormous electric refrigerator installed
in a corner of the family dining room. Its shiny white bulk
contrasted oddly with oak parquet floors and damas-

cened walls. But the palace kitchen was on the floor below, next to the state dining room, and meals were brought up to the living quarters by a dumbwaiter operated by a rope pull. It was an awkward arrangement; the convenience of the General Electric refrigerator was undeniable.

Whenever possible, President Obiri Anokye dined with his family. He was almost certain to be present for the morning meal, shared with his parents, Judith and Josiah, his younger sister Sara and younger brother Adebayo. An older brother, Zuni, his wife, Magira, and their children chose to remain in the Anokye home near Porto-Chonin on the island of Zabar.

On the Friday morning of the oil ceremony, breakfast in the palace was a light meal: melon, fresh croissants from the new pâtisserie on the Place de la Concorde, and chicory-laced coffee lightened with condensed milk. The Anokye family, in robes and pajamas, was served by a lean, grave, ebony-skinned butler. He was a Fulani, a Muslim, and wore a starched white dickey with a rather rusty black swallowtail. The Anokyes saw nothing strange in the fact that his long feet were bare. And, being a Fulani, he wore several rings and a handsome necklace of cat's-eye shells. His name was Ajaka.

The Little Captain waited until second cups of coffee had been poured and Ajaka had bowed himself gracefully from the room, closing the door gently.

"The luncheon at the Zabarian begins at noon," the President told the others. "Please be downstairs thirty minutes sooner. A car will be waiting."

"How shall I dress, Obiri?" Sara asked timidly. "Is it to be a dress-up?"

"Dress as you wish," he said. "Lightly, I suggest. The Zabarian is air-conditioned, but then we must go to the port area for the turning-on of the oil. There will be speeches. And no shade."

"You will speak, Obiri?" his mother asked.

"Oh yes," he said. "As briefly as possible," he added, smiling. "Then we will return here. The gala begins in the evening, so you will have the opportunity to rest and change. If you wish."

"Zuni?" the old man said vaguely. "Where is Zuni?"

"Zuni will join us at the Zabarian, father," Anokye explained patiently. "And after the ceremony, he will return with us to the palace. He and Magira."

"Is the boat all right?" Josiah asked anxiously. "What did Zuni say of the boat?"

"The boat is fine," the President of Asante assured him. "Zuni goes out every morning at dawn."

Then, seeing the old man's crumpled sadness, Anokye said, "Is it not better to sleep late?" And immediately cursed his stupidity for having compounded the original error.

Something had changed in his relationship with his family. He had not changed, of that he was certain. But, since his becoming President of Asante, their manner toward him had altered. He was no longer "Bibi," but was "Obiri." And frequently they avoided direct address, as if they felt "Obiri" too familiar and yet "Mr. President" too coldly formal for members of the family.

They looked at him differently, too; he was aware of it. There was love, of course, but now there was also respect and awe. Sometimes he wondered if there was not fear in their eyes as well. And if someone had suggested it was closer to dread than fear, he would have been saddened but not surprised.

They spoke awhile of Zuni's activities. The older brother continued to work as a fisherman, as Josiah had, and his father before him. Zuni was leader of the Zabarian chapter of the Asante Brothers of Independence, a veterans' organization that had aided in the Little Captain's coup. And Zuni was also head of the League of Liberty on Zabar. The League was Asante's largest political party, founded by Obiri Anokye, subservient to his wishes, dependent on his personal popularity for its success at the polls.

"Obiri," Judith said slowly, eyes lowered, "perhaps we—your father and I—should return to Zuni's home. To Zabar."

"For a visit?"

She raised her eyes then.

"I think we should return there to live," she said.

He set his coffee cup down carefully, looked at his mother and father tenderly. Age, a lifetime of hard work, a marriage of more than fifty years, had made them sister and brother, almost twins. Both with crinkled shell faces. Both with seamed skin over corded tendon and stretched muscle. Both seemingly shrunken as if they were dwindling away to the size of children, and regaining the irrational desires and petulances of children.

"You are not happy here?" he asked softly.

"The palace is very fine," hs mother sighed. "But still . . ."

"Has anyone shown you disrespect?"

"No no," she said hastily. "But your father misses the boat. I miss my kitchen and Zuni's children. All the family. Our old friends. The church. We are not needed here, Obiri."

The room was still. A few flies buzzing. Far-off hum of traffic on the Boulevard Voltaire. Distant drone of an airliner coming in for a landing at the airport. Something fading . . .

"I need you," he said gently.

She made a gesture, a small wave that said he spoke as a dutiful son. But she knew he did not need them. Or anyone.

"If you are not happy," he said finally, "do as you wish. Return to Zabar. Perhaps, after a time, you will wish to return here again. That would give me happiness."

Josiah beamed. "I will send you the best fish," he said.

The Little Captain smiled, turned to his sister. "You, Sara? Do you also wish to return to Zabar?"

"Oh no," she said quickly, "I like it here."

"And you, Adebayo?"

"I would stay with you, Obiri."

"I want you to," the President said. "You must both continue your studies. But there are ways you can be of help to me. Perhaps we should all go now to dress for the luncheon."

His mother and father rose so eagerly, moved so spryly to the doorway, that he wondered if they might not be relieved to be out of his presence. But things could never again be as they had been, and he was incapable of regret.

He called Sara and Adebayo back to the table. He waited until their parents had left the room.

"I want both of you to go to Togo," he told them. "Stay in Lomé a few days. I will have arrangements made. Sara," he smiled, "call Captain Songo and tell him you and your brother will visit."

She giggled, glanced down at her twisting fingers. She was a tall, willowy girl, hair twigged, each braid bound with a bright yellow ribbon. Her smile was of such radiant charm that it kindled the room.

"Call him now," he suggested. "You will be there Monday morning."

She paused to press her cheek against his, then flew to call her swain.

"Adebayo," the Little Captain said, "I have a task for you. An important thing you must do."

He looked steadily at the youth. Adebayo was already as tall as Obiri, almost as broad through the shoulders. His skin was darker, his features crisper. Because he wished to emulate his older brother, he was preternaturally grave, almost solemn. He tried to think deeply and speak profoundly. Only occasionally did youthful high spirits shatter that sober mien. Laughter seemed to shame him, and he bit it back.

"What is it I am to do, Obiri?"

"Escort your sister to Togo. See to her safety and comfort. It is time you learned how you must act away from home. Also, I shall give you a sealed envelope, a letter, to deliver to General Kumayo Songo, Jere's father. You are to hand it to him personally. I would prefer you give it to him in private. If that is not possible, then it will be sufficient if you hand it to him personally. Do you understand that?"

"Yes, Obiri."

"If you lose the letter, if it falls into other hands, the results will be damaging. To me and to Asante. I trust you, Adebayo."

"I will deliver the letter only to General Songo. I will not lose it, I swear it. Will he send a reply?"

"Perhaps, perhaps not. Follow his instructions."

"I will do as you say, Obiri."

The President rose, put his arms about Adebayo, pulled him to a close embrace.

"Brother," he said.

Outside, in the second floor corridor, two guardsmen stood at parade rest alongside the closed door to the conference room. Inside, President Obiri Anokye sat behind his broad desk, bending forward intently, hands clasped on the blotter. Facing him, in a semicircle of leather club chairs, were Minister of State Jean-Louis Duclos, Benin Premier Benedicto da Silva, and the Premier's aide and executive secretary, Christophe Michaux.

Duclos and Michaux were seated next to each other, having discovered during the introductions that both were Martinicains, Duclos from St.-Pierre and Michaux from Trinité. Neither had returned to his homeland after his first trip to Paris.

President Anokye sighed, unclasped his hands, leaned back into his armchair.

"There can be no doubt it was the work of Togo?" he asked. The question was directed to Da Silva, but when the Premier answered, Anokye's glance slid away to Michaux.

"No doubt whatsoever, Mr. President," Da Silva said stonily. "A Togolese army insignia was found at the scene. The murder and fire were obviously in retaliation for the killing of Nwabala. In which affair, I assure you, Mr. President, we were totally innocent."

"I find it difficult to believe that black Africans could be guilty of such sacrilege," Anokye said. "The museum was a holy place to all Africans. Centuries of our history and culture..."

"Exactly, Mr. President," Michaux burst out excitedly. "In my mind I, too, cannot believe this was an act of vandalism committed by blacks against blacks."

Anokye stared at him.

"But why..." he began, then was silent.

"Why?" Da Silva said bitterly. "Exactly—why? Who

stood to profit from this insult? Who but the Togolese would have any reason to despoil the Benin national heritage? Who else could possibly benefit from such desecration? No, no, gentlemen. Togo intended it as a deliberate provocation. There is no other explanation."

Professor Duclos shook his head sorrowfully. "That blacks should commit such aggression against blacks.... We should be forging stronger ties against the common enemy."

"With all due respect, Premier," Christophe Michaux said, "I must agree with Minister Duclos. I feel we should move cautiously in this matter, with great deliberation. We have no proof of the complicity of Togo in the attack. Surely we should wait to learn their reaction. Perhaps the fire was the work of a psychopath. Or of one who wishes to create ill-feeling between Benin and Togo."

"For what reason?" Anokye asked.

"I cannot answer that, Mr. President. But I am far from certain in my own mind that this was Togo's work. The finding of the army badge on the scene is too pat. It smells of contrivance. I am almost certain in my own mind that Togo is innocent in this affair."

Michaux was almost as light as Duclos. He was taller than the Minister of State, slender, with long, limp hands he used frequently when speaking. His hair, bleached or sun-streaked, lay flat in oiled billows, sculpted and scented. He was a young man but affected a goatee. Arched eyebrows and the spiked beard gave his triangular face a Mephistophelian cast. One looked for cloven hooves and found Gucci loafers.

"In my own mind—" he began.

"Please, Christophe," Premier Da Silva said, holding up a palm. "I don't wish to appear unkind, but what is in your own mind is of less interest to me at the moment than the political realities. Benin and Togo were already on a collision course before the burning of the museum. Whether or not Togo is actually guilty is of less importance than the fact that most Benin are firmly convinced they are. Already there is talk of reprisals. Even a war."

"Surely not that," Duclos protested. "There are other

options available. The Organization of African Unity. The United Nations. Arbitration by a third party who enjoys the confidence of both Benin and Togo. Surely all these should be explored before we speak of the possibility of war."

"There are those in my country who would gladly march tonight if the command was given," Da Silva said grimly. "How many provocative insults are we obliged to accept? Gentlemen, there is only one way to handle a bully: stand up to him. That is the advice I intend to give my government in the strongest possible terms."

"Is there any way I may be of service in this unfortunate situation?" President Anokye asked gravely.

"Mr. President," the Premier said, "I assure you every effort will be made to resolve this conflict between my country and Togo without recourse to combat. But if all peaceable means fail and open warfare becomes inevitable, where does Asante stand? What will be your reaction?"

The Little Captain drew a deep breath.

"A difficult question," he said slowly. "And one to which I cannot give you an answer now, this minute. I must give the problem careful consideration. Gentlemen, it is drawing on to noon. I suggest we adjourn and leave for the Zabarian as soon as possible. Perhaps we will have a chance to discuss the matter further this afternoon. Premier, could I have a few words with you in private? It should not take long. Jean, will you and Mr. Michaux wait for us at the cars?"

When the two Martinicains had departed, the door closed behind them, Obiri Anokye rose and stood behind his desk.

"Premier," he said abruptly, almost curtly, "several months ago, in this room, on the evening of my inaugural, I spoke to you regarding my affection for your daughter Beatrice and my desire to see her more often, to learn more about her and give her the opportunity to learn more about me."

Premier Benedicto da Silva stirred restlessly, crossed and recrossed his knees. He was a dark man, sheened skin with a ruddy underglow. Silvered hair and beard were elegantly trimmed, linen a dazzling white, all of him polished and gleaming, precisely pressed and creased. Flinty eyes saved him from soft foppishness.

"I recall that conversation, Mr. President," he said tonelessly.

"Yes. Since then, as you know, I have seen more of Beatrice, in Cotonou and Mokodi. Each time I have met with her, I have come to cherish her more. She is lovely, charming, and—and intelligent. With your permission, Premier, I wish to ask Beatrice to be my wife. To ask her tonight."

Da Silva sighed gently.

"She is so young," he said.

"Yes," Anokye agreed. "Younger than I, certainly. But old enough to marry."

"I suppose so," Da Silva said. "Although it is a difficult thing for a father to realize and admit. Since the death of my wife, Beatrice has managed my home. I know I am being selfish to hope that it might continue awhile longer, but still..."

Anokye was silent.

"And then there is a matter of religion," the Premier said, almost desperately.

"I would be willing for our children to be raised in the Catholic faith," Anokye said. "If you insist," he added, "I will become a Catholic."

Da Silva drew a deep breath.

"Ah, Mr. President," he said hesitantly, "during our conversation at your inaugural, I brought up the matter of your relationship with a certain public woman. A white woman."

"That is true. I made a promise to you at that time, a promise that I can now state has been fulfilled. The problem could not be resolved immediately. Such matters rarely can. I am certain you appreciate that. But the woman in question is no longer employed in a—a public house. I have ended my relationship with her. In fact, she is about to marry the commander of my personal guard."

"Oh?"

"So you see, your conditions have been met. Have I permission now to marry your daughter?"

"You believe Beatrice will accept you?"

"Yes, I believe it. But you have not answered my question, Premier. Will *you* accept me?"

Da Silva rose, smoothed the wrinkles from his jacket, began to pace slowly back and forth before Anokye's desk. His head was bowed, his eyes seemed to study the design of the blood-red Sarouk. He stopped suddenly, shoulders stooped, hands thrust into his pockets.

"Mr. President," he said in a low voice, "may I suggest an engagement of, perhaps, a year? To enable the families to meet and become better acquainted, to allow—"

"No," Obiri Anokye said. "A short engagement. No more than three months. I desire to marry Beatrice as soon as possible."

"Three months?" Da Silva said. His head came up. He looked directly at Anokye. "Surely such haste is unnecessary, Mr. President. I am so involved with this Togo business that I would prefer it if—"

"This Togo business," Anokye said. "Ah, yes. Premier, Benin is on Togo's eastern border. Asante is on Togo's western border. If indeed, as you fear, it comes to open warfare, why we might stand together. We might be brothers. Possibly . . ."

There was silence. The two men stared at each other.

"Three months?" the Premier said hoarsely. "Agreed."

Obiri Anokye accompanied Da Silva into the corridor. He ordered one of the guards to escort the Premier to his car. Then the President of Asante returned to his private office alone.

From the back of his top desk drawer he carefully withdrew a small tissue-wrapped package. He unfolded it slowly. A coin, a gold coin, that had been drilled and threaded onto a loop of string. It had been given to him by Auntie Tal. She told him its history. As she had been told. And her teller before her.

Centuries ago, perhaps two millennia, on this stretch of West African coast, a fleet of six ships with triangular sails had appeared, coming through the Gulf of Guinea from the north. The men who sailed these ships were white, burned by the sun, thinned by hunger. They came ashore. They spoke an unknown language. By gesture, they asked for food and drink. It was brought, and as was the custom in that place, the ancient system of dumb barter was begun.

Grain and palm wine were set out by Ashantis, who then retreated a distance. The foreigners advanced to inspect the victuals. They put down gold coins, bars of copper, knives of bronze, strings of glittering red beads. All this was placed alongside the provisions. Then the white men retreated. The Ashantis advanced to inspect what had been left. It was not enough. They retreated in silence. The strange men came forward and added more gold coins, more bronze knife blades, and retreated once more.

This happened yet again. Then the Ashantis, satisfied with the bargain, picked up the trade goods and departed. The white men loaded their grain and palm wine and sailed away. They were never seen again. They were small men, wiry and strong, with protruding lips and long, bent noses.

One of the gold coins left by these voyagers of centuries ago was the amulet given to Obiri Anokye by Auntie Tal. It had been rubbed smooth by many fingers, centuries of fingers, but the pressed images were still discernible. On one side was a leaping ibex. On the other was the head of a man. His nose was heavy and curved like a scimitar. His hair was in ringlets, rows of curls bound with a crown of laurel. His beard was also curled, but cut off squarely at the bottom. A tapering spade of a beard. Auntie Tal said this man was a great king, ruler of all the world.

Obiri Anokye unbuttoned his shirt, slipped the loop of string over his head, hung the grisgris upon his bare chest, buttoned his shirt over it. He did not believe in these things: amulets, grisgris, fetishes, juju. But he did not *not* believe.

"Honored guests," Peter A. Tangent said, in French. "Ladies and gentlemen. It is a great privilege for me, and an even greater pleasure, to present the President of Asante, Obiri Anokye."

The luncheon guests at the Zabarian Restaurant

leaped to their feet, applauding enthusiastically. The Little Captain rose slowly, shook Tangent's hand, then turned to the acclamation, smiling faintly. He stood silently, looking about the crowded room, waiting patiently until the hand-clapping ended; the guests sat down, turning their chairs so they all faced him. Black faces, white faces. All shades, all hues. Waiting...

"Friends," Obiri Anokye said. "Brothers and sisters. I thank you all for your respect and affection. I give you my love and my gratitude. Gladly and without limit." He then repeated this greeting in English and in Akan.

They bent forward, already won by his solemn words, by his grave manner. He had the gift of making the moment, and those who shared it, seem intense and significant. Even the Man from Tulsa and the Man from New York were impressed. They leaned to him as eagerly as the others, not wanting to miss a word, gesture, expression; mesmerized by this short, stocky man wearing the khakis of an Asante soldier, without decoration or indication of rank.

"Within the hour we shall witness the start of commercial production of oil from Asante waters. It is the end of a long, difficult period of exploration, discovery, and development. Success would not have been possible without the resolution and labor of Mr. Peter Tangent and his associates of the Starrett Petroleum Corporation. All Asantis are grateful for what they have done."

There was a splatter of applause. The oilmen in the audience looked at each other and grinned happily.

"But if today's ceremony marks the end of one period, it signals the start of another. A beginning. A birth. Of a new day for our beloved country. We have been blessed with a great national resource. It will enable us to provide a better life for all Asantis. Our people fed, clothed, and housed. Our children educated to the limits of their ability and talents. The land itself respected, nurtured, and made more beautiful. If we plan wisely and work diligently with love and understanding, we may create an Asante that will serve as a model for all of Africa, and that will prove to the world that Africa has the faith and determination to create a civilization of the future to rival the greatest of the past."

Then, slowly, the Little Captain assumed his familiar speaking posture: feet spread and planted, hands on hips, torso bent slightly backward, chest inflated, chin elevated so he seemed to stare at his listeners broodingly from under heavy brows. His low voice gained power:

"Africa... My Africa... *Our* Africa! So beset by trials and problems. Poor and ill. The people and the land impoverished. Drained of our wealth for so many years by others. And now struggling to create a new continent, free of the fears of the past. And yet chained to the past. It is the chain of separatism, a cruel shackle that prevents us from realizing our true destiny.

"Family against family. Tribe against tribe. Creed against creed. Race against race. Nation against nation, I tell you this infamy must end! We shall never succeed until we recognize we are Africans. Before all, *Africans!* Race means nothing. Creed nothing. Tribe nothing. Borders nothing. But our sacred land is all, demanding our total loyalty, our hearts, minds and, if need be, blood.

"I stand before you today not as an Asanti, a Christian, or a black. I am an African! And I plead with you all to renounce the evil of separatism that enfeebles our holy soil. I call upon you to give your talents, your love, your soul, every minute of the life that is in you, to the future of Pan-Africa: one beautiful continent, one strong nation, one magnificent people, one glorious future!"

With the approval of President Anokye, employees of PR Afrique, the Liberian public relations firm on retainer to the Republic of Asante, planned the evening gala to be an informal, festive affair. The palace at Mokodi, gleaming in floodlights, was festooned with garlands of fresh flowers and bunting in the national colors. Illuminated fountains on the plaza tossed sparkles into the night sky. Bands played jazz and le rock-and-roll in the streets. Vendors were allowed to set up stands on the Boulevard Voltaire, selling palm wine, millet beer, pepper chicken, and fufu. The strolling gendarmerie even smiled indulgently at games of chance flourishing on side streets.

The ardent night air was alive with the scent of sun-baked skin, exploding firecrackers, perfumed water squirted from syringes onto unsuspecting passersby. It was a noisy, good-natured crowd celebrating Asante's new wealth. There was indeed dancing in the streets, and singing, laughter, the close mingling of black natives and white tourists, all intent on enjoying the carnival mood of this memorable night. Many, in fact, wore masquerade, their outlandish costumes dimmed by the brilliance of tribal dress.

The same mood of informal gaiety prevailed inside the palace. Rather than a sit-down state dinner, a bountiful buffet had been provided in the main ballroom on the ground floor. Three bands played in as many rooms, waiters hustled to provide whatever drink might be desired and, best of all, no formal program or speeches had been planned.

Yet it was a speech that dominated the excited gathering—the short speech of President Obiri Anokye at the Zabarian. The luncheon had been covered by representatives of Reuters and Agence France-Presse. Both had taken down the Little Captain's words in shorthand. Better than that, the man from PR Afrique had tape-recorded the speech. With Anokye's permission, a transcript was made, copies were run off and distributed in answer to many requests. The only change the President made was to label his words "extempore remarks" rather than "formal speech."

Whatever he wished to call it, Anokye's ideas and phrases aroused the most intense interest in Asante's diplomatic community. Copies of the speech were sent off immediately to home offices with analyses by ambassadors and consuls stationed in Mokodi.

It was the significance of the President's remarks that caused so much spirited discussion at the palace gala. Anokye seemed to have included whites—"all races, all colors, all creeds"—in his plea for Pan-Africa. Yet he had made an obvious reference to the evils of white colonialism. And was he serious in his suggestion for "one continent, one nation, one people, one future"? In his condemnation of separatism, he went far beyond the plans of others who asked for an African unity based on a loose federation of sovereign states. Did he really mean to eliminate national boundaries in Africa? What exactly did he mean—and how did he propose it be achieved?

These questions, and others, were debated heatedly, not only by the representatives of other African countries but by diplomats of the Americas, Western Europe, the Soviet Bloc, the Far East. In fact, by everyone. And when the author of the perplexing speech was asked directly for explanation or amplification, he would only smile slightly and murmur, "Surely the meaning is evident in the words." The only consensus arrived at was that Obiri Anokye had voiced new ideas important to Africa, and to the world, and by this one short speech had marked himself a young statesman to be reckoned with. The PR representative was kept busy providing copies of the President's official biography to the world's capitals and communication media.

The ballroom was thronged, pulsing with a life of its own, the crowd growing and diminishing as guests moved to other palace rooms or out onto the terrace. Eventually they returned, drawn by the magnetic presence of President Anokye himself. He stood poised in one corner of the enormous room, Sgt. Sene Yeboa and two other guardsmen in mufti standing at his back. He greeted guests affably, thanked them graciously for their good wishes and congratulations on his speech. He sipped, occasionally, from a glass of champagne. Though he remained standing in this one spot for almost two hours, he showed no fatigue. And in spite of the demands made upon his time and attention, he seemed completely aware of what was going on in the crowded room. Once, he quietly instructed a guardsman to ask the ballroom band to moderate their volume. And once he beckoned Beatrice da Silva to his side to whisper a few words into her ear that made her blush with pleasure.

Nearby, Minister of State Jean-Louis Duclos, his wife, Mboa, and the Benin Christophe Michaux watched the President's performance with admiration.

"Poor Bibi," Mboa said. "He must be so weary."

"Bibi?" Michaux asked, greatly amused. "You call him that?"

Mboa clapped a palm over her mouth for a second.

"I should not have said that," she confessed. "But Jean and I knew him well before the coup. I still think of him as a good friend, as Bibi."

"You must address him as 'Mr. President,'" Duclos said severely.

"Yes, Jean," she said, lowering her eyes.

She was a petite woman, coal-black, wearing an Apollo shift in a blue tie-dyed design. Despite her husband's objections, she wore her hair corn-rowed. Her experiments with makeup (at his urging) had ended so disastrously that now she wore none. She had graduated from the Mokodi lycée, where Duclos had taught in pre-coup days, but she shared none of his political interests, and seemed content.

He had married her after her attempted suicide. As, he thought, she lay dying, he had realized his love, and declared it when she recovered. But now, sometimes, in moments when her placid Negro-ness infuriated him, he wondered if that attempted suicide was not a trick, as another woman might feign pregnancy to insure marriage. Mboa—or Maria, as he called her—might not be intellectual but she had, he admitted, bush shrewdness, jungle wisdom. If only she were not so black!

He was black too, of course. But so light in color that several women in Paris had told him he could easily pass. That, he would never do. He was, he told himself, proud of his blood. Still, meeting the smartly dressed white wives of foreign diplomats, imposing women who could discuss social, political, and economic theory with verve and knowledgeableness, he sometimes wondered if he had made a horrible mistake, fettering himself to this small, coal-black woman with enormous eyes and gleaming teeth, who needed only a plate in her lower lip or rings of brass about an elongated neck to qualify for a full-page portrait in *National Geographic*. Topless, of course.

"And what did you think of the President's speech, Mrs. Duclos?" Christophe Michaux asked.

She was confused for a moment.

"He wants only what is best for all of us," she said in a low voice. "I trust him."

"Do you?" he smiled loftily, a smile directed at the Minister of State, a smile of sympathy and complicity. Duclos found himself responding to that smile. Here was a man who understood.

"What was your reaction to the speech?" he asked Michaux.

The Benin Premier's aide sobered immediately, features freezing into an expressionless diplomatic mask.

"There were several things that troubled me," he said thoughtfully. "In my own mind, I cannot resolve certain contradictions. Apparently, he was saying 'Africa for the Africans.' Yet he said race was of no importance. Does he think white settlers, white colonials, are Africans?"

"It troubled me also," Duclos confessed.

"He has never discussed this idea of Pan-Africa with you, Minister?"

"Well, ah . . . no. At least not in the terms he expressed today."

"Do you agree with it?"

"Well . . . I sympathize with his vision, Mr. Michaux, but—"

"Christophe, please."

"Christophe. Thank you. As I say, I sympathize with his vision, his dream, but I believe he errs in including race as a sin of separatism. I cannot conceive of a new Africa based on anything but the highest ideals of negritude."

Michaux looked at him with interest.

"Perhaps," he said softly, "you and I hold the same beliefs. Not identical, certainly, but similar. I, for instance, in my own mind believe that the tyranny of class rather than separatism is the main obstacle to African progress."

"Class?" Duclos said. "Are you a Marxist, Christophe?"

"Oh no," Michaux laughed merrily. "No no no. I merely feel that white hegemony in Africa, economic hegemony, must be ended before we Africans may call our souls our own."

"But you are both Martinicains," Mboa said bravely. "How can you be Africans?"

They looked at her in astonishment.

"Don't be stupid, Maria," Duclos said angrily.

"All blacks are Africans," Michaux said. The lofty smile. "Originally. Whatever their birthplace."

"Jean," Mboa said earnestly, "are there not blacks in Australia? The islands of the Pacific? So you taught us at the lycée. Did they come originally from Africa?"

"Don't confuse the issue," he said furiously. "You don't have the intelligence to discuss such matters."

They stood without speaking a few moments, embarrassed. The celebration swirled about them. Music. Dancing. Laughter as brittle as shattered glass.

"Tell me, Minister," Michaux said, "how do you suppose President Anokye intends to implement his scheme?"

"Scheme?"

"His suggestion for Pan-Africa. How is it to be achieved?"

"I believe the President intended it as an ideal, a hope for the future. I do not believe it is a concrete program."

"Oh? I thought perhaps he had a plan..."

"A plan, Christophe? Oh no. Nothing like that, I'm sure."

"You should know," Michaux said dryly. "Who better than the Asanti Minister of State? You don't find some of his ideas—well...dangerous?"

"How dangerous? To whom?"

Michaux shook his head. "I cannot say. But in my own mind, I have a vague fear that the President's obvious love of Africa, his sympathy, and compassion for the masses, may lead him astray. He is such a persuasive man. What presence! It would be a sad thing if he should employ his enormous gifts only to prolong Africa's servitude to the international white power infrastructure."

"He would never do that."

"Not deliberately, Minister. Of course not. Such an implication was farthest from my thoughts. But his great personal popularity and Asante's new wealth may blind him to the realities of the racial situation in Africa today. I would not care to see him become a puppet of the whites."

"Nor I."

Michaux put a limp hand on Duclos' arm. "How

happy I am to find a man of your talents in Asante who sees things so clearly. We must speak of this again. I would deem it a great honor and pleasure, Minister, if you could visit me in Cotonou. Is such a thing possible in your busy schedule?"

"Thank you, Christophe," Duclos said, blushing with pride. "I believe it could be arranged."

"Excellent, excellent! There are some men I would like you to meet. Intelligent men with many fresh and provocative ideas. I'm sure you'll enjoy speaking with them. Mrs. Duclos, I hope you will be able to accompany your husband to Benin."

"No," Duclos said shortly. "I'm afraid that's impossible. Maria doesn't wish to fly in a plane."

"We could drive, Jean," she said timidly.

"No," he said again. "Ah . . . the President is looking at us."

The others turned to see. President Obiri Anokye was indeed staring at them. But then they realized he was not actually looking at them. He was deep in conversation with the French ambassador and was merely staring in their direction without seeing them. Or so it seemed.

Thirty minutes before midnight, the Little Captain beckoned Beatrice da Silva to his side. Making his apologies to the diplomats and oilmen surrounding him, he stepped clear of the crowd, guiding Beatrice with a light touch on her elbow. Sgt. Sene Yeboa stalked a few steps after them.

President Anokye led her from the ballroom, down a corridor toward the rear of the palace, through a suite of staff offices, and out French doors onto the terrace. Yeboa stood posted at the open door as Obiri and Beatrice strolled to the balustrade overlooking the plaza.

Because of the warmth of his manner and the ardor of his glances, the woman was certain, in her heart, that the man would ask her to marry him this evening. And when she saw he had selected the exact spot where they had first met—on the terrace, during a reception held by the late

King Prempeh IV—she was filled with love. For his thoughtfulness, for his perception, for *him*.

Actually, he had selected this place for other reasons. It was a position that could be easily observed by Sergeant Yeboa and guards posted on the palace grounds below. And he was not certain how modern young women reacted to proposals of marriage; the semi-public nature of this place, with other guests occasionally sauntering by, precluded any uncultured romantic violence on her part.

"I hope you are enjoying the gala, Beatrice," he said politely. "Is there anything you wish? A glass of champagne, perhaps? A piece of chicken?"

"Oh no," she said, giggling nervously. "I've had so much. It's good to be away from the crowd. For a few minutes."

"Your accommodations are satisfactory?"

"Marvy," she said. "A whole suite for daddy and me. Did I thank you for the flowers? They're beautiful."

He suspected they had been provided by the manager of the Mokodi Hilton, but made a casual gesture: it was nothing.

"I loved your speech at the Zabarian," she said. "Just loved, loved, loved it."

He made the gesture again, with the sudden realization of what his married life with this silly, good-natured woman might be like. But he concealed his dread and took her fingers into his. Her soft, warm, boneless fingers.

She had, he thought, gained a few pounds since he last saw her; it was not a welcome presage of what the years would bring. But now, this moment, plump flesh was springy and young, dark skin glowed. Her unlined, untouched face was alive with excitement, half-fearful, half-yielding sensuality. He was conscious of her fruity scent. Her entire body seemed bursting with expectation and hope, leaning to him. He loved her more because he knew the pain he would cause her. If not pain, then disappointment. But there would be compensations. For her and for him. They would work it out. And besides, her legs were good.

"What a wonderful night," she said. "The most wonderful night of my life!"

As always, in her superlatives, youth burbled. He thought it might be good for him, this unthinking joy. It might leaven his life, dilute his gravity, complete him. He had a sudden succulent fantasy of the smell of baked bread, a broad-bosomed wife and mother, sticky-fingered children screaming with laughter and grabbing at his legs. Home.

"Beatrice, there is something I must say to you. Ask you."

"Yes?"

"I have spoken to your father and have his permission."

"What is it, Bibi?"

"I want you to—"

He stopped. Suddenly, as she stared into his eyes, she saw the depth change. He was gone from the moment, from her.

"I must leave you a moment," he said. "Please stay here. I will return in only a minute or two."

He turned and strode away from her. She stared after him, shocked and puzzled. Had he lost his nerve? Did he need to relieve himself? What had happened to him? Why had he deserted her at such a moment?

He drew Sergeant Yeboa into the staff offices.

"Bring Sam Leiberman to me," he said. "At once. Here."

Yeboa looked at him doubtfully.

"Little Captain, you will be alone."

"Go, Sene." Anokye smiled tightly. "For a few minutes I will defend myself. You know I can."

He waited patiently, almost five minutes. Neither pacing nor smoking. Finally Yeboa returned, Leiberman following. Anokye motioned, and the mercenary came close.

"Sir?" he said.

"The aide to the Premier of Benin," President Anokye said. "Christophe Michaux. Did you meet him?"

"Yeah," Leiberman said. "I met him."

"What do you think?"

"A weasel," Leiberman said. "Or a butterfly. Or maybe a weasel *and* a butterfly."

"I want to know about him," Anokye said. "I have no one in our embassy there I can turst. Can you do it?"

Leiberman thought a moment, then nodded.

"Not me personally," he said, "but I can get it."

"Good," Anokye said. "I want everything."

"Of course," Leiberman said.

The Little Captain rejoined Beatrice da Silva at the terrace balustrade. She was almost weeping with vexation. He took her hands in his.

"Please forgive me," he said gently. "As I was saying, I have spoken to your father and have his permission to ask you."

"To ask me what?"

"If you will marry me. If you will be my wife. Will you?"

"Oh yes, Bibi! Yes yes yes!"

She flung her arms around him, drew him to her, all soft heart. And, as if arranged by the PR man from Monrovia, at that precise instant there was a loud explosion high in the sky, a crown of multi-colored torches curved out in a graceful spray. The fireworks display had started, and their lips peeled away, sideways, as their startled eyes followed the brilliant succession of red rockets, green streamers, white dripping fire, yellow falling stars, blue whirling discs, cracking, booming, thudding, snapping, roaring in the night sky over Mokodi.

Outside, from the streets of Mokodi, came the occasional crack of an exploding firecracker, a bit of song, a high drunken yell of delight. But the city was going to bed, to love or to sleep. Confetti scattering down gutters before a warm night wind. Wisps of clouds sliding across a lemon moon. From somewhere, the baritone cough of a boat whistle, siren cut off in mid-wail. And dimly, dimly, endless splash of the sea.

By 0200 the crowd in the palace ballroom had dwindled to a dozen dreamy-eyed couples. Revolving slowly to Edith Piaf tunes. Played by a somnolent band.

Waiters shuffled wearily about, cleaning up the littered buffet, overflowing ashtrays, spilled drinks and broken glass. Ancient sweepers, moving in time to the draggy music, pushed their rag brooms over the parquet floors.

In the first floor audience chamber, the barefoot Ajaka placed a silver tray of coffee and brandy on the long mahogany table, then went bowing, yawning, off to bed. They crowded around to help themselves.

"Mighty fine celebration, Mr. President," the Man from Tulsa said.

"Can't remember a better one," the Man from New York said.

"I am happy you gentlemen enjoyed it," Anokye said. "I hope you will return frequently and see more of our beautiful country."

He did not take his chair at the head of the table but selected one midway on the side. Premier Willi Abraham sat on his right, Attorney General Mai Fante on his left. The oilmen sat across from them, Peter Tangent between the Man from Tulsa and the Man from New York. For a few moments no one spoke; they sipped cautiously at hot, black coffee or touched brandy to their lips.

"I hope we're not inconveniencing you, Mr. President," the Man from New York said.

"But we're grabbing a morning flight," the Man from Tulsa said. "And this seemed like the only time to have our confab."

"No inconvenience at all," the Little Captain assured them. "I frequently work through the night. I find it more productive while everyone else sleeps."

They looked at him sharply, but there was nothing in his manner to suggest he was implying more than he had stated.

Tangent had briefed Oribi Anokye on these two Starrett Petroleum executives.

"I think of them as twins," he had told the President. "One speaks with the accent of Oklahoma, and one of New York. But they are almost identical in appearance and style. They'll wear black silk suits, light blue shirts, with either silver or striped ties. If striped, they'll be ties of British army regiments. But if I ever suggested to them that it was infra dig to wear the colors of a military regiment to which one did not belong, they'd look at me as if I were some kind of a nut. The ties come from England, don't they? The British are helping their balance of payments by selling their regimental stripes and clan tartans around the world, aren't they? So? I only mention this, Mr. President, because it is indicative of their mentality. The Bottom Line Mentality. Profit is good, loss is bad. Profit is smart, loss is dumb. So I suggest you deal with them on those terms. Like most international businessmen, they are apolitical. But do not take them lightly; they are very hard, very practical men. Shrewd as Lebanese rug merchants or Amsterdam diamond dealers. They mean to use you."

The Little Captain had looked at Tangent curiously. "Is that so unnatural?" he asked.

Now, sitting across from them, Anokye could understand why Tangent thought of them as twins. Both American executives had a polished gloss, faces in which age and experience had apparently left no interpretable marks. In spite of a long day's festivities, they were sober, spotlessly clean, unrumpled, alert and keen. The Little Captain found himself wishing he had such men working for him. They were second-rank men, but good ones.

"Mr. President," Tangent started, "we have asked for this audience to learn your reaction to a project Starrett is exploring."

"I'm glad Peter said 'exploring,'" the Man from New York said. "It's still in the talking stage."

"All smoke so far," the Man from Tulsa said. "But it's a possibility. For the future."

"What Starrett is considering," Tangent went on, "is building an oil refinery somewhere on the west coast of Africa so that crude taken from Asante wells can be broken down into marketable products in this area instead of shipping it to our Ireland refinery."

"It makes buck sense," the Man from Tulsa said. "Saves transportation costs."

"And brings us closer to our end markets in Africa," the Man from New York said. "Good for everyone. For us, of course, and because of the savings, for the consumer. Eventually."

"But refineries don't come cheap," the Man from Tulsa said.

"Far from it," the Man from New York said.

"I see," President Anokye said slowly. "And where is this refinery to be built?"

"That's the purpose of this meeting," Tangent said quickly. "As I understand it, several excellent sites are under consideration. Is that correct?"

He looked left and right, and both Starrett executives nodded.

"Several excellent sites," Tangent repeated. "We are now in the process of talking to the governments involved. Naturally, we want the most advantageous lease terms we can obtain. You understand that, Mr. President, I'm sure."

"Of course."

"One of the sites under consideration is Asante, I'm happy to say. So this is in the nature of an exploratory discussion. If we can arrive at an equitable arrangement, it's possible the refinery will be built here, and Asante will benefit from having one of the most modern, productive and profitable installations of its type anywhere in Africa."

"No doubt about that," the Man from New York said. "With a lot of local labor needed during construction, of course. That should help your employment numbers."

"With the outside technicians spending their dinero right here in Asante," the Man from Tulsa said. "To say nothing of new roads, port facilities, and other goodies."

"I see," Anokye said thoughtfully. "And you say several sites are under consideration?"

"That's right, Mr. President," the Man from Tulsa said cheerfully. "No guarantee Asante gets the prize."

"Wherever we get the best terms, like Peter said," the Man from New York nodded. "It's business."

"Well..." the Little Captain said doubtfully, "while I appreciate Starrett considering Asante, I'm not sure.... Willi, what is your reaction?"

"I'm afraid I can't express too much enthusiasm, Mr. President," the well-coached Abraham said. "While the industrializing of Asante would have some obvious benefits, I fear it would adversely affect tourism, which accounts for a very substantial part of our annual income. Tourists come to Asante because they seek a simpler, unspoiled way of life. They want to see the green hills of Africa, our villages, a lifestyle that once existed, perhaps, in their home countries, but is now gone forever. I fear we could not lure visitors if our main attraction was an oil refinery. It's exactly the sort of thing they hope to get away from, to leave behind them when they come to Asante."

"You speak the truth," Anokye nodded, very grave. "Mai, how do you feel?"

"Much as Premier Abraham, Mr. President. I must also add that the building of a refinery on Asante soil would have serious social and political repercussions. We have a growing and very vocal organization of environmentalists in Asante who would be certain to react to a proposed oil refinery with outrage. They would point out the polluting effects on their clean air and pure water. Joined in their opposition, no doubt, by fishermen and owners of coastal hotels. I'm very dubious about this project for Asante, Mr. President."

Anokye sighed. "What you say substantiates my own judgment." He looked at the three oilmen, back and forth. "I thank you for your kind offer, gentlemen, but I must request that Asante be eliminated as a possible site of your new oil refinery."

After recovering from their initial shock, the two Starrett executives moved swiftly to the attack. Tangent said little, content to—content?—*delighted* to watch and listen to this snappish dialogue.

They wheedle. Anokye scorns. They bark. He thunders. They threaten. He shrugs. They implore. He rejects. Tangent sees it as a verbal ballet—approaches and retreats, spins and leaps. To be concluded by a graceful bow from all, roses tossed from the darkness.

Aware of the professional expertise of the Man from New York and the Man from Tulsa, Tangent was exhilarated by the implacableness of the Little Captain. He was caught up in the ebb, the flow, the clash, the withdrawal, and was hardly aware of when, or by what means, Obiri Anokye introduced his demand for a no-strings grant for "national expansion."

The battle surged again, the overseas visitors rising and stalking angrily about the room. Until Anokye's steadfastness simply wore them down, physically and emotionally, and they flopped back into their chairs and asked him how much he wanted, and Tangent realized, with awe, that the Little Captain had won: he had his no-strings grant, and Asante's environmentalists disappeared as quickly as they had been invented.

The winner sat back, solemn, not gloating, and let Willi Abraham and Mai Fante hammer out the terms: Starrett got their Asante refinery site for three and a half million American dollars, to be paid in six installments over a period of eighteen months, the cash payments to be disguised in a variety of ways: advances on anticipated oil revenues, investments in worthless Asante real estate, contributions to schools and hospitals, the establishment of a Friends of West Africa foundation in the U.S. Abraham and Fante had done their homework.

When the final agreement was reached, close to 0400, the two beaten Starrett executives ceremoniously shook hands with President Obiri Anokye.

"Mr. President," the Man from New York said, "if you ever get tired of running Asante, there's a place for you at Starrett Petroleum."

"Any time," the Man from Tulsa said. "Anywhere in the world. Just tell us how much you want. Don't ask—*tell!*"

Smiling gently, the Little Captain bid them good-night and wished them a safe and speedy trip home.

Tangent drove them back to their VIP suites at the Mokodi Hilton, wondering, with savage satisfaction, if they had enough energy remaining to enjoy the pleasures J. Tom Petty had arranged for them.

Yvonne Mayer sat on the middle cushion of a wicker couch. It was covered with a rough twill in a batik pattern of harsh yellow, orange, brown, clashing with the peach-colored peignoir she wore. Her legs were crossed; she peered down through Benjamin Franklin glasses as she filed her nails with an emery board. Beside her was the evening edition of the Mokodi *New Times*, the only newspaper in Asante. It carried the President's Zabarian speech on the front page.

"It was on the radio every hour until the station went off the air," she said. "Bibi, was it wise?"

"Wise, not wise," he shrugged. "I think many Africans will react favorably. It is time to make myself known in other countries, to make friends. I cannot do it alone, from Asante. I must have men in other countries who know me, know my ideas, believe in me."

He and Sgt. Sene Yeboa had taken off their shoes and socks. They sat sprawled wearily in cushioned wicker armchairs, drinking Star beer. A single lamp burned dimly. But already, through the east windows, the black sky was thinning.

"Sene, do you have any men ready?"

"Three, Little Captain. And two more in a week's time."

"Good. We will send two to Lomé, two to Cotonou, one to Lagos. I will give them their instructions and provide funds."

"Did you ask her?" Yvonne said, not looking up from her nails.

"Yes," Anokye said. "I asked her."

"She said yes, of course?"

"She said yes."

"I had her pointed out to me at the oil ceremony," Yvonne said, finally raising her eyes to stare at him over her spectacles. "She is a dumpling."

Anokye said nothing.

"In a few years she will be a pig."

He looked at her coldly. The peignoir had fallen open. He saw her smooth knees, waxen legs. He remembered her body. Like a shaved snake. Sene Yeboa kept his eyes on his beer.

"The marriage will be within three months," he said. "My marriage. Yours will be sooner."

She made a moue and started on the other hand.

"We have the money," he told her. "From Starrett."

"How much?"

"Enough. Nkomo and I will begin examining weapons immediately. When it is learned we wish to buy and have the funds, there will be no problems."

He spoke to himself as much as to her.

"Perhaps you could go to Cotonou," he said. "No, not yet. There is a certain man, the aide to the Premier. But I will wait for Leiberman's report; then I will decide. I am tired. It has been a long day."

"You will sleep here?"

"Yes. No. Well, perhaps for an hour or two. A nap. Then I will return to the palace. There is much to be done. Much . . ."

There was silence, and when she looked up from her nails, she saw he had fallen asleep in the armchair, his chin on his chest.

"Poor Bibi," she breathed softly. "Sene, help me get him into the bedroom."

Between them, they supported the drowsing, stumbling, mumbling President of Asante into the bedroom and lowered him gently onto the bed, on his back.

"Thank you, Sene," Yvonne whispered. "I will let him sleep a few hours. Will you wait for him?"

"Oh yes. I must drive him back to the palace."

"If you wish to sleep, go to the guest room. I will wake you when he awakes."

"I am not sleepy."

"There is some beer in the kitchen, and food if you are hungry. Take anything."

"Thank you, Yvonne."

She rose up on her bare toes to kiss his cheek swiftly. He stood a moment, frozen, then smiled at her, shy and puzzled. He turned, marched from the room. She closed the door behind him.

The room was not lighted, but the bamboo shades were up, drapes open. Enough illumination to enable her to unbutton Anokye's shirt, his trousers, pull them off. He made groaning, protesting sounds as she pushed and hauled at him, trying to roll him free. Finally he was naked, lying on his back, legs spread, arms flung wide. His great, hairy chest pumped slowly. She could almost see tense force flow from his limbs as the flesh slackened, sank into sleep. He twitched a few times, mcaned a few times. Then he was still. Almost, she thought, with the stillness of death.

She sat alongside him, on the edge of the bed, staring down at his dark majesty. She put her palm lightly, fingers spread, on his thigh. His skin was hot. Her white hand looked like a fulgent sun, beams radiating.

Her hand drifted; she touched the black staff cautiously. He did not stir. She held it delicately upright, as one might hold the stem of a wine glass. At the same time her other hand pried beneath her peignoir, between her legs. She touched herself. Almost immediately she felt a flow, slick wetness.

Lost, she bent over him slowly, touched her lips to him. Her eyes were turned upward; she watched his face anxiously. It was important that he not awake. All her movements, on him and in herself, were small, sly, and without passion. The moment seemed to her of a bittersweetness she could not comprehend. As piercing as a farewell.

When his penis began to harden, she stopped immediately. She withdrew her fingers, from him and from herself. She rose cautiously, slipped quietly to the door, closed it gently behind her. In the living room she lighted one of his Gauloises, and stepped out onto the front porch. The eastern sky was greying now, changing as she watched. New sun, new day. The air smelled of it, all fresh and dewy. Flowered air, perfumed world. Hugging her elbows, cigarette dangling from her lips, she strolled around to the rear of the house, feeling the damp grass beneath her bare feet, kicking her way through a tangle of low wet groundcover whose name she did not know and a stand of tall flowers whose name she could not recall.

When she reentered the house, through the back door into the kitchen, Sene Yeboa was crouched, a snubby Smith & Wesson .38 swallowed in his huge fist, pointing toward the door. When he saw her, he slid the revolver smoothly back into a black belt holster, sat down, took up his beer and sandwich again.

"I'm sorry," she said humbly.

He chewed, grinned, waved her to the chair across from him. She took a bottle of Star from the refrigerator and joined him.

He swallowed heavily, took a gulp of beer.

"The Little Captain sleeps?"

She nodded.

"Good. A long day. He had to smile at many people. I could not have done it."

She looked at him closely. A blunt, heavy man, not as dark as Anokye. He had, Obiri said, been "made in the bush": white father, black mother. Though who they were, he did not know. Raised in a Christian mission. A silent, brooding boy. But when he was sent to the Mokodi lycée, he met Obiri Anokye, and his life began. Boyhood friends, and into the army together. He had killed for the Little Captain, and would willingly die for him.

He was Bibi's age, but without the Little Captain's magisterial quality. There was sensuousness in his dense, almost brutish features. Wide nostrils flared. Thick lips turned out, showing wet red inner skin. The smooth jaw seemed never to need a shave. Small, narrowed eyes. Wide neck. Rounded, bunchy shoulders. A blunt body. "A bull," Anokye had called him. It was there in the truculent forward tilt of head and torso. Ready to charge.

"And you, Sene?" she asked. "Are you not weary?" They spoke Akan now. Before, in the living room with Anokye, they had spoken English. The President insisted on it, wanting to improve his proficiency.

Yeboa shrugged those massive shoulders.

"I will sleep tomorrow," he said. "When I can. Yvonne, the Little Captain's marriage troubles you?"

It was her turn to shrug.

"I accept it," she said.

"Good," he said heartily, as if that settled the matter. "He will work it out for your happiness; you will see."

"My happiness?"

"Of course," he said. He waved his hand about. "You have this fine house. Servants. Now you own the Golden Calf. Is not all this better?"

She said nothing, but something in her eyes made him stare.

"You miss the life?" he asked.

She saved sympathy and kindness as another person might put money in the bank. For a rainy day.

"How did you know?" she asked. "My family came to Africa from the Saar. Not came. Were driven. My father was a thief, my mother an alcoholic. All I can remember were the hunger and beatings. So I ran away."

None of this was true, and she wondered why she said it.

"Yes, I miss the life," she said. "Not the men. The girls. The friends. It was like a family, a home. I never had any."

She had said the right thing. His eyes glistened with tears. His hand crept across the table to cover her hers.

"I also," he said. Voice low and choked. "No home, no family. Until I met Bibi. Then I could go to his family, his home. But not my own."

She nodded dumbly.

"What men are you sending to Lomé and Cotonou?" she asked.

"The Little Captain wants men he can trust in other countries. To find out things. And also here in Asante, I have men to listen and learn what is going on. Like Prempeh's secret police."

"Bibi has put you in command of all this?" she asked.

"Oh yes," he said proudly. "He wishes me to recruit and train these men. They will all report to me. It is a very important task. And difficult. I do not know if I can do it."

"Do it," she said, turning her hand over so she clasped his. "I will help you."

9.

IN MOKODI, the Rue Dumas runs parallel to the Boulevard Voltaire, one square west. It is, for the length of four squares, a popular shopping center, especially for tourists. It is dominated by Monoprix, the French equivalent of Woolworth, and by the offices of American Express and several foreign consulates.

At the corner of a narrow east-west street called Shinbone Alley is the curio shop of Lum Fong. In its small windows are displayed splendid examples of Hong Kong Renaissance: lacquered salad bowls, transistor radios, silken flowers, wire banzai trees, painted shells, bamboo backscratchers, tobacco jars shaped like human skulls, brass jewelry, "African" amulets, bead curtains, and ashtrays in the form of Negro hands, stamped SOUVENIR OF ASANTE.

When Sam Leiberman stepped into the incense-scented interior, a lissome Chinese girl came eagerly forward. She was wearing a cheongsam of electric blue silk.

"Good morning, sir," she said brightly. "Is there something I can show you?"

"Yeah," Leiberman said. "Is it true?"

She averted her eyes. "May I be of service, sir?"

"I want to see Lum Fong."

"I shall tell the master you are here," she said.

"Master of what?" he called after her. "Plastic chopsticks?"

Lum Fong followed her from an inner office. He was a wizened Chinese with wispy chin whiskers. He wore a gorgeous brocaded gown with a high collar and braided frog closures. His tiny feet were in heelless velvet slippers. He touched his long fingernails and bowed deeply.

"Ahh, Reiberman," he said. "My insignificant shop is honored by your august presence."

"Cut the Mandarin shit and talk straight," Leiberman said. "Let's go in back."

Fong led the way through a bead curtain into a large office. Larger than the shop.

Leiberman said, "You can start by offering me a thimbleful of that plum brandy you keep in the red lacquer cabinet."

The Chinese made a sound deep in his throat, a cat's purr. Leiberman supposed it was meant to be an amused chuckle.

"You forget nothing," Fong said.

"Nothing important, I don't," Leiberman agreed.

He sat in an ornately carved armchair before the desk and watched the Chinese carefully dole out minuscule teacups of the brandy. Leiberman took his, sniffed, sipped appreciatively.

"That'll put lead in your pencil," he said. He lolled back, hooked one knee over the chair arm.

The mercenary was a heavy, meatish man. Arms were thick, hairy, wrists powerful. His short-sleeved safari jacket revealed a whitened scar running from right bicep to forearm, across the elbow. He was burned a deep brick-red. Stiff iron-grey hair cut en brosse. Squinty eyes.

Small, flat ears. Nose was broad, lips protuberant. A rude face. Gravelly voice. Clotted laugh.

"How's business?" he asked.

Lum Fong shrugged. "I survive."

"Don't we all," Leiberman said. "The nose candy coming in okay?"

The other's expression didn't change.

"I do not understand what you mean, Reiberman," he said softly.

"Sure you do," Leiberman said genially. "I'm working out of the palace now; you know that. I couldn't care less about your little sideline, but I don't think El Presidente would approve. He might even have that tough sergeant of his reach up your asshole and pull you inside out. I don't think you'd enjoy that, Lummy baby."

The Chinese sat back and sighed.

"What do you want, Reiberman?"

"A small favor. Muy poco. You got cousins in Benin?"

Lum Fong nodded.

"Cotonou or Porto-Novo?" Leiberman asked.

"Both."

"Good," Leiberman said. "There's a politico named Christophe Michaux. Tall, skinny, color of sand. Greasy, marcelled hair. Looks bleached to me. Little goatee. He's the secretary or aide to the Premier. I want a rundown on him. Things *Who's Who* wouldn't be interested in printing. You coppish?"

Again Lum Fong nodded. "That is all?" he asked.

"That's all," Leiberman said. "As soon as you can. Now that wasn't so bad, was it?"

He drained his brandy, unhooked his knee, stood up. Lum Fong rose behind the desk. He touched his long fingernails, bowed so deeply the wispy chin whiskers touched the brocaded gown.

"My humble abode has been honored by your sublime presence," he said.

"Ahh, Jesus," Leiberman sighed. "Fu Manchu strikes again."

10.

"IT'S BEAUTIFUL," Tony Malcolm said. "Did you see it?"

"No," Peter Tangent said, "it was crated when I picked it up."

"A Benin bronze," Malcolm said. "Brilliant work. Ten thousand. At least. Maybe twenty."

"A small token of the President's esteem," Tangent smiled. "For your help on the refinery thing. He said to tell you he still feels obligated."

"I'm beginning to see the Little Captain in a new light," Malcolm said.

Tangent laughed. "Thought you might," he said. "Ready to order?"

They were at their favorite corner table at Brindleys. They were wearing dinner jackets, part of the pre-theatre crowd. They were going to see *She Would If She Could*, an American musical based on *Antony and Cleopatra*, which one London critic had described as "A bird for the Bard—turkey."

"What're you having?" Tangent asked, scanning the deckle-edged menu.

"Dover sole."

"I'll buy that. How about a Muscadet?"

"Why not? It'll dull the pain of the play. It's supposed to be a clinker."

"Then why are we going?"

"We don't seem to have much else to do together these nights, do we?"

"No, we don't," Tangent said. Somewhat sadly. "Ah well..."

He gave the order to Harold, their superannuated waiter, then glanced casually about the crowded room. Men and women in formal dress. Most of them young, handsome, glittering. The rattle of smart talk.

"I'm in Africa," he said to Malcolm, "the land of sweat-stained khaki. Then a few hours later I'm in the middle of this. A crazy kind of jet-lag. Call it culture-lag. Difficult to adjust so quickly."

"You're complaining?"

"Oh God, no. Tony, I didn't ask if you want an appetizer. They have smoked salmon tonight."

"Thanks, no; I'll skip. Up two pounds this morning."

"So is our stock."

They smiled at each other, comfortable again, and watched Harold lovingly uncork their wine.

"Bit of all right this is, gentlemen," he said. "Dust on the tongue, flint on the teeth."

"And acid on the liver," Malcolm said, taking a sip. "Mmm, good. So he got his refinery? And his money?"

"He surely did," Tangent said. "He's looking at guns now. The Galil system from Israel. You know it?"

"Oh yes. Very fine. As good as the Uzi. Converts to submachine gun, sniper's rifle, grenade launcher, and so forth. I think it'll go."

"He's buying more tanks and personnel carriers from France. Wants to keep them happy."

"Very wise. He thinks of everything, doesn't he?"

"Everything. He also wants some stuff from us."

"Us?"

"The U.S. Exotic stuff."

"Like what?"

"Sound-activated mines, electronic monitors, recoilless rifles, rocket launchers. Especially the eighty-seven. And a few TOW missiles."

"The TOW? That's an antitank missile. What does he want that for?"

"Who the hell knows?" Tangent said. "Maybe he just likes to play with toys. Ah, here we are. Looks good, Harold."

"Caught today, gentlemen."

"Us or the fish?" Malcolm asked, and Harold put a finger alongside his nose.

"Good," Tangent said, after trying a bite. "How's yours?"

"Okay," Malcolm said. "Caught yesterday, if not frozen."

"Eh, oui," Tangent sighed. "You can help—if you want to."

Malcolm didn't stop eating.

"He doesn't need my help to buy weapons."

"Well...you know. There may be some questions asked about why a two-bit African nation needs antitank missiles and helicopter gunships."

Malcolm stopped eating.

"Gunships?" he said. "You didn't mention those."

"Didn't I?" Tangent said innocently. "Slipped my mind. How about it? If Virginia gets behind it, the export licenses will go through with no problems."

"Oh, I don't know," Malcolm said. He patted his lips with his napkin and sat back. "I'd like to know a little more about it."

"About what?"

"Why he needs the heavy artillery. His plans."

"I've already told you what I know."

"I doubt that."

"Well, your man down there probably knows more than I do."

"Some. Wilson's eager."

"Then you can guess the rest." Tangent put down his knife and fork, leaned forward, stared earnestly at Malcolm. "Tony, please don't ask me. I have an obligation to you, but I have a bigger one to him. I know you can put it together by yourself. From what I tell you and what Jonathon Wilson sends you. Isn't that enough?"

"Apparently it'll have to be," Malcolm said. "They have tortoni tonight. Ever have a big cup of espresso with a spoonful of tortoni in it?"

"Never have."

"Magnificent."

"What about your diet?"

"Screw my diet. Let's have it."

They waited in silence while the table was cleared. Harold brought the tortoni, cups, the copper espresso pot.

"Please give it a few minutes to filter, gentlemen," he said.

"What's in it for me?" Malcolm asked.

"If Virginia makes sure the permits go through?" Tangent said. "Let's see what I've got to trade..." He thought a minute. "Is Wilson doing a good job down there?"

"Good enough. His embassy cover is blown, of course."

"How would you like someone inside? Inside the palace?"

Malcolm straightened up.

"How?" he asked.

"The Little Captain was complaining how busy he was. I suggested he bring in a management consultant to take a look at his operation and sort it out for him. You know—make recommendations for staff reorganization, office design, work flow, paper forms, and so forth. He liked the idea. Wants to modernize his administration. His word: 'modernize.' Virginia could send someone down under cover of a legit London firm, couldn't you?"

Malcolm tested the espresso pot, found it was pouring, filled Tangent's cup and his own.

"Just a spoonful of the tortoni," he said. "Float it on top. Like this..."

Tangent tried it.

"You were right," he said. "Magnificent."

"Life's little pleasures," Malcolm said. "Get enough of them, they add up, and you can endure. Interesting idea. About a management consultant in the palace. I could arrange that. Will you tell Anokye he's a Virginia spook?"

Tangent thought a long moment.

"Difficult to know where one's loyalties lie," he said.

"Always has been," Malcolm said.

"No, I won't tell him," Tangent decided. "For two reasons: one, I think he's smart enough not to reveal anything important. To *anyone*. Two, I want Virginia on his side. Not only now, but in the future."

"Clever bastard," Malcolm grumbled. "All right, I'll send a recommendation to Virginia. No guarantee. At least they'll know who he is. That speech of his kicked up a lot of dust."

They sipped their tortoni-creamed coffee. Again, Tangent looked casually about. At a nearby table there was a young, chestnut-haired woman wearing a black silk evening gown with plunging décolletage. Around her neck was a double strand of large pearls. They hung down into the cleavage between her heavy breasts.

Tangent had a sudden, shattering fantasy of a naked Amina Dunama wearing only a rope of white pearls. Glistening against her black skin. The vision was so sharp, so painful, that he caught his breath.

"What?" he said.

"Where have you been?" Tony Malcolm asked. "I said we better think about leaving. Curtain going up."

"Yes," Peter Tangent said. "Curtain going up. Tony, tell me something... I know you're Virginia, and half the members of Brindleys know it. Doesn't it bother you that your cover's so thin?"

"No, it doesn't bother me," Malcolm said. He smiled faintly. "It's designed that way."

"Designed?"

"Sure. I take the heat. What makes you think my group

is the only one in England?"

"You mean there are other—other cells in deep cover?"

"Of course."

"Do you have any communication with them?"

"No."

"Who coordinates?"

"Virginia."

"You mean," Tangent repeated incredulously, "there are other Virginia groups here and maybe in Africa?"

"That's what I mean."

"My God. It never occurred to me. There may be another Tony Malcolm operating in Asante right now."

"There may be," Malcolm acknowledged.

"Any idea who he could be?" Tangent asked.

Malcolm looked at him queerly.

"Maybe you," he said.

11.

TOGO, LIKE ITS NEIGHBORS, Asante and Benin, is a north-south slat of land. The three of them stand side by side, pickets on the west coast of Africa. And like its neighbors, Togo has a single main highway, running from Lomé on the coast to Dapango at the north. Many crossroads and trails connect the three improved highways of Asante, Togo, and Benin.

Where these east-west roads passed across frontiers, border guards were stationed. Otherwise, national boundaries were unfenced and unguarded—the "green borders" strolled across by smugglers who had their own network of unimproved crossroads, tracks, and trails.

President Obiri Anokye's letter to Gen. Kumayo Songo, of Togo, delivered by Adebayo Anokye, had requested a clandestine meeting with the general, at a place and time of his choosing. The general had sent a reply by Adebayo: Tuesday noon at a deserted village called Alampa, south of Pagala in Togo. It was not too far inside the Togolese border. Anokye could drive over the hills from Asante on a single-lane unimproved road in about thirty minutes. Or, if he elected to walk along smugglers' trails, he could be there in about two hours.

"We shall go on foot," the Little Captain told Sgt. Sene Yeboa. "I am stifled by this office. I need to get into the field again. We will take the Land-Rover to Gonja, and hike from there. Just the two of us. It will be like old times."

"Yes *sah!*" Sergeant Yeboa grinned. "Water bottles? Food?"

"No. Nothing. We will prove the good life has not softened us."

Yeboa grinned again. "Weapons, Little Captain?"

"Oh yes," Anokye nodded. "Bring the Uzi."

He would have been as elated as Yeboa at the prospect of this "outing" if it had not been for the selection of deserted Alampa for the meeting. He knew the place, and feared it. A roughly circular collection of thatched huts surrounding a packed earth compound. No one knew when this village had been inhabited, or when or why it had been abandoned. It was located near the bank of a small, sweet stream that fed into the Mono River. It was sited on a slight elevation: green land, cool breeze.

Yet the people who once lived there had walked away from it, driving their cows and goats, trundling their personal belongings, carrying squawking chickens in flopping sacks. They had left ancient fire stones, empty huts, a few rags fluttering in the wind, silence. Grass and trees had moved back in. Once-tilled fields were overgrown. Domed huts, beaten by storm, baked by the sun, had fallen in upon themselves, like shrinking old people.

Perhaps a pestilence had come. Perhaps a prolonged drought had dried the stream and withered the crops. Or perhaps, as some in nearby Pagala said, a curse had been put on the place. By a shaman, an unfriendly god, or maybe by the sins of the inhabitants. Whatever, Alampa was deserted. And despite the attractiveness of the site, no one, ever, showed the slightest desire to dwell in those crumbling huts again. The place was accursed.

But Anokye had to recognize its value as the scene of a secret meeting. No casual visitors. No wandering herdsmen. It was, in Africa, a no-man's-land.

The smugglers' trail led into and over the hills. The climb strained thigh and calf muscles. But cramps thawed on this hot, sweat-popping day, and after a while it became an excursion. They settled down to a good pace, Yeboa leading. But they played games in the bush: running madly down smooth, clear slopes, moving silently up to feeding warthogs, trying to snap the legs of feeding birds. It was their element; it was like coming home.

It was close to noon when they came up to Alampa, their camouflaged dungarees soaked. They had tracked on Pagala and then turned south. All this without map or compass. They separated then and circled the deserted village from opposite directions. No sign of visitors. No ambush indicated. They hunkered on their hams in the shade of a ruined hut, smoked crumpled Gauloises, waited without speaking. They heard no bird calls, no sounds of small animals snuffling in the bush. Only the hushed and vacant air. Finally the sound of a car moving along the Pagala-Akaba road. They listened. The motor stopped.

"Watch," Anokye said.

Yeboa nodded, unslung his Uzi, disappeared. One moment he was there, the next instant he was gone. Vanished into the green. The Little Captain heeled a depression for their cigarette butts in the dry, powdery earth, covered them over. He stepped deeper into the shadows of the dilapidated hut. He loosened the Walther P-38 in its hip holster.

Gen. Kumayo Songo came alone, puffing up the slight rise from road to village. He wore khaki uniform, peaked cap, Sam Browne belt. President Anokye watched him approach, expressionless, noting the rounded shoulders, protruding paunch, stumbling gait. The man was a clump; the bush was not his home. He came up wheezing, stopped, looked around warily. He was, Anokye realized, frightened.

He stepped slowly from the concealment of the ruined hut.

"Good morning, general," he said softly.

Songo whirled, stared, took off his cap, wiped his hand across his sweated forehead, replaced his cap, tugged down his uniform jacket, tried to smile, and bowed slightly—all this in one rapid, nervous movement.

"Good morning, Mr. President," he said.

"The shade?" Anokye gestured. "I fear we must stand. But what I have to say should not take much time."

Obediently, Songo followed him into the dimness. He was still breathing heavily. There were semicircles of stain beneath his armpits, and more sweat stains along the edges of his tightly cinched belt.

"I turst you are in good health?" Anokye inquired politely. He spoke Twi.

"I am well, praise to Allah," Songo replied. "Do you know happiness?"

"Thanks to God," Anokye returned, then switched to French. "Your family is well, I hope?"

"They are well, thank you. And yours?"

"In good health. Your son—please extend my best wishes."

"I shall."

"My sister Sara speaks of him fondly. Frequently."

"And he of her." Songo's breathing had steadied. Now he tried a small laugh. "I think perhaps we may become related."

Anokye echoed the general's small laugh.

"I think so too. How would you feel about that, general?"

"I would welcome it," Songo said promptly. He peered at Anokye in the dimness.

"I also," the Little Captain said. "There is the problem of religion. But such things can be worked out when the only desire is for the happiness of all."

"My feelings exactly," Songo said.

"If your son should come to me," Anokye said, "although he should rightfully apply to my father, I can assure you he will not be disappointed."

"Thank you, Mr. President," Songo said gratefully. "He is my oldest son; I want only the best for him."

"Of course," the Little Captain said. "And I for Sara. But that is not the reason I asked for this meeting."

"Oh?" Songo said.

The gloom bothered President Anokye. He could not see the other man's reactions, changes of expression, shift of eyes. He led the way back outside, pausing where a frayed overhang of thatch provided a latticed shade. Spindles of light illuminated Kumayo Songo's lumpish features, hairline mustache, sweaty jowls.

"What I wish to say to you," Anokye said rapidly, "must be held in the strictest confidence."

"Of course. If you say so, Mr. President."

"I must tell you that you are the only man in Togo I trust. All the others—the politicos, the diplomats, the *civilians*"—Anokye poured contempt into this last—"these men I do not trust."

As expected, General Songo swelled with pride. The paunch below his brown leather belt disappeared to inflate his chest above. His head lifted, chin elevated.

"Civilians," he repeated. "Exactly!"

"General, in all honesty I must say to you that I feel the leaders of your government are not aware of the true situation. I speak now, as you must know, of the relations between Togo and Benin."

Songo groaned softly. "Mr. President, I have tried to tell them. Many times..."

"I am sure you have, general. You are a military man. You assess the situation clearly. Without emotion and without sentiment. But I must also tell you, general, that it is more serious than even you believe. As you know, I am privy to secret reports from my embassies. Also, I have had in the last two weeks certain private conversations with persons at the highest level of the Benin government. One of the purposes of this meeting, general, is to warn you."

"Warn?" Songo almost shouted. "Of what? What?"

"I only relay this information because of our close personal friendship, the high regard I have for your patriotism, and the hope I know we both share for an even closer relationship in the future through your son Jere and my sister Sara."

"Warn me of what?" Songo agonized.

"Within the past two weeks," Anokye said solemnly, "a high representative of the Benin government asked me what Asante's reaction would be in the event of open warfare between Benin and Togo."

Songo hissed slowly.

"I gave him no direct reply," Anokye went on. "I told him Asante wanted only peace between the two nations. Between *all* African nations. But I felt I would be derelict in my obligation to our friendship if I did not tell you of this. Knowing you are the only man in Togo to whom I can speak so freely. The only man I can be certain of understanding the gravity of the situation. The civilians who control your government would..." He shrugged and left the sentence unfinished.

Gen. Kumayo Songo took a deep breath. He was sweating again, his forehead beading, stains in his uniform deepening.

"They mean to attack?" he asked hoarsely.

"That I cannot say. But their question to me indicates the possibility."

"Oh yes," Songo said bitterly. "They plan it, they plan it!"

"I do not know what you can do," Anokye said sadly. "You are a general, true. You command the armed forces. But you..."

"Not the entire army," Songo said angrily. "There are units not under my command."

"Of course," Anokye said. "But you have the northern zone. Your forces, in numbers, are the largest in Togo, are they not?"

"That is true."

"Unfortunately, you have no direct voice in foreign policy. Nevertheless, I thought it my duty to warn you."

General Songo stepped forward and placed one large,

damp hand on the Little Captain's shoulder.

"For which I extend my thanks and the thanks of my people," he said portentously.

Anokye nodded gravely. "It was my duty," he repeated. "A soldier's duty. I only wish there was some way you could alert your government to the seriousness of the situation."

General Songo gave a short, mean bark of laughter. "They won't become alert to the situation until Benin rockets land in Lomé."

"Ahh," President Obiri Anokye said slowly, as if a solution had just occurred to him. "That presents a possibility. Let us discuss it..."

He led the general out farther into the cruel sunlight, knowing how the blaze would weaken the man, deafen him to reason, scramble his wit, and make him eager to conclude any foolish agreement so that he might seek shade and comfort.

"It was the burning of the museum at Ighobo that aroused Benin," Anokye said. "Personally, I do not feel that Togo was guilty of that desecration. But what I believe is of no importance. The Benin believe you did it, and prepare for war. Would not a similar attack by Benin within your borders convince those ostrich civilians who head your government that your nation is in peril?"

Songo looked at him, wet features twisted, not comprehending.

"Well...certainly, Mr. President. A direct attack on Togo would surely make our politicos realize the dangers we face."

"You believe, in the event of war, that Togo could defeat Benin?"

"Of course."

"So do I." Here Anokye paused a moment, poked his head forward, stared at Songo keenly. "Especially with the troops and weapons of Asante."

The general caught his breath. "What are you suggesting, Mr. President?"

"That we, you and I, create an incident that will make war between Togo and Benin inevitable. That when that war begins, troops, tanks, and weapons of Asante are made immediately available—under your command, of course—to aid Togo in that war. That upon the successful completion of hostilities, you yourself—again with Asante's aid—take control of the Togolese government, nation, and people. I did it in Asante; there is no reason why you cannot do it in Togo."

This bright prospect did not stagger Gen. Kumayo Songo. Anokye was certain the man had dreamed it himself. Many times.

Songo began pacing, chin in hand, the other hand supporting the elbow. He did not look at Anokye.

"Possible," he murmured. "Possible. Not for myself, of course. But to rescue my beloved country."

"To be sure," the Little Captain said.

"The poor," Songo said. "The hungry."

"The impoverished masses," President Obiri Anokye added. "With Asante's oil money behind you, so much could be done to forge a great, strong nation. And after the military had stabilized the country, it could be returned to civilian rule. Limited civilian rule. The military would remain strong, a vital policy-making force in government."

"But Mr. President," Songo said, somewhat bewildered, "it all hinges on convincing our present politicians that war with Benin is inevitable. You mentioned creating an incident...?"

President Anokye said he had some ideas on that.

12.

PETER TANGENT, IN ENGLAND, cabled President Obiri
Anokye, in Asante, that he had contacted the manage-
ment counseling firm of Fisk, Twiggs & Sidebottom,
Ltd., of London, and suggested they send a personal
representative to Mokodi to learn first-hand from the
President what services he required.

Bemused by the names, Anokye rather hoped Mr.
Sidebottom would appear. But it was Mr. Samuel Fisk
who presented his credentials at the palace and requested
an audience with the President. He was a portly, imposing
man, clad in a white linen suit, white shirt, white tie, white
socks, white shoes. He resembled movie actor Sidney
Greenstreet. Just to see him conjured up visions of
peacock chairs, beaded curtains, fezzed waiters, and
Turkish cigarettes smoked in long ivory holders.

He addressed Anokye as "Dear sir," and was voluble and confident as he outlined what Fisk, Twiggs & Sidebottom, Ltd., could do for the Republic of Asante and for President Anokye personally. A complete on-the-scene examination of all government operations, chain of command, areas of responsibility, work flow, paper handling, production norms, future needs, and so forth. The study would be made by a senior investigator and his assistant, would require a minimum of four weeks and, preferably, would include a time study of the President's daily activities.

"Indispensably necessary, dear sir," Mr. Fisk said. That was the way he talked. Economic factors were "importantly significant." The senior investigator was "knowledgeably experienced." Even Asante was "fruitfully verdant."

At the completion of the survey, the investigators would return to London with the raw data. There, senior analysts would construct a computer model of the present Asante government, including President Anokye's role. By feeding various suggestions to the computer, they could then evolve an improved model that optimized efficiency, minimized intramural conflicts, and futurized consumer needs and production requirements. Recommendations would then be sent to the President outlining a specific program of changes in methodology to achieve the ideal, computer-created Asante.

Somewhat bedazzled by all this, Anokye signed contracts, shook the firm hand of Mr. Samuel Fisk, and showed him to the door, reflecting hopefully that the projected analysis could do no harm, even if it proved useless.

A week later, the senior investigator of Fisk, Twiggs & Sidebottom, Ltd., appeared at the palace in Mokodi, trailed by his assistant. If Mr. Fisk had been Sidney Greenstreet, Ian Quigley was Ronald Colman, and assistant Joan Livesay was Claudette Colbert. And if the Little Captain saw all these personae as movie stars, it was, he decided, because the entire project had a fictional, dream-like quality about it, theatrical and faintly ridiculous.

Quigley was English, though much given to
Americanisms—"nuts and bolts," "the nitty-gritty,"
"separate the men from the boys," "meaningful dialogue,"
"viable scenario," and so forth. He was a slender, quick
man of medium height. Brown hair receding into a
widow's peak. Innocent brown eyes. A warm smile and
affable manner. His shoes were rubber-soled. And he
wore paisley waistcoats and seemed unaffected by the
Asante sun.

The assistant, Joan Livesay, was also English, though
her accent was subtly different from Quigley's. (Tangent
later told Anokye that Quigley's accent was upper, but
that of Joan Livesay was "more upper.") She was,
perhaps, five centimeters taller than the Little Captain.
After her first meeting with him, she was careful to wear
flat-heeled shoes or sandals. She also wore white gloves.
Constantly. She was a young, quiet, pleasant woman,
subdued in appearance, but with a wry wit. She
sometimes made him laugh, for which he was grateful. He
liked her hair: brown mixed with grey, cut like a boy's,
parted on the left and brushed flat to her skull.

During their initial meeting with the President, they
explained how they hoped to operate. Ian Quigley would
roam all over the place, inspecting staff offices inside the
palace and government installations outside. He would
ask questions of everyone, armed with a letter of
authorization from the President. Joan Livesay would
dog the footsteps of Obiri Anokye, keeping a careful
account of his daily activities: where he went, what he did,
the officials he saw, etc.

"Please understand, Mr. President," Ian Quigley said
briskly, "I have no desire to intrude in those areas that are
off-limits for reasons of national security. Or for any
reasons you deem sufficient. And Miss Livesay has no
need to eavesdrop on any conversations or conferences of
a confidential nature. Goodness, that's three 'cons' in one
sentence. You'll think me a con man. Ha! But in those
cases where you desire secrecy, it would help if we could
be told the general nature of the work being done. That is,
if it concerns foreign relations or military, economic,
social, political, or personal matters. Even that much

would help us to finalize our report."

"I believe that could be done," Anokye agreed. "Miss Livesay, I fear you will find following me about something of a trial. Not very exciting."

"I'm sure it will prove very interesting, Mr. President," she said politely. Her voice was low and agreeable, and she usually kept her eyes cast down. He thought her possibly shy. Or perhaps it was a professional trick: by self-effacement to fade, as it were, into the walls, so he might come to forget or ignore her presence, and act more naturally, speak more freely.

So the project began. Ian Quigley was here, there, everywhere. He carried a pocket tape recorder into which he dictated low-voiced comments as he roamed. Occasionally he whipped out a miniature Japanese camera and took photographs of office layouts, filing facilities, the exterior of the Mokodi barracks, the fleet of cars used by palace personnel, and so forth.

Each morning, when he came down from his third-floor bedroom to his second-floor office, Obiri Anokye found Joan Livesay awaiting him, steno notebook ready, pen poised. She looked as eager as a sparrow, and after a few days he found himself welcoming her bright, "Good morning, Mr. President!" He had requested that both investigators speak English in his presence. But occasionally Miss Livesay essayed a word or phrase in Akan. She told him she was fascinated by the language and determined to learn it.

By the time Peter Tangent returned to Mokodi, the representatives of Fisk, Twiggs & Sidebottom, Ltd., had become familiar sights about Mokodi, and their presence at palace receptions caused no comment, other than frequently expressed curiosity if they slept together. And if so, did she remove her white gloves and he his paisley waistcoat? There wasn't much else to talk about in Mokodi.

Tangent introduced himself to Ian Quigley at the Mokodi Hilton bar. His first reaction was favorable; he thought Tony Malcolm had selected a good man. Quigley was easy in manner, bright, open. Nothing obviously devious or quirky about him.

Tangent asked, idly, if he had yet made the acquaint-
ance of Jonathon Wilson, the American Cultural
Attaché. Quigley said he had not. Tangent proposed
bringing them together at an informal dinner.

"You'll like him," he told Quigley. "Your kind of man."
There was no reaction to this, but Tangent expected none.
He went on: "He knows a lot about Asante, and the
government in particular. Might be able to help you out."

"Good," Quigley said. "I need all the help I can get.
Very kind of you. Speaking of help, what're my chances of
taking a look at those oil rigs of yours?"

"Just say when," Tangent said. "I'll make the arrangements."

"Thank you. Right now I'm trying to get the overview.
The oil seems important to Asante's economy."

"Essential," Tangent said. "But I'm prejudiced," he
laughed. "Anything else I can do for you?"

"Nooo, not at the moment, thanks. Joan may have
some questions."

"Joan?"

"Joan Livesay. My Girl Friday. She's doing the time
study on the President's activities. Poor girl—he works
late. Was it at it till midnight last night. And then, I
understand, he took work up to his bedroom."

"Well, she can't follow him there!" Tangent said.

"Not likely," Quigley said. An amused smile. "Not her
cup of tea at all, at all. Bit of a mouse, our Joan."

They chatted pleasantly for two drinks. Then Quigley
excused himself to go upstairs to his room and transcribe
his recorded notes.

"I hope you're getting some useful stuff," Tangent said,
looking into the investigator's eyes.

"No doubt about it," Quigley said, staring back at
him. "I think the home office will be satisfied."

At the same time Tangent and Ian Quigley were
meeting in the Mokodi Hilton bar, Joan Livesay was
seated in a straight chair in the palace corridor outside the
President's second-floor office and conference room. The
chair had been placed there for her convenience during
meetings at which her presence, however silent and
unobtrusive, was not desired. She accepted this banish-

ment as part of her job; it did not offend her. The chair was placed slightly away from the two armed soldiers guarding the room. It was not a particularly comfortable chair, but she had patience and the gift of repose. She spent her time studying a dictionary of Akan, trying the liquid syllables in a low voice.

About an hour previously, Col. Jim Nkomo, Sam Leiberman, and Sgt. Sene Yeboa had arrived within a few minutes of each other and were immediately admitted to the President's office. The visitors had already met Joan Livesay and greeted her in a friendly fashion, the two blacks calling her "Miss Livesay," and Leiberman calling her "Toots." After the three were present, Anokye had asked her to step outside.

When the three finally emerged, nothing in their expression or manner indicating if they were happy or unhappy with the conference, they nodded good-night to her and stalked away, conversing in low voices. When she reentered the office, President Anokye was replacing in his top desk drawer a sheaf of what appeared to her to be multi-colored maps. He motioned her, not to her usual station on a leather couch in a far corner of the room, but to an armchair at the side of his desk.

"Please forgive the length of the meeting," he said. "But we had much to discuss. It concerned matters of national security."

"May I list the hour as being devoted to military matters, Mr. President?" she asked.

He thought a moment. "Yes," he said. "Military. That should cover it. I think my official day is at an end, Miss Livesay. But first I intend having a cup of coffee. Will you join me."

"Thank you," she said, pleased. "That would be nice."

He lifted his phone and spoke to someone, ordering coffee—and brioche, if they were available.

"That is certainly one improvement needed," he smiled at her after he hung up. "Please make a note in your journal that when the President of Asante desires a cup of coffee in his office, he must call the main-floor receptionist, who then relays the order to the kitchen. I have no direct contact."

"I have already noted it, Mr. President," she said softly. "The palace needs a good intercom system."

"You are very efficient," he said admiringly. "Perhaps some good will come of this after all."

"I'm sure it will," she murmured.

She sat silently while he flipped through the evening edition of the Mokodi *New Times*. He was, she thought, an attractive man. Not handsome in a conventional way, but—well . . . exciting. There was no mistaking his blunt force. Much of that was physical; his energy seemed limitless. But there was something else. Psychical. His sureness, his absolute certainty. He had the same oneness Ajaka had. But in the butler it was dandyism. In Obiri Anokye it was solemnity of purpose, and absolute belief in his own destiny. She could understand his popularity, why he held so many in thrall. He was complete.

He tossed the paper aside when Ajaka knocked and came padding in with a tray of coffee and pastries.

"Good evening, my president," the butler said, in French. "Good evening, missy."

"Good evening, Ajaka," Miss Livesay said. Of all the people she had met since her arrival in Asante, Ajaka was one of her favorites. She admired the elegance with which he moved, admired his natural, flamboyant display of jewelry, admired his presence, his completeness as a human being. He obviously saw nothing menial in his job, but was proud of his smooth deftness with creamer and sugar tongs.

When the butler had bowed himself out, Anokye and Miss Livesay settled back with coffee cups. No brioche had been available, but Ajaka had brought fresh petit fours.

"You like him?" Anokye said, looking at her shrewdly.

"Ajaka? Oh yes."

"The man is an actor," he laughed. "All Fulani are actors. Fulani is Ajaka's tribe."

"I can't keep the tribes straight," she confessed. "So many of them."

"Tribes are no longer important," he said.

"So you said in your Zabarian speech, Mr. President."

"Oh?" he said. "You read my speech? I am honored.

Was the speech noted in London?" He knew very well.

"It surely was," she said. "Printed in full in the *Times*."

"A speech by an African in the *Times*," he marveled.

"Only because it was so short," she said, her smile taking the sting from her words, and they both laughed.

"I am a great believer in short speeches," he said. "If one speaks at length, there is danger of saying too much."

"Or putting your audience to sleep," she said.

"Yes," he agreed. "That, too. Are you familiar with Abraham Lincoln's Gettysburg Address?"

"I've heard of it;" she said dryly.

"Very short," he said. "Very powerful."

She leaned forward to select a pastry from the tray on the desk. Sitting slightly to one side of her, he saw the bulge of her breast. It shocked him. He had never noticed her body, never considered her as a woman. She wore prim, cover-up dresses, loosely fashioned, concealing bosom, thighs, buttocks. And those white gloves signaled memsahib to all of Africa, the Middle and Far East. Now he was suddenly conscious of what might exist beneath. Not only beneath the tent-dresses, but beneath the shy, quiet, withdrawn manner. Was there something there?

"You have never been married?" he asked her bluntly.

"No, Mr. President, I never have."

"But you are young. You will be."

"Shall I? I am not certain I wish to be. Some people, I think, should not marry."

He brooded on that for a moment.

"Yes," he said, "that is true. But sometimes it is necessary."

"I haven't yet congratulated you on your approaching marriage, Mr. President."

"Thank you. I hope you will have the opportunity to meet my fiancée. A charming girl."

"I'm sure she is. Will you be working upstairs tonight, Mr. President?"

"Working? Well, if reading is working, then I will be working. And perhaps some correspondence. Personal letters."

"What are you reading? This is not for my notebook. Just personal curiosity."

"What am I reading? Let me see.... It is my habit to keep two or three books going at once. Tonight I think I shall read more of a history of the ancient Persian empire. Do you enjoy history?"

"Oh yes. Very much."

"What is your favorite era?"

"Eighteenth-century Europe."

"Oh? My interests, at the moment, go farther back than that. Almost pre-history. Miss Livesay, may I trouble you to draw the drapes for me?"

It was such an odd request, so out of character for him, that she was startled. But obediently she set empty coffee cup and saucer on the desk, rose, walked to the windows, reached up, twitched the drapes closed.

He watched her move. The haunch showing briefly beneath the stuff of her skirt. When she reached high, he saw the strength of her back, indentation of waist. Fine hair clung to her skull like a helmet.

"Thank you," he said, rising. "Your coffee is finished? Then perhaps we will end the day and I will say goodnight. I will see you again in the morning."

She had memorized a blessing in Akan. "May you awake stronger and younger," she said.

He looked at her in pleased surprise.

"*Very* good, Miss Livesay," he said, in English. Then he spoke a sentence in Akan.

She shook her head.

"I'm sorry. I didn't catch a word of it."

"I said, 'May your dreams of tonight become the happiness of tomorrow.'"

"Oh," she said faintly. Blushing. "Thank you."

13.

"AHH, THIS IS THE LIFE," Sam Leiberman sighed. "I wonder what the poor folks are doing?"

He lolled back in the passenger seat of the white air-conditioned Mercedes-Benz limousine belonging to Starrett Petroleum Corp. Tangent was driving. With some trepidation, he had invited Leiberman and Dele to join him on a jaunt to Lomé to have dinner with Amina Dunama. They would stay for her performance, perhaps have a few drinks later.

Now the Ivory Coast girl sat happily, cross-legged and alone on the brocaded back seat, working a cat's cradle, while Leiberman slouched comfortably next to Tangent. He smoked a bent Italian cigar, watched the world whiz by as they sped along the coast road to the Togolese border.

"I thought we'd play it by ear," Tangent said casually. "If we're having a good time, we can stay over. No need to drive back tonight."

Leiberman turned his head to look at him, then laughed. "You're as hard to read as a billboard at five paces. Does the cunt know you're coming?"

"Don't call her that," Tangent said sharply.

"Pardon me all to hell, bwana. Does Miss Amina Dunama know you are arriving?"

"No," Tangent said. "I wanted to surprise her."

"Oh, you'll surprise her," Leiberman said. "Probably in the sack with some big black stud. Is that why you brought me along—in case there's trouble?"

"Don't be silly," Tangent said. Wondering if Leiberman was right. "What trouble? If she doesn't want to see me, she doesn't have to. My God, Sam, we're just friends. Acquaintances, really."

"Oh sure," Leiberman said. "And Dele is my mother. Hey, look at that—that's new."

He jerked a thumb at a roadside stand offering le hot dog and les hamburgeurs.

"Haven't seen a McDonald's yet," Leiberman said, "but it's just a question of time. Jesus, how Africa is changing. And so fast. Right in front of my eyes."

"How long have you been out, Sam?"

"Since World War the Second." He was silent a moment, then continued dreamily: "You should have seen it then. All open. Miles and miles of miles and miles. Nothing. I mean nothing. It was glorious. Now witchdoctors get around on Honda motorcycles. Well, what the hell; it had to happen. There was a lot of shit in the old days. Still is, but getting less. Now they got air pollution, hard drugs, and television commercials, just like every other civilized country. Know what did it?"

"What?" Tangent asked.

"Dry martinis," Leiberman said. "Once every gook bartender learned to mix a martini, I knew the end was near."

Tangent laughed. "Wait'll they hear about Harvey Wallbangers."

"Don't tell me," Leiberman said. "I don't want to know."

Armed with their Asante passports (handed over folded on a dash) and official documents, they had no trouble at the border.

"You dig this c—this Amina lady?" Leiberman asked.

"I enjoy her company," Tangent said carefully.

"Tell me, do you really know what the hell you're doing?"

"No," Tangent said.

"Good on you," Leiberman said. "Maybe there's more in your veins than bunker oil number six. Let me tell you something about African women..."

"Tell me, daddy."

"Screw it," Leiberman said. "Learn the hard way—like I did."

Traffic slowed them as they came into Lomé.

"Early for dinner," Leiberman said. "But we can have a few drinks somewhere while you call your ebony Cleopatra."

"Uh," Tangent said. "As a matter of fact, I took a suite at the Europa. I thought it would be handier."

"Oh, you sly goyische devil!"

"Well, they can take care of the car, and we can freshen up."

"Freshen up. Beautiful."

"Shut up," Tangent said. "It has two bedrooms and a sitting room."

"Two bedrooms," Leiberman said. "That *is* handy. One for Dele and Amina, and one for you and me."

"I'm sorry I invited you," Tangent said.

"Well, I do hope you ordered flowers for my room," Leiberman said.

But an hour later, all were in their glory. Leiberman had taken one look at the hotel suite, intoned, "Eminently habitable," had taken off jacket, tie, and shoes, and immediately called room service. Soon he was confortable with a quart of malt Scotch, a siphon of soda, a tub of cubes. Dele, curled on the floor, was spooning madly into a liter of pistachio ice cream. And, after several

increasingly desperate phone calls, Peter Tangent had
located Amina Dunama, who laughed delightedly when
she heard his voice and promised to join them within the
hour.

Which she did. Wearing strap sandals on those long,
elegant feet Tangent remembered so well. She was also
wearing something called "elephant pants"—big, green,
floppy slacks that she made at once amusing, chic, and
sexy. And a tightly fitted tanktop of bright purple cotton.
Gold hoops in her ears. A fake jewel pasted onto the flare
of a nostril. Ebony Cleopatra indeed! With a kiss for
Dele, a kiss for Sam. A kiss for Peter Tangent.

Laughter. Disco music from a local radio station.
And—Tangent pushing his luck—four bottles of champagne brought up and iced by a grinning waiter who
became their slave when he discovered that Leiberman
spoke Hausa. It was, Tangent decided, going to be all
right.

He got her over to a corner, supplied her with a glass of
champagne, one of his Players, and placed a hand lightly
on her bare shoulder.

"I thought of you," he said in a low voice. "Did you
think of me?"

"What was your name again?" she asked.

"Mr. Tangent, sir," he said.

"No." She shook her head. "Sorry. Never heard of such
a name."

He had kept a perfect memory of her: the tall, bony,
spindliness. Brown skin's midnight sheen at fold of elbow,
crease of neck. High cheekbones, high brow. Black curls
fitting as snugly as a knitted cap. Slanted, luminous eyes,
and a smile so wide, so deep, that the pink gum showed
above perfect teeth. And eely arms. He did not think it
was her exoticness that moved him. But he was not sure.

"You have been well?" he asked.

"Oh yes. I am never ill. And you?"

"Fine. We came to hear you sing."

"Such a long trip just to hear me sing!"

"Not so long. Can you have dinner with us first?"

"Of course. As usual, I am hungry."

They turned back to Dele and Sam, who were dancing,

together but separately, to rhumba rhythm.

"The hippo and the gazelle," Tangent said.

"Whites dance the step, blacks dance the beat," she said.

"And never the twain shall meet," he said.

"Do you believe that?"

"Would I be here if I did? All right, everybody, dinner-time! Where to?"

But their party seemed to be kindling its own joyous momentum, and the business of moving on would halt it. Or so they felt. Dinner in the suite would be the solution. Their very own dining room. Private service. The grinning Hausa waiter was summoned.

They plied him with malt Scotch chased with champagne, and he planned a marvelous dinner for them: prawns in a pepper sauce, whole roast kid with white truffles, baked yams and mashed plantains, a cold salad of imported asparagus and endive. This banquet would be theirs, he assured them, within minutes. And weaved his way out the door.

After thirty minutes had passed, and not even the peppered prawns had put in an appearance, Tangent got on the phone. Not only was their dinner not being prepared, but it had not even been ordered from the kitchen. In any event, a whole roast kid was not available at the Hotel Europa.

Tangent was elected, by acclamation, to investigate. Putting on his dignity with his raw silk jacket, he descended to the hotel kitchen to discover their Hausa waiter had disappeared. He was found, eventually, sleeping peacefully in the laundry room, a smile twitching his lips. After consultation with the chef, Tangent ordered four large broiled veal chops, baked yams, and a salad of mixed greens.

He returned to the suite to find that hunger pains had not diminished the hilarity. His description of the unconscious waiter produced another paroxysm, and they were still laughing, and drinking, when their dinner was wheeled in.

It was escorted by the assistant manager of the Hotel Europa, a fat, fluttery Swiss wearing a morning coat and

striped trousers. Because the suite had been reserved in
the name of Starrett Petroleum Corp., he had arrived to
offer his personal apologies. He couldn't have been
sweeter, and Sam Leiberman insisted on kissing him to
prove they harbored no ill-will toward him or the Hotel
Europa for the loss of their whole roast kid.

The dinner was uproarious, a polyglot contest of
English, French, Akan, Yoruba, and Boulé. Leiberman
declaimed a limerick in Swahili he said was so obscene
that it defied translation. Amina sang a ditty in Fon. Dele
chanted a short school verse in Pidgin English. And not to
be outdone, Tangent recited, in Latin, the opening
paragraph of Caesar's *Gallic Wars*.

Finally, it was time for Amina's performance. She was
doing one show a night at a scruffy nightclub out toward
Porto-Séguro. It was, in fact, though not even Lieberman
was aware of it, the same nightclub where Yakubu had
located the politico Nwabala and where Yvonne Mayer
had lured him to his doom.

It was crowded that night, plywood bar jammed, most
of the tables occupied. The floor creaked and groaned
under the stamping feet of frenzied dancers. The air was
milky with smoke and smelled of hashish.

"Throats cut while you wait," Leiberman commented.

Tangent paid a healthy dash, and they were escorted to
what had originally been a stall, set with a scarred table
and two rickety benches. Leiberman insisted they order
something sealed. Surprisingly, the harried waiter
brought them a half-gallon jug of California zinfandel.

"Now how did this get here?" Tangent wondered.

"Probably a disaster-aid shipment from the U.S.,"
Leiberman said. "When I was in Biafra, a shipment came
in that was ten thousand tubes of shaving cream and
sixteen crates of sanitary napkins."

After a while the three-piece band stopped playing and
picked up their bottles of millet beer. Some of the dancers
returned to the bar or tables. Many just wandered about,
carrying their drinks, greeting friends. The crowd was
mostly black, but with a dusting of tourists talking loudly
and looking as if they expected to be staked out on an
anthill any minute.

A waiter made a half-hearted effort to clear the dance floor. He didn't succeed, but there was a small, empty circle for Amina Dunama when she came strolling out slowly, carrying her mandolin. She was wearing the same gown she wore when Tangent first saw her—the silver-grey silk number, hung from her bony shoulders with rhinestone straps. The audience quieted. She strummed a few chords and began to sing.

Something had happened to her voice since Tangent last heard her. Perhaps it was just this one night. Perhaps it was due to the cigarettes she had smoked in the hotel suite, the loud talk and shouted laughter. Whatever the cause, her voice had lost that annoyingly thin, reedy sound, the mechanical phrasing. Now it was low, husky, befitting such a large woman. Maybe he imagined it, since he could not understand the language, but it seemed to him there was genuine feeling, something deepfelt in her that stirred the audience. She ended her song to enthusiastic applause.

"Son of a bitch," Leiberman said. "She's better. Did you hear it?"

"Of course I heard it," Tangent said. "What was it?"

"A love song in Ewe. Hey, she's all right. If she can keep it up."

She did. The wildly applauding audience kept her on for more than an hour. She did several types of things: ballads, fast rhythm numbers, laments. She concluded with a repetitive, guttural, half-screamed song that had the crowd yelling and stamping their feet.

"Dendi war chant," Leiberman said. "Let's go and chop their nuts off—or words to that effect. She's something, isn't she?"

She came over to their table, breathing hard and sweating. She pushed in next to Tangent, waving at the audience who were still yelling and holding their glasses up to her.

Dele, bouncing up and down in excitement, said something to her in Boulé. Amina replied in that language, and both women laughed.

"I told her my voice is changing because of the cigars I smoke," she explained to Tangent. "What did you think?"

"Wonderful," he said warmly. "I think you should stick to the blues numbers. The slow, sad things. Edith Piaf."

"Yes," she nodded. "I think so, too. I am so dry. Some wine, please?"

He filled her glass. Before she drank, she spilled a few drops onto the dusty floor.

"I haven't seen that since I got kicked out of Zambia," Leiberman said. "It's for her ancestors."

"And for good fortune," Amina said. She held up her glass. "For all of us, good fortune."

"I'll drink to that," Leiberman said. "And to anything else anyone would care to mention."

They finished the half-gallon of wine and left the nightclub, Amina still wearing her costume, Tangent carrying her mandolin. There were cabs waiting, and they selected a Peugeot they could all fit in. The driver, speaking a rapid, hissed French, offered marijuana, hashish, heroin, cocaine, opium, penicillin, quinacrine, absinthe with wormwood, milk of magnesia, or love potions. Leiberman told him to fuck off.

Tangent had devised several clever ploys to get Amina back to the hotel. He was about to essay the least fantastic when she said, "Let's go back to the hotel and have something to eat."

"My God, where do you put it?" Leiberman marveled. "You're so skinny that if you swallowed an olive you'd look pregnant. Well, I'll go for coffee and a brandy. Pete?"

"Fine with me," Tangent said carelessly.

The kitchen of the Hotel Europa was closed but a bellhop, made sympathetic with a generous dash, went hunting for an open café, and returned with a cardboard box of pepper chicken, fried shrimp, and something Leiberman called "African matzoh balls."

They sipped coffee and nibbled, more from politeness than hunger. But Amina worked her way steadily through the contents of the grease-stained box.

"Yum," she said finally, wiping her lips on the edge of the tablecloth. She dumped the naked bones into the box and clapped on the lid. "Now I feel human. What's to drink?"

"Coffee, champagne, brandy," Tangent said. "Which?"

"Everything," she said, and they stared in fascination as she first drained a cup of black coffee, then had a glass of champagne and brandy, mixed half-and-half.

"I can't watch any more of this," Leiberman said. "I hate to see a woman cry."

"I never cry," Amina said.

"Tomorrow you'll cry," he assured her. "Unless you remember that the only sure preventative for a hangover is not to stop drinking." He held the brandy bottle up to the light, then poured a large water tumbler full. "You take the glass," he told Tangent, "and I'll take the bottle. You can have what's left of the champagne."

"Where are you going?"

"Dele and I are going into the bedroom to discuss the International Monetary Fund. Care to join us?"

"No, thanks."

"Ta-ta, all," Leiberman said. "Sleep tight; don't let the bedbugs bite."

He and Dele kissed Amina. They walked slowly, hand in hand, into one of the bedrooms. Their door closed.

"Suddenly everyone's sober," Tangent said, wondering if they had ever been drunk. Not really, he decided. Just high on joy and laughter.

Amina kicked off her sandals, fished the long, thin cigars from her batik bag. She offered him one, but he shook his head. She lighted up, sprawled in a cushioned armchair. She slumped far down, sitting on the edge of her spine, long legs spread beneath the silk gown.

"Tired?" he asked.

She nodded. "Only an hour each night, but it wearies me. That is strange."

"Where do you go next?"

"They're keeping me here for another two weeks. Then on to Cotonou. A nicer place. A hotel lounge. Will you come to see me?"

"Yes," he said immediately.

"Good. I want you to. You are good luck for me."

"Am I?" he said, pleased.

She held out her glass. He divided the remaining champagne between them.

"Brandy?" he asked.

"Later," she said. "Mr. Tangent, sir."

"Oh, you do remember the name?"

She grinned, the wide open, toothy grin that ignited her entire face.

"I have a present for you," he said. "I brought it from London."

"Good," she said. "I like presents. When do I get it?"

"Now if you like."

"No," she said. "Later. After."

"After what?"

"Ho-ho," she said.

She lazily lifted a hand, pointed a long forefinger at him, thumb up, like a cocked gun. Her nails were painted green. How had he not seen her hands before? Slender hands and articulated. Nails curved like talons. Boned, supple hands. Tight knuckles shining. The pink palms were maps.

"Where in the United States were you born, Mr. Tangent?"

"Indiana."

"Is that near California?"

"Not very. It's more in the middle of the country."

"What is it like?"

"Where I was born? Flat farmland. Like most of Asante and Togo."

"Did you like it?"

"No."

"So you left to see the whole, wide world," she said, laughing and clapping her hands delightedly. "Just like me."

"Oh yes," he nodded. "Then I went east to school. Two years in the army. Back to school for two more years of business administration. Then onward and upward. Just like you."

It was the first time he had told a woman the story, the dull story, of his life. He tried to keep it short and make it amusing. But she didn't smile. Just listened intently.

"The army?" she said. "Did you fight in the army? Did you kill?"

"Oh God, no. I made out payrolls."

"But you fought in the Asante coup."

"How do you know that?"

"All of West Africa knows."

"Would you like your present now?"

"No."

"Why not?"

"Because if you give it to me now, you will think what I give to you after is a debt to be paid."

"That's nonsense," he said angrily. "I won't think anything of the sort. Yow owe me no obligation."

"You are a generous white man being kind to a poor, benighted heathen?"

He groaned, leaped to his feet, raced to her chair, stooped, kissed her upturned lips.

"Oh Mr. Tangent, sir," she breathed, and her tongue flickered like wet flame.

In the bedroom, naked together, she ministered to him, saying, "Hush, hush," to his moans, like a mother soothing a fretful child. His body was lean, smooth, sprinkled with freckles and tiny black moles. Ribs and vertebrae pressed the skin, and she scraped the bones with her talons, moved her teeth lightly across fluttering abdomen, trembling chest.

"So thin," she murmured. "So white."

Her gaping mouth scrubbed him like a small sponge. When he knew he could not endure, he tried to move her head away, but she imprisoned his hands, hissing faintly, and her tongue stabbed his breast. He looked down upon her and saw a negative of himself, embraced himself, loved himself. He could not comprehend.

He gave her the pearls then, and thought reality equaled expectation for the first time in his life. She was delighted, and doubled the long rope so that chill white spheres dripped about her neck, down between her muscled breasts, coiled about empurpled nipples, rolled into a warm navel as large as a second mouth.

He put his tongue to cool pearls and fevered flesh, his eyes glistening. He lifted one loop of beads from around her neck. Then it hung in a single rope, long enough so that pale moons gleamed between night legs. He took it all into him, night and moon, dry land and moving sea. The taste was tart, spiced, tingling on the tongue, and he didn't care.

In the morning she was gone. Nothing left of her but a dark scent on the pillow, which he kissed like a poet.

He found Dele and Leiberman in the hotel restaurant, having breakfast. He joined them wordlessly and ordered what they were having: melon, croissants, coffee, cognac.

"You can stay a few days if you like," Tangent said. "It's on Starrett."

"Nah," Leiberman said. "Thanks anyway. Let's check out. I have to get back."

"Oh?" Tangent said, not looking at him. "What's happening?"

"Fun and games," Leiberman said.

14.

OBIRI ANOKYE WOULD have been astonished if anyone aware of his actions had accused him of corrupting Gen. Kumayo Songo of Togo. Patiently, the Little Captain would have pointed out there was no corruption involved; he had merely made clear to Songo how his interests and those of Anokye coincided, and how the plan he proposed would further those interests. It was simply a matter of mutual benefit. The President had not spoken falsehoods for the sake of his own ambitions; Songo was to become preeminent in Togo, though perhaps not in the role he imagined.

In any event, having been won over, General Songo's cooperation was enthusiastic. He supplied the Little Captain with excellent maps, and revealed information concerning the strength, disposition, weapons, and combat readiness of the Togolese armed forces. Anokye did not think it wise or necessary to inform Songo of the tactics and timing of the "created incident." That way, he assured the general, he could with truth deny detailed knowledge of the raid. And though the Little Captain did not mention it, the lack of detailed knowledge would also prevent a last-minute change of heart and betrayal by the general.

Working with Colonel Nkomo, Sergeant Yeboa, and Sam Leiberman, President Anokye then planned the operation. His first inclination had been to send Leiberman in command of a group of civilian cutthroats, such as Yakubu. Then, if any should fall into Togolese hands, or be killed or wounded on Togolese soil, no proved connection with Asante could be established. (It was true that Leiberman was presently an official advisor to the Asante Government, and if captured might talk. But he was widely known in Africa as a mercenary, available to the highest bidder. Furthermore he was white and, naturally, not to be trusted.)

But as the plan evolved, it became apparent that a military operation was called for. So Anokye decided to send Nkomo, Yeboa, and Leiberman, each commanding a two-man team drawn from a special assault company Anokye had organized in 4th Brigade. It was modeled after the Commando-Ranger concept. The Little Captain hoped eventually to increase it to battalion size with amphibious and airborne landing capabilities.

The personnel having been decided upon, it remained only to plan the approach, attack, and return. The nine men would wear civilian khaki or work clothes with no labels of national origin. They would carry no incriminating identification. Obiri Anokye specified the weapons. This was the kind of thing he did well and enjoyed most.

At midnight, the three three-man teams slipped across the unguarded "green border" into Togo at a point where that country was scarcely 100 km. wide. The time of the raid had been planned to take advantage of the light of a full moon, and they spent the hours till dawn moving eastward, climbing and descending the north-south chain of the Togo Hills. They used smugglers' trails, Sergeant Yeboa's team leading the way, Leiberman's in the middle,

Colonel Nkomo's in the rear. They moved strung out on the trail, the moonlight strong enough to maintain visual contact. By dawn, they had come down onto the flat savanna, and took time out to rest, drink water, eat some food, and relieve themselves in the tall grass.

Within an hour, the three teams had separated and were on their way again, carrying their weapons in flour sacks, burlap bags, or cheap cardboard suitcases strapped to their backs. They hoped to pass as farmers coming from market or itinerants looking for work. If stopped and questioned, Leiberman was prepared to impersonate a drunken white man who had "gone native," a role in which he needed no coaching.

The Little Captain's orders allowed them considerable latitude in their method of traveling, the only requirement being that they arrive at their destination on time. So all three teams, at some point during the day, took advantage of "mammy wagons," a popular mode of transportation in West Africa, particularly favored by the market women who, in some areas, ruled the local economy.

Mammy wagons were ramshackle flatbed trucks with makeshift stake sides and wooden benches. Usually operating on no fixed schedule, stopping whenever and wherever a passenger wished to climb on or off, the rattling trucks offered perfect anonymous transport for the Asante attack teams who blended in with the motley crowds aboard. Their weapons bags attracted no attention; practically everyone else was carrying similar burdens.

As planned, all three teams passed their destination late in the evening and went on close to the border of Benin. Here, at a predetermined map position, they rendezvoused in a wooded area, drank water, ate, slept, and waited for nightfall.

The most important factor of the assault against the selected Togolese army post was that it be made from the east, as if from Benin. Tricky business, since it required that some of the Togolese defenders be allowed to live in order to report the direction from which the attack had come.

The assault was scheduled for 0200, just before the

guard was changed. Anokye reasoned that at that hour, despite the alert of Togolese army units ordered since the trouble with Benin began, many of the sentries would be bored with their uneventful tour of duty, nodding on post, or actually asleep.

The Asante force checked their weapons and gear at midnight and, with Yeboa again leading the way, began the final approach. They moved slowly in three columns of three men each, in a rough arrowhead formation, the point (Yeboa) guiding on an unimproved road leading from the Benin border inland to the Togolese army post south of the village of Kamina.

According to information supplied by Gen. Kumayo Songo, the normal strength of the garrison was thirty to thirty-five men commanded by a captain. Weapons were mostly aged bolt-action rifles, a few sidearms, and one antiquated Hotchkiss Modele 1916 machine gun. Perimeter defense was expected to be no more than five sentries. The post was not equipped with floodlights or searchlights, and the transportation was as old as the weapons: a single Ford truck, circa 1950, and the captain's personal Citroën 2-CV.

The six Asante soldiers were armed with Kalashnikov assault rifles. Of the team leaders, Yeboa and Leiberman carried Uzi submachine guns, and Nkomo a Thompson. All the attacking force wore Colt .45 pistols in holsters suspended from web belts, and each team carried a specific type of grenade: fragmentation, incendiary, and smoke. The three team leaders had combat knives. Their men were armed with glaives, the short, razor-sharp machete-swords issued to all Asante soldiers. These were carried in canvas scabbards (with one metal edge), usually worn slung across the back with the glaive hilt protruding above the man's left shoulder for an easy draw.

The Little Captain had ordered that the 4th Brigade assault company be given special training in night operations—not usual for African troops—and this attack group moved through the darkness with confidence and almost complete silence. Visual contact was maintained, and since every man's part in the action had been worked out by Anokye on a sand table at 4th

Brigade headquarters, there was little need for verbal communication during the final advance.

In a tactical situation of this nature, convention required surrounding the sleeping army post, or at least making a simultaneous attack from three sides. But as the Little Captain remarked, "Strategy dictates tactics." (He was fond of quoting military aphorisms.) So the attack was made only from the east, from the direction of the Benin border.

Col. Jim Nkomo was an enormous man, tall and broad, with a solid belief in his own invincibility. This, during battle, he translated into laughing courage. He grew a heavy black beard and a mustache that almost obscured his lips. His body, too, was covered with a pelt of thick, wiry hair. Leiberman called him "King Kong," a title he cherished. His tank corps were proud of him, although their respect was tinged with fear that he would, one day, get their ass shot off.

The Little Captain had selected Nkomo to lead the assault, Yeboa and Leiberman on the flanks.

The moon had set. As they came silently up to the compound, only the light of a small fire illuminated the dim outlines of the post itself: a low building of mud brick with a thatched roof. Two smaller outbuildings. The parked vehicles. The Asantis halted while Nkomo studied the terrain. Two uniformed men slept near the fire. After a few moments, a third soldier came from one of the smaller buildings and joined them, sitting on the ground, hugging his knees.

Nkomo sent his men to left and right to scout for additional sentries. The other Asantis lay full-length in undergrowth just short of the cleared compound. Nkomo's men returned within five minutes. They shook their heads. Nkomo then rose to a crouch and looked to both sides. Yeboa and Leiberman signaled their readiness.

The colonel straightened up. He threw a fragmentation grenade at the sentries' fire. He hurled it in a curious manner, not the recommended put-toss. He pitched it half-underhand, half-sidearm: a cross between an American softball pitcher and a British cricket bowler.

The grenade sailed through the air. It exploded almost directly in the sentries' fire.

The two sleeping men were hit by splinters and died without waking, their relaxed bodies absorbing the steel like bundles of rags taking axe blows. The sitting man was flung backward, his heart exposed by a small section of the serrated grenade that cut him open as neatly as a glaive.

All the Asantis were on their feet then, crouching. Leiberman's team hurled incendiary grenades onto the roofs of the main barrack, the outbuildings, the vehicles. Anokye's orders. When half-dressed and naked men came stumbling out into the night, Yeboa's team killed them with short bursts from automatic weapons.

The first Togolese soldiers were without guns. But those who came dashing out a few moments later fired rifles into the darkness, aiming at their attackers' gun flashes. A few weapons began to wink from the post's windows and doorways.

Nkomo pitched another grenade and, waving his men on, rushed after it, firing his Thompson, grinning. The roof of the post was aflame now; both sides could see their targets clearly.

Leiberman led his men in a rush, firing his Uzi in staccato bursts. He was not surprised to find he was screaming as wildly as the Asantis. He dropped to one knee, spraying the windows and doorways from which most of the return fire was coming. More fragmentation grenades exploded inside the main building. The roof seemed to rise a few inches, then collapsed inside the walls.

A grossly fat Togolese soldier came tiptoeing in a dainty way from the flaming ruins, firing his rifle as quickly as he could work the bolt. His face was squinched with fear and shock. He was naked. His obese body glistened; the pores seemed to exude grease. Several Asanti guns were brought to bear on this huge target, as if the attackers feared a single bullet could never bring down that great hulk. But down he went, falling face-forward into the dust, billows of suet pocked with a score of holes that oozed blood slowly.

The Asantis closed on a tight line. Anokye's orders. But not without casualties. One of Nkomo's men went spinning backward, jaw shot away. One of Leiberman's men sat down suddenly, hands pressing his belly in bewilderment. Still they crushed forward, driving the Togolese back. They were reddened by flames, blood, fury.

Into the burning building itself. Men pressed thigh to thigh, hot and screaming, eyes glaring. A few defenders battered and scrambled their way out over the crumbling rear wall. Those who chose to stand held up empty rifles in an attempt to ward off the flashing glaives. An entire head went sailing, the trunk standing a moment, spouting blood from the severed neck before crumpling to earth. An arm lying by itself in the dust, fingers slowly flexing. An ear. Things.

Then all Togolese within the post were down. The Asantis heard the sound of survivors crashing through the bush westward, heard a long, keening wail that seemed never to end.

They killed all the wounded, they mutilated all the dead. Anokye's orders. Then they regrouped. Nkomo's man, the one with the jaw shot away, was dead. Leiberman's soldier, the one with the belly wound, was still alive and conscious. He looked up at them meekly. Sergeant Yeboa stooped over him, patted his cheek, put his Colt .45 close to the man's temple, pulled the trigger once. They threw their two casualties into the burning building. There were other wounds, but minor. Everyone alive could move under his own power.

They tossed a ring of smoke grenades in case brave survivors attempted pursuit. They retreated eastward to pick up their gear, to conceal weapons in sacks, bags, suitcases. Then the teams separated, moved south as planned, struck out westward, heading home in mammy wagons.

15.

BEATRICE DA SILVA, mistress of her father's home, sat at the foot of the long glass table and peremptorily rang a small crystal bell. Immediately, three servants—one Ewe, two Cabrai—entered and began deftly to clear the table of the dinner dishes. Obiri Anokye looked admiringly at Beatrice. She sat haughty, upright, watching the servants' movements with keen eyes. He began to get a new insight into what she might be: a slave in the bedroom, a tyrant in the kitchen. He was not displeased.

She was plumpish and jolly, more girl than woman. A ruddy glow beneath the dark brown of her skin. Deep-bosomed, wide-hipped, with smooth, exciting legs. A face unmarked by experience or reflection. A tittering laugh, a swollen-eyed engrossment in anything a man might say to her. To which she would reply, "Really? Fantastic! How marvelous!" and so on. Anokye believed her a virgin, burning.

Premier Benedicto da Silva sat regally at the head of the table. President Anokye on his right. On Anokye's right, Asante Minister of State Jean-Louis Duclos. Across from them, in casual loneliness, Christophe Michaux, the Premier's aide. He touched his little goatee occasionally, once or twice patted his marcelled and oiled hair. The significant glances he aimed at Duclos did not go unnoticed by Anokye. But he was watching for them, alerted by Sam Leiberman's report.

"This Michaux cat, Mr. President," Leiberman had said. "The way I get it, he's playing footsie with the Reds. The Russians, not the Chinese. There's both varieties in Benin right now, lots of them, and more coming in. The way I hear it, Michaux is King Shit with Moscow. Maybe they're grooming him to take over."

"Da Silva is aware of this?"

"My source says no. Da Silva knows his secretary leans to the left, but he thinks Michaux is just a brainy kid kicking up his heels. I Mean, Michaux isn't an out-and-out Marxist. Not in public, he ain't. He covers it with an 'Africa for the Africans' line. Solidarity forever and let's kill all the whites. That kind of crap."

"His private life?"

"That's where it gets sticky. Back in the States they call 'em chickenhawks. Meaning he likes little boys. We all like little boys, Mr. President, but not the way Michaux does. I mean he *likes* them."

"I see," Anokye said. "Thank you."

Premier Da Silva looked at his daughter, and she immediately rose.

"Please don't get up, gentlemen," she said, smiling sweetly. She spoke a very Parisian French. "Continue your conversation. I'll see to coffee."

"Perhaps the Portuguese brandy," her father said.

"Of course, daddy," she nodded, and was gone.

"An excellent meal, Premier," President Anokye said. "I thank you."

The others also murmured their appreciation. They

spoke in generalities of the problems in Angola while coffee was served, brandy poured into proper snifters. When the servants had departed, door closed, Premier Da Silva addressed Anokye directly, his face drawn and solemn.

"I pledge you my word of honor, Mr. President," he said in a somewhat hollow, shaky voice. "We had nothing to do with it."

He spoke, of course, of the cruel raid on the Togolese army post. Men mutilated. A massacre that had brought Togo and Benin close to war.

Anokye made a gesture, as if to say he accepted Da Silva's word without question.

"But I must ask you this, Premier," he said, "is it possible the attack could have been planned and executed by your military without your knowledge? By hotheads who would like nothing better than a declared war?"

Da Silva was troubled.

"I will not say we do not have such men in our military," he said slowly. "What country does not? But I cannot believe they would go to such lengths. Christophe?"

"I agree with you, Premier," Michaux said promptly. "In my own mind I cannot conceive of any Benin engaging in such an insane act."

"Nationalists?" Duclos suggested. "Fanatics? Terrorists?"

Michaux waved the suggestion away.

"A few minor groups," he said. "Ineffectual. Ridiculous, really. And constantly under watch. They are not capable of such an attack."

Obiri Anokye looked at him directly.

"Then what is your explanation?"

"I simply do not know, Mr. President. But in my own mind, I have a—a foreboding that we are being manipulated. By an outside force. The CIA, perhaps."

"Nonsense," Da Silva said curtly. "Next you will be blaming them for our lack of rainfall."

"It is possible they staged the raid, Premier," Michaux said stubbornly. "They move in hidden ways. And, of course, they have the money to buy these things—the murder of Nwabala, the burning of our museum, the massacre at Kamina."

"For what purpose?" Anokye asked softly.

"Who can tell, Mr. President? Perhaps they merely wish to make mischief, to provoke a war that ruins both countries. Then they step in and take over."

"Take over the ruins?" Anokye said. "Why would the U.S. or any other power desire to control Togo and Benin? With all due respect, Premier, your country and Togo are not economically sound. Your national resources are not sufficient to attract any of the great powers. But you are aware of this..."

"Unfortunately," nodded Da Silva mournfully. "Christophe, I cannot swallow your theory. As President Anokye said, we and Togo, together, do not represent one fish large enough to tempt anyone to cast bait. No, I do not believe the CIA is involved."

Michaux would not give up.

"Their motives do not become clear until later," he said, his words sounding foolish even to his own ears.

Then they sat in silence. Anokye was content, letting it grow. Knowing the gloom of the Benin. Finally he looked at Duclos, at Michaux.

"Please," he said gently, "I would like a few moments alone with the Premier. Jean, I will see you on the plane in the morning."

The two aides rose, murmured something polite, withdrew. Anokye waited until the door closed behind them. Then he hitched his chair closer to Da Silva.

"Courage, brother," he said. "Things are not as desperate as they may seem."

"Not desperate," Da Silva said, waving his hand. "But bleak. Depressing."

"May we speak frankly? As brothers?"

"Of course."

"I have heard, from various sources, that Russian agents are active in your country. Very active. Is that true?"

"Yes."

"I have heard further that it may be a serious attempt

to subvert the government of Benin. Do you have any information on that?"

"It—it may well be," Da Silva admitted. "They have won many friends in high places. They have made loans, taken over farms, factories, banks. They are now a force to be reckoned with."

"How do you feel about this?"

"Need you ask, Mr. President? I am a Benin, wanting only the continued independence of my country. And now there is this business with Togo. On top of our economic problems. It is all complex. Messy."

"All life is complex and messy, Premier. We find simplicity in the grave. Meanwhile, we must look for solutions."

Da Silva looked up hopefully.

"You have a solution, Mr. President?"

"Only a suggestion. A suggestion I wish you to consider carefully. You and I are close and will soon be closer, after my marriage to your daughter. You know of Asante's wealth from the oil. That wealth could help solve your economic problems. I have also modernized the Asante armed forces. They grow stronger every day. More men. New weapons. Powerful. The best in the world. Those men and those weapons could insure the victory of Benin in the event of open war with Togo."

Da Silva began to brighten, almost growing before Anokye's eyes. He straightened in his chair, sat erect. His eyes glistened. Even the silvered beard seemed to bristle.

"So now we have solved two of the problems that beset you," Anokye went on relentlessly. "Asante wealth will help you make your economy viable. Asante weapons will guarantee you victory in case of a war with Togo. Now, how may we assure the sovereignty of Benin against the aggression of the Marxists?"

The Premier listened to this lecture with fascination. The Little Captain was saying everything he wanted to hear. It seemed to him that this evening, this talk, might prove to be a turning point. In his country's destiny, and in his own career.

"I tell you frankly," Anokye said, "and I speak the truth, you are the only man I trust."

He spoke this last in Portugese. Da Silva was touched.

"Excellent, Mr. President," he said, in French. "Your accent is improving."

"Thank you. I study hard. But in any language, my meaning is the same: you, I trust. The others, the politicos, I do not trust. They are not aware of the true situation."

"They are not," Da Silva said hoarsely. "I agree."

"I will not pledge Asante wealth and Asante weapons to a country in whose government I do not have the most complete confidence," Anokye said sternly. "Do you condemn me for this?"

"Of course not, Mr. President," the Premier said hastily. "It is only common sense."

"Exactly. Common sense. Now I shall tell you what my price is for Asante francs to shore up your economy and for Asante men and weapons to insure your victory over the Togolese."

"The price?" Da Silva said. He feared the worst. This man might demand—God only knew what this resolute man might demand! "What is your price, Mr. President?"

"That you become the leader of Benin. You are a man I can trust. We shall soon be related. I know that with you in control, I can be confident that the very considerable investment I am willing to make in Benin will not be wasted on fools or those who follow foreign ideologies."

Benedicto da Silva groaned with relief and gratification. He could hardly believe his good fortune. He knew, he *knew*, all the good things he could do if he was head of state. And for agreeing to take on this task—awesome and onerous though it might be—he would guarantee his nation the beneficence of a wealthy and powerful friend.

"Mr. President," he said, rising, "I want only what is best for my country."

"I knew I could count on you," the Little Captain said, also rising. The two men shook hands, staring gravely into each other's eyes. "And now the hour is becoming late, and I must leave. I thank you for your hospitality. But I would also like to thank Beatrice. A few words before I return to Mokodi. I think I would enjoy a final cigarette on your lovely patio. If you would—?"

"I'll send her out to you, Mr. President," Premier Benedicto da Silva said quickly, "At once, sir."

Anokye strolled up and down, smoking his Gauloise and looking at the stars. They belonged to him. One told men what they wanted to hear; it was as simple as that. But still, one never spoke a falsehood, which was a sin. Da Silva would become preeminent in Benin, just as General Songo would in Togo. And both bound to him by ties stronger than political expediency. Blood. Family. It was history, in all the books. Not dates and events. History was people.

"Bibi!" she said, coming to him with outspread arms. "You are leaving? So soon!"

"So late," he grinned, tossing his cigarette away. He pressed her to him. "First, the dinner. . . . It was a thing to remember. But I beseech you, when we are married, we cannot eat like that every night. Look at this. . . ."

He patted his growing paunch. Then smiled when she patted it, too.

"I promise," she said. "Only mixed greens and perhaps some cold rice."

"Well . . ." he said. "Occasionally, the broiled grouper as you served it tonight."

"Oh!" she said, delighted. "I knew you would like it. And the chicken?"

"Magnificent," he said. "With white wine?"

"Yes," she nodded. "And bits of this and that. I learned in Paris. At school."

They strolled up and down together, his arm about her waist. She was wearing a flowing chiffon gown. Tent-like. In green. Her favorite color. Her scent was so young, so fruity. He thought of the juices.

"You set the date," he said. "As soon as possible. Within two months."

"So much to do," she said, and shivered slightly. Not so much troubled by the planning as by the sudden vision of lying naked in bed with this man. This stranger. "I don't know where it should be."

"In Asante," he said. "The palace." He laughed. "I will declare a national holiday. We shall receive many fine gifts. From all over the world."

"Oh Bibi," she sighed. "I love you so much. We're going to have such a fantastic life."

He didn't answer, but embraced her again. Kissed her warm lips. Her mouth opened to his in surrender. As his fingers pressed her back, her soft back, her soft, yielding back. All of her yielding, and soft, and warm. Conquered.

To his surprise, Jean-Louis Duclos discovered that Christophe Michaux was driving a Renault 30TS. On the way back to Cotonou from Premier Da Silva's home near Ouidah, Duclos expressed his pleasure at riding in such a luxurious car.

"So expensive," he murmured, believing it to be a government vehicle that Michaux had borrowed for the evening.

"I was going to get a light blue," Michaux said casually. "Then decided on the black. So much more tasteful, don't you think?"

"Oh yes."

"Black is beautiful," Michaux laughed.

He drove with careless ease, relaxed, fingertips barely touching the wheel. Duclos was conscious of his scent. Sandalwood perhaps.

"I was surprised President Anokye did not desire your presence during his conference with the Premier," Michaux said. He kept his eyes on the road.

Duclos stirred restlessly.

"Sometimes more is accomplished between two men, with no third party present," he said.

"Of course," Michaux said. He laughed suddenly. "Best to have no witnesses, eh?" When Duclos said nothing, Michaux continued: "The Premier, on occasion, has not desired my presence during a conversation. But I can usually guess what is going on. I imagine their conversation tonight concerns the Togo matter. No?"

"Perhaps," Duclos said, uneasy with this conversation. "Or the marriage of President Anokye to the Premier's daughter."

"Or that," Michaux admitted. "Or both. Together.

President Anokye is a very—I was about to use the word 'devious,' but I don't mean that at all. A very *complex* man. Yes, that is better. Don't you agree he is complex?"

"No, I do not," Duclos said shortly. "It seems to me his aims are quite clear. As stated in his Zabarian speech."

"Ah yes," Michaux said. "But I was not speaking of his stated aims. I had in mind his motives; his desires. But of course you would know more of that than I. You said you have been friends for many years? Even before the coup?"

"That is true. He has been to my home frequently."

"A friend of the family, so to speak. Please forgive me for not having asked sooner, but how is Mrs. Duclos? Well, I hope?"

"Thank you, yes. In good health."

"I am delighted to hear it. I gathered from our short conversation that she has no particular interest in the business of government. Am I wrong?"

"No, you are quite right. Maria is interested only in domestic things. Our home..."

"A charming lady. You are to be congratulated, minister, for selecting an African woman to be your wife. It offends me to see so many African leaders sniffing after white bitches. Forgive the coarseness of my language, but I must speak what is in my mind. To me, negritude is of primary importance."

"To me also," Duclos said.

"Good," Michaux said. "The men we are about to meet feel as we do. I think you will like them. Not much farther now."

Jean-Louis Duclos had the right to call himself "Professor." He had been, and now he was Minister of State of the Republic of Asante. By law, he was third in rank in the Asante government, following only President Obiri Anokye and Premier Willi Abraham. His was an office of some consequence, remarkable for one as light-skinned as he. In addition, he was a Martinicain, not an African, by birth.

So, in view of these honors, why, he asked himself, should he feel such inferiority to this Christophe Michaux? The man was almost as light-skinned as he, also a Martinicain, and no more than a premier's aide.

Practically a secretary. He was, he decided finally, daunted by Michaux's almost insolent self-assurance. When speaking of Obiri Anokye, his tone verged almost on contempt. As if he knew something Duclos did not know.

In addition, Duclos was as disturbed by certain portions of the Little Captain's Zabarian speech as Michaux. The Minister of State was aware that Anokye was an expedient man. The coup would not have been successful if he were not. But now, in a position of great power, president of a wealthy African state, Anokye had no need to compromise with his enemies. Whites. Yet in his speech Anokye had publicly favored a united Africa, shared by all races, colors, creeds. It was troublesome. More so because Michaux made no effort to hide his disapproval. And Duclos, in good conscience, could not defend the Little Captain.

He had supposed the premier's aide had invited him to an informal party, a get-together. He recognized almost immediately that he was attending a meeting of sorts.

It was held in a secluded private home, near the sea, off the Porto-Novo road. There were several cars already parked in the driveway when they arrived. A few government cars and two obviously military vehicles. It was also apparent to Jean-Louis Duclos that he and Michaux were the last arrivals expected; the proceedings began as soon as Duclos was introduced to the host, a glass of warm orange juice passed to him, and the lights dimmed.

The speaker, a thin, ascetic black, introduced himself to the twenty men in the room as Sumaila Jakpa, a citizen of Benin. He had, he said, recently returned from two years in the Soviet Union, during which he had been enrolled as a student of political science in Moscow University. In answer to many requests, he was presenting this short lecture—more of a personal account, really—on his experiences in Russia.

The first part of the presentation consisted of a series of color slides (of professional quality) showing various views of the Soviet Union: the Kremlin, Moscow streets, restaurants, and hotels, a tractor factory, a resort on the

Black Sea, closeup portraits of several of the many ethnic types who composed the Union of Soviet Socialist Republics.

Then the lights were turned up again. The speaker delivered a fluent précis of his experiences in the Soviet Union: the food (unusual but palatable), the weather (extremely cold but invigorating), the hospitality of the Russian people (superlative), racism (non-existent), and sympathy for the African cause (overwhelming). The meeting was then thrown open to questions.

Q: How was his two years' stay in Moscow financed?

A: By personal funds and a scholarship from the Soviet Union, available to students from all over the world.

Q: During his studies in political science, were efforts made to convert him to socialism?

A: Absolutely not. The lectures were historical in nature, and it was frequently emphasized that students were expected to return to their native countries and make their newfound knowledge and skills available to their governments, whatever their position in the political spectrum.

Q: Had attempts ever been made to recruit him into a Soviet intelligence apparat?

A: Never. Nor was he ever, to his knowledge, spied upon, followed, his mail intercepted, or his rights of free movement and expression interfered with.

He concluded by saying:

"I do not wish to leave you with the impression that the USSR is a paradise. Of course it is not. They have many problems, serious problems, not the least of which is the constant military threat posed by the USA and China. This requires Russia to devote an inordinately large share of its gross income to national defense. This is money they would much prefer to spend for such things as schools, hospitals, housing, consumer goods, and so forth. Just as we Africans would like to do.

"One final word: At no time during my two years' stay, *no* time, was I ever insulted or made to feel inferior because of my color or national origin. At a final party, when all the black students met with our professor, he reiterated in the strongest terms the Soviet Union's interest in and sympathy for black hegemony, wherever in the world blacks were still being exploited and suffering under the grinding heel of white colonialism. And he said—I remember this well—he said, 'All we ask is that you judge us by our deeds, not our words. A helping hand will always be extended from the USSR to people of any race or color groaning under oppressive tyranny. These people, in Africa and elsewhere, will find in us a good friend who desires only to free them from the tyrants' yoke and enable them to determine their own destiny as free and independent nations.' Stirring words. I shall never forget them."

The formal program then ended, and the meeting broke up into several small groups. All were talking excitedly, most of the guests trying to press close to the speaker to ask additional questions. Duclos found himself led aside by Michaux, to be introduced to two men in the Benin government. One was a statistician attached to the Ministry of Agriculture, the other an assistant to the Minister of Transportation and Communication. Like Duclos and Michaux, both government employees wore black suits, white shirts, sedate ties. They chatted a few moments, exchanging their reactions to the presentation of the Benin student.

"What did *you* think, minister?" Michaux asked.

"Very impressive," Duclos nodded. "If we can believe what they say."

"Of course," one of the others said. "But as his professor said: 'Judge us by our deeds, not our words.' And it is worthy of note that the USSR owns not a foot of African soil, and has shown no desire for any. It may be true that they have a few minor installations here and there—refueling stations for their navy, that kind of thing—but only on sufferance of the host nation."

"I was particularly interested in his comments on their views of African hegemony," Michaux said. "Africa for the Africans. Did you find that struck a sympathetic chord, minister?"

"Oh yes," Duclos agreed. "If we can trust them. After all, they too are white."

Following the student's presentation, iced highballs, cocktails, and wine had been offered in place of the warm orange juice. And after two heavy gin and bitters, Duclos found himself with senses heightened, well able to cope with whatever subjects were introduced or questions asked by these elegant men who were so obviously respectful of his station and anxious to learn his views.

The conversation bubbled. It was years since Jean-Louis Duclos had engaged in such lively discussion and debate. He was intoxicated by it, made drunk with words, the clash of ideas, the blaze of intellects, the display of philosophical depths. He was proud of these black brothers, proud of their wit, their obvious concern for the welfare and future of black Africa. And he was proud of himself, taking another gin and bitters from Michaux's outstretched hand, proud of the things he said, the way he fielded their questions, refuted their illogic, scored intellectual points. He was, he felt, their superior in political history and political science. Somehow, the conversation came around to Obiri Anokye's Zabarian speech.

"An excellent speech," one of the Benin officials declared. "Still, I wish President Anokye had stated more clearly how he intends to achieve his dream of Pan-Africa."

"He will make it plain," Duclos said wisely. "All in good time."

"But surely, minister, you can appreciate that his comments have caused concern in some quarters. Now I specifically refer to his embracement of the whites. No one can argue against the ideal of solidarity for the African continent. But why need it include whites?"

"True," Michaux said. "And what whites does he wish to include? Rhodesian whites? South African whites? The whites who own the oil wells in his own country—the American whites?"

"A point there," the other government official said. "We cannot condemn all 'white devils' and refuse to accept aid from any."

"Still," Michaux said, "the slaves went to America, not

to Russia. But I have no objection to white aid, providing it does not diminish our independence. Do you agree, minister?"

"Absolutely," Duclos said. Vaguely conscious it came out. "Abslutey." "We have all suffered enough from white barbarism. Economic barbarism. Military savagery. Insults. Dedegration. Degradation. There must be an end to it."

"I am glad to hear you say that," Christophe Michaux said warmly. He placed his hands on Duclos' shoulders and stared solemnly into his eyes. "You have a marvelous gift of expression. You put into exact words what we all feel. We are brothers."

"Brothers!" said Duclos. So loudly that several others in the room stopped speaking and turned to glance at him.

Michaux handed him another gin and bitters, then raised his own glass.

"Death to our enemies," he said.

16.

THE RESIDENTS OF MOKODI might view the activities of Ian Quigley with amusement (calling him "Supersnoop"), but there was little doubt that the chief investigator for Fisk, Twiggs & Sidebottom, Ltd., approached his assignment with energy and zeal. He was everywhere with his tape recorder and little camera, clocking the traffic flow on the Boulevard Voltaire, inspecting the phosphate mines, charting the course of a passport application, timing the unloading, storage, and sale of perishables from the Gonjan markets.

Armed with the letter of authorization from Obiri Anokye, he was even able to inspect military installations and armories, board the several small craft of the Asante National Navy, and review operations of the air force.

181

"He will end up knowing more about Asante than I do," President Anokye said to Joan Livesay. "Mr. Leiberman tells me Quigley went far to the north, almost to Four Points, to do something called a time-motion study on goat herdsmen."

Livesay laughed. Anokye liked her laugh. Sturdy and resonant.

"I think Mr. Leiberman exaggerates," she said. "Ian did go north, but only to get a first-hand look at the economy of the region. I suppose goat-herding is a part of that economy."

It was Anokye's turn to laugh.

"In some areas, it *is* the economy," he said. "From the goat comes milk, cheese, meat, hair, skins. A very valuable national asset. How much longer will you and Mr. Quigley continue?"

"We hope to finish up in two weeks."

"I imagine you will be happy to see the last of Asante."

"Not at all, Mr. President. I can't speak for Ian, but this has been one of the happiest months of my life. I've enjoyed every minute of it."

"I am glad to hear that, Joan. You like Asante, do you?"

"Very, very much. The sun. The sea. But mostly the friendliness of the people."

"Yes. They are good people."

She looked down at the notebook in her lap, fingers twisting.

"Your friendliness, Mr. President," she said in a low voice. "It has been a great help. I know it hasn't been pleasant for you having me hang about all the time. You have been very kind."

He waved her thanks away.

"It is for my own benefit," he said. "If it aids you to— what is it Mr. Quigley says?—to optimize my performance."

He said it so wryly that she looked up at him smiling. It was early evening, the office lights not yet on. He would, he had told her, soon have a private conference with Willi Abraham, Jean-Louis Duclos and Mai Fante, concerning foreign relations. Followed by a meeting with the

Minister of Tourism regarding publicity on the new
gambling casino being built—a meeting she was welcome
to attend. This would be followed by his weekly lesson in
Portuguese, tutored by a junior clerk from the Portuguese
Embassy. This would be followed by a private conversation with Peter Tangent. She could mark in her notebook
that it would concern economic matters. Oil revenues.
And finally, he would motor to the Mokodi barracks to
observe a night operation by the special attack company
of 4th Brigade.

"Where do you find the energy?" she marveled.

"I was born strong," he said. "That is to God's credit,
not mine. But also, I have the—the determination."

"That is to your credit," she said softly.

They sat quietly in the dimness, comfortable in each
other's presence. He stared at the sleek helmet of her hair.
She had the perfect complexion of so many Englishwom-
en, rosied now by the Asante sun. He saw the crisp
features in silhouette. Her chin and throat seemed to him
so tender that if he touched them, ever so gently, they
might retain the impress of his fingers. He wondered, idly,
how old she was. Older than he, he guessed. By a few
years.

"And what will you do when you return to England,
Joan?"

"Finish up my part of the report. Make my recommendations. I'll probably have a holiday, a few days, before
my next job."

"You have family?"

"Only a father living. And some distant cousins."

"You live with your father?"

"No," she said. Something in her eyes. "He is in a
nursing home. A kind of hospital."

"I am sorry to hear that. It must be lonely for you."

"I try to keep busy."

"That is best," he nodded. "But you have friends, of
course?"

"Of course."

"And what do you do in London? Parties? The
theatre?"

"Oh yes. And museums. Concerts. Things of that sort."

"So it is not so lonely?"

"Sometimes," she said.

"For all of us, Joan," he said. "Sometimes."

Then they sat together in silence a few close moments. Their reverie was ended by the arrival of Abraham, Duclos, and Fante. The Attorney General was carrying a small black gripsack, something like a doctor's bag. As Joan Livesay was moving to her chair outside in the corridor, Sgt. Sene Yeboa arrived, and smiled at her. He went into the President's office for a moment and then emerged carrying the black bag that had been brought by Fante. Then the door of the study closed and was locked from the inside. Joan Livesay opened her dictionary and began to whisper Akan verbs.

President Anokye made his guests comfortable in armchairs facing his desk. He put out cigarettes, a box of Sumatran cigars, a decanter of Italian brandy. He lounged back in his swivel chair, picked up the painted model of the Asante army captain, turned it slowly in his fingers.

"The Togo-Benin operation goes well," he reported to them. "Please forgive me for not informing you of what has been done, but so far all activities have been of a military nature, and I did not desire that you be involved. Your time is too valuable to be spent on details better left to military professionals."

How like the Little Captain, Willi Abraham thought. To tell them they had no need to know, and to soften this implied denigration of their status by telling them they were too important to be involved.

"If all goes well," Anokye continued, "we can count on de facto control of both countries within a month or so."

There was a hissing intake of breath. Anokye looked up to see who had reacted. His gaze settled on Fante.

"Mai," he said, "you are surprised?"

"Only at the timing, Mr. President. So soon?"

"Oh yes," Anokye nodded gravely. "It must be done quickly. These things have a rhythm of their own. If we dawdle, we are lost."

"Assuming all goes as you plan, Bibi," Abraham said, "then what?"

"Precisely, Willi: Then what? The reason I have asked you here tonight. Jean, you remember that when the coup was still in the planning stage, I asked you to begin designing the government of the new Asante. So when we succeeded in overthrowing Prempeh, we were able almost immediately to present to the Asante people a complete constitution for the republic, tailored to their needs and desires. Some mistakes were made, true, but generally I feel the constitution is working well."

"Remarkably well, Mr. President," Mai Fante said. "Hardly a week goes by without my receiving a request from an African nation for a copy of our constitution, codes of civil and criminal law, and so forth."

"Very encouraging. You have worked hard, Mai. You all have. I think the stability of the country proves you have worked well."

"Thank you, Mr. President," the Attorney General said proudly. "We still have far to go, but the way forward is shorter than the road already traveled."

He was a clear-eyed older man, silver-haired, who moved lithely, youthfully. He wore suits of polished grey silk, always casual, always elegant. It was said he was related, closely or distantly, by blood or by marriage, to half the citizens of Asante. There was no doubt he had the natural politician's gift for remembering names, faces, familial ties. Which was one reason Obiri Anokye had appointed him national chairman of the League of Liberty, the Little Captain's political party.

"To continue," President Anokye said. "I believe the time has come to consider how we may administer the governments of Togo and Benin. And other countries that come under our hegemony in the future. Not only in the best interests of those countries, but to further our aim of a Pan-Africa. You three men are my best trusted advisors. You know I speak the truth. I ask you now for your ideas on the nature of the union we must form with other African nations. Jean?"

"A—a sort of United States of Africa?" Duclos said slowly. "Based on the American model of several states joined in a partnership by and to a federal government?"

"Not another USA," Willi Abraham smiled. "We

would have to call it United African States, UAS, to avoid confusion. But I am not certain the American model is suitable for Africa."

"Nor I," Anokye said.

"Perhaps a looser federation," Mai Fante suggested. "Similar to the British Commonwealth."

"Too loose," Duclos said. "That is just a sentimental club of sovereign states."

"I think," Anokye said, "rather than attempt to adopt or adapt an existing system, it would be best if we first decide what characteristics we desire our system to possess, and then design it with those requirements in mind."

"Very sound, Bibi," Abraham nodded approvingly. "As usual, you go to the basics. I will start off. Our federation, first of all, must have a single monetary system."

"Good," Anokye said. "I agree. Now you, Mai."

"A single code of law," Fante said promptly.

The others were silent.

"Desirable," Abraham said finally, "but unrealistic, considering tribal customs. Perhaps a very brief, basic code of criminal and civil law, but loose enough to allow local interpretation. Elastic enough to cover the traditions and habits of different areas and different peoples."

He was a small, neat man, somber in dress, educated at the Wharton School of Finance, very hard, incorruptible. His calm bravery and cool assurance during the coup had contributed greatly to the outcome. And his had been the chess player's brain behind the financing of Anokye's coup.

"I will accept that, Willi," the Little Captain said. "Jean, you wish to add something?"

Duclos rubbed a palm across his forehead.

"Some form of democratic participation in the government. Perhaps elected legislatures in each country, but with the chief executive appointed by you, Mr. President. It is a very difficult problem that requires much thought and careful planning."

"Which is why I want to get started on it at once," President Anokye said. "I hereby appoint you gentlemen a committee of three to draw up a blueprint for the new—well, for the time being, let us call it the United African States. The UAS. It is not a bad name. I would like from you a design, as detailed as possible, of exactly how this union will be constituted."

"And when do you want this, Bibi?" Abraham asked.

"Two weeks," Anokye said. "No later."

He smiled at their groans, and rose to his feet. They stood up promptly and moved toward the door. But they stopped when he spoke.

"None of you has asked what my requirement is for the new union," he asked.

"What do you suggest, Mr. President?" Mai Fante asked.

"One army," Obiri Anokye said. "One uniform. One flag. The army of the United African States to be headquartered in Asante. Under my command."

Yvonne Mayer and Sgt. Sene Yeboa had been married in a quiet civil ceremony, presided over by a magistrate of the Asante National Judiciary. The only witnesses were President Obiri Anokye, best man, and Mboa Duclos, matron of honor. Following the brief wedding, the Yeboas returned to the home of the bride for a short, sedate reception attended by a dozen of their friends. The guests included a few of the girls from the Golden Calf and some of the sergeant's army buddies. Everyone behaved well.

Yvonne and Sene then settled down to a quiet, contented married life. To all appearances. They both seemed intent upon acting in what Asante's social arbiters called "a cultured manner." The wife, with the aid of servants, kept a clean, cheerful home for her husband. There was hot food awaiting him whatever time he arrived, and cold beer in the refrigerator. In turn, he allowed her to handle all their finances, spoke to her in a respectful tone, never beat her or struck her in anger or drunkenness. It was known in Mokodi, via testimony of the servants, that the Yeboas slept in separate bedrooms.

But no one, ever, doubted the manhood of Sene Yeboa. Bush wisdom decreed that it was only a question of time before the door between their adjoining chambers was unlocked, thrown open. It was said that in the Mokodi barracks, wagers had been made on when this event might occur.

On the evening that President Anokye met with his advisors to begin planning the United African States, Sergeant Yeboa returned home about 2130. He had not left the palace until, as usual, he had satisfied himself that the guards assigned to the Little Captain for the remainder of the night were adequate, armed, sober, and mindful of their responsibility. "Mother Yeboa," he was called. Not, of course, to his face.

When he entered his home, through the rear entrance that led directly into the kitchen, Yvonne was waiting for him with a warm smile and a cold bottle of Star. It was difficult for him to choose which gave him more pleasure, the friendly greeting or the frosty beer. But as Yvonne took from him the gripsack he carried, he leaned forward to kiss her scented, flaxen hair. She laughed and patted his cheek. He felt very good.

Only one servant, Chantal, the maid, lived in. But this was Chantal's weekly night off. She spent it moonlighting at the Golden Calf. She liked the opportunity of earning extra money, of having fun. And she also served as an unwitting spy for Yvonne, enabling her mistress better to estimate revenue and calculate the malfeasance of the sly Yakubu.

So this evening, Yvonne, having already dined, served her husband's dinner with her own hands. The main dish was pepper chicken, prepared in a way she knew pleased Sene: enough hot spices to bring sweat to his scalp. But there was beer to cool his palate and, if he wished, brandy afterward in the living room, and a good cigar.

He did so wish, and they relaxed together, both barefoot. Sene puffed importantly on his cigar, touching the brandy balloon to his lips occasionally. Yvonne had taught him that it was uncultured to toss the drink down in one wild gulp.

She, with her own gin sling, sat coiled at the opposite end of the couch. Watching him with amused affection. She did feel affection for him. As one might feel affection for a splendid stallion. Or even a massive bear, shambling on its hind legs.

"What is in the black bag, Sene?" she asked casually.

"Money," he said, grinning at her. "Much money. French francs."

She was very quick.

"It goes to Togo and Benin?"

"Yes," he admitted. "To men who favor war. You understand?"

"Of course. The Little Captain plans well."

"He does," Sene agreed. "I must assemble the packages tonight. Tomorrow I will cross the borders and deliver them."

"You alone?"

"Bibi wishes his brother Adebayo to accompany me. He says the boy must learn."

"Adebayo?" she said. "A child."

"Not so much a child. Already taller than the Little Captain. When he puts meat on his bones, he will be a good man. Strong."

"You can trust him?"

"Adebayo? Of course. Bibi has told him to follow my orders in all things. Adebayo learns quickly. He speaks little, but he listens carefully. And he never complains."

"Adebayo," she repeated. "I still think of him as a child. Does he have a woman?"

"Ho!" he laughed. "Give the lad time."

In truth, he was not enamored of brandy; it was too small, gone too soon, and did nothing to calm the fire of the pepper chicken. So when the snifter was empty, he fetched another cold beer from the kitchen and brought Yvonne a fresh gin sling.

"The Little Captain has left it to me to decide how much money the men in Togo and Benin are to receive," he told her. "It is a great responsibility. Will you help me?"

"Of course," she said. "Need you ask? But what of your men here in Asante? Do you also pay them?"

"I pay them, personally, but Bibi has set the amount each man gets."

"You pay them, and they report to you?"

"That is true."

"How many men do you have, Sene? Here in Asante and in other countries? In your entire private army?"

"Now? Today? I cannot say exactly. Perhaps fifty men. And Bibi says we must have more."

"Interesting," she said thoughtfully. "Let me get my glasses, and we will decide how the money is to be divided."

She had been wearing a man's sapara of unbleached muslin, the voluminous folds cinched at the waist with a narrow scarf of vermilion silk. She had learned the off-hand, taunting chic of African women, their high-rumped flair. And she made the plain sapara a ballgown. But when she came from the bedroom, wearing her glasses, she had changed into a blue pegnoir over a lighter blue nightgown. The same costume she had worn to invite Nwabala to his death.

They sat close together at the teak table in the dining area, and she began to organize his affairs. He had pockets of paper scraps, jotted notes, some hastily scrawled hieroglyphics that even he could not decipher. But gradually, as they worked, she was able to draw up lists, of names and assignments.

They opened a jug of palm wine, poured it over ice cubes, and sipped occasionally as they worked. He supplied her with details, furrowing his heavy brow as he sought to recall the personalities, virtues and vices, of the men who worked for him. They did not include members of the President's personal guard, who were uniformed Asanti soldiers. They dealt only with Yeboa's secret army, the domestic spies and the agents who had been sent abroad, to Togo and Benin, Nigeria, one to Zaire, one to Gabon, one to Cameron.

When they had finished, they stared in astonishment at their lists. Many more than fifty. Sene personally commanded almost a hundred men in undercover work in Asante and beyond the borders. Gathering information. Funneling it only to Sergeant Yeboa.

"I didn't know," he admitted, ashamed of his inefficiency. "But it has all happened so quickly. The Little Captain tells me more men, more men, more places. I want to know everything, everywhere."

"I am glad you spoke to me of this," she said, putting a comforting hand on his arm. "From now on, you must tell me everything. Whenever a man is added, or when a man is sent from here to there, you must tell me, and I will keep a record of it. I will set up a file for each man."

"Good," he said gratefully. "Who each man is, how much has been paid, if he is to be trusted, and so forth. Yvonne, you will do this for me?"

"Of course," she said. She laughed lightly. "It is exactly what I need to keep busy."

He looked at her, understanding. The first few weeks of their marriage had been difficult for her. He knew that. When she realized, slowly realized, that Obiri Anokye was not coming to their home, not coming to her bed, ever again. But she was no stranger to pain, physical or emotional, and had the stripped sinews of a survivor.

"Now you must do something for me," she said. "Tell Bibi you need more men. Men to gather information. To go everywhere in Africa. If he wishes to create one nation, he must have friends in Angola and Kenya and South Africa and Mali and Chad. Everywhere. Tell him this, and he will agree. Never fear. He will find the money for all these men."

He looked at her a long, long moment. Then his hand crept across the tabletop, a dark beast walking on strong fingers. It clamped about her wrist.

"I will tell him that," he said. Throaty voice. "I will do as you say, Yvonne."

"Good," she said. "Also, I wish you to hold a higher title than sergeant. I know Bibi has offered you officer's rank. I want you to accept it."

His eyes went opaque; she felt something close to fear. Perhaps because she could not read what he was thinking.

"No, Yvonne," he said softly, still holding her wrist. "It is something to be a sergeant in the Asante army. The President is called the Little Captain and is proud of it. I will not ask him for officer's rank."

She had not been a successful whore for nothing. She knew when to be hard, when to be soft.

"All right," she said. "Do not ask him. But if Bibi suggests it again, grumble but accept. You agree?"

"I agree," he said grudgingly. "But only if he suggests it."

"He will," she said. "I know the Little Captain," she added bitterly. She twisted her wrist in his grasp, bent her fingers down, stroked his pink palm with her fingertips. Then scraped with her nails. "And now we shall go to bed," she said staring into his eyes.

"Yes," he said.

She had never seen him naked before, and caught her breath. His blunt body was a geography of scars: thin rivers of white, puckered valleys, torn ravines and crooked crevices. Bullet wounds, knife cuts, purpled blows. She could hardly believe that his flesh had borne this punishment. Like her, he was a survivor.

He made love like the splendid stallion engorged, the massive bear maddened and no longer exhibiting his tame tricks. He showed his teeth, and she surrendered willingly beneath that ferocious assault. She could not counter his brute strength, his grunting fury. But opened her pale and hairless thighs to him, wondering if she would die from that throbbing bludgeon that rent her, split her, and drove her steaming.

"My master!" she gasped. "My ruler! My king!"

"I do not wish to be paranoid about the French," President Obiri Anokye told Peter Tangent. "Still, I know they are aware of the situation between Togo and Benin, and it must puzzle them."

"I'm sure it does, Mr. President. You anticipate interference? By the French?"

"No," Anokye said. "Not really. But it—what is the English word?—it frets me. Yes. Frets. I thought perhaps there is something I can do. We can do. I leave as little to chance as possible. I would not care to see a thousand

French paratroops dropping on Mokodi."

He stood suddenly and began stalking about his office. He glanced, several times, at the gold Patek Philippe he had taken from the wrist of the dead King Prempeh IV. The band had been shortened, and the Little Captain wore the watch—originally a gift to Prempeh from Peter Tangent—with comfort and pride.

"I'm already late for a night operation at the barracks," he said, almost angrily. "They are waiting for me. We must conclude this quickly. I have only one thought on the matter: the Russian Marxists are active in Benin. Also, somewhat, in Togo. But in recent months, very heavily in Benin. I know this to be true. Do you think the French are aware of it?"

"Undoubtedly, Mr. President."

"This is my idea: Is there any way we can convince the French that the Togo-Benin dispute is the result of a Communist plot? To divide the two countries. Inflame hatreds that will lead to open warfare. So that, in the resulting confusion, the Marxists may come to power, or perhaps act as arbitrator, enforcing their own policies, elevating their own men. Could the French be made to believe this?"

Peter Tangent smiled slowly. "A red herring," he said softly.

"Red herring? I do not know the meaning, Peter."

"In my country, the phrase has two meanings, Mr. President. Primarily, it means a false trail. But in government circles, it also means using the Red Menace as a means of promoting policies—appropriations, and so forth—that might otherwise have no viability. You understand, Mr. President?"

"Of course. Very ingenious. We will give the French a red herring. Could your friend in London be of assistance to us in this matter?"

Tangent considered a few moments.

"I think he could," he said finally. "But I do not believe he would be willing to act only on my word, on my assurance of the Russians' complicity in the Togo-Benin dispute. If we could present him with evidence..."

"Evidence? You mean, perhaps, a statement by a third party? A confession? Perhaps a document that has come into our possession?"

"Something like that."

"I will provide it," President Anokye said.

"And perhaps another gift of African art," Tangent said.

"That, too," the Little Captain said.

17.

THE POPULAR "Haut Monde" column in the Mokodi *New Times* carried the following account:

Mokodi society, and even the au courant of the hinterlands of Gonja and Kumasi, are all atwitter over the visit to Asante of General and Mrs. Kumayo Songo and their oldest son, Capt. Jere. Songo père commands the northern zone of the Togolese army, and Songo fils serves as his father's Chief of Staff. The beautiful and gracious Mrs. Songo, the former Bakwa Bawo of Bassari, is active in Lomé society and renowned for her many charitable activities. Last season, the Songos hosted the annual Society Club Ball at their lovely home near Ountivou. It was a glittering event that brought together the very brightest ornaments of West African society, with glamorous party-goers galore arriving from such distant locales as Senegal and Gabon.

Haut Monde has learned from a usually reliable source that the visit of the Songos to Mokodi has nothing to do with military matters or foreign relations. No, indeed! It is rumored that the oh-so-handsome Capt. Jere and Sara, the lovely younger sister of President Obiri Anokye, are an item, and an announcement of their engagement is expected to be made shortly, perhaps during a formal dinner being given in the visitors' honor tonight at the palace.

Best wishes to all!

The "usually reliable source" mentioned by the author of "Haute Monde" was the public relations man retained by the Asante government, and the newspaper account was reasonably accurate. The dinner was a family affair, attended by the three Songos and the complete Anokye clan, including Judith and Josiah, and Zuni and his wife, Magira, who had come over from Zabar on the afternoon ferry. And, of course, Sara and Adebayo.

Sara and Captain Jere were seated side by side at the long table in the state dining room. They were the center of attraction, blushing targets of mild joking, embarrassed recipients of dire warnings of the pitfalls of marriage.

Sara had never looked lovelier. She wore a long gown of russet silk, with ribbons of the same material threaded through her twigged hair. The excitement of the evening gave her eyes a brilliance, her smile a flash. She attempted to appear composed and mature, but youthful high spirits broke out in giggles and snorts of laughter. Once, when Zuni warned Captain Jere that his bride-to-be could not boil water without burning it, Sara covered her face with her palms in uncontrollable mirth.

The captain blushed as frequently. He was shy, almost to the point of inarticulateness. But "Haute Monde" had not exaggerated; he was "oh-so-handsome" and, in his dress uniform, was a prince charming perfectly capable of making Sara forget the photograph of Alain Delon that hung above her bed.

After dessert and coffee were finished, President Anokye nodded to Ajaka, and champagne was served. The Songos were Muslims, but happily ignored the prohibition on alcohol in honor of this festive occasion. The Little Captain rose to his feet at the head of the table, and the others quieted.

Speaking French, he said: "I ask you all to join me in celebrating the engagement of my beloved sister, Sara Anokye, to Captain Jere Songo." He raised his glass. "To this charming young couple. May they know happiness for the remainder of their days, and may their union be blessed by Allah, God, and all the gods of our ancestors. Sara and Jere, you have all our love and all our hopes for a long life of good fortune."

All drank to that, willingly, and then clustered around to embrace and kiss Sara, who was now weeping with joy, and to shake the grinning captain's hand, slap his back, congratulate him and wish him well. Even the servants in the room came forward to kiss Sara's hand and the captain's, and to bestow blessings in several tribal dialects. Ajaka made a cabalistic sign over the young couple and whirled thrice, rapidly, on his bare feet.

"A moment of your time, general?" President Anokye murmured, touching Songo's elbow.

"Of course, Mr. President."

The Little Captain led him from the dining room down the corridor to his office. Joan Livesay was sitting outside with her Akan dictionary. She looked up briefly as the two men approached, then went back to her book. Anokye made no attempt to explain her presence, and Songo didn't ask.

Inside, the door locked, the President took maps from the top drawer of his desk, rolled them open, motioned the general close.

"You can depend upon the loyalty of the Army of the North Zone?" he asked abruptly.

"Absolutely, Mr. President," Songo said, somewhat shocked by the question.

"And the South Zone?"

The general hesitated. "That I cannot say with certainty. I would guess they will remain neutral."

"Or wait until they see how you progress in the north. Then, if you appear to be succeeding, they will join the attack."

"That is possible, Mr. President."

"Yes. Possible. But I count only on their neutrality for a short period of time. I ask only that they do nothing. You understand?"

"Of course, Mr. President."

"Now," the Little Captain went on, pointing to wide red arrows marked on the map with grease pencil. "I wish you to advance in this area south of the hills. A three-pronged attack from Sokodé, Kpessi, and Atakpamé. All three columns are to strike directly eastward into Benin, guiding on these roads here, here, and here. Any objections so far?"

"Is it wise to divide my forces, Mr. President?"

"It would not be if a single large force of the enemy was in position to oppose you. But intelligence reports indicate there are only a few scattered outposts in this area of Benin. The only place that might give you trouble is here, at Savalou. If you meet determined resistance, I advise you to flank the village and continue your advance. Try, in all events, to avoid a confrontation. Move as swiftly as you can. Your objective is to slice directly across to the Nigerian border. Cut the north-south highway and divide Benin in two, so that troops cannot be brought south to the coast from Kandi and Parakou. Is that clear?"

"Yes, Mr. President."

"I will coordinate my attack with yours. By moving in vehicles on the improved coastal road, I should be in Ouidah, Cotonou, and Porto-Novo before you are well inside Benin. You see my plan now, general?"

"A classic pincer," Songo said admiringly. "You striking northward from the coast, and I striking coastward from the north!"

"Exactly," the Little Captain said. "But do not begin your move southward until your advance troops have reached the Nigerian border. I will send you word when to turn southward. I can count on you to await that word?"

"You can."

"Good. I anticipate hard fighting in the Ouidah-Cotonou-Porto-Novo area. It is where the bulk of the Benin army is presently positioned. But I have the men and weapons to move them, to shove them northward. Then, after you have cut the country in half, you will make your ninety-degree turn southward. We will have the enemy trapped between us. And we will smash him."

"Excellent, Mr. President! A brilliant plan! There is but one thing..."

"And that is?"

"To reach Benin, your army must come through Togo on the coastal road. You said you ask only the neutrality of the officers and men of the Army of the South Zone. But what if they should offer resistance to this invasion by the Asante army?"

"Hardly an invasion, general. We will merely be passing through to Benin."

"I understand that, Mr. President, but will they? All they will see are armed men pouring into Togo from Asante. They may fight. It is something to be considered."

Obiri Anokye straightened. He tossed down the pencil he had been using as a pointer. He stood at the map, feet firmly planted, hands on hips, chest inflated. His head was lowered; he stared at the map broodingly from under his brows.

"I have already considered it," he told General Songo. "I have made contact with certain officers of the Army of the South Zone. Money has changed hands. Pledges have been made. They will remain neutral. There will be no resistance offered to Asante forces passing through to Benin."

Gen. Kumayo Songo looked at the Little Captain with wonder.

"You think of everything, Mr. President."

Anokye didn't answer, and after a moment of silence, Songo became uneasy.

"You intend to lead your troops in person, Mr. President?" he asked nervously.

"I do. I will be with Colonel Nkomo's tank corps. I will try to keep you informed of my progress. During the next two weeks, you will receive several private messages from me. These will concern timing, passwords, radio wavelengths, flare signals, and so forth. The messages will be delivered to you personally by my brother Adebayo. If you wish to reply, he will carry your letters back to me. After your return to Togo tomorrow, I suggest we have no more direct communication by telephone or mail."

"I agree, Mr. President."

"Begin organizing your striking forces at once. Please keep me informed of your progress and exact dispositions. I expect you to be ready to move within two weeks."

"Two weeks!"

"It can be done."

"I am not certain I can..."

Songo's voice faltered. President Anokye raised his head. He stared coldly at the general, starting at his feet, and letting expressionless eyes move slowly upward: bandy legs, bulging paunch, uniform straining at breast and arms, tight collar, fat neck, flushed face glistening with sweat, damp hair. Then lowered to stare at Songo's rapidly blinking eyes.

"But I am certain you can," he said softly. "I have great faith in you, general. I would not care to find that faith has been misplaced. Two weeks. After that, be prepared to move on twenty-four hours' notice. You will be informed of the code word that will signal the attack. And twenty-four hours after *that*, Benin will be crushed, and you will be the leader of Togo."

"Nothing can stop us!" General Songo said excitedly, regaining his nerve.

"Nothing," Obiri Anokye said gravely. He replaced the maps in his desk and started toward the door. Then he paused. "One other small thing," he said casually. "I need a certain document from you...."

18.

THEY SAT LIKE landed gentry in the library of Brindleys in London. Slumped in deep leather armchairs. Nursing their brandies. Feet up on a brass fender before the fireplace. Genial flames flickering, lighting ruddy faces in the darkened room. Peter A. Tangent from Crawfordsville, Indiana. Anthony J. Malcolm from Altoona, Pennsylvania. And there they were . . .

"A beautiful mask from the Congo," Tony Malcolm said lazily. "Shells and ivory, human hair and odd things. Must be centuries old. I'm embarrassed by his generosity. And to think he wants nothing in return."

Peter Tangent laughed. Lightly.

"Cynical bastard," he said. "As a matter of fact, he wants to do something for you."

"Does he, now?"

"Well...something for the French, actually. But he thought it might benefit you if you brought it to their attention."

"Very kind of the Little Captain."

"He can't go directly to the French with it, you see, because he fears their embassy in Mokodi is riddled with Marxists. Makes sense, doesn't it?"

"Peter," Malcolm said dreamily, staring squint-eyed into the dancing flames, "just what the fuck are you talking about?"

"This..." Tangent said. He took an envelope from his inside jacket pocket, withdrew a folded sheet of paper. He shook it open, held it out to Malcolm. "Read this," he said.

"Must I?" Tony murmured.

"You must. I assure you, you'll find it interesting."

Malcolm sighed, straightened up in his chair. He took a pair of rimless spectacles from his breast pocket and put them on as slowly as a fussy bookkeeper. Then he took the paper from Tangent's hand. He turned sideways in his chair to illuminate it by firelight.

"You read French?" Tangent asked.

"My mother tongue," Malcolm said, and Tangent chuckled.

Malcolm read it through, then read it again. He raised his eyes to stare at Tangent over his glasses.

"Let's see if I've got this straight," he said. "This document is submitted to me as being a photostatic copy of the third page of a three-page Top Secret report sent to the Togolese Minister of Defense in Lomé by a certain General Kumayo Songo, and signed by him. The report concerns an investigation carried out under the general's orders into the circumstances of a raid by persons unknown on a Togolese army base near the village of Kamina. In their investigation of the unprovoked attack, the general's men discovered the body of one of the attacking force. He was identified, by papers found on the corpse, as being one Indris Obodum, a Benin student who was also, apparently, a card-carrying member of the

Benin Communist Party. Have I understood all this correctly?"

"You have," Tangent said solemnly. "The document came into the possession of President Anokye by means that need not concern us. You are aware of the Marxist activity in Benin?"

"I am aware," Malcolm said.

"So is President Anokye. And very concerned about it. I need hardly tell you. He believes this document is added evidence that the Reds are fomenting the trouble between Togo and Benin. He thought he should bring this document to the attention of the French, who still consider Togo and Benin in their sphere of influence. For the reasons I've already stated, Anokye prefers to do it this way—to ask you to inform the French of the Communist plot."

Tony Malcolm took off his glasses, folded them slowly, tucked them back into his jacket pocket.

"You fucking amateurs," he said softly.

"What?" Tangent said, jerking upright. "What do you mean?"

Malcolm rose to a crouch, leaned forward, scaled the paper into the flames.

"What are you doing?" Tangent cried.

The paper burst into flames, curled, crisped. In a few moments it was ashes. The two men settled back in their club chairs, heads turned so they could stare at each other.

"A piece of bumf," Tony Malcolm said calmly. "The French could make one phone call and discover it was as phony as a three-dollar bill. I'm surprised at you, Peter. Is that what you think my business is like? Falsified documents? Micro-miniaturized bugs and cameras in cigarette lighters? Unspeakable torture and fiendishly clever assassination?"

"Well, I—well, isn't it?" Tangent said confusedly.

"About five percent," Malcolm said.

"And the other ninety-five?"

"People. Just people. Getting them to tell you what you want to know. To do what you want done."

"Manipulating them, in other words?"

"Nonsense. Most of them are quite aware of what they're doing. Do it voluntarily, happily."

"But . . . *why?*"

"Why do they do it?" Malcolm asked rhetorically. "Idealism. The dream of a better world. They feel they can strike a blow against the forces of evil and darkness, make some small contribution to a future of freedom and liberty, a world in which political fear and tyranny no longer exist."

His speech began to take on the singsong accents of an evangelist. Tangent listened with astonishment, wondering if (1) it was an elaborate put-on; (2) Malcolm really believed this shit; or (3) the man was crazed with drink.

"There *are* good people in this world," Malcolm continued what sounded like a soliloquy. "People determined to leave this life just a little better than they found it. If I am able, in some small way, to harness that high resolve, to further it, then I feel it is my moral duty to do exactly that. But I will not aid in any way whatsoever the advancement of those dark forces of political absolutism that threaten everything I and the people who work for me hold dear."

Tangent, seeing a side of Malcolm he never knew existed, was thoroughly flummoxed.

"Then I gather," he said, "that you know what the Little Captain is trying to do."

"Of course," Malcolm said. "He doesn't want the French to make any good guesses about what he's up to. So he's trying to sell them the Russians as the *agents provocateurs* behind the Togo-Benin dispute."

"Something like that," Tangent said grimly. "Another drink?" he asked, determined to be polite.

"Why not?"

The bottle of Remy-Martin was on the floor alongside Tangent's chair. He poured a finger or two into their glasses. Malcolm was in charge of the soda siphon. He gave them each a splash. They settled back again, slumping down onto their spines.

"Oh well," Tangent sighed. "You win one, you lose one."

"What makes you think you've lost this one?" Malcolm said.

Tangent's head jerked around. He stared at Malcolm again.

"If you make confusion a deliberate policy," he said, "you're succeeding admirably. Whee! You mean, after that lecture, you're willing to—"

"The document was stupid. It would never have convinced the French. Except that Anokye has this General Songo in his hip pocket."

"But now you say you'll—"

"That I'll do it? Yes, I'll help the Little Captain. Tell him that. I'll get the French all excited about the Red threat in Togo and Benin."

"And how will you do that?"

"Trade secret," Malcolm said smugly.

"Come on, Tony, you can tell me. How will you do it?"

Malcolm considered a moment, then smiled sweetly.

"I'll tell them," he said. "That's all. Just tell them to beware the Russians."

Tangent looked at him in wonderment.

"And they'll believe you?" he asked. "Just like that?"

"Just like that," Malcolm nodded. "They know I'm a very honest fellow."

"Ho-ho," Tangent said. "Tell me, honest fellow, why are you willing to do this for the Little Captain?"

"I like the gifts he sends me," Tony Malcolm said. "I'm building up one of the finest private collections of African art in the world."

"Bullshit!" Peter Tangent said promptly. "There's something more..."

The two men sat in silence for almost five minutes. Once, a uniformed attendant came into the library, and they took their feet off the fender to allow him to lift another small log onto the fire. Then, without speaking, went back to their former positions, their brandies and soda.

"Got it!" Tangent said finally.

"Oh?"

"You've heard from Ian Quigley. He's filed with

Virginia. You think the Little Captain is going to pull this off, and you want to be on the winning side. That's why you're willing to help."

"Is that what you think?" Tony Malcolm said sleepily.

Shortly afterward, drink finished, Tangent rose, stretched, yawned. He mumbled something about a busy tomorrow, told Malcolm he was welcome to whatever remained of the Remy-Martin, and made his exit. Tony Malcolm flapped a languid hand in farewell.

Tangent left the club through the bar. There were several men there, including the Frenchmen Julien Ricard. Tangent kept his head down and hurried past. For once Ricard didn't grab his arm and start another of his unpleasant conversations. The club's commissionaire whistled up a cab, and Tangent headed back for his suite at the Connaught, phrasing in his mind the tender, clever letter he would write that night to Amina Dunama.

"He's gone?" Tony Malcolm said, as Julien Ricard slid into the armchair vacated by Tangent.

"Took off in a cab," Ricard said. He laughed shortly. "Rushed past me like a thief. Learn anything?"

"Yes," Tony Malcolm said, staring again into the flames. "Tell your people in Paris that the Russians are stirring up the trouble between Togo and Benin."

"I don't believe that," Ricard said, touching the purple birthmark that glowed in firelight.

Malcolm turned slowly to look at him.

"You don't have to believe it," he said coldly. "You played at Canby's last night, didn't you?"

"You know I did," Julien Ricard said surlily.

"And you won, didn't you?"

"I did," Ricard said. "But not enough."

"Don't get greedy," Tony Malcolm said.

19.

THE LIMOUSINE CAME directly from the airport. When it arrived, President Obiri Anokye was waiting on the steps of the palace. He was flanked by Premier Willi Abraham, Minister of State Jean-Louis Duclos, and Col. Jim Nkomo.

The long, black Mercedes-Benz rolled slowly to a stop. Guards hurried forward to open the doors. Out stepped Premier Benedicto da Silva of Benin, his daughter Beatrice, his aide Christophe Michaux, and a Benin army officer, Col. Kwasi Sitobo, whose aiguillettes denoted his staff rank.

President Anokye moved down the steps smiling, holding his arms wide in welcome. He embraced Beatrice first; a chaste kiss on her cheek.

"Welcome to your new home!" he said, and then laughed when she did.

He shook hands formally with Da Silva and Michaux, and then was introduced to Colonel Sitobo, a dark, thin man with fiery eyes. In turn, Anokye presented his aides to all the others. After introductions, the party was sorted out:

Col. Jim Nkomo commandeered the limousine and took Colonel Sitobo off to a review of the Asante tank corps, planned in the visitor's honor.

Premier Abraham and Minister of State Duclos took charge of Da Silva and Michaux, and led them to the main floor audience chamber for preliminary discussions on a cash loan President Anokye had promised to make to Benin.

The Little Captain escorted Beatrice up the wide mahogany staircase to the second floor where his sister Sara was waiting, Joan Livesay hovering in the background. The two fiancées, who had met several times before, embraced and kissed with expressions of girlish delight. Joan Livesay was introduced to Beatrice, and the three women were shooed off to the upper regions of the palace that, everyone agreed, needed redecoration—new rugs, new drapes, new furniture—before they would be suitable for a married president.

"Go spend the taxpayers' money," Anokye called, in high good humor, and the three women went upstairs giggling, already chattering about color schemes and the pros and cons of calling in a professional decorator.

Obiri Anokye had an hour to himself in his office. He spent it reviewing, once again, the maps and battle orders he had prepared for the Togo-Benin campaign.

There had been a time, not too long ago, when he would not have planned a military operation of any magnitude without the counsel of the Englishman Alistair Greeley, chief teller of the Asante National Bank. Greeley, a strange man, a cripple, had one passion in life: military history and his collection of antique model soldiers. And it was with the aid of those brilliantly painted miniatures, moved about on maps and diagrams, that Captain Anokye and Greeley had plotted the attacks against the Marxist rebels in Asante.

But the rebels were destroyed now, or at least reduced to insignificant numbers. And Greeley was gone, faded away, after his wife and sister deserted him, together. Some said he was in South Africa. There were rumors he had been seen in the slums of Durban, filthy and besotted. But no matter. No one cared.

His advice was no longer needed. Obiri Anokye, alone, had planned and commanded the successful coup d'etat that deposed King Prempeh IV. The Little Captain himself had devised the tactics, sent these men here, those men there. And then, in person, had led the final assault on the palace.

That victory made him his own man. He knew now what he must do, and how he must do it. If he patterned his fighting style after any military leader's it was that of the American general Ulysses S. Grant: move in the greatest force you could muster, bulldoze, crush, take your losses without faltering and come on, implacable, unstoppable, a juggernaut.

This did not mean that you should not be adroit in your planning. But cleverness took you only to the instant the first gun was fired. Then planlessness took over, and winning then depended on resolve, instinct, and a kind of fury. All growing from a belief in your own invincibility. "I fight: therefore I am." The philosophy of every successful general.

So Obiri Anokye, the Little Captain, pondered his maps, diagrams, orders. Knowing this was only the start, the beginning. Intelligent enough to question what drove him, what lashed him on. It was an odd thing, he acknowledged, for a man to be in awe of himself. And yet he was.

Africa was filled with captains, and colonels, and generals. Some commanding numbers of men ridiculous in the blue eyes of white military leaders. An African captain might command ten, a colonel fifty, a general a few hundred. Sometimes African soldiers wore the castoffs of the world's armies. Weapons were frequently ancient, and malfunctioned. An army might need a dozen calibers of rifle ammunition. Close-order drill was a laugh. Discipline lasted until the first mortar round landed. And yet . . . And yet . . .

Obiri Anokye knew all this, worked within these limits. He knew the men who served under him, their shortcomings and their capabilities. Knew all these things better than his foes. But he could see no reason why a well-trained, well-fed, well-uniformed, well-armed, proud African soldier could not be the equal of any soldier on earth. Superior, perhaps, if the man with the rifle could be won to the Little Captain's dream: one nation, one people, one Africa.

So he was awed by his own ambition, his hunger. Knowing he could not hesitate nor doubt. He was familiar with Shakespeare's "There is a tide . . ." and was determined his life would not be leaked out in shallows and miseries. Auntie Tal had cast the stones for him and had seen a glorious future. He could not deny his destiny.

Col. Jim Nkomo's personal tank was called "Ami," the name painted on the side in crimson script. And it was from the opened turret of *Ami* that the bearded Nkomo and visiting Benin colonel Kwasi Sitobo reviewed the maneuvers of the Asante tank corps. After a corps parade, they watched through field glasses as a V-formation of the new AMX-30 tanks plunged down into a ravine, raced up the other slope, and blasted away with their 105mm cannon at paper targets, scoring impressive hits.

Colonel Sitobo growled softly.

"Now here is something that may interest you," Jim Nkomo said casually. "Our first TOW missile from America. You are familiar with this weapon?"

Sitobo nodded uncertainly.

"Wire-guided," Nkomo said. "Designed for antitank work, but useful on anything within a thirty-five-hundred-meter range. Especially moving targets. Crew of 'four. All the gunner has to do is keep his crosshairs on the target. A computer makes in-flight corrections. The missile can't miss. About fifteen centimeters in diameter. Speed is about a thousand kilometers per hour. The warhead is shaped. Armor-piercing. We have this one on a portable tripod mount. The ones on order will be mounted on Jeeps. I understand the Americans have also had good results with the TOW on helicopter gunships. Watch this."

They stood in the turret of *Ami* and stared through their field glasses as a squad of soldiers, somewhat apprehensively, dragged the burned-out hulk of a Volkswagen on a long rope across an open field. A thousand meters away, the TOW crew worked swiftly.

"Three launches in ninety seconds," Nkomo murmured. "If needed . . ."

The TOW gunner brought his crosshairs to bear. Pressed the trigger. There was a surprisingly small whoosh as the missile streaked toward the moving target. The gunner worked his sights; the missile, uncoiling its wire from two spools, curved toward the hauled Volkswagen body. It hit squarely; the rusted hulk dissolved in an explosion of steel and earth. The squad pulling the target fell to the ground, then rose shakily to their feet.

Col. Kwasi Sitobo made a sound.

"Nice," Nkomo said. "Well, that concludes our little show. I'm afraid the limousine has returned to the palace, but I can run you back in one of our Berliet armored personnel carriers. A fine piece of machinery. I think you'll like it."

Colonel Sitobo sighed.

The guests arrived promptly, wooed by an invitation to "a Portuguese evening" in honor of visiting Premier Benedicto da Silva of Benin. They gathered for a pre-dinner drink at one end of the grand ballroom. A rum-and-lemon punch was served, and appetizers included hot peppers, marinated hearts of palm, black olives, pickled mushrooms, and tiny prawns in a garlic sauce. At the other end of the long room, a five-piece African band played rhumbas, sambas, and mambos in execrable rhythm.

As usual, the guests soon divided into two gossiping groups: men and women. Only Joan Livesay and Ian Quigley stood together, a bit apart from the others.

"No punch, Ian?" she asked. "It's quite good."

"I'll pass," he said. "I'm hoping to work tonight, and a buzz I don't need. Where's his nibs?"

"Upstairs. Locked in his office with the visiting premier and that funny little colonel who never speaks."

"Ah?" Quigley said. "That's interesting. Wonder what they're up to?"

"Foreign relations," Livesay said. "At least, that's what President Anokye told me. Said he'd join us at dinner."

"Decent of him to invite us," he said. "Makes me feel less of a nuisance. Ready to go home?"

"Whenever you say."

"A week perhaps. Maybe less."

"Then you've got everything you want?"

"Just about. A few more details. What do you think of the Little Captain's fiancée?"

"A child," Joan Livesay said. "Still has her baby fat."

"Maybe that's what he fancies," Quigley laughed.

"Don't be crude, Ian."

"Sorry, old girl. One of these days you must draw me a blueprint of that high moral sense of yours. So I'll know—"

"Oh, shut up," she said.

"Where's Bibi?" Beatrice da Silva asked, looking about anxiously. "I hope he won't be late."

"He's upstairs with your father," Sara Anokye told her. "I'm sure they won't be long. Mboa, you look so pretty. I love your Apollo. Did you make it?"

Mrs. Duclos flushed with pleasure.

"Thank you, Sara. Yes, I printed the cloth myself. You do not think it is too—too crazy?"

"Of course not. It's fun!"

"Jean says it is crazy," Mboa said sorrowfully. "His friend, that man Michaux, agrees."

"They're both full of beans," Sara said. Then she giggled. "Or they will be after dinner. That's what we're having—beans. Feijoada."

"Feijoada!" Beatrice da Silva exclaimed, clapping her hands. "How wonderful! How thoughtful of Bibi to have this for us."

"Where is the President?" Christophe Michaux asked, looking about, frowning. "He appears to be missing. And Premier Da Silva."

"I believe they are upstairs," Jean-Louis Duclos said. "In conference."

"Ah? And where is Colonel Sitobo? He is also in conference?"

"I believe so."

"Interesting," Michaux said. "I must say that in my own mind I am somewhat annoyed that we weren't asked to join them. Are you not annoyed?"

"Perhaps it is a private matter, Christophe. The marriage..."

"A private matter with Sitobo present? I doubt it. It must concern military matters. They are planning something?"

"I don't know."

"Don't know or won't say?" Michaux laughed lightly. "I'm afraid you do not—" But then he stopped what he was about to say.

"What is your impression of Premier Da Silva's aide?" Mai Fante asked Willi Abraham in a low voice.

"Michaux?" Abraham said. "A capable man." He turned slowly to glance at Duclos and Michaux deep in conversation. "Very knowledgeable. He was shrewd in the negotiations this morning. But there is something about him..."

"Exactly," Mai Fante said. "Something.... My reaction exactly. You think he may make trouble?"

"Let him," Abraham shrugged. He quoted an Akan proverb: "Let the child pick up a live coal; you won't have to tell him to drop it."

"Well, I hope Jean is keeping his mouth tight," Fante said.

"He'd better," Willie Abraham said grimly. "I have seen the Little Captain in anger. Mai, do me the honor to exchange favors?"

"What may that be?"

"If I talk to your wife, will you talk to mine?"

"Done," Fante laughed.

In his private office, the door locked, President Obiri Anokye stood behind his desk and traced map positions with a blunt forefinger. It was not the same map he had shown to Gen. Kumayo Songo. Now the red arrows ran from east to west, from Benin into Togo.

"A broad attack in the north," he was saying. "Aimed toward Sokodé, Kpessi, Atakpamé. Your objective is to cut the north-south highway, divide the country in two so that reinforcements cannot be brought south to the coast from Sansanne-Mango and Lama-Kara. Is this plan clear to you so far?"

Premier Da Silva stroked his silvery Vandyke and looked to Col. Kwasi Sitobo. The colonel, his eyes on the map, bobbed his head and grunted. Anokye took the sound for acquiescence.

"I will coordinate my attack with yours," the Little Captain went on. "I will come down the coast road to Lomé. I, personally, with Colonel Nkomo's tank corps in the lead. I believe you saw with your own eyes what that force is capable of, colonel. Infantry will follow the tanks. I intend to take Lomé and push the enemy northward along the improved road. When you have achieved your objective, colonel, and Togo is cut in two, turn south and we will have what is left of the Togolese army between us, and we will smash them."

Colonel Sitobo looked up briefly, eyes flashing. Obiri Anokye had a profile on him, supplied by the Asante embassy in Porto-Novo and by Sergeant Yeboa's agents in Cotonou. On the strength of this information, he had instructed Premier Da Silva to select Sitobo as his military chief.

This Sitobo was a young hawk, fierce. Apparently, he

was apolitical, but combined excessive patriotism with excessive zeal for military ideals: discipline, discipline, and discipline. It was said he had once shot and killed one of his own men when his orders were disobeyed. Surprisingly, in one whose whole existence was devoted to command, he had a ridiculously high-pitched voice and spoke as infrequently as possible.

"During the next two weeks," President Anokye continued, "you will receive a number of messages, delivered by my brother Adebayo. These will concern timing, code signals, radio wavelengths, and so forth. I want you ready to move in two weeks. You can do this?"

Again Da Silva looked to Sitobo. The colonel nodded.

"Good," Anokye said. "At the end of two weeks, be prepared to begin your attack on twenty-four hours' notice. I believe it will only take us another twenty-four hours to crush Togo completely and end this threat to your national security."

Col. Kwasi Sitobo spoke for the first time.

"I agree," he squeaked.

The crystal chandeliers in the state dining room gleamed wickedly. The table was trigly dressed with stiff napery and polished silver. A staff of grinning servants, commanded by the lordly Ajaka, skipped merrily about to keep glasses filled with Portuguese wine, to rush in more and more platters, bowls, and kettles of the fabulous feijoada.

A dish as much African as Brazilian, feijoada is an orchestration of tangy flavors: garlic and pigs' tails, onion and smoked fatback, collard greens and ham hocks, spareribs and manioc, pigs' ears and rice, fufu and Tabasco, black beans and sausage. It is a kitchen sink of a dish. Prepared for a company as large as this one, it took the palace cooks almost two days to prepare; the Piper Aztec of the Asante National Air Force was dispatched to Cotonou for the paio sausage, to Accra for the smoked beef tongue.

Feijoada is a festive dish, and suited the mood of the

guests, appetites already whetted by the rum punch and spicy things. Platters were passed, bowls spooned, kettles ladled, and great mounds of feijoada grew on the plates of the diners, to be hacked away, whittled down, demolished, as the beaming waiters scurried in with more steaming rice, more greens, more hot sauce, more peppers and jerked beef.

President Anokye looked on benignly from the head of the table, making certain no guest was in want. Premier Da Silva was to his right, Beatrice to his left. The others sat along the sides, men and women alternating, with Sara at the foot of the table, learning to act as hostess.

The room was noisy with the loud appreciation of the diners, clash of cutlery, clink of bottle against glass, clack of spoon on bowl, ladle on kettle.

"The best, Mr. President," Premier Da Silva said, closing his eyes in rapture. A smear of garlic sauce clung to his silvery beard. He raised his glass to Anokye. "I swear to you, the best I have ever tasted. It is an evening to remember." He leaned across the table to Sitobo. "Well, colonel, what do you think of this? Eh? Eh?"

Sitobo grunted, not pausing to look up, shoveling into his waiting mouth yet another spoonful of black turtle beans.

Even the ladies, who had started picking daintily at their food in a cultured manner, could not resist the contrast of succulent flavors. Soon they ate as energetically as the men, calling for more salt pork, more cold orange salad, more hot malagueta peppers. Then women and men alike were sweating from the spices and from their labors. Chilled Mateus and beer were brought, and bowls of ice chunks which some of the guests rubbed across their fevered foreheads.

Obiri Anokye selected carefully, avoiding the beans and rice, filling up on beef, tongue, spareribs.

"You are not eating, Bibi," Beatrice chided.

"Enough," he protested. "Well, perhaps a few ribs more and some sausage. I must store up strength. After we are married, it will be only cold rice and green salad. We agreed!"

"Of course," she giggled. "Oh, it's so good!"

"Your suite at the Mokodi Hilton is satisfactory?" he asked, leaning toward her to be heard above the hubbub.

She nodded, wide-eyed, her white teeth too busy gnawing a pig's foot to reply.

"And Colonel Sitobo and Christophe Michaux—they are comfortable?"

She paused a moment to dab her greasy lips with a starched napkin.

"I'm sure the colonel is," she said. "But he never says anything about anything!"

Anokye smiled, nodded understandingly.

"And Michaux?" he said.

"Oh, he didn't want to stay at the Hilton. Said it was too American. He's staying in a safari bungalow at the Hôtel Africain. Do you know it?"

"Oh yes," the Little Captain nodded slowly. "I know it."

Then, when they could eat no more, when every guest swore another mouthful, a bite, a nibble, would cause him to burst asunder, the plates, platters, bowls and kettles were whisked away, the table cleared, and mounds of sherbet were served, in three flavors, with chilled Madeira to reduce the possibility of their palates' igniting. Champagne, beer, and brandy were also available, and chicory-coffee, tea, and Perrier water.

As usual, Obiri Anokye drank sparingly, touching a glass of cold Star beer to his lips. He sat back comfortably, hearing the happy, chattering company. Soft smile on his lips. Eyes away somewhere.

But not so far away that he was not the first in the room to see Sgt. Sene Yeboa standing framed in the suddenly opened door to the dining room. The Little Captain rose immediately to his feet, murmured quiet apologies to right and left, and was gone from the table before most of the guests realized their host was leaving. He drew Yeboa out into the corridor, closed the door against the noise.

"What is it, Sene?" he demanded.

But the sergeant's eyes were brimming with tears. Massive shoulders slumped. Muscled arms dangled.

The Little Captain gripped him, shook him gently.

"What is it, man?"

"Your father," Yeboa whispered, his eyes turning slowly downward. "Forgive me, Bibi."

Anokye looked at him.

"Dead?" he asked.

Yeboa nodded dumbly.

"When?" Anokye asked.

"Not so long ago, Little Captain. Zuni called the duty officer here. I was out at the barracks. They called me. Then I spoke to Zuni. He said Josiah was helping to pull the boat up onto the sand. And then he fell over and was dead. Bibi, I . . ."

Anokye nodded. The two men embraced, holding each other tightly.

"He was my father, too," Yeboa said, his voice muffled and shaky.

"I know, Sene, I know. You have done well. Now there is more you must do. Call the naval base. Have a launch prepared. Sara and I will go at once."

"May I go also, Bibi?"

"Of course. You are family. Go now and have the launch ready. I will tell Sara. Thank you, brother."

They embraced again. Then Yeboa turned away and began to run. Anokye stopped a servant about to enter the dining room and asked him to send his sister Sara out to him. She was with him in a moment. He told her. She fell into his arms, her wails of anguish smothered in his shoulder. He comforted her as best he could, saying their father was an old man, it was to be expected, he had lived a good life and harmed no one, now he was with God, and so forth.

When she had calmed, he told her to go to her room and pack a suitcase to take to Zabar; her mother would need her, for how long no one could say. When she ran upstairs, he took a deep breath and reentered the dining room. The guests, surprised by the sudden, unexpected departure of the two Anokyes, looked at him, silent and troubled.

"Dear friends," he said in a steady voice, "I regret that a family matter has arisen that requires the presence of my sister Sara and myself. I apologize for our absence. Please do not concern yourselves, but finish your dinner and enjoy the evening. Premier Abraham, may I ask you to serve as host in my absence?"

"Of course, Mr. President."

"I thank you all for your company," Obiri Anokye said, smiling bleakly. "Please do not let this unfortunate interruption spoil your pleasure."

"What a tragedy," Jean-Louis Duclos mourned. "The Little Captain will be devastated."

"He was an old man, wasn't he?" Christophe Michaux said.

"Very old."

"Well then?"

Sitting alone in the back seat of the Duclos' Simca, Mboa listened to the conversation and decided she did not like this man Michaux. She hoped he would stay for only one drink at their home, and then depart. Black he may have been, but he was not African; there was no feeling in him for Bibi's loss.

"Is there a grog shop on the way?" Michaux asked.

"Yes," Duclos said, "but there's no need to stop. I have wine, beer..."

"Let me get you something good," Michaux said.

When they stopped in front of the lighted store, Michaux hopped out and went inside.

"Jean—" Mboa began.

"Maria, do not tell me I have already had enough to drink," he said angrily. "I am in no mood for lectures tonight."

"When have I ever lectured you?" she asked.

"Your manner," he said furiously. "Your silent, reproachful manner. It is lecture enough."

"I do not understand," she said faintly.

Michaux came bouncing out, carrying a string bag containing bottles wrapped in old newspaper.

"Two Beefeater gin," he said, "and one Glenlivet Scotch whisky. That should be sufficient."

"Raw-ther," Duclos drawled in a burlesque English accent, and both men laughed hysterically.

They pulled up before the Duclos' home, on an ordinary street off the Boulevard Voltaire. In this section, the sidewalks were unpaved, the roads laterite or packed earth.

"We're looking for a new place," Duclos said casually, "but haven't been able to find anything suitable. With all the oilmen in town, good housing is scarce."

"The Americans spoil everything," Michaux said.

Inside, the premier's aide looked about amusedly. "Roughing it?" he laughed. He patted his marcelled waves. "You do have ice, I trust?"

"Of course," Duclos said angrily. "Maria, two glasses with ice."

"As I recall from Cotonou," Michaux said languidly, "you fancy gin and bitters. Do you have bitters?"

"No," Duclos said shortly. Then he brightened. "But two fine fresh limes. We shall have gin gimlets."

"Enchanting," Michaux drawled.

Mboa went into the bedroom, closed the door. She sat on the edge of the bed, stared down at her clenched fists.

"Maria!" Duclos bawled from the living room. "Where are you? Glasses! Ice!"

She rose, changed into a nondescript housedress, a loose shift of unbleached muslin laundered so many times it was as thin as silk. It clung to hips, haunch, nipples. She went padding out in bare feet, deliberately the African slattern.

She fetched the men their glasses. Fetched their ice. Sliced a lime and fetched that. Fetched a small pillow to put behind the back of Christophe Michaux so he might be more comfortable in the raddled armchair. Then she retired to the kitchen and sat quietly in the darkness, listening.

She was a small woman. Flat-breasted, lean-shanked, tunnel-black. But there was a slim sinuousness to her body. A grace. Her features were classically African: convoluted lips and nostrils boldly splayed. Eyes liquid and almost Oriental. Nose strong and almost Semitic. She was a Hausa. Proud women. And, when need be, stone. In the darkness of her kitchen she sat as stone, motionless and listening.

"How will the death of his father affect President Anokye?" asked Christophe Michaux.

"Affect him?"

"His public activities," Michaux said impatiently. "Will there be a period of public mourning? Will the loan talks be postponed?"

"Oh no, no," Duclos said hurriedly. "It is a private matter. I imagine the President will want the day-to-day activities of the government to continue without interruption."

Michaux laughed shortly. "You imagine," he said ironically. "Duclos, exactly how much do you know of what Anokye intends?"

"I know his intentions," Duclos said hotly. "I am as close to him as any man in the Asante government."

"Of course, of course," Michaux soothed. "I did not mean to imply you were not. But surely you will admit he may have plans which he has not revealed to you. Military plans, for instance."

Duclos grumbled something unintelligible, swilling his gin, sulking.

"How I wish I could have a private audience with the Little Captain," Michaux mused. "A short audience. There is so much I would like to ask."

Duclos looked up with interest.

"Ask him what?"

"Oh... about his political philosophy. How he intends to achieve the Pan-Africa of his Zabarian speech. Whether his inclusion of all races is something he really believes, or is just expediency. Public relations."

"The President is an expedient man," Duclos acknowledged. "But is that to be condemned? All the world's great political leaders have been pragmatists."

"I couldn't agree with you more," Michaux said warmly. "With your deep knowledge of history and political science, who would dare disagree?"

He laughed lightly, and Duclos laughed in return, feeling better. He poured himself another drink after noting that the premier's aide still had half a glass.

"Expediency," Michaux nodded. "Now, that is wise. I believe almost any compromise might be justifiable if the goal can be achieved. The end justifies the means—what?"

"Oh yes," Duclos agreed. "But not always. No obsalutes. Absolutes."

"Correct, minister!" Michaux cried. "Not always, and no absolutes. For instance, if I knew in my own mind that the unification of Africa could be achieved by the inclusion of whites in high political and economic posts. I would be tempted. I admit it, I-would-be-tempted."

"Wouldn't we all?" Duclos muttered.

"But knowing the past history of whites in Africa, their cruelty and racism, could we dare include them? Could we in all conscience include them? I say no."

"No," Duclos said.

"A dilemma, is it not? We agree the end justifies the means, but here is one means we reject out of hand. What to do? You know, Duclos, with all my heart I hope Obiri Anokye has solved this problem. That he has devised a way to achieve African solidarity with the aid of whites without the danger of giving them a stranglehold on our future."

"He has!" Duclos shouted, beaming. "He has!"

"Has he, now?" Michaux said smoothly. "That's encouraging. I think I'll have a refill."

Duclos poured gin with a wavering hand. Michaux added ice and a squeezed lime wedge. He stirred the drink slowly with a long forefinger and polished nail. Then he settled back, stroking his little goatee lovingly.

"I can't tell you what a pleasure this is," he said. "To have such a stimulating conversation with a man of your learning. Just to listen to your words, minister, gives me renewed faith in Africa's destiny."

"Thank you," Duclos said, preening. " 'Preciate that."

"Africa, Africa," Michaux sighed. "What are we to do with her? But I am glad to hear that at least one man knows the answer. Obiri Anokye can unite the continent if any man can."

"Correct!" the Minister of State said excitedly. "He has not told me this, mind you.... This is strictly my own idea...."

"Of course, minister."

"But I believe Bibi—the President, that is—

unconsciously senses an evolution of political form. That is to say, no man of intelligence believes democracy is the ideal form of government for every country, regardless of its stage of political and economic sophit— sophistication. That is to say, in India, for example, authoritarian rule may be necessary, temporarily. And then, evolving, we arrive at a limited monarchy, constitutional monarchy, something of the sort. And then, when the electorate has been educated and is capable of understanding the issues involved and choosing representatives wisely to deal with those issues, why then we—you understand what I'm getting at?"

"Of course, of course," Michaux said enthusiastically. "Government not as stasis, but a growing organism, evolving as the people evolve."

"Exactly!" Duclos said. "Christophe, you've grasped it immediately. The state growing as the people grow. Say, from a military dictatorship to a fully participant democracy. Over a period of years, naturally."

"Naturally," Michaux said. He hunched forward on his chair, hands on knees, staring at Duclos intently. "And you feel this is what President Anokye believes? Unconsciously, of course."

"Induti—indubitably," Duclos said. "The Little Captain has faith in the inherent good sense of the comman man."

"The common man," Michaux repeated. "His inherent good sense. How right you are! But first, a start must be made. Even if it's a military dictatorship. Correct?"

"Correct," Duclos said, staring at his guest somewhat glassily. "It's only a start. A first step."

"Granted. Toward something much better. Much finer. I agree. But how is this first step to be made? Africa is an enormous continent. More than sixty nations. How would one take the first step? To bring all these diverse nations and peoples under one rule?"

"Ah!" Jean-Louis Duclos exclaimed. He held up a finger, shaking it. "Impossible for any other man. But Obiri Anokye can do it. He has a plan!"

"Oh-ho," Christophe Michaux nodded, as if with satisfaction. "A plan. And what might that be?"

The Asante Minister of State began to talk.

Mboa, huddled in the kitchen, listened with dismay. She knew little of history, nothing of Realpolitik. But she knew her husband was drinking too much, and talking too much to a man from another country. A man she did not trust. One did not have to be a professor to know this. Or a politico. One had only to be a smart bush nigger—which was, she acknowledged, exactly what she was—to know that her husband, whom she loved, was acting the fool. And fools in Africa were no different from fools in America, France, or Esquimau-land. Fools anywhere could bring to nothing all the agonized thinking and careful planning of wise men. A smart bush nigger knew that from the age of three.

So she let her husband talk, and drink, and did not interrupt. She merely sat tensely, noting grimly how Michaux flattered her foolish husband, massaged his ego, agreed with him in all things, and drew from him, eventually, the story of how Obiri Anokye intended to become the ruler of both Togo and Benin in two weeks' time.

Finally, after another drink—Mboa had lost count—her husband fell asleep in his chair, snoring softly. Christophe Michaux took the empty glass gently from the limp fingers. "Maria!" he said imperiously.

When she entered the room, he stretched lazily and tried to yawn.

"Good talk," he said. "What is it you say—good palaver? I have enjoyed it. As you can see, your husband is asleep." He laughed. "The cares of state," he said. "I must get back to my hotel. Call a taxi for me."

"They do not run at this hour," she said stonily. "I shall drive you."

He looked at her bare feet.

"Well, well, well," he said. "Will wonders never cease?"

She put on sandals to drive the Simca. Michaux sat close beside her. It seemed to her he sat too close.

"It is a delight to see an African woman capable of handling modern machinery," he said. "You drive very well."

When she said nothing, he poked around in his jacket

and came up with a packet of cigarettes.

"Would you care for a smoke?" he asked. She shook her head, and he laughed and said, "Not strong enough for you?"

The cigarette had a sickening, perfumish odor. She leaned her head toward the open window to escape the smoke.

"You are a funny little woman, Maria," he said. "Or would you prefer that I call you Mboa?"

"Whatever pleases you," she said.

"What pleases me?" he said. "Are you good at pleasing men, Mboa? Are you an expert?"

Suddenly she realized this evil man was as big a fool as her husband. Bigger. She had a vagrant thought that perhaps these light-skinned Martinicains, these pale-skinned men, had been bled of their sense as well as their color.

"I like to please men," she said boldly, determined to test the depth of his stupidity.

"Do you?" he chuckled. His hand fell onto her thigh. "Would you like to please me, Mboa?"

"Perhaps," she said archly, and he laughed.

She knew the way. South on the Boulevard Voltaire, and then west on the coastal road past the Mokodi Hilton. It was quite late; there was little traffic.

When they came to the turnoff to the Hôtel Africain, he directed her along the laterite road to the row of safari bungalows. His was last in line, the one farthest west. She had heard talk about this hotel, but could not recall it. Idle gossip was of no interest to her.

His soft hand had remained on her thigh. When she switched off the motor and killed the lights, the hot hand moved upward.

"I find you African women very understanding," he said. "Very sympathetic. I am so alone, Mboa. So lonely."

"No man should be alone," she said, knowing she ran no risk.

Then he did laugh, his hands fondling her small breasts roughly through the thin cloth.

"Nigger whore," he said, still laughing. "No, Mboa. I

already have company. And I would not soil myself with you. Now drive carefully going back, sweetie. Tuck hubby into bed and play with yourself awhile."

Still laughing, he got out of the car, unlocked the door of his cottage, entered. She heard the door lock behind him. She leaned from the car window, spat on his track, muttered a curse in Hausa.

Then she started the car and drove directly to the home of Yvonne and Sene Yeboa.

His wife, Judith, and Zuni's wife, Magira, had washed and patted dry the corpse. Scented it with cloves and spices artfully placed. Dressed it in clean linen and a shiny black suit. Now the small, dead body lay on the kitchen table, arms crossed on the chest. The eyelids had been lowered. A small bundle of white cock feathers, bound with Judith's hair, had been concealed beneath the shirt, over the heart. The Baptist burial had been scheduled for early morning. In that climate, it was wise.

Obiri Anokye, Sara, and Sene Yeboa had arrived. They had waded ashore from a launch of the Asante National Navy. Under orders, it rode at anchor, bobbing, a hundred meters off the Zabarian beach. They embraced Judith, Magira, Zuni. Then kissed the wrinkled cheek of the dead man. The family sat about the corpse in the kitchen, drinking coffee and discussing funeral arrangements.

"Bibi, you will speak over the grave?" Judith asked.

Obiri looked to Zuni. He was the oldest son; it was his right.

"You, Bibi," Zuni said. "It will be more honor if the President of Asante speaks."

"I will speak," Obiri nodded. "You have arranged for the carriage? The grave?"

"Pastor Moeller has promised to take care of all," Zuni said. "We asked for a private burial, but he said friends will wish to be there and we cannot say no."

"Let them come," the Little Captain said. "He had many friends. Let them show their grief."

"Bibi," Sene Yeboa said in a low voice, "an honor guard? Rifles fired over the grave?"

"No, Sene," Obiri said gently. "Nothing like that. Let us keep it simple and quiet. Mother, you are tired?"

She shrugged. "I will sit up," she said.

"No, no," he said quickly. "You are all tired. You have had much to do. Go to bed. I will keep vigil."

"And I," Yeboa said.

"And Sene," the President said. "Sene and I will sit together. The rest of you go to your beds."

"I will not sleep," Judith warned.

"Then rest," Obiri smiled. "Just rest. Tomorrow, you will need your strength."

She was as old, as worn and wrinkled, as her dead husband. Veins, sinews, tendons pressing out the parchment skin. But her eyes were unclouded. As lively as Sara's. And her children knew her determination. She might, they hoped, live on another ten years or more, struggling against death as she had struggled all her life, never questioning the need.

"Adebayo?" she asked suddenly.

"I have sent him to Togo," Obiri Anokye said. "He cannot be recalled in time."

She looked at him but said nothing. She rose slowly. The others followed her from the room. Obiri and Sene were left alone with the corpse. They took off their shoes, jackets, loosened their collars. The Little Captain poured them more coffee.

"Sene, call the palace duty officer and tell him where we are."

When he had become President, he had insisted that a telephone be installed in Zuni's home. It was the second phone in the village of Porto-Chonin. The other belonged to the fish merchant.

Yeboa spoke briefly, then returned to take a chair to the right of the Little Captain and slightly behind him.

"The dinner has ended," he reported. "The guests have all departed. Premier Da Silva wishes to convey his condolences. And the others, also."

Anokye nodded. The two men settled down, in comfortable silence. They both had the ability to wait, in quiet and tranquillity. On the trail, ambush, or whatever the circumstances. Waiting, patiently, was a gift as important as fury in battle. Acceptance was the other side of resolve.

Obiri Anokye stared at the body of his dead father. He saw the old man's face in profile. Features already softening. Waxen sheen of blood stopped. Ironic expression of repose.

Death did not come new to him. Neither natural death: among kin or friends, field or road, face whirled suddenly to the sun, soil warm beneath the back. Nor violent death: the body torn and shocked, ripped from life. The Little Captain knew it all.

"Sene," he said slowly, "do you fear death?"

"Fear it?" Yeboa said, just as slowly. "No, I do not, Bibi. We go to a better world. The sun shines. The rain is sufficient, and so there is food. Old friends and laughter. How should I fear it? Millet beer and palm wine. All a man can drink. And the hunt of splendid animals. The hunt might take the turning of the sun, but in the end the beast is slain. And a good-hearted woman who cooks well and never complains. The sea is there, also. Fish. The hills. Great savannas of grass and forests of green trees. Everything a man could want. In the next world. Do I speak the truth, Little Captain?"

"You speak the truth," Anokye said.

"It is true I have not always been a good man," Yeboa went on in his stubborn way. "I have killed. But always for sufficient reason, Bibi."

"I believe it."

"Other things I have done I did from bad feelings or drunkenness or from weakness. But Little Captain, if we are all God's creatures, as our church says, then God has given us the bad feelings and the weakness. The drunkenness, I admit, might be mine. But if we are truly God's creatures, then we must do what we must do, and the fault is not in us. Is that not true?"

"It is true, Sene."

"So we do what we must do," Yeboa nodded, satisfied. "I am a sergeant, and you are a captain. But God is the general who commands us all. And we obey His orders because we are good soldiers. That is how I see it."

"You are a wise man, Sene."

"No, Bibi, not so wise. I am just a soldier."

Their palaver ceased then. Neither slept, but both sat upright with the corpse of Josiah Anokye since it would not be seemly for the dead man to be left alone before his interment. It was long past midnight when the new phone shrilled. Neither man was startled, but both turned slowly to stare at the black instrument. Yeboa rose to answer it, and Anokye watched his expression.

"Yes? Yes, Yvonne, he is here and awake. Yes. Tell me; I listen."

He listened a long time, turning his head to stare at President Anokye.

"All right, Yvonne," he said finally. "Now you must repeat what you told me to Bibi. Yes, it is necessary. I want him to hear it in your words."

His eyes had become blank, his face frozen. He held the phone out to the Little Captain.

"It is Yvonne," he said, his voice cold. "From our home."

Anokye rose and took the phone.

"Yes, Yvonne?" he said.

First she expressed condolences on the death of his father, for which he thanked her. Then she told him what she had just told her husband: that Mboa Duclos had come to the Yeboa home and awakened her. That Mboa had told her that Minister of State Jean-Louis Duclos had become befuddled with drink and had spoken foolishly to Christophe Michaux. That Duclos had revealed details of the Togo-Benin campaign to the premier's aide. That Mboa believed Michaux was an evil man who was Obiri Anokye's enemy, and Mboa wished Yvonne to tell all this to the President.

"Thank you, Yvonne," Anokye said evenly. "You and Mboa have done well. I shall not forget it. She is there now?"

"Yes. Weeping."

"Keep her there. Sene and I will be with you in an hour. You understand?"

"Yes, Bibi."

He hung up and turned to Yeboa.

The sergeant stared at him and imagined he saw, far in the back of Obiri Anokye's dark eyes, a red light begin to flame. No larger than a candle in a tunnel, but burning, burning...

"Call Sam Leiberman," Anokye said. Voice hard and without tone. "Tell him to meet us at the naval base. A black car. Not a government car. A full tank of fuel."

The sergeant nodded.

"I will wake Zuni to keep vigil with our father. Then I will go down to the beach and signal the launch to come in for us. Meet me there. We must move as quietly as we can. I do not wish to awaken the women."

He started from the room, then turned back.

"Sene, are you armed?"

"I have a revolver, Little Captain."

"Good. But I have nothing. Tell Leiberman to bring me a weapon. A Uzi."

"Yes *sah!*" said Sgt. Yeboa.

Sam Leiberman was waiting for them at the head of the ramp. The car he had brought was an old, bulge-bodied Buick. It had been repainted a dozen times. The top coat was a dulled, grainy black, covering ancient dents and scars. Even the pitted chrome had been painted over. President Anokye and Sergeant Yeboa climbed into the wide back seat.

Leiberman turned, arm resting on the back of the front seat

"Listen," he said roughly to the Little Captain, "about your old man—I'm sorry."

Anokye patted the meaty arm.

"Thank you, Sam," he said. "Your father is still living?"

"Who the hell knows?" Leiberman said. "He took off when I was a kid." He bent over, picked up the Uzi from the floor at his feet, handed it across to Anokye. "The safety's on," he said. "I cleaned it. Full magazine. It throws a little high and to the right."

"I'll remember," Anokye nodded.

"Where to now?"

"First to Sene's home. Here is what has happened..."

Mboa was still there, no longer weeping. President Anokye took her aside and spoke gently to her a long time. Holding her hands, looking into her eyes as he questioned her. Leiberman, Sene, and Yvonne sat in the kitchen, smoking Gauloises and drinking Star beer. Leiberman told them a funny story of how, while serving with the U.S. Army in Sicily, he had fallen out of a truck, dead drunk, broken his arm, and had been awarded the Purple Heart. Then Mboa and the Little Captain came into the kitchen.

"We will need two cars," the President said. "Sam, you and Sene and I will go in yours. The women will follow in Mboa's Simca. When we get to the turnoff for the Hôtel Africain, switch off your lights. Michaux is in the last safari cottage, the one farthest west."

Leiberman finished his beer in two heavy gulps and belched. He rose to his feet, hitched up his pants.

"We go there first?" he asked, knowing.

"No," Obiri Anokye said. He turned slowly, looked at the trembling figure of Mboa. "First we go to the Duclos' home and take Jean."

She took a quick step forward, put a hand hesitantly on his arm.

"Bibi?" she said. "Please?"

They stared at each other. The others did not speak. Did not move.

Then Obiri Anokye touched the woman's cheek and nodded once.

"For you," he said.

The door of the Duclos' home was unlocked. They went in fast, grabbed Minister of State Jean-Louis Duclos from where he sat, still snoring gently in the armchair. They hustled him out of there, stumbling, grumbling, legs flopping under him. They threw him into the back seat of the Buick. Leiberman drove sedately toward the Hôtel Africain.

The windows were down. A cool night breeze came billowing in. Duclos gulped, came awake, shook his head, looked about. Puzzled. Not yet fearing.

"Sene?" he said. "Bibi—Mr. President?"

"Yes," Anokye said.

"What—where are we going?"

"To visit your good friend Christophe Michaux," the Little Captain said. The fire in his dark eyes blazed brighter. He leaned close to Duclos. Face to face. "You understand?"

Duclos looked into those eyes. Then he feared.

"Thank your wife that you live," Anokye said. "I do it for her. She is correct; you are a fool."

"A fool," Duclos agreed, beginning to weep. "I am a fool."

Anokye thrust the man from him, turned his face away. They drove the rest of the way without speaking; the only sounds were Duclos' sobs and snuffles. The Simca followed closely.

They came to the turnoff. Switched off their lights. They toured slowly down the line of separated bungalows. Coasted silently to a stop near the last.

"Wait here," Anokye whispered.

He slipped out of the Buick, faded into shadows. They sat patiently. Duclos had stopped crying. Now he sat bent far over, face hidden in his hands. In a few moments, Anokye returned.

"Lights," he reported in a low voice. "Two of them inside. Michaux and another. In the rear of the cottage. The door is locked, but not strong. Here is how we shall do it: I go in first. If I cannot kick the door open, I will shoot the lock."

"Bibi—" Sene Yeboa started.

"No, Sene," Anokye said sternly. "I go first. You two bring Duclos between you. Close behind me. We go in very fast. Is all understood?"

They got out of the car. Reached in, hauled out Duclos. He was blubbering again. Hardly able to stand. Leiberman and Yeboa got a good grip under his arms. Hustled him after Anokye, feet barely touching the ground. They moved quickly around to the front door.

Anokye glanced back. In the darkness the whites of his

eyes seemed enormous. Flaming centers. Entire face old and stretched.

"Ready?" he asked. Voice gritty.

They nodded. He drew up his right leg. Knee almost touching chin. Uzi held in firing position across his chest. Heavy boot drove forward. Wood splintered. Lock wrenched off. Door went slamming backward, Anokye rushed, crouching. Muzzle of gun searching. He ran short, quick steps toward the lighted bathroom. The moaning Duclos was pulled after him.

Bathroom door slammed back. Into the scented room. A naked black boy, ten perhaps, or twelve, in the water. Lolling. Head over the tub rim. Michaux atop him. Glistening. Looking back over his shoulder. Face coming apart. The full tub soaped and steamy. Bubbles of bath oil. Perfume.

Anokye stepped to one side. Duclos was dragged to the doorway. Yeboa grabbed his hair. Yanked his head back so he must look. Obiri Anokye opened fire.

The Uzi thundered in the small room. He held the trigger depressed and ran through the entire twenty-five-round magazine. Back and forth. Bodies of the two stitched again and again. Leaping first. Then twisting. Turning. Driven back. Down. Under. Soapy water churned to bloody froth. Mouths open but no screams. No sound but thunder. The 9mm slugs hit, pierced, broke, hammered, killed.

Sudden silence. Christophe Michaux, one arm draped over the tub edge. Head out. Silky goatee dripping crimson soap. Eyes staring at the floor. The boy completely under. Swirling. Floating in ink.

Obiri Anokye turned away, motioned to the others. They supported the gagging, retching Jean-Louis Duclos outside, threw him into the back seat of the Simca. Mboa got in alongside him, cradled him in her arms.

"Thank you," she said softly to Anokye. "The other?"

He stared at her a moment, slowly calming. Then he nodded.

"Good," she said.

President Anokye turned to Leiberman and Yeboa.

"Handle it," he said. "For those who have heard the gunfire, it is a police matter, not to be questioned. Forget the damage. The manager will wish to keep his license for this shit pot. But give him money also."

"It shall be done, Bibi," Sergeant Yeboa said. "As for the bodies, there are deserted phosphate pits up near Gonja."

"I know them," the Little Captain nodded. "Excellent. Better than the sea. Questions will be asked about the disappearance of the premier's aide and the boy. An exhaustive investigation will be made by the gendarmerie. Take care of it, Sene. Sam, here is your Uzi. Thank you. You are correct; it throws high and to the right."

He got into the front seat of the Simca, next to Yvonne. She drove back to the Yeboa home. She and Anokye got out. Then Mboa drove her husband back to their home. Yvonne and the Little Captain got into the sergeant's military Land-Rover. Yvonne drove him back to the naval base.

"I am in your debt," he said shortly. He drummed fingers on his knee. "Yours and Sene's. Is there anything you wish?"

"Yes," she said promptly, and he turned in surprise. "Sene wishes to become an officer."

"I offered him rank after the coup," he told her. "Sene said he wished to remain a sergeant."

"I think he now knows he made a mistake," she said. "But Sene is a proud man. You must ask him again."

"Yes," Anokye agreed, "Sene is proud. I shall ask him again. How does Captain Yeboa sound?"

"Colonel Yeboa sounds better," she said.

He laughed at her impudence and touched her arm lightly.

"Very well," he said. "Colonel Yeboa. Now you shall be the colonel's lady."

"So I shall," she said.

They drove the rest of the way in silence. She pulled up at the ramp at the naval base. Anokye reached over, turned off the engine, the lights.

"Yvonne," he said. "You and Sene. . . . All goes well?"

"Very well," she nodded. "Better than I expected."

"Good. Yvonne, you are still in my heart. I have not deserted you. You know that?"

"I know it, Bibi. You will marry soon?"

"Yes. Very soon."

"I hope you and your wife will be as happy as Sene and I."

"Thank you," he said. They had been speaking French. He switched to Akan: "May you have happiness all the days of a long life."

"May good health be yours," she replied in the same language. She paused. "And may the gods grant all you deserve," she added.

When he was in the launch, heading out to Zabar, he looked back. The Land-Rover was still parked at the head of the ramp. He thought he could see her pale face. Staring at him from the opened window.

Once again he waded ashore. When he came into the kitchen of the Anokye home, his older brother was seated next to the corpse. But Zuni's head was down on folded arms on the table. Judith Anokye sat nearby, awake and erect. She looked up as Obiri came in.

"There has been trouble?" she asked anxiously.

"A matter of no importance," he said. "Please return to bed."

She rose wearily to her feet. She seemed to him so old, so worn by life, that he took her into his arms, held her tightly. Refusing to weep.

"You are not happy, Bibi?" she asked.

"Yes, yes. I know happiness. All goes well, mother."

"You are not happy," she decided, and sighed.

He would not argue, but stroked her cheek and pushed her gently off to bed. Then he awoke Zuni and told him he would resume the vigil. His older brother nodded, embraced him sleepily, started out. He turned, the two of them standing on opposite sides of their father's corpse.

"A good catch today, Bibi," Zuni said muzzily.

Obiri Anokye, fisherman's son, was immediately interested.

"I have heard the runs have been good," he said. "What did you get?"

"Bass, grouper, and three fine, fat tuna. Tomorrow, I

will send the fattest tuna to the palace for you."

"Thank you, brother."

Zuni departed, and Obiri took his chair next to their dead father. Who, the Little Captain knew, would have been pleased by this short conversation between his two oldest sons. He took off his wet shoes and socks again, removed his jacket. He stared at the blurred, dissolving features of Josiah Anokye. He began, in his mind, to compose the eulogy he would deliver at the burial of this good man.

20.

THERE WAS A hard knock on the office door. Anokye frowned, slid the maps he was working on into his top desk drawer, called out, "Come in." The guard on corridor duty stepped inside, snapped off a sharp salute. "My president," he said, "the English lady wished to speak with you."

"Livesay?" the Little Captain said. "Yes, it is all right. Show her in."

He rose and moved from behind his desk. She came into the room flustered and, he thought, blushing. She was wearing the white gloves again.

"Joan," he said, smiling, "I thought you had gone back to the hotel to pack?"

"I had, Mr. President," she said, trying to smile. "But now Ian tells me we're flying out quite early in the morning. I was afraid I wouldn't have a chance to see you again, and I did want to say goodbye and thank you for your kindness. I'm sure it was a very trying time for you."

He made a gesture.

"Come sit down for a moment, Joan," he said. "You do have a moment?"

"Oh yes."

"Good. Sit here on the couch."

He crossed the room to close the door firmly, then went to the cabinet behind his desk.

"Now here is an excellent Italian brandy," he said. "Shall we have a drink together and toast our friendship and also, perhaps, our meeting again soon?"

"Thank you," she said faintly. "I'd like that."

He poured them each a small bit, then sat on the couch with her. Each turned sideways to look at the other. Raised glasses.

"Go in good health and return in good health," he said in Akan.

"May you know happiness," she said in the same language. They touched glasses and sipped.

"Your Akan is very good," he said, in English. "I hope you will continue your studies."

"Oh yes," she said. "I intend to."

"Good," he said. "I think you will find that after you have mastered Akan, then all the others—Twi, Ewe, Hausa, and so forth—all will come much easier. But of course, you must return to Asante to practice!"

She smiled, looking down at her glass.

"I hope I'm not keeping you from your work, Mr. President."

"Not at all. I was about to finish up. It is late, is it not?"

"Yes. Almost midnight. But I don't suppose you consider that very late."

"No, I do not," he laughed. "There is still some reading I must do. Upstairs. In my chamber."

"Oh," she said. "Then I'll just stay a moment."

"As long as you wish," he said gallantly. "Tell me, Joan, have you decided what recommendations to make? How things may be improved in Asante?"

"I have some ideas, Mr. President," she nodded. "I

really shouldn't mention them to you because the analysts in London may turn them down. They'll run them through the computer, you see, to determine if they're sound. Economically sound, you know, or justified in view of Asante's priorities. The 'overview.' They're always talking of judging suggestions in relation to the 'overview.'"

"I understand that," he said. "But what suggestions will you make?"

"Mostly small things," she confessed. "Like efficient intercom systems for the palace and other staff offices and ministries. A centralized government motor pool. Better organization of the school system. More bus routes. And have you considered a railroad from Mokodi to the north?"

"It has been discussed off and on for many years," he said. "But it hardly seems necessary with the paved highway going all the way to Four Points. Trucking takes care of all our needs."

"It does today," she agreed. "But phosphate production increases every year, and so does the shipment of hardwoods from the hills. Perhaps in five or ten years, a railroad would prove valuable. It would certainly help open the north country. New villages. New factories."

He was bemused by her insistence. "Perhaps you are right," he said doubtfully. "But I would have to see the results of a study by transportation specialists. Projection of future needs."

"And a television station," she said. "I think Asante should have TV."

"A television station! But would that not be very costly?"

"Very," she acknowledged. "But I was wondering if you might get a big British or American or French or German company to build it for you. In return for an exclusive franchise to sell their sets in Asante."

He looked at her admiringly.

"Clever," he said. "Very clever, Joan."

"You have so little time for domestic politics, Mr. President. It is an area that, frankly, I think you neglect. Not because you fail to recognize its importance, but simply because you don't have the time to travel all over the country giving speeches and meeting voters. Television might be the answer."

"Yes," he said thoughtfully, "that is true. And would I also be able to appear on television sets in neighboring countries? Say, Ghana and Togo?"

She shook her head, the short, fine hair bouncing about her ears.

"I don't know the answer to that, Mr. President. You would need technicians to tell you. But your speeches could always be taped for showing in other African countries. And overseas, too, of course."

"Yes," he said. "An interesting idea. You will suggest this to your company in London?"

"I intend to."

"Good. Do you have any more recommendations?"

"Just in the organization of your personal office, Mr. President." She took a deep breath, a sip of brandy, another deep breath, and plunged ahead. "I think you need a private aide. An executive secretary. Someone like that. To oversee a personal staff. To relieve you of all the day-to-day details of your office. About a week ago you spent most of one morning straightening out a squabble between your cook and the man who delivers fresh vegetables to the palace. There were other times when you had to call repeatedly to get a car or make certain the plane would go to Cotonou to pick up Premier Da Silva and your fiancée. Your time is too valuable to spend on such matters. A good executive staff could take care of those annoying details."

"Oh, what a blessing that would be!" he exclaimed. "Joan, you are a very intelligent, honest, and understanding young woman. I believe your suggestions are going to be a great help, and for that I thank you. Would you care for more brandy?"

"Well... all right," she said shyly. "A wee bit, thank you. I really just came to say goodbye."

He poured them each a little more. Then sat back in the corner of the couch, crossed his legs. He sniffed his brandy, regarded her with some puzzlement. She sat on the edge of the leather couch, back straight, knees together, elbows close to her body. Her head was bent. He could see the curved nape of her neck, a halo of fine hair outlined in the lamplight. There was about her, in that child's pose, a tenderness, a soft vulnerability.

As usual, her loose dress revealed nothing. It fell in generous pleats and folds, billows of cloth. She could be a stick beneath. Or a child. Or a naked woman. And beneath the blushing manner, the hesitant wit, might be... what?

He stood suddenly and put his brandy glass aside. He came over to stand directly in front of her. She looked up. He took her glass from her and set that aside also. Then he cupped her head in his hands, lightly, feeling the sheen of her hair. Pressing. Still she looked up at him, rigid, but showing no fear. Slowly her hands rose and clamped about his wrists. Not pulling him away. Pulling him closer.

He leaned from the hips, lowering his head until their faces almost touched. So he could stare directly into her deep, swimming eyes. She raised her chin slightly and brushed his lips with hers. A swift brush. A pause. Then her lips returned. A pause. And brushed again. And again. Until they lingered. Her hands gripping his wrists harder, pulling. Then leaping suddenly to the back of his head, his neck. Straining. Lips... tongue...

Still leaning, still kissing, he unbuttoned her high-collared dress, slipped a hand inside. Heard her sound. Felt her move. Touched a naked breast. As slick as silk. Large, coolly limpid, with a peak that hardened instantly between his blunt, twisting fingers.

"Is the door locked?" she said.

21.

ASANTE, A FORMER FRENCH COLONY, achieved independence in 1958. King Prempeh IV was crowned first ruler of the new monarchy, and as a gesture of goodwill, the French gave Asante a small corvette. Of Le Fouqueux class, the craft was 52 meters long and displaced 325 tons. It was powered by four Pielstick diesels, and had a range of 3,000 miles at 12 knots. Main armament included two 40mm Bofors and two 20mm antiaircraft guns, as well as deck mortars and depth charge racks.

The gift turned out to be a shrewd investment for the French. The profligate Prempeh spent almost five million francs in Toulon shipyards converting the fighting craft to a pleasure yacht with luxurious sleeping accommodations, a grand piano, marble bathtubs, and bidets in the

Asante national colors. The pride of the Asante Royal Navy, it was renamed *La Liberté*, and was reserved for the King's exclusive use. Prempeh made several short cruises, close to shore, but by the time the conversion was completed, Asante's balance sheet was in a deplorable state; little money was available for fuel. So *La Liberté* was moored at the Mokodi naval base, and used as a setting for diplomatic receptions or as a kind of private club for the King's relatives and cronies, who, all being Muslims, welcomed the opportunity to escape occasionally from the suffocating presence of their many wives and the strictures of their faith against the use of alcohol.

When Obiri Anokye deposed, and killed, King Prempeh IV, and became the first president of the Republic of Asante, *La Liberté* was one of the prizes that fell undamaged into the hands of the dissidents. President Anokye was more interested in guns than colorful bidets, and during the early months of his regime, *La Liberté's* armament was restored to working order. The baroque furnishings, gilt-framed paintings, grand piano, tapestried bulkhead panels, and Oriental rugs were taken to the presidential palace. Because of the cost of removal, it was decided that the marble bathtubs (and the famous bidets) would remain in situ. But generally *La Liberté* was returned to fighting trim. Instructors were brought from Toulon to teach Asante sailors how to operate the antiaircraft batteries, deck mortars, and depth charge racks. With Asante's treasury beginning to show signs of wealth, money was available for practice ammunition. And money was available for fuel.

It was a hazy, sun-spangled morning when the crew of *La Liberté* cast off lines from the Mokodi pier and headed slowly southward out to sea, under the proud command of young Capt. Niblo Ojigi, highest ranking officer of the Asante navy. (There were only five other officers, all lieutenants, three of whom commanded motor launches.)

Aboard, in addition to officers and crew, were President Obiri Anokye, Col. Sene Yeboa, Col. Jim Nkomo, Peter Tangent, and Sam Leiberman. Despite the shimmering glory of the day, and the special provisions brought aboard, this was not intended as a pleasure cruise. It was, in fact, to be the final planning session for the Togo-Benin campaign.

In the main wardroom, where the late King Prempeh had once shown Laurel and Hardy films and Chaplin comedies, the men gathered about a long steel table bolted to the deck. President Obiri Anokye spread his maps and outlined his plan to pit Togolese and Benin armies against each other in the central areas of both countries while Asante forces invaded and occupied the centers of government on the coast.

They listened with growing amazement as Anokye's scheme became clear to them. Sam Leiberman, in particular, was almost hysterical with amusement.

"I love it," he said, coughing and holding his ribs. "It's going to be as fucked-up as a Chinese fire drill. How long do you think it'll take them to coppish what's happening?"

"By the time they understand," Anokye said, "it will be too late. We will have taken Lomé, Cotonou, and Porto-Novo."

"And then?" Colonel Nkomo asked. "Surely they will turn south? Come at us?"

"Let them try," Sene Yeboa growled. He was wearing his new gold leaf with pride.

"Possibly they will turn south," Anokye nodded. "Probably. But I believe they will be bloodied. Demoralized from having found a hard fight when they expected to be unopposed. If they come south, then we must fight on two fronts. In Togo *and* Benin. It will be necessary to divide our forces. But with the new tanks, trucks, and personnel carriers, we have mobility. They do not. I will shift men and weapons as events develop. Now here is our first order of battle. Listen closely and learn your assignments. Ask questions if everything is not clear. It is the timing that concerns me most. We must move swiftly, hit hard, move on again…"

They spent three hours in preliminary discussions as *La Liberté* continued cruising, cutting smoothly through a calm sea. South of the island of Zabar, Captain Ojigi set a new course, on the second leg of a triangle that would bring his ship, eventually, back to the Mokodi base.

Shortly after noon, the wardroom was locked. President Anokye and his guests went topside for an alfresco luncheon on the afterdeck. The cold chicken, sandwiches, salad and fruit had been prepared in the palace kitchen and packed into individual boxes. Chilled beer was available from *La Liberté*'s capacious refrigerator.

They sat on the teak deck between depth charge racks and mortars, and looked about at the curious day. The sky was pearlescent, sea a thin milk. They merged at the horizon with no juncture. So all the world seemed a steamy, lustrous globe, slightly bluish, faintly gleaming, and *La Liberté* was its center. All else revolved slowly, dazzling and dreamy. They fell silent, drank their beer, and felt dizzy, transported.

Finally, they returned to the wardroom, and in the cool dimness regained their purpose and resolve. They bent over the maps once again.

"I will lead the attack personally with Nkomo's tank corps," the Little Captain told them. "Following us will be Fourth and Sixth brigades in trucks and personnel carriers. We will pause in Togo only long enough to neutralize Lomé. Then we advance across the Benin border to take Cotonou and Porto-Novo. Hopefully, during the siesta. Sam, you and Sene, with the Third and Fifth brigades, will remain in Togo. When the coastal section is secure, begin moving northward in case Songo discovers what has happened and turns south in an attempt to retake Lomé. Jim and I shall do the same in Benin to counter Colonel Sitobo. I do not underestimate that man. I am assigning you field artillery and the TOW missiles that are operable. We shall be in constant communication on radio. Broadcast in clear. I do not care. If you face a situation you cannot handle, tell me and I will send tanks. In addition, *La Liberté* will cruise off Lomé. The Bofors may prove of value in the event buildings near the coast must be shelled."

"What are you leaving in Asante?" Leiberman asked curiously.

"Very little," Anokye admitted. "The Corps of Engineers, the palace guard, the gendarmerie. Border guards. The country will be practically stripped bare, undefended for at least twenty-four hours. A calculated risk. With the aid of Peter and his friends, we have done all that can be done to turn the attention of the French elsewhere. But if they decide to drop paratroops or bring in a landing party, they will stroll into the palace, probably without firing a shot. But we cannot allow that possibility to affect our plans. Sene, I want you and Sam to work out your attack and movement toward the north tonight. I will go over your maps tomorrow morning at the palace."

"When does the balloon go up?" Leiberman asked. Then, when Anokye looked at him, puzzled, the mercenary said, "When does the party begin?"

"I have determined, after studying all the factors involved, that we shall move at dawn on August the seventh. Almost exactly a year to the day after the coup. An auspicious date."

He wondered what their reaction (particularly that of the whites) might be if they knew "all the factors involved" included secret consultations with certain astrologers, necromancers, and Auntie Tal, who had cast her magical stones to determine the most favorable time to launch an undertaking of great magnitude, importance, and danger.

"I want every Asante soldier to wear clean camouflaged dungarees," the Little Captain went on. "Polished boots. Regulation headgear. All weapons to be inspected. Extra magazines. We have spelled it out in a general order to be distributed to all officers and noncoms."

He continued to speak in flat, emotionless tones, all the more dramatic for that, but Peter Tangent was no longer listening. It was Anokye's unexpected use of the royal "we" that had caught his attention and started him wondering. He moved quietly away from the map table. Left the others discussing the logistics of the attack and wandered to one of the windows. Prempeh had them installed in the main wardroom in place of portholes. Tangent stood looking out, bending slightly from the waist. He watched Asante come up on the starboard bow.

At this distance, the land rose from the sea like a green dream. Cloud puffs hung almost motionless in a pellucid sky. Palms along the shore were as sharply etched as Japanese prints; and beyond, the white ribbon of the coastal road and the haze of the city. It was a floating fantasy, a vision of what all the world might be, perfumed and verdant.

"A beautiful land," Obiri Anokye said quietly at his elbow. "You agree, Peter?"

"Oh yes. Beautiful."

"But not your land. I do not expect you to die for it. That is why I have not planned your participation."

"I noticed that."

"I am sure you did. You have already done much to make our plan possible. I am in your debt; you know that. I do not think it wise if an American citizen, a representative of the oil company, joins Asante in this invasion of other African nations."

"You're probably right," Tangent sighed. "Still..."

"Still?"

"I would like to be there. To take part."

He turned to face Anokye. The two men stared gravely at each other.

"If that is your wish," the Little Captain said softly, "I cannot say no." He thought a moment. "Where is your lady? The singer? Amina Dunama?"

"She is presently in Cotonou, Mr. President. I believe she is performing in a hotel lounge."

Anokye nodded. "Perhaps you might join her there. A day or two before the attack. When we arrive at Cotonou, you might then join us. As an observer. Would that please you?"

"Very much, Mr. President."

Anokye grinned suddenly, clapped Tangent on the shoulder. "Good. I told you once you bring me luck. I will be happy to have you with me. But be cautious. You need not die to prove your manhood. There are other ways."

"Ah?" Peter Tangent said. "Ah," he agreed sadly.

22.

SHE WAS STILL sleeping when he awoke. He lay
motionless, staring at the ceiling. He thought, this is the
day I may die. He waited to feel something significant, but
felt nothing. He slid cautiously from the bed. The sheet
had wadded on his side. She slept naked, back bowed,
knees drawn up. She made an elegant Z shape. The pearls
were still around her neck and hidden beneath her body.

He padded quietly to the hotel window, parted the
curtains cautiously, peeked down. A dusty Cotonou
street. A few people shuffling slowly on the shady side. A
car now and then. Dogs. A woman with a frayed market
basket balanced on her head. Two soldiers laughing and
pushing each other. Tangent listened intently, but heard
nothing. No gunfire. He looked at his watch. Coming up
to noon.

He went into the bathroom. He recalled reading

somewhere that men going into battle should, if possible, wash thoroughly and wear clean clothing. To help prevent the infection of wounds. Like having your head blown off, he thought sourly. Still, he soaped and scrubbed more thoroughly than usual, brushed his teeth, shaved carefully. The dandy preparing for an assignation.

When he came out, a towel modestly knotted about his thin hips, Amina Dunama was awake. Lying on her back, legs spread wide. She was smoking one of her long cigarillos. He bent to kiss her cheek.

"Good morning, darling," he said.

She grunted, but when he started to straighten up, she grabbed his head, pulled him down again, kissed his lips.

"I'm hungry," she said.

"Oh boy," he sighed. "Last night, after that half a cow you ate, you said you'd never be hungry again."

"That was last night," she said. "Mr. Tangent, sir."

"I thought you agreed to drop that 'Mr. Tangent, sir' crap," he said.

"When did I agree to that?"

"About two o'clock this morning."

"I didn't know what I was saying," she said lazily. "I was crazed with lust."

"Yes," he said, laughing. "So you were. Do you remember standing on your head?"

"Did I?" she said. "I thought it was you who was upside down."

He went to the window again, looked at his watch again.

"Got a date?" she asked.

"No, no. Just seeing what kind of a day it is."

"What kind is it?"

"Usual. Hot. Sunshiny."

"What is it?" she asked.

"What is what?"

"You. You're acting funny."

"Funny?"

"Well . . . strange. All wound-up."

"Nonsense. I'm the same sweet, understanding, calm, dependable, lovable slob I've always been."

"Come to bed," she said. "Mr. Tangent, slob."

"Well, ah, no," he said. "I don't think so. Not at the moment. I have to dress."

"Why?"

"People usually do. Sooner or later."

"What's wrong with later?"

"Come on," he said. "You're hungry; you said so. Let's dress and get a big breakfast. Maybe bifteck aux pommes frites. How does that sound?"

"Look at me," she said.

He turned to look at her. She was doing his favorite stunt: sitting up in bed, bending forward, her ankles hooked behind her neck. Her bearded vulva protruded like a pouting mouth. She looked up at him meekly. He couldn't help laughing, went over to sit on the edge of the bed, kissed the insides of her thighs.

"One of these days you're going to get stuck in that position," he said. "Spend the rest of your life like that. A little boy will have to pull you around on a cart."

She unhooked her ankles, curled around, put her head in his lap.

"There was a leper in my village like that," she said. "He had no legs. Or hands either, for that matter. Or ears. A child pulled him around on a little cart."

"I don't want to hear about it," he said stiffly.

She slowly raised her head. Slowly straightened up. Stared at him.

"Don't want to *hear* about it?" she said. "Lepers. People with their bodies eaten away. Also elephantiasis. Ever see a man who had to carry his balls in a wheelbarrow?"

"Why are you talking like this?" he said angrily.

"You think you know Africa," she said.

"Did I ever say I knew Africa?" he demanded. "You're determined to quarrel, aren't you?"

"You don't know Africa," she said sullenly. "Never will."

He stood, stalked away, ripped his towel off. He began to dress, tried to step into his undershorts, got his toes caught, had to hop about.

"Now we get it," he said furiously. "White men can never understand the secret heart of Africa. Englishmen can never understand Italians. Protestants can never understand Catholics. But everyone in the whole wide world understands the crass, money-grubbing, vulgar Americans. Right?"

"Go fuck yourself," she said coldly.

"Except, the first chance they get, they see American movies, read American novels, eat American food, drive American cars, drink American whisky. They have nothing but contempt for American culture, and they'll tell me all about it while eating a hotdog and drinking a Coke."

"I didn't say a word about Americans," she said. "All I said was you'll never know Africa. Not if mention of leprosy makes you sick. Just the *mention* of it. Let alone getting outside the Mokodi Hilton and trying to see what this country is really like."

"Eyeball to eyeball with a tsetse fly?" he said. "You think I don't know the sickness and the hunger and the poverty? You want me to wallow in it, is that it? Go into the villages and cry over the lepers, weep because children have swollen bellies from starvation, despair because some tribes eat the livers of the enemies they kill? Would that satisfy you?"

"You *don't* understand," she cried.

"*You* don't understand," he said hotly. "I'm helping bring dollars to Africa. And the only reason there's not more being done with those dollars is because you've got the most rotten, most venal, most corrupt political leaders in the world, and you damn well know it!"

They glared at each other, quivering with their fury. Eyes bulging. Fists clenched. She sitting naked on the bed, trembling. He in his long white cotton drawers, knobby knees shaking. But the moment was too taut to hold. It twanged tight and broke.

"What are we arguing about?" she asked.

He shook his head bewilderedly.

"Beats me," he said.

She leaped out of bed, raced across to him, pearls streaming behind her. She jumped up onto him, arms about his neck, long black legs curling about his hips. He staggered back and just did manage to keep his balance.

She plastered her lips to his, and at the precise instant their darting tongues touched, there was a rumble of thunder in the distance, a high-pitched warble overhead and, in the street below, someone began to scream and seemed never to stop.

She slid down him, like coming off a greased pole, and ended up sitting on the floor at his feet. They stared at each other, mouths still open, tongues still protruding.

"Now what the hell?" she said.

He strode quickly to the window, looked down, saw a deserted street. He came back, pulled her roughly to her feet. He held her close, staring into her eyes.

"Listen carefully," he said. "Stay right here. Stay inside. Lock the door after I leave, and keep it locked. Don't go out. You understand that?"

She looked at him.

"It's an invasion," he said. "Asante soldiers are coming. Are here. There may be fighting in Cotonou. I don't know. I want you right here."

"Where are you going?" she said quietly.

"I'm going," he said. "I'll be back. But don't you go anyplace. Stay right here. Wait for me."

He began to dress, pulling on clothes she had not seen before, clothes she didn't know he had in his suitcase: khaki jeans, bush jacket, denim cap, heavy woolen socks, boots. And a 9mm Parabellum automatic in a shiny new holster. He tucked pistol and holster into his belt, under his jacket.

He went to the window again, pulled the curtain aside, searched the empty street. The scream had ended. There was no more warbling overhead. But the thunder of guns was louder now, coming from the west. As he stood at the window, realizing he had planned no way to join Anokye's forces, wondering how he might get to them, Amina Dunama came up behind him.

"Going off to war, are you?" she said.

"Ah yes," he said, still peering down. "Into the breach, lads, for Harry and for England. Shot and shell. And all that."

"Well, well, well," she said. Alongside him now. Staring out the window with him. "My conquering hero.

Braving death. Then dying with my name on his lips."

"Something like that," he said lamely. "You know—machismo. Or whatever."

She pushed his shoulder suddenly, spun him around, struck him across the face with her clenched knuckles. His head flung back, and he blinked.

"You," she said. "*You!* But what about *me?*"

Then she was in his arms, and they were both weeping. He was saying, "I must I must I must," and she was saying, "I know I know I know."

In this area of West Africa, distances between national capitals are short: little more than 180 kilometers between Mokodi, in Asante, and Porto-Novo, in Benin. The invasion could have been made on foot. But the Little Captain insisted on tanks, personnel carriers, and trucks. Not for the comfort of his troops, but to achieve speed and surprise. And to overwhelm the enemy with the abundance of new Asante vehicles and weapons.

It was almost 0700 before the long column began to move. But Anokye had allowed for slippage in his schedule; the delay was not important. If all was going well, Gen. Kumayo Songo of Togo and Col. Kwasi Sitobo of Benin were beginning their attacks at approximately the same time.

President Obiri Anokye led the Asante invasion, riding in the front seat of a Jeep preceding Col. Jim Nkomo's tank corps. Following orders, Asante border guards had closed the coastal road to traffic from Ghana on the west and Togo on the east at midnight of August 6th. The only vehicles encountered were the cars of Asante citizens or tourists in Asante. These were ordered off the road by Mokodi gendarmerie on motorcycles, acting as outriders for the military column.

At the border, Togolese guards took one look at the rumbling file of AMX-30 tanks and hastily raised their barricades. The tanks clanked through. A squad of infantrymen, detailed for the duty, dropped off to take

possession of Togolese border installations. No shots had
yet been fired.

At the juncture of a secondary north-south road before
the approach of Lomé, a company of 3rd Brigade moved
out of the column and took up positions to guard against
a flank attack. This force was commanded by Lieutenant
Solomon, who was also assigned three 105mm M-50
howitzers and three 60mm mortars.

The main invasion force continued rolling eastward
and, at 0749, on the outskirts of Lomé, came under
intermittent rifle fire, badly aimed. Col. Sene Yeboa then
led an assault company of 5th Brigade troopers who
advanced on a skirmish line, firing their Kalashnikovs
briskly over open ground. Opposition melted away and,
as far as could be determined, no casualties resulted, on
either side.

Lomé itself proved to be undefended. The airfield,
railroad terminal, and presidential palace were seized
without serious resistance, although there was a great deal
of shouting, shoving, and brandishing of weapons by the
Togolese gendarmerie and troops assigned to the capital.

But the sight of Nkomo's enormous tanks had the
desired effect. As did the truckloads of smartly uniformed, well-armed Asante infantrymen. Within an hour,
all important government offices were occupied. The
railroad station and airfield were temporarily closed to
traffic. Asante troops held the power station, telephone
exchange, and cable office. The newspaper and radio
stations were closed down. The port area was patrolled by
armed guards.

Under strict orders, Asante soldiers treated the curious
(but not fearful) populace with grave courtesy. The
sophisticated Togolese were no strangers to coups and
assassinations. They did not find this invasion of soldiers
of another land particularly alarming, especially since the
"foreigners" spoke French, Ewe, Twi, and Hausa, just as
they did, and most of them were animists, as they were. So
the business of Lomé continued uninterrupted, for the
most part; restaurants, cafés, and shops remained open,
the tourist hotels were not affected, and vendors on the

Rue du Commerce did a brisk business with the invading army. Raising prices, naturally.

A command post was established on the Rue Pelletier in a building housing the Asante Embassy, where communications equipment had gradually been accumulated in the week preceding the invasion. After making a quick tour of the key targets, to make certain they were firmly in Asante hands, President Obiri Anokye wished Col. Sene Yeboa and Sam Leiberman good luck, and set out for Benin, once more leading the tank corps, followed by 4th and 6th brigades.

Yeboa and Leiberman set up a loose perimeter defense of Lomé and established roadblocks on the two main highways leading into the city from the north. They then formed company-strength probes to provide advance warning of any attack in force from General Songo's troops to the north. Yeboa led the 3rd Brigade foray in person, and Leiberman headed the 5th Brigade reconnaissance. The white mercenary, commanding forty men in two trucks, proceeded up the improved highway. He came under heavy rifle and machine gun fire near the village of Tsévié. The time was approximately 1045.

They were far from being the Wehrmacht, Leiberman knew. And maybe they weren't as good as a company of Ibo scouts he had led in Biafra. But those men knew they were dead, and didn't give a damn. Still, these Asantis were okay soldiers and would be even better after a few firefights. Preferably wins. Leiberman had helped train them; he knew what they could do, and what would be foolish to expect.

When the guns opened up, they didn't panic. But they didn't waste any time getting off the trucks, down into a foul-smelling ditch alongside the paved road. Then they scuttled back to a scraggly growth of oleander, elephant grass, and thorn bush, Leiberman right along with them. They had a tendency to bunch up, like all new soldiers, so he got them spread out in a line paralleling the highway. The fire from the other side hadn't slackened. It was directed mostly against the two deserted trucks. One of them blew with a crimson whoosh of exploding gas and black smoke. Grenades and extra ammunition left behind kept cracking off after the flames dwindled.

Leiberman was happy to see his radioman nearby. His backslung equipment appeared intact. The mercenary slithered along the ground and told the radioman to stay put. He then pointed out two two-man teams, and told them what he wanted them to do: one team drift to the right flank, the other to the left. They were to determine the size and position of the enemy force. The only way to do this was to fire their weapons directly ahead and see if that drew return fire. If not, they had to stand, or at least crouch, to draw enemy fire. They weren't happy about this assignment. Leiberman didn't blame them.

He waited patiently, repeatedly cautioning his men not to fire since, from their position, they could see no targets. The raised roadbed hid their enemy. It also, of course, provided effective cover. As far as Leiberman could determine, his casualties so far were two men killed jumping from the trucks. Their bodies lay on the road. A brindled pyedog came nosing around.

His flanking teams eventually returned and reported. Allowing for their exaggeration, and adding what he could judge from the volume of rifle fire, Leiberman estimated he was pinned down by a force of fifty to seventy-five men armed with bolt-action rifles and two light machine guns. They seemed to be spread along a 100-meter line, slightly bowed, the two ends closer to the road than the middle. The mercenary did not believe they had mortars, or they would already have used them.

He knew Sene Yeboa was moving along an improved road that ran northwestward. The farther Yeboa went, the farther he moved from Leiberman's position. Consulting the Michelin map he carried, Leiberman saw there was an earth track connecting Yeboa's road and his.

Assuming the colonel had not been bushwacked, and his trucks were still rolling, he could turn eastward at Assahoun, go through Gape to Agbélouve. There he would join the highway that Leiberman was on. By turning south, Yeboa could come in behind the Togolese force that had ambushed the mercenary. Yeboa had about fifty men with him, and two 87mm rocket launchers. If they could join forces, Leiberman figured he and Yeboa could take the Togolese, who were still wasting ammunition on the other side of the road. According to the map, Sene could be there in an hour.

He motioned the radioman over and tried to raise the colonel, calling in clear. Nothing. Either the radios were kaput—hardly unusual in Africa's climate—or Yeboa's radioman was fucking off. Or dead. Lots of possibilities. Leiberman then tried the command post in Lomé. This time he got through. Much interference, but he was able to explain his predicament and ask them to contact the colonel. They said they would. The operator in Lomé signed off by crying, "Long live Asante!" and Leiberman grinned sourly.

He told his men help was on the way. He felt a lot better about the situation, and settled back behind the thickest tree trunk he could find. He was about to light a black, twisted Italian cigar when a grenade came sailing across the road, exploded, killed one of his men, wounded three, and he bit his cigar in two.

Grenades were an added factor; he pulled his men farther back into the bush and had them cover the crest of the road. If a rush came, it had to come from there, and for a very brief time, the attackers would be silhouetted against the sky. If Leiberman's force couldn't stop them there, the only alternative was to run. As fast and as far as they could.

The mercenary did what he could for the wounded. One of his corporals had been designated as a medic. In addition to his AR-15, he carried sterile pads, sulfa powder, quinine pills, and morphine syrettes. Leiberman gave each of the wounded men a shot. After a while they stopped screaming.

Another grenade came lobbing across the road, but fell short and did no damage. But Leiberman had two men send up shrieks of terrible anguish. It did no harm and just possibly might make the attackers overconfident and careless. They were using their grenades so sparingly, tossing one at a time, that Leiberman figured their supply was limited.

He also figured the Togolese on the other side of the road, still firing at nothing, were not part of Songo's disciplined forces, coming down from the north, but were just a ragtag outfit, perhaps from a garrison at Tsévié, who had heard about the invasion and wanted to get in on the fun. He hoped he was correct. In Africa, it was hard to judge. Maybe right now they were getting a snootful of hemp or something stronger, and listening to a shaman tell them they were impervious to bullets. If all that happened, they'd come floating across the road, silly grins on their faces, and if there were enough of them, they'd waltz right through Leiberman's troops, kill them all, and gnaw on their roasted knuckes. It was possible.

The firing from the other side of the road suddenly ceased. Leiberman heard a shrilling, exultant screams, battle cries, wails that went up and down the scale. He didn't have to tell his men what that meant. They aimed their weapons at the road, pressed their bodies harder against the warm African earth, waited. No one bugged out. He loved them then.

Togolese came over the road in a long, leaping line, capering and shouting. Even as he raised his Uzi, he thought it was bad leadership; they should have hit in a single, hard-driving wedge. They'd have gone right through him. As it was, his men had a field day. They cut down the attackers with short bursts, as they had been taught. A few Asantis even rose to their feet to pursue the fleeing Togolese. Leiberman had to scream them back.

He looked again at his watch. Yeboa had to be nearing the paved highway, soon to turn south. *Had* to be. Then Leiberman checked what was left. Four more dead, seven more wounded. But three of the wounded were still able to function. He redistributed weapons and ammunition. He called Lomé again. They swore they had passed his first message on to Yeboa, and the colonel had acknowledged. There must have been something in Leiberman's voice; this time the operator didn't cry, "Long live Asante!"

They waited, shifting uneasily. Showing their teeth to each other. Leiberman watched them carefully. It wouldn't do to let one man break. The others would stampede after him. With the mercenary bringing up the rear, bellowing, but running just as hard as his men. No one broke. No one ran. But he saw the amulets and grisgris were out. His men were preparing to die.

The second attack came in silence. A sudden wave of high-stepping men coming over the road, down into the ditch, up and into the grass, through the thorn, firing wildly. The Asantis shot them down again. But not all, not all. Men leaped to their feet, glaives flashing. Leiberman, back against a tree, half a cold Italian cigar clamped in his teeth, potted targets as they came, turning left and right, but never sure if he was doing any good. It was all hot and close, grunts and cries of fury, smells of blood and sweat, burning things. And shit. And fear.

A few fled back across the road. This time no one attempted to pursue. Half his men were gone, dead or staring wide-eyed at the empty sky, holding arms, legs, chests, bellies, faces, while blood bubbled out between their fingers. The flies were there.

Once more, he thought. That's all it will take. If they have the will to come across that road one more time, they have our livers.

He lighted his cigar stub. He moved up and down his punished line.

The Little Captain is with you, he told them. He told them they should stay and fight to the death for the Little Captain. He will know of your bravery, he assured them. He will honor you as great Asanti soldiers. As great as the Ashanti warriors of the past. Do not run now, he said to them. Your brothers will be with you soon. The Little Captain has great magic, great juju. Fight and die bravely for the Little Captain, he urged them.

He spoke to them in Akan. They listened and nodded their agreement, pledging their blood. Not to him, he knew, but to the Little Captain. And to Asante. Son of a bitch, he thought suddenly. With faithful, trusting children like these, a man could go anywhere, do anything. Win the world.

He never questioned why he was staying. If you got paid for a job, you did the job. He admitted the stupidity of that. But all men were stupid—in different ways. Staying was his brand of stupidity. He reloaded and wished he had been kinder to Dele, his Ivory Coast girl.

When the third attack came over the road, he and all

his remaining men stood. Even the wounded dragged themselves to their feet, those who could, and there was a tight action so confused he was conscious of nothing but explosions, screams, cries of terror, cries of triumph.

And then, unmistakably, he heard the rush of a rocket on the other side of the road, a fresh screeching of fury. He was aware of more men, many men, in clean Asante uniforms. There was a great silvery flashing of glaives, stuttering of automatic weapons, a Hausa chant of victory he recognized, and he wondered—theirs or ours?

He straightened, turned toward the road, and something hit his back, low, whirled him, slammed him down. The Uzi bounced from his limp fingers. He tasted dirt and bile in his mouth, rolled, said aloud, "Goodbye, goodbye."

He lay there on his back, fully conscious, listening to the slowly quieting sounds of battle. His pants felt full of blood. He raised his head slowly, saw the dark stain spreading across his groin. His first thought was that his genitals had been shot away. He opened his belt and fly with fumbling, nerveless fingers. His penis and testicles were still there.

"Hi, fellers," he said.

He felt around to the back with cautious fingers, probing through the greasy blood. The pain was starting, but nothing he couldn't handle.

He discovered what had happened: he had been shot through both buttocks, from right to left, the slug apparently exiting. Mortifying, but comforting. He would play the violin again—if the wounds were treated before his ass turned green.

He was lying on his stomach, pants and drawers down, trying to stop the blood with strips torn from his shirt, when he saw a pair of dusty combat boots planted next to him. He looked up. Col. Sene Yeboa.

"You grinning ape," Leiberman said to him. "Get me some sulfa powder and a morphine shot."

Yeboa nodded, trying not to laugh, and not succeeding.

"Sam," he said, "I think you eat standing up for a while."

"Ah, what the hell," Leiberman said. "I'm young again.

I got dimples in my ass."

From Lomé, the Asante invasion force rolled eastward along the coastal road, President Obiri Anokye leading. Baguida and Anécho fell without resistance. The border of Benin came into view. Anokye signaled a halt. Men slapped dust from their uniforms, sought the shade, drank some water, beer, or palm wine.

Offshore, *La Liberté* moved slowly along the coast. Since the corvette had not been needed in Lomé, Anokye had signaled Captain Ojigi to proceed eastward and stand off Cotonou. Escorted by three motor launches, *La Liberté* moved on ahead of the halted column, an oversize Asante flag whipping back from the mainmast.

The Little Captain remained in his Jeep, listening to his field radio. Since leaving Baguida, he had been aware of the ambush of Sam Leiberman's force below Tsévié. He had heard the mercenary's first laconic call for aid. The relay to Sene Yeboa, Leiberman's second, more desperate plea, and Yeboa's assurance he was on the way.

Then there was silence. Anokye sat stolidly, not revealing his tension to his driver or radioman. He could easily visualize what had happened, what was happening. He believed in the skill and loyalty of Leiberman and Yeboa, but it was difficult to resist the temptation to turn around, lead his force in a dash to the rescue, flags snapping, plunge into the battle, fight, *win*.

But during the brief halt before the Benin border, the radio crackled into life. Anokye learned that Yeboa had arrived in time. Leiberman was wounded, but not seriously. Opposition had been annihilated.

The Little Captain sat back, but could not relax. He mused on how his destiny was coming to depend more upon the faithfulness and bravery of others. Before the coup, he had been a junior army officer relying on his own determination and the belief of a few. Today he led an invasion of thousands, tomorrow a political crusade of millions. He could not do everything himself; he needed the minds, strength and blood of others.

The problem was trust. His own family he could trust without limit. Sene Yeboa perhaps. The Asantis, his brothers. But now there were others: Yvonne Mayer, Sam Leiberman, Peter Tangent. And soon there would be his wife, Beatrice, Benedicto da Silva, Kumayo Songo. And then many, many more not of his family, blood, or people.

They would cleave to him because they wished to share his destiny. But he was realist enough to know that he must give to each what no one else could offer. Always there was the peril of a higher bidder. Obiri Anokye stared at the shaved neck of the Jeep driver in front of him, and thought this man might very well turn suddenly and empty his pistol into his president's face. Because another had bought his loyalty with a bigger reward or a greater promise.

He sighed with sorrow, knowing he would never be sure, of anyone. But he could never let doubt hobble his will. He must be alert, constantly, and secretly command one to watch the other. And so, by turning his aides and confederates against each other, he might escape the consequences of their greed, venom, ambition, or jealousy. It was not a way that was sweet on the tongue, but he saw no other choice.

He signaled the advance. In a few moments, the men returned to their vehicles, the column rolled forward. Obviously, news of the Asante invasion had spread; Benin border guards fired upon them with rifles. Anokye waved one of Nkomo's tanks forward. Machine guns spat. The border guards were killed, and Obiri Anokye crossed into Benin.

Now speed was increased and Anokye's Jeep pulled out of line to let the giant AMX-30 tanks take the lead. They raced through Comé and Guézin, and although there was no resistance, Anokye ordered his men to spray automatic rifle fire at guard huts and gendarmerie offices. Heavily armed squads were dropped off at each village captured, and a reinforced platoon, a tank, and an armored personnel carrier were left in Ouidah. The airfield outside of Cotonou was taken after a brisk skirmish with soldiers and guards. Anokye took his first casualties here—two men of 4th Brigade killed, four wounded—but he seized the airport and plunged on.

The Little Captain commanded that a roadblock be set up at the juncture of the coastal road and the tarred north-south highway. Then 6th Brigade, reinforced with two tanks, a TOW missile, and a mortar company, was sent on a wide sweep north of Cotonou to attack Porto-Novo, the capital. In addition to the government buildings, their mission was to occupy the customs post at the Nigerian border.

Anokye and 4th Brigade moved against Cotonou, ponderously and in force. When the invaders were fired upon from gendarmerie headquarters, the gaudy presidential palace, ministries, and from buildings in the Akpakpa area, the Little Captain radioed *La Liberté* to fire 40mm rounds into the city.

When resistance continued, Col. Jim Nkomo's tanks brought their 105mm cannon to bear. The tanks clanked slowly ahead through deserted streets, turrets questing, turning this way and that, blasting. Several buildings crumbled; others shuddered from point-blank hits, but stood shakily, showing blue sky through holes in walls and roofs. Casualties included civilians.

Within an hour, all resistance ceased; a Benin official approached under a white flag and surrendered the city. Asantis took control of the radio stations, and repeated broadcasts were made—in French, Yoruba, Dendi, Fon, and Mina—asking the populace to remain calm. The telephone exchange and power station were occupied. Asanti soldiers patrolled the streets. Gradually, slowly, the Cotonois peeked out, ventured out, picked up the tempo of their daily lives.

Peter Tangent joined President Obiri Anokye by strolling along dusty streets past the Hôtel de la Plage. He approached the tanks drawn up in the parking lot before the Hall des Congrès. He waved jauntily. A grinning Little Captain. Came out to meet him. They shook hands.

A few moments later, Tangent was seated alongside Anokye in the back of the President's Jeep. They led a convoy of tanks and trucks back to the north-south highway. The Piper Aztec of the Asante National Air Force, scouting the Abomey-Bohicon area, had reported a large force of troops, in trucks and on foot, moving south toward the coast.

"That will be Colonel Sitobo," Anokye said grimly. "He has guessed what is happening. He has reacted very quickly. A good man."

Col. Kwasi Sitobo's attack had kicked off on schedule, at 0600 that day, and had almost immediately run into trouble. The advance westward, which President Anokye had assured him would be against undefended or lightly defended areas of Togo, slammed head-on into strong columns of Togolese apparently on the march eastward.

If Sitobo was surprised, the only thing that saved him was that the Togolese forces seemed just as shocked. Both sides, after sharp skirmishes, drew back cautiously. The Benin colonel ordered a series of small reconnaissance probes. By 1100, he had learned that three columns of Togolese had crossed the border under orders to seize the north-south highway in Benin and press on to the Nigerian frontier. Most of this intelligence was obtained from a captured Togolese lieutenant whose initial obduracy disappeared before the first strip of skin was wholly peeled from his chest. He began chattering. Within minutes, Sitobo had the details of Gen. Kumayo Songo's plans.

Shortly after that, a radio broadcast from Cotonou reported the Asante invasion of Togo and the capture of Lomé. Subsequent bulletins said the border of Benin had been breached, Ouidah had fallen, the airport seized, and Asante tanks were approaching Cotonou. The radio station then went off the air.

Col. Kwasi Sitobo was a man of such fervent nationalism that the thought of foreign troops on the sacred soil of Benin was as great an abomination to him as another man's hands on his body. He wasted no time in considering whether or not Benedicto da Silva might be a party to this plot; his only desire was to defend his country, drive out the invaders and, if possible, drink the blood of Obiri Anokye.

He moved swiftly. He left a dangerously light screening

force in the Savalou area to counter Togolese attacks, and then marshaled the bulk of his troops and vehicles on the highway for a dash southward to defend Cotonou. There was a small plane overhead, identified as a Piper Aztec belonging to the Asante National Air Force. Sitobo had no doubt that the Little Captain would be kept informed of his position and strength. He didn't care. The sooner the battle was joined, the sooner Benin would once again be free.

His column rolled south on the highway, through Bohicon. He picked up additional troops from Abomey, a few kilometers away, and continued the advance through the great palm groves of Zogbodomé. At Ouagbo he learned that Cotonou was under attack. At Allada he learned that Cotonou had fallen. He halted the column and called his officers to a conference at his Jeep.

At the junction of the coastal road and the north-south highway, Obiri Anokye halted his Jeep and called his officers to him again. He spread his maps on the hot, pinging hood, and they clustered around to learn his orders.

The majority of Col. Jim Nkomo's tanks were needed in Togo, and at Ouidah, Cotonou, and Porto-Novo. But two AMX-30s could be spared, with a single armored personnel carrier, and enough trucks to carry sixty men. This mobile force was assigned rocket launchers and recoilless rifles, and designated Task Group Able, under command of Colonel Nkomo. He was ordered to proceed westward to Ouidah, then to turn northward on a secondary improved road to Allada. With luck, Task Group Able might take the tarred north-south highway behind Sitobo's force. Exactly the same tactics that had worked for Leiberman and Yeboa in Togo. Anokye was willing to try it once again, but doubted if Nkomo could arrive on time to influence a pitched infantry battle he now saw as inevitable.

As for him, he would command what remained of 4th Brigade in a march northward to stop Sitobo. He sent a captain of the special assault company and three troopers on ahead in the presidential Jeep, to serve as advance point. Then he led his troops on foot, setting a steady pace, guiding on the tarred highway. Peter Tangent walked alongside him, looking about curiously as the heavily armed men trudged steadily, dust rising as they cut along the borders of fields of cotton, corn, coffee, and a precisely planned, beautifully groomed orange grove.

"Probably Chinese," Anokye commented, pointing at the gently curving rows of trees. "Africans could never be that neat!"

"Is this the type of terrain where you expect to meet up with Sitobo, Mr. President?"

"It will probably be similar, Peter. I do not know this land as well as I would like. I know the palm groves are farther north, and the rice fields to the east. This section is mostly plantations. Some orchards. All flatland."

"Not much cover," Tangent said.

"No," Anokye agreed, "not much cover. But it is not always possible to select an advantageous site. We must manage with what exists."

They tramped on, Anokye leading his men farther west, off the road. He explained to Tangent that by the time he turned to meet Sitobo, the sun would be setting, and he wanted it at his back, so that Benin riflemen would be dazzled and blinded by the fulgent rays.

The late afternoon was hot, caught in the stillness of a wind-shift. Dust raised by the marching men hung almost motionless in the air, chalked their faces, clogged their throats. The sky was cloudless, a salt-rimmed blue, and, if one looked upward, seemed sprinkled with a million twinkling points of white light, diamonds or dancing motes.

"Mr. President," Tangent said hesitatingly, "if Sitobo is coming south, then he must be aware of your presence in Benin."

"That is true. Probably from the radio before we captured Cotonou."

"If it had been broadcast that Premier Da Silva was the new ruler of Benin, do you think Sitobo would still have reacted?"

"Probably not," Anokye said blithely. "He is a fanatical patriot. It is the thought of foreign troops in his country that maddens him. If I had broadcast Da Silva's elevation to power, I believe Sitobo would have accepted a fait accompli. I considered such a course, but rejected it."

Tangent said nothing; they hiked on in silence. At this time of day, the sun cooling, it seemed the greater heat came from the baked earth itself, radiating upward in glassy waves. They swam through this sea, uniforms soaked, bare skin raw and swollen.

Perhaps Anokye took Tangent's silence for rebuke. He said: "I told you that personal bravery, in combat, is the root of political power in Africa. It is so for men and so for nations. It is necessary that Asante fight a battle and win it, if we are to be respected and feared. What is the Oriental expression—a paper tiger? We cannot allow ourselves to be thought a paper tiger. A decisive military victory now will save lives in the future. It will dismay our enemies, hearten our friends. It will encourage the Asante army."

"And help spread the legend of your magic," Tangent said, without irony.

"Yes," Anokye said tonelessly. "That too."

Tangent looked about. He estimated about 150 men were in the line of march. It seemed incredible to him that a commander would lead these soldiers into a needless battle for such intangibles. He stared at the short, stocky figure of Obiri Anokye, striding ahead so purposefully, and wondered if he would ever get to the end of this man.

The presidential Jeep came bouncing off the highway, across a field of reaped wheat. Anokye held up an arm; the marching column halted, men hunkered on their hams or leaned on their rifles. Several stood casually on one foot, the other knee bent with the sole of the foot pressed against the inside of the straight knee. Like cranes. They could stand so for hours without strain.

The captain commanding the advance point leaped from the Jeep, came trotting, saluting Anokye as he came. He was a short, muscular man, wearing a black beret, chewing on a kola nut. He carried an M-16 under his arm as easily as a swagger stick.

"Made contact, my president," he said laconically. "Drew fire. Here is the situation..."

He squatted, and Anokye squatted next to him. Other officers came up, and they squatted, sitting comfortably on their heels. Only Tangent remained standing. The captain drew a combat knife from a scabbard inside his boot and used the point to sketch a diagram in the earth.

"The coastal road is here," he said. "The tarred highway runs slightly northeast, then turns northwestward to Allada. Here. This is your position. Soon you will come to the village of Abomey-Calavi. The news of your coming has spread; the village is deserted."

"And the enemy?"

"South of Allada, just before the bend in the road. About here. On a front extending across the road and into the fields on both sides. Through the glasses I saw no tanks or artillery. But at least five machine guns. Perhaps more. Far behind are parked trucks. Perhaps there are men in the trucks. A reserve. I do not know. The men I saw appear well-armed. Grenades. Automatic weapons."

"Mortars?"

"I saw none."

"They are advancing?"

"No, my president. They are sitting or lying down. Resting. There is a picket line out in front of the main force. The pickets are standing, patrolling."

"How many men in all?"

"I would guess two hundred, my president. There may be more in the trucks."

"You have done well."

Anokye studied the rough sketch drawn in the dust. No one spoke. Then Anokye took the combat knife from the captain's hand and pointed with the tip.

"Here, where the road turns northwest—is it a sharp turn?"

"Perhaps forty-five degrees, my president."

"Good. We will take them at that turn. Half the men on this side below the turn; half on the other side above the turn."

"But they are not moving southward, my president."

"So you said. I will take the assault company up the road, make a frontal attack. Their flanks will wheel and close in. I will then retreat down the road to the turn. They will follow, smelling victory. Then we will spring the trap."

"Let me take the assault company, my president."

"No. I will command. How far to their position?"

"Perhaps fifteen kilometers if you go by road. But if you go northward across country from this position, then only half that."

"Then we will go across country. Quickly now, before it grows dim. Here are your orders, and this will be our timing."

He gave commands rapidly, showing officers on the earth sketch where troops were to be placed at the turn so their fire would enfilade the road.

"Give me two hours, precisely," Anokye said. "If I have not returned within that time, then I am dead. If that should happen, wait for the arrival of Task Group Able, and smash them between you."

The officers nodded, went to their commands. The specially trained assault company, thirty men, stood, slung their weapons.

"May I come?" Peter Tangent asked.

"If you wish," Anokye shrugged. "We will move fast. If you cannot keep up, we must leave you."

"I understand."

"Do you have a weapon?"

"I have a pistol," Tangent said.

"Unfortunately we have no extra rifles," Anokye said. Then he added, "Later, there will be many extra rifles."

The Little Captain took one quick glance at the setting sun, turned, set off at a fast pace. Not quite a jog or trot, but stretching his legs in a ground-covering stride across plowed fields, through orchards, down rows of corn, over paths, into and out of shallow ravines, drainage ditches, irrigation canals. Tangent tried to keep up, stumbling, breathing heavily through his nose. The heat was beginning to melt his knees, drain his reserve. After them came the Asante soldiers, stolidly pounding in a steady rhythm all their own, rifles and equipment clanking, picking up a cadence of boots thudding on packed earth.

Anokye did not look at the men behind him, and did not stop. A Kalashnikov assault rifle was slung across his back. He swung his arms as he hiked, the momentum pulling him forward. To Tangent, the Little Captain seemed to be leaning, always in danger of falling, his feet coming up at the last second to smack the earth, peel back, tilt him on, push him ahead.

They marched steadily for almost an hour, dust swirling about their churning legs, and never exchanged a word. They stopped when they came to the highway. Anokye signaled everyone down. They fell limply to the ground, chests heaving, mouths open, throats taut in the hunger to suck in air. But the Little Captain took his rest standing, his weapon now in his hands. His eyes searched the road ahead, a stretch of bougainvillea, a stand of dusty eucalyptus trees.

Slowly, one by one, the soldiers climbed to their feet, checked their weapons. Anokye looked at them, then at Tangent.

"All right?" he asked.

Tangent nodded.

They moved up the road cautiously in two files, along the verges, five meters between them. Anokye led, crouched, head swirling. Then he held up a hand, signaled down. They crawled then, bellies and knees scraping loose gravel. The Little Captain signaled a halt. Tangent raised his head slowly, fearfully.

On the road ahead, two Benin soldiers stood close together, rifles slung. They were lighting cigarettes. Anokye came up to one knee, looked back. With hand signals, he moved his men out into the fields on either side of the road, then waved them forward until they formed a ragged line.

The Benin sentinels had separated, were strolling into the fields. Anokye stood up. Fired a short burst to left. Then to right. He jerked the barrel of his gun forward. His men began screaming, firing, plunging ahead.

They raced on, cutting down the pickets. A hundred meters away, the main body of troops scrambled to their feet, shouting, grabbing up weapons. Tangent, followed closely, saw the Little Captain go down, fire a burst, roll swiftly to the right, fire another burst. He tried to do the same, popping away with his pistol, the sound lost in the crackle of fire all around him.

Then they were all down, reloading, setting up to take
the first charge of Sitobo's troops. They came howling
across the fields, firing their automatic weapons in long,
unaimed blasts, leaping as if demented, and shrieking in
warbling wails.

The disciplined fire of the Asantis slowed them, halted
them, killed them. Some ran. Some threw away their
weapons. But behind them came more, and more, and
more. Tangent heard the sound of motors starting; the
trucks in the far background began to move. Anokye
stood bent, turned, waved his men to withdraw. Tangent
saw his face: lips tightened in death's head grin. Wet teeth.
Eyes blazing. They pulled back, turned, fired, retreated,
turned, fired.

Then they began to run—those still alive. Not in the
fields now, but pounding down the highway, sobbing,
reloading as they ran, turning to fire wildly, blindly, and
running again. Men dropped and crawled. Men dropped
and lay still. But no one paused to give aid or comfort.
The Benin trucks were in sight now, gears grinding, and
the pursuing enemy foot soldiers were close enough so
Tangent could glimpse faces, glaring eyes, straining
chests, mouths open and screaming.

Pistol empty, Tangent flung it insanely at men who
wanted him dead, and without breaking stride swooped
and snatched up an AR-15 from a fallen Asanti. He saw
Anokye was still on his feet, still functioning, the last to
pull back, the man closest to the enemy. He thought that if
the Little Captain lived, then he would live, and he kept
pulling the trigger of the unfamiliar weapon, not aiming
it, but just pointing it and firing and cursing and filling
with a wildness he had never known before because now
he was on the edge, and felt it, and perhaps he was
sobbing, but whether from hot joy or cold fear or both, he
did not care.

Then they were coming to the sharp bend in the
highway, and pounding around, the trucks closing now,
the running enemy scenting the kill and pressing harder.
Then they were through the turn, the road soft beneath
their jolting feet, and as Tangent started a scream of

exaltation, the guns of 4th Brigade opened up, a hurricane, and Tangent was slammed down by the thunder, fell, rolled, ended up on his face, hands crossed atop his head, and couldn't stop whimpering.

The storm would not end, but grew, and now there were louder explosions, and gradually a feral roar as 4th Brigade rose up and came on, glaives catching the last crimson light, and there was Peter A. Tangent, white man, oil executive, native of Crawfordsville, Indiana, on his feet again, right along with them, bony knees pumping, thin arms waving crazily, a glaive in his fist now, and not seeing or hearing or knowing, but wading like the others into the madness, his own shriek lost in the world, a face looming up, a slash, and the face opening like a sliced casaba, eyes springing apart, and then 4th Brigade was through, turned, came back, winnowed the ground again and again, until the enemy was not only dead but minced, shredded, hacked, kicked, stomped and made to vanish utterly from the earth, including the patriot, Col. Kwasi Sitobo, and when it was over, the Little Captain had to twist the glaive hilt from Tangent's frozen fingers, and patted his cheek with a bloody hand.

It was almost 2100 before Peter Tangent returned to Cotonou. He had watched, a fascinated observer, as Obiri Anokye met with his officers and diplomatic staffs, and issued orders to consolidate his power in Togo and Benin. Army units were dispatched to the northernmost sections of both countries, beyond the Atacora Mountains, to insure the loyalty of small, isolated villages and outposts. Meetings were scheduled with Gen. Kumayo Songo and Benedicto da Silva. Statements were released to Reuters and Agence France-Presse claiming that the "Twelve-Hour War" had ended; Asante, Togo, and Benin were at peace, and Obiri Anokye wanted nothing but close friendship with all nations, "in the true spirit of equality and brotherhood."

Tangent hitched a ride back to Cotonou in a black Citroën belonging to the Asante Embassy. His fellow

passengers were embassy officials who could not stop
exclaiming in wonder at the day's events and extolling the
wisdom and bravery of the Little Captain. When one
referred to the new Asante as a "world power," the others
took up the phrase with delight. Tangent listened to these
young, elegant Asantis chatter of hegemonic spheres,
axes of influence, and dichotomous interactions. It
saddened him, but he supposed it was inevitable.
Something gained; something lost.

The hotel seemed untouched by the change of
government. The air-conditioned lobby was bustling, the
bar jammed, a line waiting for tables in the crowded
dining room. Tangent couldn't see the merry, jostling,
brightly dressed throng. His mind was clogged with
denser images: hot, earth-colored, without laughter.

He was about to open the door of his suite, then
stopped, hearing an odd sound. He put an ear close to the
panel. A dull chant, almost a singsong mumble, in a
language he could not understand. Yoruba, he guessed, or
perhaps Adj. He opened the door slowly. The short
hallway was in darkness. But a dim, flickering glow came
from the sitting room. He closed the door softly, moved
quietly.

Amina Dunama, naked, her basalt body gleaming with
oil, sat crouching on her thighs before a small clay lamp in
which scented fuel burned bluely. The rope of pearls was
doubled about her thin waist. On her high brow, cheeks,
and breasts were strokes of what appeared to be grey ash.
On the rug in front of her were several things: a small
bundle of feathers, a stone, a bone, a brass amulet...

Her head was back, face lifted. Her body swayed
slightly as she droned the endless dirge. Tangent could
guess what it was: ritual for the dead in battle. His eyes
stung. Then he moved silently back to the outside door.
He opened it, slammed it loudly shut. When he entered
the sitting room again, she was standing, staring at him
with enormous eyes.

He looked at her, then down at the objects on the floor.
She bent swiftly and snuffed the little lamp. Now the
room was in darkness, faint illumination coming from the
street through drawn curtains.

"You thought I was dead?" he asked.

"You didn't return," she said. "So..."

He was fretted by the sudden notion that they were speaking as strangers, meeting as strangers. Whatever they had been to each other in the past was eliminated, gone. They were starting anew, having to fumble their way to a fresh relationship. Better than the old or worse than the old. But different.

He stumbled his way to an armchair, sat heavily. He saw her crouching on hands and knees in front of him. Light gathered on her oiled back, curved spine stretching the skin.

She opened his pants, took the tip of his penis between her lips. More gesture than caress. Then she moved close to him, clasped his legs.

"They say the Little Captain has great magic," she said. "Is that true?"

"It's true," he nodded. "Even in my country it would be recognized. In one day he has conquered two nations."

"And sent you back to me."

"Yes."

"He knows of us?"

"Oh yes."

"He approves?"

"I think so. I think he believes it is another link that..." He didn't finish the sentence.

"That chains you to Africa?" she said.

"That is what I was about to say, but that is not what I feel. May I turn on the light?"

"If you wish."

He reached up to turn on a table lamp. In the bright light he saw something else on the floor. With the bone, feathers, amulet, was a long, dry, black thing, wrinkled and mummified. She saw him staring at it.

"It is very old," she said. "Very holy. A relic."

"What is it?"

"Very old," she said evasively. "Why do you smile so strangely?"

"An odd thought. This ceremony in a hotel that takes American Express credit cards. You were right this morning: I shall never understand Africa."

She unbuckled his boots, took them off. Peeled away his wool socks.

"Your feet are all red and swollen," she said.

"We marched," he said.

"And fought?"

"Yes."

"But you are alive," she said, with satisfaction.

"Sort of," he said.

"Do you wish to talk about it? Palaver?"

"No palaver now. Maybe later. Now I wish to shower and be clean."

She took off the pearls and came with him into the shower. She soaped him and herself, scrubbed both their bodies with a sponge. She handled him gently, patted him dry, powdered him. When they came out of the bathroom, she led him by the hand to the bed.

He wanted to beg off, to plead weariness, or to say honestly that love was of no interest to him at the moment. But she knew better, and her instinct was true. Kaleidoscopic visions of that bloody day stretched his mind, and almost against his will he became turgid and hard. He was astonished, but she was not.

She put him into her with delicate thumb and forefinger. She was hot, hot and tight, and he pressed himself down upon her swallowing body as he had sought the protection of the earth when death came howling across the field.

She clamped him with strong muscles inside her. She grasped his buttocks to pull him deeper. Her hips began to move, to pump slowly. Her long, sleek legs hooked about his waist. She raised her head from the pillow, and with closed eyes, swollen lips, whispered obscenities into his ear. Which was exactly what he wanted.

23.

Fog hung low over the Thames. It swirled across parks, rolled down narrow streets in billows of grey lambs' wool, greasy and clinging. The sun was gone forever; air stuffed the throat. The sky itself pressed down, an enormous weight that bowed heads, curved backs.

In spite of the day's gloom, the two men sauntered through Green Park, careless boulevardiers. They were identically clad: putty-colored Burberry topcoats, black bowlers. They both carried tightly furled umbrellas. They might have been twins—or refugees from a chorus line of flashers.

"Were you surprised?" Peter Tangent asked.

"Not really," Tony Malcolm said.

"Ah," Tangent nodded wisely. "Ian Quigley tipped you off what to expect, eh?"

Malcolm didn't answer. They strolled on in silence.

Finally, Malcolm said: "I suppose Anokye will go after Nigeria next."

"What makes you say that?"

"It's obvious, isn't it? Togo and Benin weren't worth the tick, except to get a border contiguous with Nigeria. *That's* worth the tick."

"Don't know," Tangent said shortly. "I really don't, Tony. I know nothing of his military plans. Hasn't Ian Quigley given you a clue?"

"No," Malcolm said. "By the way, did you see the report Fisk, Twiggs and Sidebottom submitted to the Little Captain?"

"Yes, I saw it."

"What was your reaction?"

"Some excellent recommendations. Some silly stuff. But all in all, worth the cost."

"That's what I thought. Well, Quigley is a professional."

"You should know," Tangent said.

Tony Malcolm stopped abruptly at an empty bench. "Let's sit a minute."

"Tony, look at it; it's all wet."

"Nonsense," Malcolm said. "Just a bit dampish." He took a clean white handkerchief from his jacket cuff, wiped off the seat rapidly. "There you are. All dry."

"Nut," Tangent said, but he sat down cautiously. "We look a couple of proper cuckoos, we do, sitting on a park bench in this weather."

He offered Malcolm a Players. The two men sat quietly, smoking.

"How is he going to organize it?" Malcolm asked. "Do you know?"

"Well..." Tangent said hesitantly, "I really shouldn't talk about it, but it won't be a secret for long. The United African States, a federation of semi-sovereign nations. Each with its own chief executive appointed by Anokye, but with national legislatures elected by popular vote. One law code for the entire UAS, but elastic enough to allow for local traditions and tribal customs. A single monetary system. One flag. One army."

"Commanded by Anokye, of course?"

"Of course."

"He remains president of Asante?"

"No, he becomes president of the United African States. The chief executive of each member nation is actually a governor. Zuni Anokye—he's Obiri's older brother—takes over in Asante."

"Interesting," Malcolm said. "What about taxes?"

"Each nation collects its own, with a percentage going to the UAS. Willi Abraham is setting it up, putting in his own men."

"Naturally. I think the Little Captain has been reading Persian history."

"Why do you say that?"

"The whole shmear is right out of Cyrus. Satrapies."

"Could be. He reads a lot of history."

"Perhaps he'll be able to avoid the Persians' mistakes," Malcolm said.

"Do I detect a note of hope?" Tangent asked sardonically. "Are you really on his side?"

"All the world loves a winner," Malcolm said.

"My, we are sententious today. As a matter of fact, you're right. He's already received confidential inquiries from Sierra Leone and Niger asking on what terms they might join the United African States."

"Why not?" Malcolm said. "With all that oil money he's got. More, if he takes Nigeria."

Tangent leaned over to stub out his cigarette on the park path. He spoke while still bent over, his voice muffled.

"Going to back him then?" he asked casually. He straightened up, looked at Malcolm.

"Thinking about it," Malcolm said.

"Don't think too long," Tangent advised. "I'd like you to get in first. Before the French or British. Or anyone else. He'd be a valuable friend in Africa for the U.S. That's the line I'm going to sell in Washington. You can help."

"I'll think about it," Malcolm repeated.

They sat in silence a moment, hunched over, poking at the ground with their umbrellas. Then Tangent glanced at his watch, rose to his feet.

"I've got to get back," he said. "Give you a lift?"

"Thanks, no," Malcolm said. "Think I'll sit here awhile and enjoy the damp."

"All right," Tangent laughed. "Dinner Saturday? At nine? The club?"

"Sounds good."

"See you then," Tangent nodded, and stalked off.

Tony Malcolm sat quietly, hardly moving. He didn't even stir when a woman wearing a plaid mackintosh took the seat vacated by Tangent. Her head was uncovered; droplets of moisture glistened in her sleek hair.

"I thought he'd never leave," Joan Livesay said.

"My sentiments exactly," Malcolm said. "Well, you're looking fit. Nice tan."

"I never get much darker than this. That sun was glorious."

"I can imagine. The deposit was made to your account."

"I know. Thank you. Was everything all right?"

"Everything was fine."

"I had some trouble with that bloody camera. Thought I'd botched it."

"No, no," he assured her. "Everything was quite clear."

"The maps?"

"Especially the maps."

"Good. What are you going to do with that lot?"

"Oh..." Malcolm said vaguely. "File it all away somewhere. You never know..."

"Anokye's quite a man, isn't he, Tony?"

"Oh yes. Quite a man."

"I got a letter from him this morning. At the office."

He turned slowly to stare at her.

"Did you, now? About what?"

"Guess."

"I like guessing games," he smiled. "How many do I get?"

"One," she said.

"The Little Captain wants you to return to Asante as his executive secretary."

It was her turn to stare at him.

"You son of a bitch," she said.

He laughed. "A little respect for your elders, dear."

"What do you think I should do?" she asked him.

"It's your choice," he told her. "Go or don't go. You're a freelancer; you can do anything you effing well please."

"Watch your effing language," she said. "I just don't know what to do. The salary he offers is splendid. That, plus what you'd pay me.... You would pay, wouldn't you? For more of the same?"

"Oh yes, I'd pay for more of the same. You need money badly?"

She nodded violently, teeth gnawing her upper lip.

"Your father?" he asked gently.

"They put on a new attendant at the home. My father gave him five pounds to smuggle in a bottle. Doctor Gaither said it almost killed him. He's back where he was a year ago."

"I'm truly sorry," he said softly.

She turned suddenly to glare at him, eyes widening.

"You didn't plant that new attendant in there, did you?"

"I? Joan!"

"To bring dad the bottle? So I'd have to..."

He groaned. "Do you really think I'd do such a thing?"

She wasn't entirely convinced. "Well... you are a bastard at times, you know."

"My, my," he said. "A son of a bitch *and* a bastard within ten minutes. This *is* my lucky day."

She sat forlornly, and he said nothing. He looked at her twisting hands, bowed head, the fog-slicked hair.

"Well?" he said finally. "What have you decided?"

Her head rose slowly. Face turned upward. Eyes searched for the Asante sun. But the sky was falling.

"I'll go back," she said.

"That's best," said Tony Malcolm.